# AT THE CROSSROADS MAGIC AND MURDER PREPARE TO BE SPELLBOUND . . .

**"Witch Sight"** by Roberta Gellis: Innocence is not always what it seems in this tale of a young witch charged with the murder of her best friend.

**"Doppelgangster"** by Laura Resnick: Somebody is whacking mobsters all over town, from Skinny Vinny Vitelli to Johnny Gambone. But if Vinny and Johnny are six feet under, who are these wiseguys who look and talk just like them?

**"Dropping Hints"** by Lawrence Watt-Evans: The wizard's murderer was one of five identical homunculi. One of them was lying . . . but how to tell which?

**"Au Purr"** by Esther Friesner: From a Nebula Award–winning maestro noted for her love of wicked puns comes a catty tale that is sure to give "paws."

**"A Tremble in the Air"** by James D. Macdonald: Family secrets aren't the only things buried in this drawing-room mystery featuring Orville Nesbit, psychic researcher.

MURDER by MAGIC

# MURDER

## by

# MAGIC

**Twenty Tales of
Crime and the
Supernatural**

Rosemary Edghill, *editor*

ASPECT®

NEW YORK   BOSTON

This book is a work of fiction. Names, characters, places, and incidents are the product of the authors' imaginations or are used fictitiously. Any resemblance to actual events, locales, or persons, living or dead, is coincidental.

Contributions copyright: Introduction, copyright © 2004 by Rosemary Edghill; "Piece of Mind," copyright © 2004 by Jennifer Roberson; "Special Surprise Guest Appearance by . . . ," copyright © 2004 by Carole Nelson Douglas; "Doppelgangster," copyright © 2004 by Laura Resnick; "Mixed Marriages Can Be Murder," copyright © 2004 by Will Graham; "The Case of the Headless Corpse," copyright © 2004 by Josepha Sherman; "A Death in the Working," copyright © 2004 by Debra Doyle; "Cold Case," copyright © 2004 by Diane Duane; "Snake in the Grass," copyright © 2004 by Susan R. Matthews; "Double Jeopardy," copyright © 2004 by Peggy Hamilton-Swire; "Witch Sight," copyright © 2004 by Roberta Gellis; "Overrush," copyright © 2004 by Laura Anne Gilman; "Captured in Silver," copyright © 2004 by Teresa Edgerton; "A Night at the Opera," copyright © 2004 by Sharon Lee and Steve Miller; "A Tremble in the Air," copyright © 2004 by James D. Macdonald; "Murder Entailed," copyright © 2004 by Susan Krinard; "Dropping Hints," copyright © 2004 by Lawrence Watt-Evans; "Au Purr," copyright © 2004 by Esther Friesner; "Getting the Chair," copyright © 2004 by Keith R. A. DeCandido; "The Necromancer's Apprentice," copyright © 2004 by Lillian Stewart Carl; "Grey Eminence," copyright © 2004 by Mercedes Lackey; Afterword, copyright © 2004 by Rosemary Edghill.

Copyright © 2004 by Rosemary Edghill and Tekno Books
Introduction copyright © 2004 by Rosemary Edghill
All rights reserved.

Aspect® name and logo are registered trademarks of Warner Books.

Aspect/Warner Books
Time Warner Book Group
1271 Avenue of the Americas, New York, NY 10020
Visit our Web site at www.twbookmark.com.

Printed in the United States of America

First Printing: October 2004
10  9  8  7  6  5  4  3  2  1

Library of Congress Cataloging-in-Publication Data

Murder by magic / edited by Rosemary Edghill.
    p. cm.
    ISBN 0-446-67962-3
    1. Fantasy fiction, American. 2. Detective and mystery stories, American. 3. Supernatural—Fiction. I. Edghill, Rosemary.
    PS648.F3M87 2004
    813'.087209—dc21                                        2003012754

Book design by H. Roberts Design

# Contents

# Part III: Murder Most Genteel  /  171

# Part IV: Murder Fantastical  /  243

# Part V: Murder Most Historical  /  293

# Introduction

Rosemary Edghill

I t is a truism of publishing that sooner or later every author wants to commit murder, and I have proof: a new take on the mean streets from Laura Resnick, a charmingly chilling story from Carole Nelson Douglas, alternate police procedurals from Josepha Sherman and Keith DeCandido—detectives amateur, private, and decidedly outside the law, in settings ranging from the haunted galleries of Elizabethan England to the worlds of the Eraasian Hegemony. And from Jennifer Roberson, perhaps the strangest detective of all.

I hope you'll enjoy these twenty stories ranging from the past through the future, set both here and . . . Elsewhere.

When I set out to assemble *Murder by Magic,* the contributors had only two rules to follow to write a qualifying story: there had to be a crime (preferably murder), and magic and the supernatural had to be somehow involved, either in the commission or in the solution of the crime.

1

As you will see, that left plenty of room for variation, from James Macdonald's very traditional psychic investigator to Will Graham's wisecracking supernatural adventurers to Josepha Sherman's deadpan hilarious civil service magicians to Diane Duane's lyrical tale of a policeman's last case. And, yes, in Debra Doyle's Eraasian country-house "murder," a homage to detective fiction of the 1920s and a tragedy in the Classical sense of the word.

When it came time to choose an order for the tales in *Murder by Magic,* I found that the stories seemed to fall naturally into five categories that turned out to pretty well encompass most of the variations on today's supernatural detective story. Some stories were easy to fit into my five pigeonholes—a historical occult mystery certainly is, after all, and a historical mystery with animated chairs is naturally fantastical. But others I hesitated over until the last minute—was "Overrush" a Murder Most Modern or a Murder Unclassifiable? Which subgroup did "The Case of the Headless Corpse" *really* belong in? Was "Snake in the Grass" Unclassifiable or Fantastical? At last, with much trepidation, I made my final decisions. You may agree with me, or you may not—the fun of getting to be the editor is that I get the final say about what goes where. And certainly you'll have your own favorite stories out of all those presented here, as I have mine (I'm not telling which ones mine are, but here's a hint: there are twenty of them).

Opinions exist to differ, but one thing I'm sure we'll both agree on is that, based on the evidence, the Occult Detective is alive and well a century and more after his "birth"—though Doctor John Silence might be hard put to recognize some of his literary descendants.

And whether it's a story of clandestine and unexpected magic set in the real world, or a tale set in an alternate universe in which magic openly replaces science, the rules for a good mystery—supernatural or otherwise—are always the same: find the killer and bring him (or her, or even it) to justice.

I hope you'll enjoy your foray into the shadows, where impossible crimes are commonplace. I've gotten you some excellent guides.

Come.

There's nothing to fear.

PART I

# Murder
# Most
# Modern

# Piece of Mind

## Jennifer Roberson

Jennifer Roberson has published twenty-two novels in several
genres, including the Cheysuli and Sword-Dancer fantasy series and
the upcoming Karavans saga. She has contributed short fiction to
numerous anthologies and has edited three herself. Though the
story's heroine is indisputably *not* the author, she does nonetheless
live with ten dogs, two cats, and a Lipizzan gelding and has
frequent—if one-sided—verbal conversations with all of them.

n the Los Angeles metro area, you can pay $250K-plus for
a one-bedroom, one-bath bungalow boasting a backyard so
small you can spit across it—even on a day so hot you can't
rustle up any sweat, let alone saliva. And that's all for the privilege of
breathing brown air, contesting with a rush "hour" lasting three at the
minimum, and risking every kind of "rage" the sociologists can hang a
name on.

But a man does need a roof over his head, so I ended up in a weird
little amoebic blob of an apartment complex, a haphazard collection of
wood-shingled boxes dating from the fifties. It wasn't Melrose Place,
and the zip wasn't 90210, but it would do for a newly divorced,
middle-aged man of no particular means.

Interstate 10 may carry tourists through miles of the sere and fea-
tureless desert west of Phoenix, but closer to the coast the air gains

moisture. In my little complex, vegetation ruled. Ivy filled the shadows, clung to shingles; roses of all varieties fought for space; aging eucalyptus and pepper trees overhung the courtyard, prehensile roots threatening fence and sidewalk.

I found it relaxing to twist off the cap of a longneck beer at day's end and sit outside on a three-by-six-foot slab of ancient, wafer-thin concrete crumbling from the onslaught of time and whatever toxins linger in L.A.'s air. I didn't want to think about what the brown cloud was doing to my lungs, but I wasn't motivated enough to leave the Valley. The kids were in the area. Soon enough they'd discover independence, and Dear Old Dad would be relegated to nonessential personnel; until that happened, I'd stay close.

Next door, across the water-stained, weather-warped wooden fence, an explosion of sound punched a hole in my reverie. I heard a screen door whack shut, the sound of a woman's voice, and the cacophony of barking dogs. She was calling them back, telling them to behave themselves, explaining that making so much racket was no way to endear themselves to new neighbors. I heartily concurred, inwardly cursing the landlady, who allowed pets. She was one of those sweet little old widow ladies who were addicted to cats, and she spent much of her income on feeding the feral as well as her own; apparently her tolerance extended to dogs, now. Dogs next door. *Barking* dogs.

Muttering expletives, I set the mostly empty beer bottle on the crumbling concrete, then heaved myself out of the fraying webwork chaise lounge with some care, not wanting to drop my butt through *or* collapse the flimsy aluminum armrests.

The dogs had muted their barking to the occasional sotto voce *wuff* as I sauntered over to the sagging fence, stepped up on a slumping brick border of a gone-to-seed garden, and looked into the yard next door. When they saw me—well, saw my head floating above the fence—they instantly set off an even louder chorus of complaint. I caught a glimpse of huge ears and stumpy legs in the midst of hurried guard-dog activity, and then the woman was coming out the back door yet again to hush them.

I saw hair the color some called light brown, others dark blond, caught up in a sloppy ponytail at the back of her head; plus stretchy black bike shorts and a pink tank top. Shorts and tank displayed long, browned limbs and cleanly defined muscles. No body fat. Trust her to be one of those California gym types.

She saw me, winced at renewed barking, and raised her voice. *"Enough!"*

Amazingly, the dogs shut up.

"Thank you," she said politely, for all the world as if she spoke to a human instead of a pack of mutts with elongated satellite dishes for ears and tails longer than their legs. Then she grinned at me from her own wafer-thin, crumbling, three-by-six concrete slab. "They'll quit once they get used to you."

"Those are dogs?"

Her expression was blandly neutral. "Not as far as *they're* concerned. But yes, that is what their registration papers say."

"They're not mutts?"

"They're Cardigan Welsh corgis." She made a gesture with her hand that brought all three of the dogs to her at a run, competing with one another to see who'd arrive first. "I work at home much of the time, or I'm not gone for long, so I'll try to keep them quiet. I'm sorry if they disturbed you."

I didn't really care, but I asked it, anyway, because once upon a time small talk had been ingrained. "What do you do?"

Abruptly, her expression transmuted itself to one I'd seen before. She was about to sidestep honesty with something not quite a lie, but neither would it be the truth, the whole truth, and nothing but the truth. "Research."

And because I had learned to ignore such attempts, and because it would provoke a more honest response, I asked her what kind.

Across the width of her tiny yard, the twin of mine, and over the top of a sagging fence that cut me off from the shoulders down, she examined me. A wry smile crooked the corner of her mouth. "You must be the private detective. Mrs. Landry told me about you."

"Mrs. Landry's a nosy old fool," I said, "but yes, I am." I paused. "And I imagine *she* could tell me what kind of research you do."

Unexpectedly, she laughed. "Yes, I imagine she could. But then, we met when she hired me, so she ought to know."

"Hired you to do research?" I was intrigued in spite of myself; what

kind of research would a little old widow lady want of my new neighbor, who looked more like an aerobics instructor than a bookworm?

"In a manner of speaking," the neighbor answered. She eyed me
speculatively a moment, as if deciding something. "Do you have any
pets?"

"A cockroach I call Henry."

She studied my expression again. Something like dry amusement
flickered in brown eyes. "Sorry, but I don't do them."

And with that she went into her shingled, ivy-choked box along
with her three dogs and let the screen door whack closed behind her.

I was morosely contemplating the quaking clothes dryer from a
spindle-legged chair when the Dog Woman arrived. She lugged a cheap
plastic clothes basket heaped with muddy towels. Mrs. Landry's apartment complex hosted a small laundry room containing one dryer, one
washer, and three chairs. Most everyone drove down the street to a
Laundromat, but I'd always felt the Landry Laundry was good enough
for me. Apparently for the Dog Woman, too.

She glanced at me as she came in, noted the washer was available,
and dumped her load inside. I watched her go through the motions of
measuring detergent and setting the washer dials. Once done, she
turned to face me. "I hope the dogs haven't bothered you lately."

I shook my head. "You were right. Now that they're settled in, they
don't bark much." I couldn't help but notice she was bare-legged and
bare-armed again, this time in ancient cutoffs and a paw-printed sleeve-
less T-shirt. I hadn't seen her in weeks, though I did hear the screen
door slam from time to time and her voice in conversation with the
dogs outside. One-sided. "You think a lot of those critters."

My neighbor's eyebrows arched. "Sure. They're good company.
Smart, interactive . . ." She stopped. "You're not particularly interested,
are you? Don't you like dogs?"

I sighed. "They're okay."

Her eyes examined me. "Mrs. Landry said you were divorced."

"Yeah. So?" I wondered if she was considering hitting on me. Then
decided it was a pretty stupid thought: I didn't look like much of a
catch.

"I'm sorry," she said. "I know it's difficult."

I grunted. "You divorced, too?"

"No. Never been married." Something in my expression must have told her something. "And no, I'm not gay. It's just not always easy meeting an understanding man in my line of work."

"Research," I said neutrally.

She shrugged. "More or less."

Unless she was some kind of sex surrogate, I couldn't see what kind of research might scare a man off. She wasn't hard to look at. "Maybe it's the dogs," I muttered.

"What?"

I hadn't meant to say it aloud. "Well, some men don't like dogs."

"And some dogs don't like men." She smiled as I glanced up sharply. "What goes around—"

"—comes around," I finished, and pushed out of the chair. My load was done drying. It was a simple thing to pull clothes out of the hot barrel and dump them into my plastic basket. Why fold?

"Mrs. Landry told me you used to be a cop."

My jaw tightened, but I kept stuffing clothing into the basket. "Yep."

"But now you're a private detective."

"Just like Magnum," I agreed; too often I watched the reruns on daytime TV. " 'Cept I don't look much like Tom Selleck, and I lost the Ferrari in the divorce."

That did not elicit a smile. "She said you told her you walked away after a bad case. Quit the LAPD."

It was a night I'd downed far too many beers, and Mrs. Landry had knocked on my door to ask if I could help her with a leaky pipe underneath her kitchen sink. I'd managed to get the leak stopped, but in the meantime I'd talked too much.

"It was time," I said dismissively.

Brown eyes were very serious. "It must have been a difficult decision."

I grinned crookedly as I gathered up the brimming basket. "You don't know the half of it."

She waited until I was at the door of the tiny laundry room. "Then maybe you should tell me."

I stopped. Turned. "What?"

"The half I don't know."

"Hell, lady, *I* don't know the half of it. I just knew I had to get out."

Her eyes drilled into me. For some reason, I couldn't move. Her voice sounded odd. Pupils expanded. "She said you saw in black and white. Your wife."

I stared at her, stunned.

Her tone was almost dreamy. "That you had no imagination."

I wanted to turn my back, to walk away. But couldn't.

"That you lived too much inside your head."

Finally, I could speak. "Among other things." My voice was rusty. "Are you one of her women friends?"

She smiled oddly. "I've never met her."

"Then how in the hell do you know what she said?"

She blinked. It wasn't one of those involuntary movements, like a heartbeat, but something she did on purpose. As if she flipped a switch inside her head. "Have you ever had any pets?"

It broke the mood. I shrugged, turned to go. "Not since I was a kid."

"*Wait.*" The crack in her voice stopped me. I swung back. She was staring at me fixedly again, pupils still dilated, and said in an eerily distant voice, "Your father killed your dog."

I felt a frisson slide down my spine. "Listen—"

"Your father killed your dog."

"Because the dog had been hit by a car," I said sharply. "He was badly hurt and in pain. My father had no choice."

"So were you," she said. "In pain. You knew what he was feeling. You *felt* what he was feeling. The dog. You saw the accident."

I shook my head. "I wasn't there."

"Yes, you were."

"I was on my way home from school. I didn't see it."

The color had drained out of her face. She put out a hand to steady herself against the washing machine.

"Are you sick?" I asked sharply. Or on drugs.

Even her lips were white. "You don't see in black and white."

I lingered in the doorway, caught on the cusp of wanting to go and wanting to stay. "What are you talking about?"

"You see in color. *Too much* color."

I dropped the basket and made it to her before she collapsed. I hooked the chair with a foot, yanked it over, put her into it. She was all bones and loose limbs. She muttered an expletive under her breath, then bent forward. Splayed fingers were locked into light brown hair.

"What are you on?" I asked.

She shook her head against her knees. "No drugs."

I stood over her. "This happen to you often?"

She muttered another expletive.

"Look, if you feel sick, I can get the wastebasket."

"No." She shuddered once, words muffled. "No, it doesn't take me that way."

Alarms went off in my head. "What doesn't 'take' you *what* way?"

She heaved a sigh, sat up, pulled fallen hair out of her face. Her color was somewhat improved, but a fine sheen of sweat filmed her face.

I'd been married; I couldn't help it. "Hot flash?"

She grimaced. "I wish. No . . . no, it's just—something that happens." She closed her eyes a moment, then looked up at me. "Would you do me a favor and help me to my apartment? I'm always a little shaky afterwards."

"Is this a medical problem?"

Her hands trembled on the chair arms as she pushed herself to her feet. "Not medical, no."

I hooked a hand under her arm, steadying her. "Come on, then. We'll take it slow."

She nodded. It looked for all the world like a rag doll's head flopping back and forth.

I took her to her apartment, pushed open the door, and was greeted by three highly suspicious dogs. I wondered uneasily if I was about to lose my ankles, but she said something to them quietly and they stopped barking. The trio stood there at rigid attention, watching closely as I got her to an easy chair.

"Thank you," she said. "Would you . . . would you mind getting me some iced tea? There's some in the fridge already made."

The dogs let me go to the kitchen, but only under close supervision. I hunted up a glass, found the pitcher of tea in the refrigerator, poured it full. The liquid was cloudy, and lemon slices floated in it. I sniffed suspiciously.

"It's sweet tea," she called from the other room. "No drugs. I promise."

I walked back into the front room with the glass. "You psychic or something?"

She glanced at the dogs, who clustered around my legs, and reached out for the tea. "You're a detective. Detect."

A chill touched me at the base of my spine. "We worked with one or two in the department. I never believed there was any merit to them. Their claims. Their *visions*. I never solved a single case using them."

She drank tea, both trembling hands wrapped around the glass. The sugar left a glistening rim along her top lip. "It's a wild talent," she explained. "It comes and goes in people. Very few can *summon* a vision at a given time, so it's not surprising cops don't believe what they say if they can't perform on command." She looked at the dogs. "We're not a circus act."

"Research," I said dubiously. "Paranormal?"

She drank more tea, then smoothed the dampness from her lip with three steadying fingers. "Mrs. Landry asked me to read her cats. That's how we met."

*Read* her cats. If she heard my doubt, she gave no sign.

"Two of them were with her husband when he died. He was at home, you know. Mrs. Landry was out grocery shopping. She always worried that he was in pain when he died, that he was terribly afraid because he was alone." Shoulders lifted in a slight shrug. "I did what I could."

I kept my tone as neutral as possible. "You read her cats."

"It was very sudden, his death. There was a moment of pain—he died of an aneurysm—but it passed. He was gone very quickly. He didn't have time to be afraid."

"The *cats* told you this?"

"No." She set the drained glass down on the table next to the easy chair. "No. They *showed* me." She saw the look in my eyes. "The same way your dog showed you, when he was dying. On your way home from school."

I opened my mouth to reply but found myself unable.

"You don't see in black and white," she said. "You see in color. Or did. Very vivid color, in a much broader spectrum than anyone else. They are the colors of the mind. But you've shut them down. I think you must have done it that day, because it was too painful to see from behind your dog's eyes. Or else you said something, and your father told you it was just your imagination. Parents often do that when they don't understand what the child is saying."

I murmured, "My wife says I don't have any imagination." Then I caught myself. "*Ex*-wife."

"Most of us don't get married. Or don't *stay* married." Her tone was dry.

"Us? You're counting me in with you?"

"Of course." She leaned back against the chair, slumping into it. "Thank you. The sugar helped. But I need to rest now."

"You *read* me back there? In the laundry room?"

"No. I can't read humans. Not clearly. But there were edges . . . pieces." The bones stood out beneath the whitening skin of her face. "I'm sorry. I have to rest now."

One of the dogs growled. Very softly. Almost apologetically.

I didn't have to "read" him to know what he meant. I took myself out of the apartment and back to my own, where I opened the bottle of single malt I kept for special occasions. The first and only time I'd availed myself of it was when the divorce papers arrived in the mail.

Outside, I sat in the fraying chaise lounge and drank Scotch, remembering a dog, and a car, and the unremitting pain that ceased only when my father ended the dog's life. But before that, in the final moment, I had felt the unflagging trust in the canine heart: *the human will save me.*

I swore. Downed Scotch. Fell asleep—or passed out—as the moon rose to replace the sun.

My neighbor opened the interior door just as I knocked on her screen door, and stared at me through the fine mesh. She wore nice slacks, silk blouse, a well-cut blazer. Hair was neatly brushed and shining, hanging loose to her shoulders. Makeup told the story.

"You're going out," I said inanely.

One hand resettled the purse strap over her shoulder. "I have an appointment."

"Reading more cats?"

"As a matter of fact, no. It's a Great Dane."

"Should you be doing it so soon? I mean, it was only yesterday that you nearly passed out in the laundry room."

"I'm fine." Her eyes were cool, her tone businesslike. "Is there something I can help you with?"

I found myself blurting, "You can let me go with you."

"I'm sorry," she said, "but that wouldn't be a good idea."

"Why not?"

"Because you don't believe what I told you. You want to go only to prove to yourself I'm lying."

I opened my mouth to deny it. Closed it. Shrugged. "Maybe so. I guess you *are* psychic."

"Not really. This particular gift goes far beyond that."

"But you told me—"

She interrupted. "I told you what you wanted to hear. You said you worked with psychics when you were a cop. What I do is different."

"But you said 'us.' As in you and me."

"Because it's in you, too. Buried very deeply under years of denial, but there."

"You can't know that."

Her tone was tinged with humor. "Of course I can." Then abruptly, she pushed the screen door open one-handed and stepped back. "Are you coming in?"

"You have an appointment, you said."

"Appointments can be rescheduled."

"But—"

"You came here for a reason."

It was very lame, but I offered it, anyway. "Cup of sugar?"

She smiled dutifully, but the eyes remained serious. "Come in."

"Won't the Great Dane be offended?"

"The Great Dane would just as soon be a couch potato." She stepped aside as I moved past her. "It's his owner who believes the dog knows something."

"And it doesn't?"

"Probably not. Sometimes dogs are just dogs. But this *is* California, home of the Great Woo-Woo, and some people identify a little too much with their pets." She slipped the purse from her shoulder and put it on the console table behind the sofa. "I got over feeling guilty years ago. If it makes the owners feel better, it's not wasted money."

"You mean they hire you even if there's nothing to read?"

"There's always something to read." She gestured to the sofa, then sat down in the easy chair. "But sometimes what I read is merely a dog's inarticulate longing for food, or a cat's annoyance with the fly buzzing around its head." She smoothed the slacks over one knee. "What can I help you with?"

I glanced around. "Where are your dogs?"

"Outside, basking in the sun." Her eyes were steady. "Well?"

"Can you read something that belonged to an animal?" I asked. "Like a—a food dish or something?"

"Sometimes. Is that what you want me to do?"

I drew in a breath, released it. Then dug down into the pocket of my jeans. I pulled out the collar. "This."

She looked at it in my hand. A simple braided nylon collar, tan, stained dark in spots, the kind called a slip collar, with a metal ring at each end. You threaded the nylon through to make a loop and slipped it over the dog's head.

I watched her eyes. The pupils went pinpoint, then spread like ink. Her hand came up, lingered; but she dropped it back to the chair arm. "Wait a moment. Please."

She pulled a cell phone from her purse. Ten numbers were punched in. In a moment she was explaining quietly that something had come up and she'd have to reschedule; and, likely in answer to what was said, explained it was very important. Then she disconnected, dropped the phone back into her purse, and leaned forward.

Her hand hovered. I pushed the collar into it. Her fingers grasped it, closed tightly—and then spasmed, dropping it.

She was standing. Trembling. *"My God—"*

I looked at the collar lying on the carpet. Then at her.

"My God—" she repeated. "Do you know what that is?"

"Do you?"

"*Yes,* I know what that is! But—" She broke it off, bit deeply into her lip, drew in a shuddering breath, then took a visible grip on her emotions. "If I do this—and yes, I know what you want—then you have to come with me. Put yourself behind the dog's eyes."

"Me? But I can't do—"

"Yes, you can." We stood three feet apart, stiff with emotion. The collar lay between us. "Yes. You can."

I felt saliva drying in my mouth. "You think I didn't *try*? Hell, we were all ready to try anything by then! I took that thing home with me, practically *slept* with it, and never saw a single thing. Never felt anything." I sucked in a breath and admitted it for the first time in thirty years. "Not like with my dog when I was a kid."

She shook her head. "I can't do this alone."

"I don't know how. I shut it away, just like you said. My parents told me I was imagining things . . . that I'd had a shock, and they understood, but that I couldn't let it upset me so much." I made a gesture of futility with empty hands. "I don't know how to do it."

"I'll help you. But you have to agree to come with me. All the way." Her eyes were unexpectedly compassionate. "You were a cop once. You'll have to be one again."

After a moment I nodded. "All right."

She sat down on the carpet and gestured for me to do the same. The collar lay between us. "We will reach out together, and we will pick it up together."

"Then what?"

"Hold it," she said simply.

"How will I know if it's working?"

"You will."

"What if it *doesn't* work?"

"It will." She saw something in my face. She extended her left hand. After a moment I closed my right around it. "Now," she said.

I saw our free hands move out, move down, then close upon the collar. I felt the braided nylon, the slightly frayed strands where something had rubbed, the cool metal rings.

And tasted—

—*blood in my mouth. Blood everywhere. It splattered my legs, matting fur together; drenched my paws. Leathery pads felt it against the sidewalk, slick and slippery, drying to stickiness. I smelled it everywhere, clogging nostrils, overwhelming my superior canine olfactory sense.*

*Movement. The scent, the sharp tang of human surprise, fear, panic. Hackles rose from my neck to the base of my curled tail in a ridge of thick, coarse hair. I heard a man's voice, a blurt, a bleat of sound, shock and outrage. Another man's breathing, harsh and rasping; smelled the anger, the hatred, the cold fury that overwhelmed any comprehension of what he did beyond stopping it, stopping them; ending it, ending them; ending HER—*

*—crushed grass, leather, torn flesh, perfume, aftershave—*

*—aftershave I knew—*

*—had lived with—*

*—it was him, HIM, the man, the man I knew—*

*Knife. Long blade, red and silver in the moonlight. A woman on the ground, slack across the concrete, pale hair a tumbled mass turning red and black and sticky.*

*—I know the man—*

*—the man who once fed me, walked me, petted me, praised me—*

*HIM. But what is he—*

*So much blood.*

*Everywhere.*

*Blood.*

*—and the other man, falling. Bleeding. Breath running out. Two bodies on the ground.*

*Blood is everywhere.*

*I lift my voice in a wailing howl.*

*In the moonlight, I see him turn. In the streetlights, I see him look at me. Black face. Familiar face.*

*Knife in his hand.*

*Blood on the knife.*

*Blood is everywhere.*

*He turns. Walks away. Back into the darkness.*

*I bark.*

*But he is gone.*

*Two bodies on the ground.*

*I bark and bark and bark—*

I yanked my hand away from hers, let go of the collar. Felt rage well up. "That son of a bitch!"

She was white-faced and shaking. Like me, she had released the collar. It lay again on the carpet. "That poor woman."

"And the kid," I said. "Poor guy, wrong place at the wrong time, like everyone said." I closed my eyes, then popped them open again as the memory, the *smells,* threatened to overwhelm me. "I was the dog."

"Yes."

"We saw what *he* saw. The Akita."

"He was the only witness," she said, "except for the murderer."

"That son of a bitch . . ." I rocked back, clasped hands on top of my head. Breathed noisily. "And it's not admissible."

"Double jeopardy," she murmured.

"But I know now—*we* know . . ." I squeezed my eyes shut.

Her voice was very quiet. "You left the department after the trial. That was the case that went bad."

I opened my eyes. "After the lawyers got through with us, I had no heart for it anymore. We *knew* we had the evidence. But they played the department. Played the media. And cherry-picked the jury."

Tears shone in her eyes. "You took the Akita's collar home. To find out the truth."

I grimaced. "I was desperate. I knew even if it worked, even if somehow it worked, no one would believe me. Are you kidding? But I thought maybe it would give me a lead if I could put myself there that night, behind the dog's eyes—find something we missed, something no one could manipulate . . ." I shook my head. "Nothing. I couldn't do it. I didn't have the *magic* anymore."

She smiled. "Is that what you called it?"

"Magic? Yeah, as a kid. Hell, I didn't know what it was. I *still* don't. It's as good a word as any."

"I'm sorry," she said.

I nodded. "Yeah." Then the world revolved around me, began to gray out. "Whoa—"

"Lie down. I've got some energy bars in my purse. Lie down, Mr. Magnum."

"Mag—" Then I got the reference. Laughing, I lay down as ordered, sprawled on my back. Heard the rustle of torn paper peeled away. Felt the nubbly surface of a granola bar shoved into my hand.

"Eat it. Then eat another. In a few hours you may feel like getting up. It's just backlash from the energy expenditure. It's always best to do this on a full stomach, but, well . . . sometimes it doesn't work out that way."

I bit off a hunk of granola bar. "What about you?"

Her words were distorted. "I'm already eating mine."

I lay there a moment, chewing. Contemplating. "Will my life ever be normal again?"

"Nope."

"Didn't think so." I finished the first bar, accepted a second from her. "It's a curse, isn't it?"

"Sometimes. Now you know what happened that night in front of the condo when two people lost their lives because of an ex-husband's jealousy. You will never be able to forget it. But it's a gift as well."

"How is it a *gift,* when you can experience something like that?"

"It's a gift when you can tell a frail, terrified old woman who's had nightmares for years that her beloved husband did not die in pain and wasn't afraid because he was alone. It's a gift when you offer peace of mind." Her smile widened. "A *piece* of mind."

I considered it. "Maybe that'd be all right." I sat up slowly, steadying myself against the floor. "I need to leave. But I want to come back . . . talk to you more about all of this."

She watched me stand up, noted my unsteadiness. Refrained from suggesting I wait. "Where are you going?"

"Cemetery," I said. "There's someone I need to visit. To tell her I know the truth." I glanced back. "That *we* know the truth. Finally."

She nodded. "Peace of mind."

I paused in the doorway, stretching open the screen door. "Never found a man who could understand you, huh?"

"Not yet."

"Yeah, well . . . my wife didn't understand me, either. Maybe it's better if we stick to our own kind."

"Maybe," she said thoughtfully, climbing to her feet. She paused in the doorway, caught the screen door from my hand as I turned to go. "Excuse my bluntness, but, well . . ." She plunged ahead. "You're bitter and burned-out, and dreadfully out of shape. Now that you know what you are inside, what you can do, you need to clean up your act. It takes every piece of you, the"—she paused, smiling—"magic. You need to be ready for it."

I grimaced, aware of my crumpled shirt, stubbled face, bloodshot eyes, the beginnings of a potbelly. She wasn't ultrafit because she was a narcissistic gym rat. It was self-preservation in the eye of the hurricane.

I turned to go, grimacing. "Yeah."

"My name, by the way, is Sarah. Sarah Connor."

I stopped short and swung back. "You're kidding me."

Color stole into her cheeks. "I take it you saw *The Terminator.*"

"Hell, I *own* the movie. On DVD."

She thought about it. "I guess if your name isn't Arnold, we'll be okay."

I laughed. "No, not Arnold. That I can promise you."

"Well?" she asked as I turned away again. "What is it?"

I threw it back over my shoulder as I reached my little sidewalk. "Clint East—"

"No!" she interrupted, wide-eyed. "Really?"

"Just *East*," I said. "But the guys in the department, well . . ." I grinned. "They called me Woody."

Sarah laughed aloud.

As she closed her door, still grinning, I stuffed hands in my pockets and went whistling next door to mine, feeling good about myself for the first time in months.

# Special Surprise Guest Appearance by . . .

## Carole Nelson Douglas

Ex-journalist Carole Nelson Douglas is the award-winning author of forty-some novels, including nine fantasy and science fiction titles. She currently writes two realistic mystery series with light fantasy content. *Good Night, Mr. Holmes* introduced the only woman to outwit Sherlock Holmes, American diva Irene Adler, as a detective, and was a *New York Times* Notable Book of the Year. The series recently resumed with *Chapel Noir* and *Castle Rouge,* a two-book vampirish take on Jack the Ripper. Douglas also created hard-boiled feline P.I. Midnight Louie, whose part-time first-furperson feline narrations appear in sixteen novels set in contemporary Las Vegas. *Cat in a Neon Nightmare* and *Cat in an Orange Twist* are the latest titles. Douglas's short fiction has appeared in seven *The Year's Best* collections.

She collects vintage clothing as well as stray cats (and the occasional dog) and lives in Fort Worth, Texas, with her husband, Sam.

agic is a man's game," he told the reporter for the *Las Vegas Review-Journal* who sat beside him in the audience.

"In this town, for sure," she answered. "Except for Melinda at the Venetian, a female illusionist has never headlined in Vegas before. That's why I'm interested in your take on this one."

His "take" on this one was he could take her or leave her, and she had left him, long ago, not on her terms.

"Even you must admit," the reporter said, eyeing him slyly, "that her Mirror Image trick is a winner."

"It's all mirrors," he answered, snorting ever so slightly. No sense in demeaning his own act while dismissing that of a rival.

Rival?

Chardonnay LeSeuer was one of those tall black women with a whole lot of cream in their coffee. Looked like a freaking supermodel.

Now she was "Majika" and making hay by playing both the sex and the race cards: not just the second woman ever to headline on the Strip but the first black magician.

She was also an ex-assistant he had sent packing years ago for packing on a bit too much poundage. Sure, she looked pretty sleek now, but usually it was all downhill with women once the weight started piling up. How was he to know she'd get over putting on fifteen pounds because her kid had gotten that annoying disease? She'd missed a lot of rehearsals with that, too.

Time had added assorted swags and sags to his six-foot frame as well, as if he were an outmoded set of draperies, but his magician's costume could be designed to hide it, as did the ignominy of a custom corset that doubled as a handy storage device for assorted paraphernalia that shall remain nameless, at least to readers of the *Review-Journal*.

"Actually," he added, trying to sound affable, "I haven't seen this infamous Mirror Image trick yet."

"Why do you say infamous?"

"From what I've heard, it smacks more of a gimmick than legitimate magic."

"Aren't all magic tricks a gimmick?"

"Please. Not 'tricks.' It makes magicians sound like hookers. We use the term 'illusions.' We are frank about what we do, but we don't debase it. There's a fine line."

"And how has Majika crossed over it?" the reporter asked, pencil poised. She was a twenty-something twerp with an overstudded left ear and an annoying manner, as if she knew something about him that he didn't.

*By overstepping her bounds,* he wanted to snap. Instead, he displayed that mysterious and vaguely sinister smile that was pasted on billboards high above the Strip and had been for fifteen years. It was pasted on his face now, too, thanks to Dr. Mengel. "We'll find out tonight, I'm sure."

Marlon Carlson sat back in the seat, startled when it tilted back with him. The damn Crystal Phoenix Hotel and Casino had gone first-class in designing a house for this upstart woman. He'd had an exclusive gig at the Oasis down the Strip—as Merlin the Magnificent—for years, but the fact was the joint was getting a bit tacky. Every older stage show seemed shabby after Cirque du Soleil had hit town. That was the trouble with Vegas: it took millions to set up a theater specifically for a designated show meant to run for decades . . . and then the star got millions, too.

Refurbishing in midstream was the name of the game, and he was getting tired of it. He was getting tired, period, especially of the cosmetic surgery that had tilted his eyes to a Charlie Chan slant and drawn his neck skin back like a hangman's noose. At least he had never looked as artificial and aerodynamically taut as the eerily ageless Siegfried and Roy. Yet. And at least he didn't have to work with cats, animals almost as annoying as the clichéd rabbit. He understood that Majika still resorted to producing the expected (another word for rabbit) in the illusion trade.

When he couldn't help shuddering at the indignity of resorting to the rabbit, which was literally old hat, the snippy young reporter had the gall to ask if he was cold, like he was somebody's Uncle Osbert instead of a first-rank stage magician at the top of his game.

He forced his attention to the stage, where the woman who now called herself Majika, slim and limber in spangled leopard leotard, was going through the motions of various sleight-of-hand illusions.

She was slight of form again, he noted nostalgically. Always a looker, but not very cooperative. Usually, his assistants considered it a signal honor to sleep with him. Well, maybe it was a less signal honor these days, but it was still a tradition.

She had no real assistants, except for various members of the audience she called onstage.

That's what was wrong with magic shows nowadays. They had all gone over to the proletariat. There was Lance Burton with his kiddie brigade at the Monaco, as if magic were still something meant to amaze and amuse the preteen set instead of a multimillion-dollar con game with almost 40 million tourists a year to milk and bilk. There was, until recently, the afore-considered Siegfried and Roy, in their off-hours breeding rare albino lions and tigers and, perhaps someday, even some bloody bears. *Oh, my.* All for the good of the planet and mankind.

All Merlin the Magnificent did was mystify and collect his millions. At least Majika had no politically correct cause on display along with her lean form and her skimpy magical prowess.

His nose wrinkled despite itself, quite an achievement given his last surgery, as she coaxed a shy, fat middle-aged woman in a (sigh) floral-decorated sweat suit from one of the first rows of the audience onto the stage.

The usual cabinet had been wheeled center stage by the black-clad ninja stagehands. They came and went like ebony fog, no posing, no muscle-flexing. In fact, there was something weirdly boneless about their silent, supple forms, like electric eels gone upright. Frogmen in wet suits, that's what they evoked in their shiny spandex jumpsuits covering head to toe to little finger. Disgusting.

This time the eternal magician's prop was presented with the mirror in plain view on the outside front, even framed in ornate gilt wood, as if it were made to hang on a wall. The simpering cow from the audience, obviously a plant, was finessed into the cabinet by the door swinging open on a dead matte-black interior.

Once the dupe was inside, the shadowy ninjas sprang from somewhere to spin the cabinet sideways. Majika stood proudly edgeways behind it, her figure as sleek as a diver's.

To the uneducated eye, the cabinet looked no more than two inches wide, like an ordinary mirror frame. *Please!* Marlon was getting a headache.

"How does she do that?" the reporter was whispering, nagging in his ear.

"Mirrors!" he snapped.

But he wasn't sure. How irritating.

The frogmen spun the cabinet . . . once, twice, three times.

Its side profile was always as black and narrow as a dagger's, and Majika made sure to stand behind it fully visible, as if it were really that thin an edge.

He rapidly calculated angles, checked the wings and floor for hidden mirrors.

The audience gasped.

. . . for out of the narrow edge of the dark mirror the woman in the gaudy sweat suit stepped, blinking as if emerging from the dark.

"My goodness," she murmured like the tourist born she was.

What a stooge! So annoying as to appear absolutely natural. He wondered what casting director Majika used.

The lithe magician gestured the woman to stand at her right side, then nodded to the dark men to spin the mirror again.

And this time the very same image of the sweat-suited woman stepped out from the other edge of the mirror. Majika moved between them, her own figure reflected to infinity in the bland mirrored face of the cabinet front.

The split images of the woman from the audience eyed each other and then began addressing each other.

"You can't be me."

"You must be me."

Twins. Simplest trick in the book. One backstage waiting to go on, the other planted in the audience. What a sucker ploy!

"How'd she do that?" the reporter prodded, her pencil waving in his face.

*Watch the fresh peel, baby!*

He leaned away from the unwanted contact. Twins, he was about to say when Majika waved the two women together and they slowly converged *until they melted into each other* and only one stood there, looking like she needed to be pinched to wake up.

"How'd she do that?" the reporter persisted, insisted, as that ilk will.

"Mirrors," he said shortly, rising so he could beat the rest of the audience to the exit doors. It was hard work. They were all standing, blocking the rows and the aisles, giving Majika a standing ovation for the final illusion of her act. He didn't even glance stageward to catch the vaunted final fillip of the show: a white rabbit pulled from a black top hat that moments before had been flatter than a Frisbee. Even flatter than the edge of the spinning mirror.

"Chardonnay," he greeted Majika when she finally returned from the multiple bows to her dressing room, which he had managed to enter as if he had appeared there by design. It stank of opening-night floral arrangements, but the show had been running for eight months.

"Merlin," she answered. "I mean, Marlon. Dare I ask how you got in here?"

"Started early, honey. Shut the door. We have things to discuss."

She obeyed, just as she had when she needed the paycheck.

His confidence perked up. He was the maestro, she the upstart. "That mirror thing is a fairly effective trick," he said, smiling. *God, it hurt.*

"Works for me." She sat at her dressing table to swipe the glitter highlights from her face.

He wished she would wipe off that new expression of elegant self-satisfaction. Or had she always looked that way?

"Seriously," he added, "I think you might have something there."

"Really?" She spun toward him, barefaced, looking as taut as a teenager.

He blinked like a tourist in the limelight. Something was wrong here. Unfair. Why should she be slim and unwrinkled when she'd passed off his babe-scale years ago?

"So how's your kid?" He had searched for the given name and given up.

"He died."

Silence always made him uncomfortable. He supposed firing her in the middle of that medical melodrama could have made it hard on . . . someone. He didn't like to hear about people dying. He never knew what to say, so he said nothing.

She seemed to expect no less from him. "So, did you like the show?" she asked.

"What's not to like?" *Everything.* "Glad you made such a great . . . comeback. You look terrific." Spoken softly, like an invitation.

"Thanks. It's good to see you again, too." She seemed pleased that he was here.

Oddly, that cheered him. He hadn't realized he'd needed cheer until now. "Really?"

"Well, you *are* the maestro. I'm flattered that you bothered to see my show."

"It's that Mirror Image trick that's the draw."

"Illusion," she corrected as swiftly as he had corrected the reporter.

She leaned an elbow on the dressing table, then her chin on her fist. Her image reflected to infinity behind her, thanks to the room's traditional parallel aisle of dressing table mirrors. It was all done with mirrors, and he was never done with mirrors, for he saw himself, small and wee, in a tiny corner of the reflected room behind her. His trademark mane of hair, now a dramatic white, was mostly extensions now. He was the sum of all the parts of his former illusions.

His heart fluttered. This moment was important. He knew it. For her, for him. He couldn't tell for which one it was more vital, just as one couldn't tell the twins from the Mirror Image illusion apart, even when they merged at the end.

"It's twins, isn't it?" He spoke without wanting to, hungry, urgent, worried.

"No, not twins."

"Not twins?"

She smiled gently, as at a slow-witted child. "This is something totally new, my illusion."

"Nothing's new in magic. Nothing! It's the same dodge and burn the photographers use to enhance photographs, only it's performed on the audience's eyes instead of a negative."

"Dodge and burn," she repeated. "I like the way you put that."

"Listen. I'm curious as hell, and I admit you've got me wondering. I really want to know how you do that."

She was silent. Signature illusions were a magician's bread and butter, big-time.

"A million dollars," he said, unable to stop himself. "I'll give you a million dollars if you show me the secret of that trick."

His words had surprised her as much as they had him.

"A million dollars." She savored them like bittersweet chocolate. "A million dollars would have saved Cody's life."

"Cody?"

"My son."

"Oh. Sure. Sorry. Sorry about that. So the disease, whatever, was terminal."

"Then it was. Not now."

He didn't know what to say, so he left his offer hanging there.

Apparently, she saw it still twisting in the wind. "You have to promise not to tell anybody."

"Sure. I mean, no. Not ever."

"And you can't use it yourself without paying me a . . . royalty."

"I wouldn't want to use it. I mean, I'm not a copier. Haven't ever been. I just want to know." He realized this new, unexpected need was the deepest he'd felt in some time. "I don't understand it. It's not magic like I know it. I need to—"

"I understand need," she said, cutting him off as if uninterested in the sudden flood of genuine feeling that engulfed him. "I'll show you how the trick works."

"A million dollars," he repeated, awash in a foreign wave of gratitude.

He really had to know, more than anything in his life. What life? It was all magic show. She'd probably give the million to some foundation for the disease that had killed her son. So he'd have helped her, after all. Life was strange, but magic was even stranger.

It would be quite an event. She would only reveal her illusion by using him in it. He was to be the stooge hauled from the front rows of the audience. His hotel and her hotel had agreed to copromote the one-time union of two major Strip magicians as if they were world-class boxers having a ballyhooed rematch.

Maybe they were.

She also stipulated that he wear his stage costume: glittering black sequined vest and satin cummerbund, the vaguely frock-coat-style jacket with the capelet in the back. Even his corset. He had felt like blushing when she mentioned it. How did she know?

It was obvious, though, that she had to know the stooge's apparel before the illusion began. He knew he had no twin, but maybe she could make one. No one came to take an impression of his face beforehand, but makeup people could do incredible masks even from photos these days. More and more it was special effects instead of old-fashioned magic, like everywhere else in the entertainment industry.

He was even announced on the program, a parchment flyer tucked into the glossy photo-book about Majika and her show that cost the marks nine bucks a throw: "Special Guest Appearance by Merlin the Magnificent by arrangement with the Goliath Hotel and Casino."

He sat down front, cricking his neck to look up at the stage he was used to looking down on people from. He felt like a kid dragged to a cultural outing, the local symphony maybe. There was a lot of show to sit through, and for a pro, it was all routine stuff, although the audience around him gasped and applauded.

He patted his palms together; no stinging claps from him. The racket, music to his ears when he was onstage, only hurt them now, especially the enthusiastically shrill whistles. His act never got whistles, but that was because it offered an old-fashioned dignity. He shrank a little in the disconcertingly mobile seat. Old-fashioned dignity did not sound like where it was at these days. He wouldn't outright copy Majika's mirror illusion, but borrow the best of it. And being part of it, going through it, was the easiest way to master another magician's illusion. You saw how it was done in an instant. Amazing that none of her audience stooges had been tempted to give away the trick, since it was the talk of Vegas and exposing it would cause a media frenzy. He was surprised that the Cloaked Conjuror at the New Millennium, who specialized in laying bare the mechanisms behind the magic, hadn't touched Majika's Mirror Image illusion.

When the mirrored cabinet was finally whisked onstage by the black-spandexed minions, Marlon stared hard at the space above the wheels. No mirror halfway back to reflect the front wheels as if they were the back ones and disguise an escape or entrance through the stage floor. In fact, Majika writhed underneath the cabinet like a sex kitten— or Eartha Kitt in heat—just to show the space was open and empty.

But not to worry. He'd soon know the way his "twin" would enter the box, although how she got that "two melt into one before your eyes" effect would be interesting to know. Probably mirrors again. So embarrassingly often, it was mirrors.

When she singled him out in the audience, he stood, nervous as a schoolboy at his first magic show. He was used to being in control, the king of the board, not a pawn.

As he headed for the six stairs to the stage, he heard an audience member hissing, "Look at that kooky old guy, that big white hair! Televangelist showman. Las Vegas!"

He held his cherished snowy pompadour high. It gave him an ecclesiastical air, he thought. He liked to consider himself as the high priest of magic in a town riddled with cheesy acolytes.

Chardonnay went through the usual chitchat with him: name, where he was from, what his hobbies were. The audience quickly caught on that he was more than the nightly guinea pig, that he was a noted magician himself, and laughed at his coyly truthful answers.

"Are you ready to face my mirror of truth and consequences?" she asked at last.

He glanced over his sober, caped, black shoulder at the gaudy thing. "Of course. I am even more ready to meet myself coming *from* it than going *into* it."

That earned a few titters from the audience, and then the gilt-frame door was swinging toward him like a horizontal guillotine aiming at his sutured neck. He ducked when he stepped up to enter the dark space behind the silvered door, thinking the opening might be too small for his height.

But nothing impeded him, and in a moment the door swung its matte-black-painted interior shut on him with a finalizing snap.

He turned at once, feeling up . . . down . . . around for any panel that might give.

Nothing did. In fact, he felt no edges of anything, no limits.

Surprised, he took a step or two forward. Or four or five. Six, seven, eight! Backward. Sideways. Nothing. And he could hear nothing, no muffled covering lines from Majika while the transfers were accomplished inside the mirrored cabinet. No transfers were accomplished. He couldn't even feel the cabinet jolted and manipulated by her accomplices as they spun the unit on the stage.

Nothing spun but his own baffled speculations. No way could such a paltry cabinet be so vast inside. No way, no illusion . . .

He was in a void. A soundless, motionless void. Not a hair's-width of light entered or escaped that void. It was as pitch-black as a childhood confessional booth.

Used to mentally tracking time, Marlon tried to tote up the seconds, minutes, he had been thus isolated. He couldn't compute it. Had no idea. His every expertise failed him here.

He would have pounded on the cabinet walls, broken the illusion, if he could have. But there was nothing to pound upon except the solid floor upon which he stood. *Upon which he stood.* He stamped an angry foot, a child having a tantrum. No sound, not even the pressure of an impact.

He searched his throat for a cry of protest or fear, but found it too tight and dry to respond to his panic.

And then, just like in that long-ago confessional, a small square of gray appeared in the darkness.

"At last! Where have you been?" he demanded. "There can't be much time to make our reappearance together."

"Time?" asked an odd, wheezing voice. "What's that? Be still. I need to absorb you."

*Absorb him?* "It's a little late for Method acting," he fussed. "If you can't do a reasonable impression of me right now, this entire illusion is ruined."

*Hmmm.* A botched illusion wouldn't do much for Majika's hot new career. Perhaps this mess-up was for the best. One less rival was one less rival. "Where do we exit this crazy thing? I'm first."

"And the first shall be last," the wheezing voice noted, laughing soundlessly, or rather, with something like a death rattle.

"I don't understand," he said.

"This is where she fulfills her bargain. I have provided the faces and bodies of hundreds of mortal souls for her nightly exhibitions. It was always understood that I, the eternally shifting one, should eventually acquire a mortal body and soul of my own and escape this endless lonely dark."

Perhaps his eyes had finally adjusted to the sliver of gray light that shared the darkness with him. He imagined a wizened, warty figure not at all human, as perhaps the cat-suited and masked ninja men might look if stripped of their shiny black skins.

The glimpse was enough to convince him that this was no derelict hired double, but something far less ordinary.

"You're a genie," he guessed, "like in a lamp, only in a mirror. And she found you somehow and you gave her a wish, her resurrection as a youthful woman and a magician, only she had to promise you . . . something."

"Not very much." The tone implied the creature had been studying him and found him wanting. "I did require a soul that had squeezed itself bare of attachments to this world, that had shriveled enough that there would be room for me to expand."

"You can't just . . . take me over!"

"Ah, but I can. That is my sole talent. I can replicate any being, any body. I got into trouble about that millennia ago, and some wicked magician—a real one—sentenced me to my lonely mirror."

"What kind of demon are you?"

"Explaining that would take too long. Although time is endless for me, I see by the spinning of my senses that we are expected to make our appearances upon the stage. I will warn you about one thing: my gift of replication responds only to the genuine. I can't control that. So it is and so shall you be and so shall I be when I become you. But freedom is worth the price."

"Freedom! And you would imprison me in your place? For eternity? No mortal soul deserves that."

"You are right." The creature's gray aura faded as it appeared to think.

Marlon knew a moment's relief and a sudden surge of hope for a new life, a better life, a kinder, gentler life. It was not too late . . .

"I will not abandon you to the dark," the croaking voice whispered, very near now, but no more visible. "I will not deprive you of your beloved limelight. I am a master of transformations, and I can manage that. Watch and believe."

Marlon . . . Merlin the Magnificent . . . found himself blinking like a tourist under a bank of gel-covered spotlights. Red, blue, green they blazed, Technicolor stars in an artificial sky.

He was . . . himself. Standing on a stage as he did almost every night, and Majika was lifting one graceful arm to indicate his presence. His reappearance from the box. His deliverance. His rebirth. *I will be good, I will, I will. Well, better.*

He took the stage, spread his arms and cape, rejoiced in the magic of his vanishing and recovery.

Applause.

And then more applause, accompanied by fevered whispers and then shouts of wonder.

Majika had thrust her left arm out to introduce the second half of the illusion, the other Merlin the Magnificent standing on her other side.

Marlon turned his eyes uneasily, expecting to see the gray, shriveled, scrofulous thing from the dark.

Instead, he saw a tall, white-haired man in fanciful evening dress . . . a man whose snowy mane had dwindled to a few threadbare strands . . . whose lumpy frame slumped like an overstuffed sack of extra-large baking potatoes . . . whose neck had become a jowly wattle, whose eyes were sunk in ridges of suet flesh.

For the first time he truly felt the horror in the story of Dorian Gray. *Gray!*

And before he could do or say anything, or even make a few more frantic mental promises to what or whom he couldn't say, before he could even take in the enormity of it all and the loss that loomed before him, the foul thing moved toward him—the man he was before he had changed his own mirror image—and sank into him like fog, or like an exiled part of himself.

Marlon drowned in the engulfing presence of Merlin, a Merlin cursed to live and die looking exactly as Marlon had not allowed himself to look, and happy for that.

Where Marlon went he couldn't say. It was dark. And narrow. And he heard and felt nothing and knew he'd go mad if he was kept here.

And then . . . slap! Snap! A sharp small sound and the world exploded again with light and applause. He gulped a deep, anxious breath of light-heated stage air, lifted his head, and almost sniffed the sound of the applause. It was thunderous. Better than ever. He'd survived whatever nightmare the mirrored box had put him through.

Then it became too much. The continuing racket crashed on his sensitive ears. He shrank again, cowered, even as Majika lifted her arm the better to display him to the admiring audience.

His heart pounded against the palm of her hand.

His long white hair was full and thick again, luxurious, and she stroked it with her other hand.

Majika's giant face stared down with piercing eyes. His sensitive ears flattened at the horrid screeching of her voice in the microphone as she displayed her triumph of illusion: him.

Her face came close, smiling.

"You've been such a good boy tonight, Marlon," she whispered giddily as if to a confrere, "you'll have extra veggies in your after-show supper, and maybe even a big carrot from Mr. MacGregor's garden."

While his ears and tail drooped with self-recognition, he spied his former form, now bent and shuffling, hastening out of the theater before the crowd began its rush for the exits.

# Doppelgangster

## Laura Resnick

Laura Resnick is the Campbell Award–winning author of several fantasy novels, and more than forty SF/F short stories. She is also the award-winning author of a dozen romance novels published under the pseudonym Laura Leone. In her copious spare time, she wrote *A Blonde in Africa,* a nonfiction account of her journey across the continent. You can find her on the Web at *http://www.sff.net/ people/laresnick.*

It wasn't no surprise that Skinny Vinny Vitelli got rubbed out. I mean, hey, I'd nearly whacked him myself a couple of times. So had most guys I know. Not to speak ill of the dead and all that, but he was an *irritating* bastard. Vinny could pick an argument with a plate of pasta. He could piss off the Virgin Mother. He could annoy the dead—so it wasn't exactly a big shock when he *became* one of them.

A couple of nuns taking a cigarette break found his body in an alley early one morning. He'd been done with four slugs straight to the chest. Which was a little strange, actually, because Vinny always wore the bulletproof vest he got the time he whacked that fed.

It's not what you're thinking. It was personal, not business. Vinny caught the guy in bed with his underage daughter. The vest was lying right there on the floor, and after Vinny impulsively emptied a whole clip into the guy's torso, he decided the vest was A Sign. (Did I mention he was a pretty religious guy?) See, Vinny had always been afraid of dying exactly the way he'd just killed the fed who'd been stupid enough to take off his bulletproof vest before humping a wiseguy's seventeen-year-old daughter right there in her father's house. (Feds. They breed 'em dumb.)

So Vinny picked the vest up off the floor, put it on, and never took it off since. I mean *never.* Just ask his wife. Well, if you can find her. She hot-tailed it straight down to Florida before the corpse was cold and ain't been seen since. She was making plans for her new life right there at Vinny's funeral, yakking on her cell phone with her real estate agent while the casket was being lowered into the ground.

"It's a funny thing," I said to Joey "the Chin" Mannino while the grieving Mrs. Vitelli kicked some dirt into her late husband's open grave with the toe of her shoe while telling her real estate agent she expected to be in Florida by nightfall.

"Huh?" Joey didn't really hear me. He was stroking his scarred chin as he stared lovesick at the Widow Butera. She was glaring back at him. A very beautiful woman, even at forty-five, but bad news for any guy.

"Give it up, Joey," I advised.

"I can't." He shook his head. "I've asked her to marry me."

I slapped my forehead. "Are you nuts?" One of the mourners frowned at me, so I lowered my voice. "She's had three husbands, and they're all dead. Don't that tell you something?"

"She's been unlucky."

"Her *husbands* have been unlucky. All three of them. So I'll lay odds that number four is gonna be real unlucky, too."

"It's not her fault, Vito."

"No, but being married to her is so unlucky it crosses over into dumb."

Her first husband got hit just because he was having dinner with Big Bobby Gambone at Buon Appetito the night Little Jackie Bernini decided to kill Bobby and didn't feel too particular about who else he sprayed with his Uzi. That was the start of the first Gambone-Bernini war. Well, a beautiful woman like that couldn't stay widowed forever. So three years later, during the second Gambone-Bernini war, she married a hit man from Las Vegas who the Gambones brought into town to teach the Berninis a lesson. But then the Berninis brought in their own hit man from Boise to deal with him, and ain't *nobody* tougher than those Boise guys. So the Widow was widowed again. Then, maybe because she was tired of marrying Gambones who got whacked out, the Widow shocked everyone by marrying Bernini Butera, who was everybody's favorite pick to head the Bernini family next—until Joey clipped him last year. That hit pretty much ended the third Gambone-Bernini war. But from the way the Widow Butera was glaring at Joey across Skinny Vinny Vitelli's grave now, it didn't look like she had forgiven Joey for stuffing her third husband into a cement mixer in New Jersey.

"What'd she say when you asked her to marry you?" I asked Joey.

"She told me she'd rather fry in hell." He shrugged. "She'll come round."

I shook my head. "Joey, Joey, Joey . . ."

He gave a friendly little wave to the Widow Butera. She hissed at him. The priest, Father Michael, smiled vaguely at her and said, "Amen."

So, to take Joey's mind off the Widow, I said, "Anyhow, like I was saying before, it's a funny thing."

"What's a funny thing?"

"About Vinny."

"No, no," Connie Vitelli was saying into her cell phone as she shook Father Michael's hand, "the condo's got to have an ocean view, or no deal. Understand?"

"Funny?" Joey said. "Oh! You mean about the vest, right?"

"Yeah." I shook my head when Father Michael gestured to me to throw some dirt onto the coffin. Hey, I didn't kill Vinny, so no way was I doing the work of deep-sixing him. Not my problem, after all. "Why'd Vinny take off that vest for the first time in five years? It ain't like him. He was a religious bastard."

"I think you mean superstitious." Joey's an educated guy. Almost read a book once.

"Okay, superstitious. Vinny always thought he'd get killed if he ever took that thing off. And, sure enough, look what happened. So why'd he take it off? It don't make sense."

"You mean you didn't hear, Vito?"

"Hear what?"

Connie was shouting into her cell phone. "Speak up! Are you driving through a tunnel or something? I'm getting tons of static!"

Vinny's daughter, now twenty-two years old and reputedly still a virgin, stepped up to the grave, made a face at her father's coffin, and then spit on it.

"Poor Vinny," said Father Michael, who looked like he'd taken a fistful of Prozac before coming here. "He will be missed."

"Not by anybody I ever met," muttered Joey.

I said to Joey, "What is it that I didn't hear?"

"Oh! The strange thing is, Vito, Vinny was still wearing his vest when they found his body."

"Huh? So how'd four slugs wind up in his chest?"

Joey shrugged. "It's a mystery. No holes in the vest. No marks at all, like it was never even hit. But as for Vinny's chest . . ." Joey grimaced.

While I thought about this, Connie Vitelli said, "But how big is the master bathroom?"

"So, Joey, you're saying that someone clipped Vinny, then put that vest back on him? For what? A joke?"

Joey shook his head. "That vest never came off him, Vito."

"Of course it did. How else did four bull—"

"The cops said the fasteners on Vinny's vest were rusted and hadn't been disturbed for years."

"Jesus. So it's true what Connie said. Vinny even *showered* in that thing!"

"Uh-huh."

I frowned at Joey. "But what you're saying . . . I mean, how did the bullets get past the vest and into Vinny's chest?"

"That's what's got the cops stumped."

"And why'd the cops tell *you* this?" Cops don't usually say nothing to guys like us besides, "I'll get you into the witness protection program if you cooperate."

"I don't think they meant to tell me," Joey said. "It just sort of slipped out somewhere during the seven straight hours they spent interrogating me yesterday."

"Oh, *that's* why you weren't at the wake."

Joey nodded wearily. "I'm thinking of suing them for the emotional trauma caused by missing a dear friend's wake, as well as the stain they have placed on my good reputation."

"How come they think you're the one who whacked him?"

"Well, you know, I had that argument with Vinny last week at Buon Appetito."

"So what?"

"So it turns out there were three undercover feds in the place at the time, and they took it the wrong way when I held a steak knife to Vinny's throat and said I'd kill him if I ever saw him again."

"Man," I said, sick of how unfair it all was. "You just have to be so careful these days. Watch every damn little word."

"Tell me about it."

"Whatever happened to the First Arraignment?" I said.

"Amendment."

"Whatever."

"I admit," Joey said, "I thought about whacking Vinny."

"Sure."

"Who didn't?"

"You said it."

"But it's not like he didn't deserve it," Joey said.

"Absolutely," I said as Vinny's son opened his fly and pissed on his father's grave.

"So I don't see why the cops have to get so bent out of shape just because someone finally *did* whack Vinny."

"Me, neither."

"And just because I'm the last guy anyone saw threatening to kill him, the cops ruin my whole day. Now, is that fair? Is that the American way?"

"It really stinks." I patted Joey on the back. "Just out of curiosity, *did* you kill him?"

"No. I was proposing to the Widow Butera at the estimated time of death."

"Did she alibi you to the cops?"

"No."

*Women.*

"So I wonder who did it," I said.

"Could've been any one of a hundred guys," Joey said.

"More," I said.

"Yeah."

The Widow Butera stepped up to Vinny's grave and looked down at it for a long moment. Then she crossed herself, glared once more at Joey, and started walking to her car.

When Connie Vitelli got off the phone for a split second, Joey and I paid our respects so we could get the hell out of there.

"Such a shame," Joey said politely to Vinny's widow. "Him being so young and all."

"Not that young." Connie shook her head. "And I think dementia was setting in already. He was seeing things."

"Seeing things?" Joey said. "Then 'dementia' probably isn't the right word, because that's when—"

"Oops! I gotta take this," Connie said as her cell phone rang.

"Wait a minute," I said. "What things was Vinny seeing? Feds stalking him? Hitters from the Bernini family coming after him?" If we knew, we might be able to figure out who'd whacked him.

Connie rolled her eyes. "Himself, if you can believe it."

"Huh?"

"The day before Vinny died, he came home in a cold sweat, babbling about how he had just bumped into the spitting image of himself on the street outside Buon Appetito. The guy was even dressed like Vinny. Right down to the bulletproof vest. Go figure." Connie shrugged off the idea that her husband's perfect double was out there somewhere and added, "Now, I've really got to take this call. Thanks for coming, fellas." She turned away and said into her cell phone, "Hello? Oh, good! Thanks for getting back to me today. Yes, I'll be out of the house by tonight, so put it on the market right away."

"So Vinny was losing his mind," I said.

Joey nodded toward Connie and the kids. "And you're surprised by this?"

"No, I guess not."

Which is why I didn't think any more about it. Not then, anyhow. Not until three days later, which was when a dinner-and-dance cruise accidentally found Johnny Be Good Gambone's body floating in the Hudson River.

"But it can't be Johnny," I said to Joey Mannino when he told me about it.

"It is. Positive ID, no doubt about it."

"No, it can't be, because—"

"Vito, pull yourself together," Joey said. "Two of our guys dead in one week. We're going to the mattresses."

"It can't be Johnny, because I saw him alive at the same time they were fishing that corpse out of the river."

"It must be the Berninis doing these hits. Who else would have the nerve? Those bastards! Well, if they want another war, we'll give them another w—"

"Joey, are you listening to me? I'm telling you, whoever they found in the Hudson, it wasn't Johnny Gambone, because I had dinner with him last night!"

Joey stared at me. "Are you losing your mind, too?"

"No! They're just putting the wrong name on the corpse."

But when we showed up at the mortician's to inspect the body, I saw there'd been no mistake. That was Johnny Gambone lying on that slab, no doubt about it. Who else in the world had a purple tattoo of a naked broad on his shoulder with the word "Mom" written across it?

"So you're not still denying that's Johnny?" Joey prodded.

"Couldn't be anyone else, but . . ."

"But?"

"But I'm telling you, I was having dinner with him that evening. We talked about Vinny's death. Johnny told me that no matter how much we hated Vinny, it was our job to find out who'd clipped him, because we can't just let people go around killing made guys without even asking first. Especially not *our* made guys."

"Vito, that's impossible. According to the cops, Johnny had already been dead for thirty-six hours by the time you had dinner with . . . with . . ."

"Something's not right," I said.

And whatever was not right became even more wrong a couple of days later when Danny "the Doctor" Bardozzi, best known for chopping up four members of the Gambone family and passing them off as ground ostrich meat at an East Village restaurant which went out of business soon after Danny was indicted, was found dead.

I know what you're thinking, but we didn't do it. We didn't even *know* who did it, just like we didn't know who'd clipped Johnny and Vinny. We were knee-deep in bodies by now, and we had no idea who was stacking them up.

"And the *way* the Doctor was killed," Joey told me as we walked along Mott Street, "is really strange."

"You mean compared to the normal way Vinny was killed, with four bullets pumped into his chest and not a scratch on the bulletproof vest he was wearing at the time? Or the normal way Johnny Gambone was found floating in the river while I was watching him eat linguine and bitch about his indigestion?" Okay, I was feeling irritable and got a little sarcastic.

Joey said, "Listen, Danny showed up at Bernini's Wine and Guns Shop in a panic, armed with two Glocks and a lifetime supply of ammo, and locked himself in the cellar. There's no way in or out of the cellar except through the one door he'd locked, and—because Danny was acting so crazy—there were a dozen Berninis standing right by that door trying to convince him to come out."

"And?"

"Next thing they know, they hear a few shots go off. So they break down the door and run downstairs. Danny's alone. And dead." Joey grimaced. "Shotgun. Made a real mess."

"But you said he had two Glocks."

"That's right. And, no, there wasn't a shotgun down there. Not before Danny locked himself in . . . and not when the Berninis found him there."

"Then it wasn't a shotgun. He blew his own head off with a Glock."

"No. His guns hadn't even been fired, and there was buckshot everywhere. Just no shotgun."

"In a locked cellar with no windows and no other door? That's impossible."

"Like it was impossible for you to be eating dinner with a guy whose two-day-old corpse was floating in the Hudson River at the time?"

"We're in trouble," I said. "We've got something going on here that's bigger than another war with the Berninis."

"That's what they think, too."

"What? You mean they ain't blaming us for Danny's death?"

"How could they? I just told you what happened. They know we're not invisible, and neither are our guns. In fact, they knew something strange was happening even before we did, because they knew they didn't kill Johnny Gambone."

"We've got to have a sit-down with the Berninis."

"I've called one for tonight. At St. Ignazio's. I gotta have dinner at my mother's in Brooklyn first, but I'll be there."

St. Ignazio's was dark and shadowy, lit only by candles. The whole place smelled of incense and lingering perfume—the Widow Butera's perfume, I realized, as I saw her kneeling before a statue of St. Paula, patron saint of widows.

Father Michael and two guys from the Bernini family were waiting for me in an alcove on the other side of the church.

"Is Joey here yet?" I asked the Widow Butera.

"What do I care? What do I care about any of you fiends?" She rose to her feet and came toward me. "I hate you all! Every single one of you! I spit on you! I spit on your mothers' graves!"

"So you haven't seen him?"

She shook her fist at me. "Stay away from me!"

"Hey, I'm not the one trying to make you a widow for the fourth time. So don't yell at *me,* sister. And . . ." I frowned as wispy white things started escaping from the fist she shook at me. "Are those feathers? Whatever happened to praying with rosary beads?"

She made a real nasty Sicilian gesture and stomped toward the main door in a huff just as Joey entered the church. The poor guy's face brightened like he'd just met a famous stripper.

He asked her, "Have you thought any more about my proposal? I mean, take all the time you need. I just—"

"Get out of my way!" she shrieked. "Don't ever come near me again! Don't even look at me!"

"Maybe we'll talk later?" Joey said to her back.

She paused to look over her shoulder at him. "Amazing," she said in a different tone of voice. Then she left.

"You're late," I said to Joey.

"Sorry. Couldn't be helped."

"Gentlemen," said Father Michael, smelling strongly of sacramental wine as he came close to us, "the Berninis are eager to begin this summit, so if you—"

"Summit?" I repeated.

"Sit-down," said Joey.

"Oh."

"So if you'll just take your seats . . ."

"You're fucking late," said Carmine Bernini. He was Danny "the Doctor" Bardozzi's cousin by marriage, and also the world's biggest asshole.

"But we haven't been waiting too long," added Tony Randazzo. He was a good-looking kid who'd been a soldier in the Bernini family for a few years. A stand-up guy, actually, and I'd let him date my daughter if I didn't think I'd probably have to kill him one day.

"Would anyone care for some chips and dip?" Father Michael asked. "Maybe some cocktails?"

"We ain't here to fucking socialize," said Carmine.

"Don't curse in church," said Joey.

"Well, please fucking excuse *me*."

Like I said—the world's biggest asshole. "Never mind the refreshments, Father," I said. "This'll just take a few minutes." I looked at Carmine. "Let's lay our cards on the table."

So we did. And what these guys told me about Danny Bardozzi's death got my full attention.

"He said *what*?"

Tony said, "Danny came into the shop that day and said he'd just seen his perfect double, his spitting image."

"His doppelgänger?" said Father Michael.

"Yeah, his doppelgangster," said Carmine. "He was fucking freaking out. In a cold sweat, shaking like a virgin in a whorehouse, babbling like a snitch with the feds. Scared out of his mind."

"Because he'd seen this doppelgangster?" I said.

"Yeah. He said it meant he was gonna die."

"He was right," I said. "But how did he know?"

"Perhaps," said Father Michael, "he knew that, traditionally, seeing your doppelgänger portends your own death."

"No shit?" said Carmine.

"No sh—um, yes, really," said Father Michael.

"But we got more than people *pretending* their deaths here, Father," I said.

"No, *portending*," the priest said. "Seeing your doppelgänger is, in popular folklore, a sure sign that you're going to die."

"Weird shit," said Carmine.

"Even weirder," I said, "Danny ain't the only one around here who's seen a doppelgangster." I told them about Skinny Vinny telling Connie he'd seen his own perfect double the day before he died.

"Johnny Gambone did, too!" said Father Michael, swaying a little. "My God! I didn't realize . . ." He wiped his brow. "Just a few days before his body was found, Johnny told me after Mass that he'd seen a man who looked very much like himself, dressed the same, even bearing the same tattoo—but nowhere near as handsome."

"He always was a vain son of a bitch," said Carmine.

"So he saw his double, too, then," I said. "All three of these guys died after seeing their doubles."

"And died in such strange ways," Tony added.

"Yes," said Father Michael. "Almost as if meeting the doppelgänger doesn't just presage death, it actually curses the victim, making him utterly defenseless against death when it comes for him."

"So once you see this fucking thing, that's it?" said Carmine. "You're as good as whacked?"

"That would explain how bullets somehow got past or around Vinny's vest," I said.

"And how someone walked past all of us without being seen," said Tony, "and got through a locked door to kill Danny."

"So we're dealing with what?" I said. "Witchcraft? Some kind of curse? The evil eye?"

"It's some weird fucking shit," said Carmine.

Father Michael fumbled behind the skirts of the shrine of the Virgin and pulled out a bottle of wine. He uncorked it, gulped some down, and then said, "Black magic. What else could it be?"

"Fucking creepy."

"And whoever is doing it is damn good," I said. "I had dinner with Johnny Gambone's doppelgangster and didn't even know it wasn't the real guy."

"But no one has seen Vinny, Johnny, and Danny since they were found dead, right?" said Father Michael. "I mean, no one has seen their doubles since then?"

I hadn't even thought about that. "No," I said. "That's right. The last time I saw Johnny's double—the last time anyone saw it, as far as I know—was before his body was found."

"So . . ." Father Michael took another swig. "So whoever is doing this sends a doppelgangst—doppelgänger after the victim to curse him with inevitable death. And then, after the victim is dead, the perfect double continues carrying on the victim's normal life until the death is discovered."

"And then what?"

"Then it . . ." Father Michael shrugged. "It probably disintegrates into whatever elemental ingredients it was originally fashioned from."

"So if you hid the fucking body well enough, it would be years before anyone even knew you'd made the hit. Hey, this black magic is some fucking great stuff! If I could learn to do it—"

"Whoever *has* learned to do it," I said, "is out to kill all of us. Get it? We've got to stop him before we're all dead!"

"Vito's right," said Joey. "We're all in danger."

My cell phone suddenly rang, making us all jump a little. (Hey, if you thought someone was about to kill you that way, wouldn't you be a little jumpy, too?) I pulled the phone out of my pocket. "Hello?"

"Vito?" said Joey at the other end. "I'm coming from my mother's, and I'm still in Brooklyn. Stuck in traffic. You'd better start the sit-down without me. I'll get there as soon as I can."

My blood ran cold as I stared at the Joey sitting here with me, absently stroking his chin the way the real one often did. Choosing my words carefully, I said to the Joey on the phone, "Seen anything strange lately?"

"Huh?"

"Anyone familiar?"

"Well . . . my mother, obviously."

"No one else?"

"What are you talking about?"

"Okay, good," I said with relief. I like Joey. I'd miss him if he was the next one to die. "Listen to me very carefully. *Stay right where you are.* Call me back in an hour."

"But, Vito—"

"Just do it!" I hung up.

"Who was that?" asked Joey.

I jumped him, took him to the floor, and started banging his head against the stone. "Vito!" he screamed. "Vito! *Stop!* What are you doing? *Ow!*"

"Vito!" cried Father Michael. "Stop!"

"Fucking maniac," said Carmine.

"Thought you'd get Joey Mannino, did you?" I shouted at the doppelgangster. "Well, think again, you bastard!"

"This is one of them?" the priest shrieked.

"Yes!" I kept banging its head against the floor. "And it's gonna tell me who's behind these hits!"

Its eyes rolled back into its head, it convulsed a few times, and then its head shattered like dry plaster.

"Whoa!" said Tony.

I looked down at the mess. Nothing but crumbled dust, lumps of dirt, and feathers where the thing's head had been. Then its body started disintegrating, too.

"I think you whacked it, Vito," said Tony.

Father Michael poured the whole rest of the bottle of wine down his throat before he spoke. "Well . . . I guess this means that Joey is safe now?"

"Not for long," I said. "Whoever did this will make another one the moment he knows this one has been—wait a minute!"

"Vito? What is it?" said Tony.

"Maybe it's not a *he*," I said.

"Huh?"

"Think about it! Who would hit the Berninis *and* the Gambones? Who hates *both* families that much? Who wants all of us dead?"

"You saying the fucking feds are behind this?"

"No, you asshole! I'm saying the one person who hates both families equally is behind this!" I grabbed a handful of the crap that had been Joey's doppelgangster a minute ago and waved it at these guys. *"Feathers!"*

"Vito, this is a very serious accusation," said Father Michael, slurring his words a little. "Are you absolutely sure?"

"Huh?" said Tony.

"Just fucking follow him," said Carmine as I ran for the same exit that the Widow Butera had taken.

I kicked in the door of her apartment without knocking. I'd figured out her scam by now, so I expected the feathers, the blood sacrifices, the candles, the chanting, and the photos of Bernini and Gambone family members.

I just didn't expect to see my own perfect double rising out of her magic fire like a genie coming out of a lantern. I pulled out my piece and fired at it.

"*Noooo!*" screamed the Widow Butera. She leaped at me, knocked my gun aside, and started clawing at my face.

"Kill it! Kill it!" I shouted at the others.

Carmine said, "I always wanted to do this to you, Vito," and started pumping bullets into my doppelgangster while I fought the Widow. Father Michael ran around the room praying loudly and drenching things in holy water. Tony took a baseball bat—don't ask me where he got it—and started destroying everything in sight: the amulets and charms hanging everywhere, the jars of powders and potions stacked on shelves, the cages containing live chickens, and the bottles of blood. My perfect double shattered into a million pieces in the hail of Carmine's bullets, and the pieces fell smoldering into the fire. Then Tony kicked at the fire until it was scattered all over the living room and started dying.

"It's a fucking shame about the carpet," Carmine said as chickens escaped the shattered cages and started running all over the room.

". . . blessed art thou among women, and blessed is the fruit of thy womb . . ." Father Michael was chanting.

"What else can I break? What else can I break?" Tony shouted.

"I'll kill you all!" the Widow screamed. "You're all dead!"

"Too late, sister, we're onto you now. You've whacked your last wiseguy," I said as she struggled in my grip.

"Three husbands I lost in your damned wars!" she screamed. "I told them to get out of organized crime and into something secure, like accounting or the restaurant business, but would they listen? *Noooo!*"

"Secure? The fucking restaurant business? Are you kidding me?"

"The Berninis and Gambones ruined my life!" the Widow Butera shrieked. "I will have vengeance on you all!"

"Repent! Repent!" Father Michael cried. Then he doused her with a whole bottle of holy water.

"*Eeeeeeeeee!*" She screamed something awful . . . and then started smoking like she was on fire.

I'm not dumb. I let go of her and backed away.

The room filled with smoke, and the Widow's screams got louder, until they echoed so hard they made my teeth hurt . . . then faded. There was a dark scorch mark on the floor where she'd been standing.

"Where'd she go?" I said.

"She'll never get her fucking security deposit back now," said Carmine, looking at the floor.

Tony added, "No amount of buffing will get that out."

"What the hell happened?" I said, looking around the room. The Widow had vanished.

Father Michael fell to his knees and crossed himself. "I don't think she was completely human. At least, not anymore. She had become Satan's minion."

"Huh. I wondered how she kept her good looks for so fucking long."

"That's it?" I asked Father Michael. "She's just . . . gone?"

He nodded. "In hell, where she belongs." After a moment he added, "Mind you, that's only a theory."

"Either way," I said, "I'm kinda relieved. I know we couldn't just let her go. Not after she'd hit three guys and tried to hit me and Joey, too. But I really didn't want to whack a broad."

"What a fucking pussy you are, Vito."

"Carmine, you asshole," I said, "the sit-down was successful. We found out who's behind these hits, we put a stop to it, and there ain't gonna be no new war. So now get outta my sight before I forget my manners and whack you just for the hell of it."

"Did I mention how much fun it was pumping a whole clip into your fucking doppelgangster?"

My cell phone rang, making Father Michael jump.

"Damn." I knew who it was even before I answered it. "Hello?"

"Vito," said Joey, "I've been sitting here in my car, not going anywhere, just like you said, for a whole hour. Now, do you want to tell me what the hell is going on?"

I looked at the scorched spot the Widow had left in the floor and tried to think of the best way to break the news to him. "So, Joey . . . would you still want to marry the Widow Butera if you knew she'd been trying to whack you and everyone you know?"

# Mixed Marriages
# Can Be Murder

## Will Graham

Will Graham is the pseudonym of a private investigator in Texas specializing in computer forensics and electronic evidence. This is his first short-story sale.

 looked at my cigarette as the flame caught, while the coffee finished brewing. It was an old trick, but still a fun one, and I liked being able to do it after all these years. Another beautiful day. Leaning against the counter in the kitchen, I glanced out the tinted window to see the city before me. Critics be damned, San Francisco had a magic all its own. We'd been here for many years, and it still struck me that some cities can truly hold you in their spell. The faint streaks of predawn were appearing. I fought a yawn.

A noise behind me made me turn. Emma came in from the living room, her white fur robe belted tightly around her, auburn hair spilling loosely around her shoulders. "Darling," she said. "Must you?"

I smiled at her. "It keeps me human. So to speak."

She wrinkled her pretty nose and looked at me with a combination of irritation and fondness. She doesn't like my smoking, she never did, but as I've pointed out to her, I smoked when she married me, so she has no real grounds to complain. It's a game, an old one, a familiar one, the type that people who have been together forever and a day can play with each other.

I turned, reached into the cabinet, and got her favorite cup. Precisely one spoon of sugar (raw, imported from Jamaica), mixed well. Her newest fad was heavy cream, delivered every morning. A heaping splash of that, again mixed well until blended into the coffee. When it was ready, I put the cup on a saucer and presented it to her with a flourish. I could see into the living room, the heavy curtains moving as a breeze came in from the open window.

She took a sip, smiled, and said, "You'll do. I think I'll keep you."

"I certainly hope so." I took my own coffee to the table and joined her. If it matters, I like mine black, no sugar, but I'm not fanatical about it. Over the years, I've had everything from nectar of the gods to stuff that tasted like it leaked from a broken crankcase in a truck from Kentucky. Coffee is coffee is coffee, and I've loved it from the first time I ever had it.

"Well," she said in a teasing tone, "there are things you are good for." Her smile widened. "Such as the other night . . ."

"That's enough about 'the other night,'" I said in reply. Her smile grew even brighter, and it amazed me, as it always does, that she could still take my breath away, to use a cliché.

She looked over my shoulder at the sun rising. "It's beautiful, isn't it?"

"It always is. But then, it's not the only beautiful thing I see." I gave her my own version of a sex-crazed leer.

She fought a blush. "Now, darling . . ."

"'Ah, to be young and in love . . .'" I let it trail off.

A perfect morning. The sun rising, the woman I loved with me, in our home, safe, warm, and secure. It was all perfect.

Well . . .

Except for the body in the living room.

Just a week ago, we'd been working a case.

We'd met the client at a small restaurant, a favorite of ours called Café Elégant.

"Mr. and Mrs. Steele, it is a pleasure to meet you," he said as he stood to greet us.

"And you, sir," I replied as we shook hands. It was obvious that he was instantly and forever dazzled by Emma, but she has that effect on most men. We sat down after he asked us to do so.

Arthur "Call Me Art" Harrison was unremarkable in every physical way—average height, average weight, average hair loss, average glasses—but for some odd reason he reminded me of a weasel. He had the air of someone who had deciphered the meaning of life and the secrets of the cosmos. After spending ten minutes with him, I could almost believe that he had indeed.

"You come highly recommended," Art Harrison said. "Your reputation is remarkable."

"We've had some luck," Emma said as the wine steward approached. Harrison ordered the single most expensive wine on the list, without even wondering if it would go with our meals. Since Emma and I had been regulars here over the years, the sommelier brought only two glasses, setting one before Emma, the other before Harrison.

"You don't drink, Mr. Steele?" Harrison asked.

"Not wine," I said with a small smile.

Out of the corner of my eye, I could see Emma fighting the giggles. We'd been through this before, and it always amused her. Why it did was beyond me, but any man who claims to understand a woman, any woman, is either a liar or living in fantasyland. Ever since she bought me that silly movie with the actor and his sillier Hungarian accent . . .

Harrison explained his situation. Nothing major, but someone had come up with a new twist on an old twist in the computer software arena, and competitors were out to steal it before it could reach the production phase.

"That is impressive," Emma said. She had the marvelous ability to focus on someone so totally and completely as to give the person the feeling that her day would not be complete without their having met. She was sincere about it. People fascinated her, and always would. I was a more private type of individual, preferring to stay at home with her, my books, a bit more distrustful of people. The clichés are true: opposites do indeed attract, and it's a wonderful thing when it works.

"How long will you need us?" I asked as the dinner was served. Harrison had ordered lobster flambé, Emma and myself steak Diane.

"A week," he replied. "One week of your time is all we need."

I nodded. "It will be expensive."

"As they say, cost is no object."

Emma nodded to him, acknowledging the compliment. "As I mentioned, we've had some luck."

"Luck has little to do with brilliance," Harrison said. "I had the two of you researched."

I kept my face impassive, but felt Emma stiffen just a touch. She always got a little nervous when people started asking too many questions. "What do you mean?"

Harrison smiled, pleased with the chance to show off for us. "Jonathan and Emma Steele, private investigators. Low-key, quiet, but a one hundred percent success rate. Rumor has it that the FBI uses you as consultants occasionally, and it's a known fact that Mrs. Steele worked for the CIA at one point."

Emma relaxed. Unless you knew her very, very well, it would have been impossible to detect either the sudden tension or its release.

"I was in Hungary for a time, true. But I was nothing more than a student, out to see the world," she said with one of her most dazzling smiles.

Harrison gave her a look that, verbalized, would have been, "Okay, we can play the game if you wish. But I know better." "Then there was the business with that killer, the serial killer who ate his victims. He escaped from the state hospital he was being held in. Is it true that you left him bound and gagged on the steps of the police station?"

I shrugged. "You know how rumors are, Mr. Harrison." I shut my mind to the memories that came rushing back. For the first time in a long time, I had been actually frightened when all that happened.

"Call me Art, please," he said with a smile as he forked some more lobster from his plate. "According to the story, whatever happened with that man has left him quite quiet, subdued, with a serious sudden interest in religion. Did you really shave his head and paint it bright orange?"

I shrugged again, pretending I didn't see the look in Emma's eyes. "Who knows what made him do what he did? And who knows what made him change his ways?" I ignored the question about head shaving and orange paint; Emma does have her moments of whimsy.

"You two are the best there is," Harrison said after he swallowed his food, "and that's what we want. The best."

"Well, we'll see what we can do for you," I told him.

He reached into his pocket and handed me a check. The zeros on the end made my eyes blink several times. "That's what it's worth to us," he said with a satisfied smile.

Emma leaned over just enough to see the amount, then turned back to Harrison. "I believe we can accommodate your needs, Mr. Harrison."

"Call me Art," he said again, and looked around for the waiter.

Alistair came out, discreetly removing the dinner plates. Emma's was almost spotless. If there's one thing in this world she adores, it's steak Diane.

Dessert was, as always, an event. Bananas Foster, prepared table side. I pushed it around on my plate, not actually eating any.

Emma patted her lips with her napkin, then smoothly stood. "If you gentlemen will excuse me for a moment." She left us at the table, and I gave Harrison credit for trying not to watch her as she walked away, long legs flashing. As I mentioned, she does have that effect on men.

He and I sat quietly for a few moments, then began discussing the nuts and bolts of the matter at hand. While I could appreciate the importance to him, it was a simple case of industrial security. We'd done this sort of work many times before, and I felt confident it would be easily handled.

Emma returned to the table, joining the conversation. We came to the agreement that we would start the next evening.

It was a pleasant night, and we walked Harrison to his car. After reassuring him that things were under control, Emma and I decided to walk to our home rather than ride. Harrison started his gleaming Porsche and took off with tires squealing. As the taillights rounded the corner, I looked at Emma. "He was showing off, of course."

"Of course, darling. Do you find that annoying?"

"Amusing, to be honest. If he only knew . . ."

She laughed with me, her perfect teeth flashing. "Yes. If he only knew. Are you hungry? You didn't eat much tonight. You never do, but tonight seemed different."

"Just not in the mood, I guess."

And we walked home, arm in arm in the moonlight. "It's still beautiful, isn't it?" she asked me, glancing upward.

"Most of the time," I replied.

She giggled. "Three-quarter time?" she asked, pointing at the three-fourths moon.

"That, too."

She hit me with the full force of her eyes, and I was mesmerized. Come to think of it, that's how she got me to fall in love with her. In all my years, I've always marveled how men plan, plot, scheme, romance, and seduce. When a woman makes up her mind that a man is hers, a wise male simply accepts it, as there's no use fighting. A mutual friend once asked me when I had fallen in love with Emma, and my immediate response was, "As soon as she told me to."

We were silent for a time, enjoying the night, then she tightened her grip on my arm. "Mr. Steele, I do believe there's something in the air."

"Indeed there is, Mrs. Steele," doing my best Sean Connery imitation. "Something's come up."

Her hand slid up and down my arm, and she looked at me with the eyes that a woman saves for the man she loves. "Well, we'll see what we can do about that."

And when we got home, we did.

The next night we were ready.

Four days passed with nothing happening. Nothing at all. On the fifth night . . .

Shortly after midnight, there was a delicate sound of breaking glass from the foyer. Emma had been lightly dozing, and her eyes snapped open. She was alert and on her feet in the space of a heartbeat. Knowing each other well enough, we had no need for words as we moved to our respective hiding places. One of the things Harrison insisted upon was that we identify the thieves.

A scratching sound told us someone was trying to pick the lock to the front office door. I'd been tempted to leave it unlocked, but decided against being too obvious about the setup. I had an infrared camera ready, and as the door opened, I hit the button to start the film rolling. Specially modified to be completely silent, it did its job perfectly, recording everything from that moment on.

As the intruder came into the room, I could see night-vision goggles over the eyes. The would-be thief went directly to the safe where the software was stored, and began manipulating the dial. I fought a small smile of admiration: in this day and age of smash and grab, take the money and run, it was refreshing to see someone who was a craftsman.

The camera was still working quite nicely, the tiny light on my side of it blinking steadily. I waited until the thief had the safe open and the package in his hands. I couldn't resist any longer, snapped off the camera to protect the sensitive film, and hit the light switch. With a hoarse cry, the thief straightened and tore the goggles from his face. Since they were designed to take any ambient light, however faint, and amplify it to the nth degree, a sudden blast of real light had to be agonizing. Of course I'm always sympathetic to those who have problems with light.

I flicked a small switch on the side of the camera as I turned it on again, switching to regular film to get a good shot of the intruder's face. Emma came up behind him. While he was still rubbing his eyes, she took the package from his hands and gently guided him to the floor.

I came out from the filing cabinet where I had squeezed myself, and didn't waste time. The thief was still trying to focus his blasted eyes, so it was simple to pat him down until I found his wallet. Emma stood a little closer to him, in case he made any sudden moves. Flipping the wallet open, I read his name aloud from his driver's license. "Mark . . . Harrison? Any relation to Arthur Harrison?"

Mark managed to get his eyes open and look at me. "So what? Who the hell are you?"

Emma tapped him on the back of his head, gently for her but with sufficient force to get his attention. "Manners, my friend."

He tried to turn his head toward her, but she held his neck in her hand easily, forcing him to look at me.

"Since you asked so nicely," I said to him, "my name is Steele, Jonathan Steele. The lovely lady holding you is my wife, Emma. Your brother hired us to prevent this very thing from happening."

Mark looked up at me, his eyes still streaming. "He would."

I glanced at Emma. She was still holding his neck securely, but her eyes narrowed. "What do you mean?" she asked.

"He stole it from me," Mark said. "I spent years on it, and he took it. Now he claims it's his, all his."

"Can you prove that?"

He looked everywhere but at me. "I could explain it, but never prove it."

"Try me."

He took a deep breath. "My brother used black magic to get my share of the company."

*As the actress said to the bishop,* I thought, *it's cute, but a bit hard to swallow.*

Over the years, both Emma and myself had developed contacts and connections, some of which were literally out of this world. It didn't take much to learn that Mark was telling the truth. His brother, whom I now thought of as Art the Weasel, had hired a *bofour,* a voodoo priest, to perform a spell of change. Translated into English, the brothers briefly traded bodies. Art/Mark kept Mark/Art drunk and drugged, posed as him, and met with an attorney to sign over complete control of the company. After the spell wore off, the real Mark had only hazy memories, but one night the entire episode came back to him.

I glanced at Emma. She nodded slightly. "It happens like that sometimes," she said. She knows far more about that than I do, and I, as usual, deferred to her on such subjects.

"Let's have a little fun," was my suggestion.

"What do you have in mind?"

"Something massive, I think."

Simply put, we stole the code.

Doesn't sound like much, does it? We found out that the code to the safe had been changed, but, I, um, got around that fairly easily.

Once the safe was opened, the written software code was there, along with more than a dozen diskettes. Mark clutched them fiercely, almost sobbing in relief. "I don't know how to thank you," he said.

"We'll cash the check your brother gave us," Emma told him. "I assume that won't affect you at all?"

"Not a bit. When this gets out, and if it does as well as I think it will, I'll double it."

"That's not necessary," I told him. "We've already been paid."

Later, Emma asked, "Any guesses?" as she came into the living room, offering me a glass.

"None," I said as I took a sip, feeling the warmth trickle down my throat. "For all I care, he can rot."

She sat next to me for a while, then stood, stretching. "I think I'll take a bath," she said, leaning down to kiss me. "And then . . . well, we'll see . . ."

"Tonight's the night," I reminded her.

I stayed where I was for a moment, savoring both the drink and the night.

The picture window exploded inward in a shower of glass.

I went over the back of the couch, crouching low. A figure came through the window, a pistol in hand.

When I saw who it was, I stood.

"Hello, Art," I said as I brushed glass fragments from my clothing.

"Shut up," Art Harrison said. "Where's your wife?"

"Leave her out of this."

"You ruined me, you bastard. You both did. So you both pay."

"How did we do that?"

"You were supposed to kill him!" Art yelled. "Kill him once and for all and get him out of my life!"

"We don't do that kind of work."

I could see old Art was building himself into a rage. "I had it all planned, damn you. He was supposed to break in, and you'd kill him. That would have been the end of it."

"The best-laid plans and all that," I said.

His eyes glazed over. He aimed the gun at me and pulled the trigger. The shot was explosive.

He stared in shock. I staggered a little; these new heavy-caliber weapons are annoying, but I was still standing, and I smiled at him.

Art pulled the trigger again. The bullet hit me in the upper right chest, tearing through my shirt. "You know," I said to him, "I just bought this shirt."

"My God," he moaned. "What are you?"

"Arthur old boy," I said as I brushed powder from my shirt and glass from my hair, "your inquiries about us were not as good as you thought they were."

He'd made me angry, very angry, and there was nothing I could do about my fangs beginning to show.

His head was shaking back and forth, not believing. Whatever. I was used to it and didn't really care anymore.

He kept pulling the trigger. One of the bullets hit me in the head, and that really pissed me off. While hardly fatal, the damn things *hurt*. I sent a fervent thanks that we had no neighbors on the top floor and that Emma had insisted on soundproofing the entire place a few years back.

"Fun's over, Art," I said as I moved toward him.

There was a growling sound from the darkness. Before I could reach him, a huge white creature shot out of the blackness. Covered with fur, moving with lupine grace.

Art screamed.

Once.

"What should we do?" Emma asked me the next morning.

"I'm open to ideas. This one won't be easy to explain."

"We've got the shattered window," Emma said, a flick of her head indicating the stirring curtains. "He did have a weapon. He was trying to kill you."

"Just his bad luck he tried on a night when the moon was full, I guess."

She smiled at me. "Never try and kill a woman's husband. We get cranky."

I nodded. "And mortal women think they have problems every twenty-eight days."

"I suppose we could clean this up ourselves."

I nodded as I lit yet another cigarette. Emma frowned as the tip burst into flame when I glanced at it, but, as I said before, it was a trick I liked doing. Okay, so I still liked showing off for her a little bit. "We're going to have to, I think. A quiet and clean disappearance is best, I think."

"Agreed. I'll go get dressed, and we can get this done. Will the sun bother you while we clean this up, darling?"

I shook my head. "Between the tinted windows and heavy curtains, I'm fine as long as it doesn't hit me directly."

She went into the living room, heading for the bedroom, her clothing in the bedroom closet. "Jonathan, I've been thinking," she called out. "We need a pet. A bird or something. Perhaps a dog. Maybe another cat."

"Darling, the last time we tried that, you *ate* the cat."

"Picky, picky, picky . . ."

# The Case of the Headless Corpse

## Josepha Sherman

Josepha Sherman is a fantasy novelist, freelance editor, and folklorist whose latest titles include *Son of Darkness* (Roc Books), *The Captive Soul* (Warner Aspect), *Xena: All I Need to Know I Learned from the Warrior Princess, by Gabrielle, as Translated by Josepha Sherman* (Pocket Books), the folklore title *Merlin's Kin* (August House), and, together with Susan Shwartz, several *Star Trek* novels, including *Vulcan's Forge* and *Vulcan's Heart*. She has also written for the educational market on everything from Bill Gates to the workings of the human ear. Recent titles include *Mythology for Storytellers* (M. E. Sharpe, 2003) and the *Star Trek Vulcan's Soul* trilogy.

She is a fan of the New York Mets, horses, aviation, and space science. Visit her at *http://www.sff.net/people/Josepha.Sherman*.

he body was male, strongly built, clad in an elegant midnight-blue robe, and without a doubt, dead.

Murdered. Very few suicides manage to tear off their own heads. The crime had made a mess of the expensive-looking Oriental carpet. And, I thought irrelevantly, they were never going to get the stains out of that nice oak floor.

My partner, Raven, was looking about the extravagantly large living room. "Where's the head?"

The cops gave us both a wary glance. "We haven't found it yet."

I was doing my own scouting. With all this mess, you'd have expected bloody footprints, or at least a trail of—

Whoa. "Here it is," I called. "Here, behind this sofa," which was an expensive white leather affair. "Must have rolled."

"Or been thrown," Raven said, crouching to study the head.

My partner is a tall man, dark-haired, lean and good-looking in a rangy sort of way. I'm female, brown-haired, not exactly lean, and half his height. We've been partners long enough to be surprised by pretty much nothing.

The head was that of a man in perhaps his late fifties, blond hair fading to gray. The face was strong but with slightly sagging jowls, and looked vaguely annoyed by the whole affair. It was a face I recognized from the news: Randolph Dexter, head of Dexter Arcane Industries, a major supplier of magical goods to the trade, though not a magician himself. Divorced, if memory served, with offspring.

Yes. A quick glance at my handheld Wizard told me that there was indeed an ex–Mrs. Dexter, Eleanor, and that there were two of those offspring, a son and a daughter. None of them were magicians, either: in fact, there were no magic licenses on record for any of the family.

There was only one problem in getting accurate data and with us being here at all. Because of Dexter's profession, the place was full of magical trophies: a silver chalice on the mantelpiece, a colorful, intricately woven mandala hanging on one wall, and so on. Handsome stuff. All of them together cast a psychic fog of magic, yet nothing had that unmistakable mental jolt that says "I've been used." There was neither sign nor *feel* of any grimoires or other magic manuals, which are the only methods by which a nonmagician can even hope to cast a spell.

In other words, magic fog or no magic fog—well, my partner was already explaining it to the cops.

"He wasn't killed by magic. It's not our jurisdiction."

Raven and I are agents for the MBI, the Magical Bureau of Investigation. We take on those cases of murder, espionage, and matters of national security involving the arcane arts.

(And no, Raven isn't his real name any more than mine is Coyote: the MBI has a perverted sense of humor when it comes to giving its agents handles.)

No murder by magic. No trace of spells. Just to be on the safe side, I softly recited the reveal-spell charm that's supposed to be foolproof. Granted, the magic haze was a nuisance, but . . . Nope, assuming the readings were accurate, no spells.

But something else was bothering me. I murmured to Raven, "Why aren't there any footprints?"

He shrugged. "Clever killer?"

"Oh, come *on*."

"Maybe he stood on a chair. Maybe he ran across the sofa."

"And the head? If it had rolled, there'd be a blood trail on the carpet. If it had been thrown, there'd be blood on that nice white sofa."

"Good point."

There was also the small problem of who or what would be strong enough to rip a man's head off his body.

"Raven, *there's* the magic. Some sort of strength-enhancement spell—no, never mind," I corrected myself before he could comment. "That would have shown up on our scans, too."

With no magical evidence, we were forced to turn the case over to the cops. But later, as we returned to the small office we share in the MBI Building—which looks, deliberately, like any other bland gray governmental building, were other governmental buildings warded—I couldn't get the murder out of my mind. "Raven . . ."

"Yes. It's nagging me, too. We're missing something."

"But what?"

"I haven't a clue."

"Yes. That's exactly the problem. No clues."

Just then a message sprite formed between us with the smallest *pop* of displaced air. Like all the sprites, it was a sexless, slight, green-skinned figure with wings that blurred as it hovered.

"Agents Raven, Coyote, boss man wishes seeing you *now*!"

With another small *pop* the message sprite was gone. Raven and I exchanged a resigned glance and headed off to Chief Wizard Merlin's office.

Needless to say, Merlin isn't our superior's real name any more than Raven and Coyote are ours. He is a heavyset man of indeterminate age, the sort who looks like an ex-jock who was probably a fullback in college—but with eyes that hold a *lot* of cold, hard experience.

He acknowledged us with his usual curt nod. "New case. A woman claims that her poodle is being possessed by the ghost of her deceased husband."

"You're putting us on," Raven said.

Merlin seemed to be enjoying this a little too much. He shook his head, face absolutely without expression. "Seems that the poodle has started talking to her."

"Uh . . . of course. Chief, I understand that talking poodles might be an MBI matter, but we'd really like to keep working on the Dexter case."

Merlin raised a bushy eyebrow. "You already filed that one as a nonarcane murder."

"Well, yes," Raven began, "but—"

"*Is* it?"

"It seems to be, but—"

"*Seems?*"

I took pity on my floundering partner. "We merely want to follow up on a few new leads. Be absolutely sure."

Merlin's quick wave of a hand brought a computer screen into view. Scrolling down the files, he commented, "Neither of you sensed any magic other than peripheral haze due to unused arcane objects. The reveal-spell charm revealed nothing. There is no evidence of any arcane talent in any member of the immediate Dexter family. What leads?"

"The family," I said. "Dexter's company. There might be something . . ." I stopped. That sounded lame, even to me.

At Merlin's second wave, the screen and computer obediently vanished again, and he turned to fix us with a look as cold and hard as that of a basilisk. "I'm well aware that a murder investigation is more glamorous than a case of a dead husband giving stock tips to his widow through her poodle."

"Stock tips?" I asked.

"Good ones?" Raven added.

"Excellent ones, to all accounts."

"And she wants to get rid of *that*?"

"Apparently," Merlin drawled, "the dog is big on insider trading."

"But—"

"We can't—"

Merlin silenced us by fixing us with a look that would have pierced a demon's disguise. "Is this reluctance of yours due to magical intuition? Or are we merely playing hunches?"

There was an awkward pause. Then Raven said, "I really wish we could claim the former, but . . ."

"We just don't know," I finished.

Merlin sighed. "You two should have been named Bulldog and Terrier, you know that? Very well, you have"—he glanced at his watch—"exactly one minute to convince me why I should keep you on the Dexter case."

Raven and I both knew that he meant it literally. Hastily, counting off the seconds in my mind, I summarized the lack of footprints, the lack of any blood trail. "Yes, I know it could have been the work of a really clever killer—"

"One with inhuman strength," Raven cut in.

"Or, perhaps, a very efficient power tool," Merlin said dryly. "The minute, agents, is up." He held up a hand to stop us from interrupting. "As I say, you two should have been called Bulldog and Terrier for your sheer tenacity. Or is that simple stubbornness? Still, I have to agree that the case of the insider trading poodle can wait a day."

"Thank you!"

"*Only* a day."

"Chief—"

"A day. You two have exactly twenty-four hours in which to prove the use of magic with intent to kill in the Dexter case. After that . . ."

"Poodle," I said.

"Precisely."

A second trip to the murder scene netted us nothing but impatient cops. Of course they had already questioned the Dexter family and employees, but not being MBI, they hadn't gotten more than surface answers. We had an advantage, needless to say: magic. One of the reasons Raven and I work so well as a team is that our magics are perfectly compatible. This means that our powers don't fight each other, a problem that has happened to other, failed partnerships.

Unfortunately, though, since the murder hadn't been caused by a spell, we couldn't use our joined talents to simply track the spell backward and conjure up the killer's name. But at least we could whittle down the list of "possible" suspects to "more likely" suspects.

Sure enough, a scroll materialized between us even as we finished reciting the last spell-syllable.

"That's *it*?" I asked. "That's all?"

"Not the most promising of lists, is it? Let's see . . . Dexter's ex-with-kids . . . one business rival . . ." Raven shook his head. "That's it, all right: two adults, two kids. Nary a friend or even an acquaintance on the list."

"Either everyone loved him except for his wife and/or rival, or he had no friends at all."

"Want to bet me it was the latter?"

"No bet," I said. "I *feel* that, too. Unfriendly fellow, the late Mr. Dexter. Ah, you know, the killer *could* have been some random lunatic. 'Random' wouldn't show up on the list."

"Oh, thank you *so* much."

"Just a possibility."

There is an annoying rule in the MBI that no agent may interrogate a witness or suspect alone. As it happens, there's a perfectly good reason for it: a solo agent was once slain by a suspect who, much to his surprise, turned out to be mostly demon. But the rule was going to cut down on our precious time, since we couldn't split up to make separate investigations.

"Mrs. Ex-Wife first," I decided, and Raven agreed.

Dexter had apparently believed in doing right by his ex, or else she had a very good lawyer. Ex–Mrs. Dexter lived in a penthouse apartment that could just as well have been called a penthouse mansion, on top of the sort of building usually described first as "luxury."

Then we met the ex-wife, who opened the door herself with the air of someone who'd just been interviewed by cops and was prepared for a return bout. Her appearance pretty much screamed top designer, and her beige suit probably cost the same as my whole year's salary. I couldn't completely envy her, though. She desperately wanted to be young, at least as much so as cosmetics could manage (no cosmetic magics, though, which surprised me, since a lot of folks use them these days), and was fiercely svelte and blonde, hair caught up on the latest artfully tousled style. I stopped myself just in time from self-consciously touching my own less elegant hair.

What Mrs. Ex-Wife didn't look was grieving. Angry and weary, yes, and thoroughly sick of answering questions, but not grieving. "Your people were already here, ah . . ."

"Call us Raven and Coyote, ma'am. We're not with the police, but with the MBI."

I've seen many reactions to that announcement, ranging from anger to wary alarm. This one surprised me: the woman recoiled from our IDs in genuine horror, and I *felt* fear blaze up in her like a psychic wildfire. She was clearly only barely keeping from slamming the door in our faces. Raven and I exchanged quick glances: Mrs. Ex-Wife would never have had anything to do with the arcane.

Odd fear for someone who was married to the head of Dexter Arcane Industries. But then, money could overcome a lot of things. Including any scruples she might have had against taking her ex's life? "Ma'am," I prodded gently, "could we come in? We'll try not to take up too much of your time."

She would probably rather have told us, *Go to the devil,* and meant it. Instead, Mrs. Ex reluctantly invited us into a vast living room that was all either beige fabric or white marble and, like its owner, fairly screamed top designer.

Raven and I sat on matching chairs that had been designed more for style than for comfort. Mrs. Ex perched uneasily on a third. We asked her the usual opening questions, trivial stuff about maiden name, number and age of children, none of which were intended to do anything but relax her a little.

No go. So I went straight for the proverbial jugular. "Ma'am, please do accept our sincere condolences. But I have to notice that you're not exactly in mourning."

"Should I be?" she snapped.

"Well, uh, surely—"

"Raymond brought it on himself! Dealing in, well, in *that!*"

"Dexter Arcane Industries, you mean?" Raven asked.

"I warned him, but he wouldn't listen to me. Raymond was so good, so kind in every other way." She stopped, staring fiercely from Raven to me and back again. "I already told the police all this! Even after the divorce—it's true, we didn't have anything to do with each other after that, but Raymond never complained about the settlement, never stinted on child support."

"Did he visit the children?"

"No! I wouldn't risk it!"

"I . . . beg your pardon?"

"Oh—oh, I don't mean he would have abused them. He never even showed much interest in them. Raymond was—you've heard that old line about being married to a job? It wasn't quite that bad, not at first. But Raymond just would not listen to my warnings! He could have sold the company, gone into something safer, something more wholesome. But he never listened to me, not even when his love for that sinful business was costing us our marriage."

"Ma'am, we know he was the owner and CEO of Dexter Arcane, but are you saying that he was also a practitioner?"

"God knows what he was into!"

That wasn't exactly hard data. Carefully, Raven and I continued to question her. No, she'd never caught her husband attempting any spells. The only time he'd brought home any objects from the company, she'd tossed them out and had their home purified by a priest.

Clear enough. What we had here was a true antimagic bigot. If it weren't for our MBI IDs, we'd probably already be out on the street. If Dexter had tried anything arcane, he would have had to work it on the sly, and so far there just wasn't any evidence of that.

However, we weren't quite finished. "Ma'am," Raven said, "do you mind if we question your children?"

"They know nothing about this! They haven't even seen their father for years."

"I understand," I said in my gentlest woman-to-woman voice. "But this must still be very difficult for them."

"I haven't told them how he died. But those cops, those stupid, stupid cops, let them know that he was murdered. At least I stopped them before they could throw in how he'd been—how he—how he died."

She'd just gone up a notch in my opinion: concern for her kids.

"I'm sorry," Raven said, and I knew he meant it. "We'll try our best not to upset them. But we really do need to ask them a few questions."

The kids turned out to be named Tiffany and Blaine. Tiffany was a slim little blonde doll, maybe five or six, very pretty and just a touch too cute in her pink ruffled blouse and neat jeans. Blaine was a lanky young blonde teen, maybe fourteen at the most, wearing the inevitable band-advertising T-shirt and artfully worn designer jeans. They sat side by side on the sofa, Tiffany's feet, encased in pink sneakers, dangling, both kids looking as if they'd rather be anywhere else. Not that I blamed them.

They didn't look particularly grief-stricken, just bewildered. Then again, judging from what their mother had told us, they hadn't even seen their father for years. Maybe Tiffany didn't even remember him.

Very clearly, no magic coming from Blaine. Children as young as little Tiffany are more difficult to read, since Power usually doesn't focus itself until adolescence. All I got from her was purely mundane child: confusion over the loss of a man she didn't know, uneasiness over the presence of two strangers her mother clearly didn't like.

Very gently, Raven and I edged around the details of the kids' father's death, trying to learn, first from Blaine, if the man had, indeed, been attempting magic on his own. Blaine blustered as only a frightened teenage boy can do. "My father wasn't a dirty, double-damned *sorcerer!*"

"Neither, I trust, are we," Raven said somberly.

Mrs. Ex, to do her credit, didn't comment.

What else we got from Blaine was that he didn't care (a lie), he didn't miss his father (a lie), and he didn't like us (true). He was not a singularly complex kid, but to be fair to him, Blaine was also struggling with adolescence. Hormones were overriding pretty much everything else in his psyche.

When we asked Tiffany similar but more simply phrased questions, she shook her head, refusing to admit that her father could ever have done anything wrong. Our questions quickly showed that she had only a vague concept of "father," namely as someone who didn't want her, since he'd never come to see her, and a feeling, just below the surface, that something must be wrong with her because of that. Her fear and despair were rapidly growing so strong that when tears welled up in her eyes, they almost welled up in ours as well.

We'd gotten all the information we could from her. Excusing ourselves, we fled.

"I hate questioning kids," Raven said, fighting himself back under control.

"So do I." I ran a not-quite-steady hand through my hair. "They have no clues at all about not broadcasting their emotions."

"That was one genuinely scared, unhappy little girl. Not that I blame her for any of that. Dexter sounds like a real sweetheart. Bet Tiffany winds up in therapy in a few years. And—"

"Raven, look at the time. Child psychology's going to have to wait."

We grabbed quick cups of coffee and sandwiches from the nearest coffee shop and hurried on to our next destination. From all we had been able to learn—and from all that our brief magical listing had let us see—Dexter Arcane Industries had had only one genuine rival: Mandala Inc.: Supplies for the Right-Hand Path. Expensive merchandise, mostly handmade, usually out of the range of MBI agents' salaries, and guaranteed Darkness-free.

"Whatever we learn," Raven said dryly, "it'll be a pleasure to question an *adult*!"

Mandala Inc. was located in what is usually called a business park: gleaming white buildings surrounded by plenty of grass and trees. Squirrels raced across the cement paths, and sparrows chirped all around us.

"Where are the aerobics classes?" Raven muttered.

"Or the Druid wanna-bes. You'd never know this place manufactured magic equipment."

Just then something flapped quickly by us—something that wasn't a bird.

"*Almost* never know," I amended.

The office of Mandala Inc.'s owner and CEO was a quietly elegant place, with plush moss-green carpet, a few pots of discreet greenery (the ivy sort that doesn't shed), and gleaming wood and chrome furnishings. A wall-length window looked out over the tranquil business park and a decorative lake. Disconcertingly clean office, I thought. Not a paper out of place. A neat desk is a sign of a troubled mind and all that. Or else Mr. Sinclair simply delegated *everything*.

Just then the door opened and a slight man in a neat navy-blue business suit hurried in. His face was absolutely ageless, narrow and rosy-cheeked, unmarred by any lines: really good cosmetic magic or else incredibly clean living. His longish hair was pure white, possibly prematurely so, and he had the clearest blue eyes I've seen in a human.

"Forgive me, agents. I was just inspecting the latest lot of thuribles. As you surely already know, I am Amadeus Sinclair."

We duly shook hands, and he took his seat behind that gleaming, too-clean desk. "Please," Sinclair said, gesturing to two of the leather and chrome chairs, "be seated. Now, you wish to ask me some questions."

Of course he knew who we were without needing to check our IDs: Sinclair fairly radiated magic. But his magic seemed so utterly untainted by anything nasty that it *felt* downright wholesome.

"I wonder what Mrs. Ex thought about *him*," I murmured to Raven.

Of course Mr. Sinclair had already heard of his rival's death; it wouldn't have taken magic for that, not where business was concerned.

"I warned him, many times I warned him. Put up a warding, hire some arcane guards, do *something*. Working in such an industry without any talents of his own—"

"He wasn't killed by magic," Raven cut in.

That stopped Sinclair dead in his tracks. "No? But—no?"

"Does that surprise you?"

"Well, yes! I just never thought . . . It seems so, well, ignominious for poor Raymond to have been murdered by mundane means."

Tearing off someone's head didn't strike me as mundane, but I wasn't about to say that. Instead, I asked, "You're not glad to see a rival removed?"

"Powers, no!" He leaned forward, and for the first time there was something sharp on his face, something that said *businessman*. "Look, I don't deal with Darkness, but that doesn't make me a saint. Dexter Arcane takes too many shortcuts, and their products undercut mine in manufacturing costs and distribution. If the whole company disappeared overnight, I wouldn't exactly weep. But we're speaking of a human life! How . . . how *did* he die?"

Raven told him, and I watched Sinclair shrink back in a shock that looked and *felt* genuine. "Good God, how horrible! Poor Eleanor. She's had to put up with so much from him, and now this! And the children—terrible, terrible! Do they know? No? There's a mercy. What spell could have caused—no, you said there was no magic involved. But—"

"I'm afraid we can't disclose any more details."

"Of course not, of course not."

We let him dither on for a time. But all the while, like any good magician, he kept up a strong mental warding. We could only take him at his babbling words. And nothing in that babbling, for all our careful questions, revealed anything useful.

Except . . . "You and Mrs. Dexter are friends?"

"Social acquaintances. We saw each other at the same events, and only rarely spoke with each other, but I always knew she was unhappy."

"Oh?"

Sinclair stared at us, taking a moment to interpret that monosyllabic question, and then burst into laughter. "Agents, please! First of all, she would never have had anything to do with a magician. And second, I've never had anything to do with women. No, my feeling toward Eleanor is pity, nothing more."

Damn. We could both sense that he meant it. Another possibility squashed.

"We have nothing further to ask," I said.

Raven added, "I assume that the police have already warned you not to leave town."

"They think *I'm* a suspect, me! But of course I was his rival, of course they'd think—but *me*! How could they . . . ?"

We left him engrossed in a new round of babbling.

"That," Raven said as we headed down the path, birds and squirrels doing their birdie and squirrelly activities all around us, "is either the most innocent man we've ever met or the finest actor."

"He's gay. That was true. He pities Mrs. Ex. That was true, too. And he really didn't know how Dexter died."

"That doesn't mean Sinclair didn't send an assassin: 'Just do the job; don't tell me how you do it.'"

I glanced at my partner. "Remind me never to get you really teed off at me."

"Hah," Raven began.

Then all hell broke loose, almost literally. Magic alarms blared out on all sides, nothing audible to the nonmagical but forceful enough to us to nearly stagger us.

"Sinclair!" we exclaimed as one, and raced back the way we'd just come. IDs out and yelling the mantra "MBI! Let us through!" we forced our way through the confused crowds of workers and grim-faced guards to Sinclair's office. What had been the door to his office was now just so many splinters. Where were his wards? They should have slammed into existence the moment there was—

No, they'd only have formed in the case of a magical attack. The . . . thing menacing Sinclair, backing him against a wall, had no magical aura at all.

"What the hell is that?" Raven asked.

"Not from hell—not a demon . . ."

What it was, though, I couldn't say. Something huge that looked like a weird cross between a lithe black panther and a heavy-furred ogre out of Faerie. But it lacked the sharp psychic tang of anything out of that Other Realm, and besides, no Faerie thing would be caught out in the daylight—

That didn't really matter. The thing wasn't being stopped by any of the defensive spells Sinclair was throwing at it, though all around the creature, glass was breaking and wood shattering.

Great. Not only wasn't the monster magical in itself, it was also immune to magic. But this was definitely the thing that had killed Dexter, because judging from those powerfully massive arms and clawed hands, it was planning to tear Sinclair's head off, too.

It's at times like this that I really wish MBI agents carried guns.

Raven didn't waste time in regrets. Seeing a man about to have his head torn off is a pretty good incentive for one of those feats of strength emergencies give us. Raven snatched up one of the heavy chrome and leather guest chairs as though it weighed nothing, and hurled it at the thing. The chair slammed into the monster between the shoulder blades, and it staggered—but didn't fall. Instead, the thing whirled with alarming speed, and we saw a face like something out of a nightmarish storybook: eyes that were too big, too flaming red, nose like that of a dog, a wide human mouth filled with just too many rows of fangs.

No wonder we hadn't sensed any magic at the murder scene—the damned thing was extra-dimensional, outside the scope of our talents.

In fact, it was so alien that it looked like a kid's idea of a monster. Maybe that's what inspired me—besides the realization that my partner, who was now panting from the strain of throwing a heavy chair, was about to be lunch. But some vague memory from childhood surfaced, from those days before I knew that things like this did exist outside the storybooks.

"Stop that!" I shouted at the monster—and the startled thing froze. Feeling like an idiot, I scolded, "Bad monster! Bad monster!"

It actually whimpered, a confused, puzzled sound.

"Go home!" I commanded, and stamped a foot. "Shoo! Go home!"

It snarled, but it didn't attack. The thing turned somehow sideways—and vanished.

Raven didn't waste time asking questions: another of the reasons we make such a good team. Ignoring Sinclair's confused stammerings of thanks, the two of us raced off straight to ex–Mrs. Dexter's apartment.

After all, I had told the creature to go home.

The doorman didn't want to let us in, but he was too frightened of our MBI identities to resist. Ex–Mrs. Dexter really didn't want to let us in, regardless of our IDs—or, rather, because of them—but she didn't have much of a choice. We burst the lock with a well-placed gesture and all but forced our way in past her.

"The children," I panted. "Where are they?"

Her eyes widened in horror. "Blaine's with a school friend. Tiffany—oh my God, *Tiffany!*"

There was a roar of wind, then the shrill scream of a terrified child. Not a chance of beating a frightened mother racing to the defense of her daughter, but we came in a close second.

We found ourselves in a large, brightly colored room like a child's dream, full of toys and plushy stuffed animals. *Larger than my whole apartment,* flashed through my mind, but there wasn't time for nonsense. There, looking utterly impossible amid all the sweetness, was the monster, towering over Tiffany, who huddled in a corner.

"Mommy!" she wailed.

Only our quick grab of the woman's arms kept her from rushing blindly to her daughter's side.

Looked like we had been right—and yelling "Go home!" to the creature wasn't going to work this time. It *was* home, at least as close to home as it could get in this dimension. And the monster was going to kill the one person who was holding it here.

Not if we had a say in the matter!

"Let go of me!" Mrs. Ex was shrieking.

"Mommy!" Tiffany was wailing.

"Got any ideas?" I whispered to Raven.

"Not a one. You?"

"No."

"Damn. I really don't feel like getting killed today."

With that, Raven let go of Mrs. Ex and charged the monster, hitting it low, for all the world like a football player trying to stop the offense. He sent it stumbling sideways, away from Tiffany. Mrs. Ex charged in, snatched up her child, and raced back toward me. I gestured to her, *Get out of here!* The monster would follow, but at least we'd bought a little time.

Unfortunately, the monster hadn't fallen. Recovering with super-human reflexes, it whirled, catching Raven with a backhanded swing of a hand that sent him flying. My breath caught in my throat—but for-tunately for Raven, there was enough carpeting and all those stuffed an-imals for him to land relatively softly. But he was clearly stunned.

My turn. I yelled inelegantly, "Hey, you monster!" to get it away from Raven, and hunted frantically for something I could use as a weapon. What, a doll, a stuffed rabbit, a beach ball—what was I sup-posed to do, *play* with the thing?

Whoa, maybe I could. A quick illusion spell brought the bunny to life, grown to monster size. A second gave the beach ball jet propulsion. It smashed into the monster, hurling the creature off its feet, and the bunny came after it, pummeling the monster.

More time bought. Letting go of the bunny and beach ball spells, I grabbed up the nearest lamp and brought it down on the monster's head as hard as I could. Damn! The thing's skull was like concrete! At least Raven was on his feet again, slamming the monster's head with a second lamp.

No go. All we were doing was keeping the creature from regaining its feet. That was at least something, but it was cursed frustrating know-ing that Raven and I had spells to stun or kill, yet the strongest of them would be useless against a thing that shed magic like water.

Or like us. With a roar, the monster was on its feet again, brushing us aside like two flies. And of course it was heading after Tiffany. I'd hoped Mrs. Ex would have the sense to leave the apartment, get the hell out of the building, and give herself and us a fighting chance. But no, in true panicked human fashion, she'd just managed to corner herself in the living room. Pushing Tiffany behind her, she stood at bay, a mother protecting her young, a beautiful, brave, primal, and stupid thing to do. Stupid, because all the maternal will in the world wasn't going to help. The monster batted her aside almost absently.

"Mommy!" Tiffany shrieked.

Raven and I exchanged the quickest *You do that and I'll do this* glance. He started throwing things at the monster—fruit, the fruit bowl (ow, cut-glass crystal, heavy), books from the nearest bookcase, anything to distract the monster. Anything to give me the opening I needed.

Yes! I dove past the monster, almost landing on top of Tiffany.

"You can stop this," I told her.

"Mommy!"

"Tiffany, listen to me!" No, don't yell, the kid is scared enough as it is. "It just wants to go home, Tiffany. It needs its mommy, too."

Which was a ridiculous thing to say about something that had torn off her father's head. But Tiffany didn't know that. And she was only five, after all.

"Mommy?" she whimpered.

"That's right. It's scared"—oh, *right*—"and that's why it's angry. Send him home, Tiffany. Send him home."

"*Go away!*" she screamed at the monster with all the impressive power of a five-year-old's lungs. "*Go home!*"

Yes. Right words, right amount of will—and the monster did that sideways turn and vanished.

"Mommy!" Tiffany cried, and zoomed to her mother's side.

Mrs. Ex wasn't badly hurt, fortunately, just shaken and bruised, as well as winded from having a five-year-old-child-shaped bullet hit her. But she clung to Tiffany with frantic strength, even as she stared at us in complete confusion. "What . . . ?"

"Tiffany," I said gently.

She turned a tearstained face to me. "I didn't do it. I didn't!"

"Tiffany, honey, no one's angry at you. We just want to know how the monster got here."

"I didn't . . . It was for Mommy." Her eyes were innocent. "I mean, Mommy always said that magic was bad, that it had hurt Daddy. I knew it was why he didn't like me. I thought if I tried very hard, the bad things would go away."

And instead, she'd drawn the creature out of its rightful dimension and dumped it here. With the command to kill Daddy's magic. But Daddy hadn't had any magic. So it had tried to tear it from him. Then it had gone after the next magic it could find that was related to him, Dexter Arcane's rival. Next probably would have been the MBI. But we'd driven it back to as close as it could get to its home. By killing Tiffany, it would have broken the link to this dimension.

Mrs. Ex was looking, understandably, like someone who has just had the underpinnings of her life kicked out from under her. How do you explain to someone that her own prejudices had led to her ex-husband's death? How do you tell someone like that that her own daughter was a powerful wild talent?

We left that for the MBI counselors.

"Not exactly a happy ending," I said to Raven as we headed back to the office.

"Not many murder cases have one."

"Good point. Come on, Raven. We still have a couple of hours left on this case. Coffee?"

"Yeah."

"Good. It's your turn to buy."

# PART II

# Murder
# Unclassifiable

# A Death in the Working

An Inquestor-Principal Jerre syn-Caselyn mystery story by Haef Teliau
Translation and footnotes by Sommes Vinhalyn,
Diregis Professor of Contemporary History and Lecturer
in Eraasian Culture, University of Galcen

## Debra Doyle

Debra Doyle was born in Florida and educated in Florida, Texas, Arkansas, and Pennsylvania—the last at the University of Pennsylvania, where she earned her doctorate in English literature, concentrating on Old English poetry. While living and studying in Philadelphia, she met and married her usual collaborator, James D. Macdonald, who was then serving in the U.S. Navy. Together, they traveled to Virginia, California, and the Republic of Panama, acquiring various children, cats, and computers along the way.

A NOTE ON THE AUTHOR: Haef Teliau, pseudonymous author of the Jerre syn-Caselyn mysteries, began his writing career during the early period of the Eraasian Hegemony. Although the highly popular series was not overtly political, both the setting—some three decades before the first Eraasian contact with worlds beyond the interstellar gap— and the overall tone of nostalgia for those bygone days suggest at least an unconscious agenda on the writer's part. One of the book-length works, *Death of a Star-Lord,* was in fact suppressed during the sus-Peledaen purges of 1151 E.R., though later reissues of the series saw the book restored to its proper place in the sequence. —S.V.

igh summer in Hanilat, and the climate controls in the Center Street Watch Station weren't working. Again.

"I would give a great deal," said Inquestor-Principal Jerre syn-Casleyn, "to get out of this office for just a day."

"The universe hears you when you say things like that." Station-Commander Evayan tapped Jerre's desktop with a broad forefinger. "Check your files."

Jerre complied and read through the documents with increasing disbelief. "Lokheran Hall? Wide Hills should have gotten this one, not us."

"Wide Hills, in this case, defers to Hanilat Center Street with a sigh of profound relief," the Station-Commander said. "And you've been asked for special."

"Why me?"

"Take a look at the victim."

Jerre paged through the form. "Deni Tavaet sus-Arial.[1] Inner family, senior line. Just what I needed to make my day complete." He began transferring the documents to a travel pad. "Of your kindness, Station-Commander, send word to the Center Street Circle and ask them for the loan of Rasha *etaze*[2] for a jaunt in the country."

"You'll have to do without this time, I'm afraid."

"What do you mean?"

"Protocol," said the Station-Commander. "Look at the file again."

Jerre called up the desktop copies; read them; frowned. "Deceased was an unranked Mage in the Lokheran Circle."

"And Refayal Tavaet's baby brother," the Station-Commander fin-

1. Deni Tavaet sus-Arial: For Teliau's original readers, the names in this passage would carry a considerable weight of implication. The "sus-" prefix to the family name indicates birth membership in the higher nobility—either the old (and at the time of the story, still powerful) land-based aristocracy, or the newer, and newly ascendant, star-lords. Inquestor-Principal syn-Casleyn is himself identified by the "syn-" prefix as a member of the lesser nobility; the prefix could also serve (though not in Jerre's case, as other tales in the series make clear) as an indicator of adoptive membership in a hypothetical sus-Casleyn family.

2. *Etaze* is the traditional title accorded to one of the ranked Mages in a working Circle—those who are, in the vulgar usage, "Magelords." The title is loosely equivalent to "Master" or "Mistress" among Adepts, though not all Mages will carry the rank. Rasha Jedao of the Center Street Mage-Circle is Jerre syn-Casleyn's regular consultant on cases involving Magecraft.

ished. "The Circle claims it was a death in the working. The head of the sus-Arial doesn't believe them. Hence your country vacation."

Jerre couldn't take Rasha *etaze* with him to Lokheran, but he could take her to the Court of Two Colors[3] for dinner and discussion—purely in the interest of laying a proper groundwork for his investigation prior to departing for the Wide Hills District. Over a shared platter of grilled meats and vegetables at a quiet table, Jerre laid out his questions.

"The first thing I need to know," he said, "is why Refayal Tavaet considers himself entitled to a say in this investigation."

"The dead man was his brother. I suppose that's enough if you're sus-Arial."

"Deni Tavaet was a Mage. He would have left the family altars years ago."

Rasha looked thoughtful. "Well . . . there's leaving, and then there's leaving."

"What do you mean?"

"Not everybody who goes to the Circles has their name stricken from the tablets and purged from the files." She sounded a bit wistful. "Some of them even go home for weddings and holidays and things like that."[4]

"And you think Deni was one of those?"

"He might have been." Rasha skewered a curl of shaved meat and dipped it into the puddle of sauce. "Or there could have been other reasons."

One more thing remained for Jerre to do before leaving Hanilat for the Wide Hills District: he paid a social call on Refayal Tavaet.

3. Teliau's choice of setting here can be taken as an indication of his political sympathies. The Court of Two Colors, in its heyday perhaps the best, or at least the most notable, hotel and restaurant in downtown Hanilat, would have been in operation for perhaps five years at the time of this story. For Teliau's readers, the Court—having been largely destroyed by an incendiary device in 1142 E.R. as part of the ongoing power struggles among the star-lords—would have signified nostalgia for the older regime of land and merchant aristocracy, and would have stood as a covert rebuke to the ruling fleet-families.

4. Rasha Jedao's family ties and Circle life are explored in depth in the second Jerre syn-Casleyn novel, *An Unkind Corpse,* which introduces the Center Street Magelord to the series as a continuing character.

The head of the sus-Arial family kept a town house in one of the most elegant of Hanilat's residential neighborhoods. Jerre presented himself to the doorkeeper-*aiketh*[5] early in the forenoon and identified himself as Jerre syn-Casleyn rather than as Center Street's Inquestor-Principal. Refayal Tavaet might have asked the local Watch for assistance in the matter of his brother's death; but that didn't mean he wanted its official presence intruding on his household.

Jerre drank red *uffa*[6] from a crystal glass and asked the head of the sus-Arial, "Why don't you accept the Circle's account of your brother's death? Is there bad blood between your family and the Lokheran Circle?"

"I hadn't thought that there was," Refayal said. "But my brother is dead."

"I don't wish to make light of your grief, but he was a Mage, after all.[7] The possibility was always—"

"I know all about the possibilities." Refayal's voice was harsh; Jerre, listening, supposed that his anger and sorrow might well be genuine. "Deni's private funds and property go to the Circle. And not even Mages are above temptation."

The Lokheran Circle lived and worked in a three-story brick building two blocks off the central street of Lokheran proper.[8] The Mage

5. *Aiketh* (pl. *aiketen*): Prior to the pacification of the Mageworlds in A.F. 980, the people of the Eraasian Hegemony made extensive use of these robotic servitors. The *aiketen* relied upon quasi-organic components rather than silicon for their computational power, making them difficult to mass-produce but capable of handling instruction sets of great subtlety. Whether or not an *aiketh* could achieve true sentience remains unknown; no *aiketen* have been made or instructed in the classical manner since the fall of the Hegemony, and even the savants of Eraasi's own golden age disagreed on the theoretical possibility.

6. *Uffa*: a mildly stimulating herbal drink, similar in its effects and social uses to cha'a, and like cha'a, usually served hot; it comes in dark and pale—or "red" and "yellow"—varieties.

7. Of all the practices of the Mage-Circles, the raising of power through ritual combat—always real and sometimes fatal—is the one most alien to the rest of the civilized galaxy. It is a common misconception, even today, that those Mages who meet their deaths in this fashion are unwilling sacrifices. In fact, such duels for power are consensual and (as Jerre syn-Casleyn obliquely points out in this passage) one of the known hazards of life in a Circle.

8. Once again Teliau's unstated political agenda makes itself apparent, this time in the attention paid to the autonomy and strong local focus of the Lokheran Circle. Teliau wrote during the Early Transitional period; he would have been a witness (perhaps even a participant—see Hithu and Bareian, *Survey of Eraasian Literature,* for a good summary of the arguments pro and con in the Teliau-as-Magelord controversy) to the struggles out of which came the Classical and Expansionist tradition of hierarchical structure and of shared and subordinated power.

who answered was painfully young and earnest, reminding Jerre of Center Street's recruits-in-training. He made a note to interview her as soon as possible, before her superiors could take her aside and instruct her in what to say; she wouldn't have been with the Circle long enough to know in her bones which things were spoken of to outsiders and which were not.

Unfortunately, good manners and standard procedure both required that he speak with the First of the Lokheran Circle before asking to speak with any of its members.

"I'm Inquestor-Principal Jerre syn-Casleyn of the Center Street Watch," he said. "My message preceded me, yes?"

Her eyes widened. Jerre suspected that she'd never dealt in person with a member of the Watch before this, and that she didn't know whether to be frightened or embarrassed about it. "Yes, *etaz*—sir. Lord syn-Casleyn. He's waiting for you in the downstairs office."

Grei Vareas, First of the Lokheran Circle, was a stocky, graying man who could have been own cousin to Station-Commander Evayan back at Center Street. Like the young Mage who had answered the door, he wore everyday clothing in the local style,[9] a season or two behind the fashions of Hanilat.

"I'm sorry that Refayal Tavaet is still grieving for his brother," he said to Jerre. "Nevertheless, Deni's death was as we reported it."

Jerre nodded. "'In the line of duty' can be hard for family members to take sometimes."

"Yes."

"Especially if it's unexpected . . . Lokheran doesn't seem like the kind of place that would demand a great working."[10]

9. Mages in the pre-Transitional period for the most part dressed in the garments customary to the region or community they served, donning the already traditional black robes only for Circle meetings and group endeavors. Nor did the Circles yet work masked; the *geaerith*, or full-face hardmask, did not become universally worn until well into the Expansionist period. Then as now, however, a Mage and his or her staff were inseparable, and the black wood cudgels—formidable weapons even without a Circle's intention to add strength to the blows—were worn even with everyday garb.

10. The so-called great workings—those endeavors and intentions where the combat results in the death of one or more participants—are much less common than popular opinion in the Adeptworlds (and sensational fiction on both sides of the interstellar gap) would have us believe; available statistics (see, once again, Hithu and Bareian for a concise summary) confirm that a Mage in an ordinary Circle could reasonably expect to see only one or two such workings in the course of a lifetime.

"No," said Vareas—lured into confidence, as Jerre had hoped, by the show of sympathy. "Farming, banking, a bit of light industry. The last great working before this one was back in '59—the drought year. A fire in the factory district threatened to burn out of control and destroy the center of town."

"Before your time?"

"Almost. I was even younger than Keshaia, whom you must have met."

"The little doorwarden?" Jerre took advantage of the opening Vareas had provided. "I'd like to speak with her next, if I may. Purely in the interest of rounding out my report."

Jerre met with Keshaia in a small office near the back of the building's ground floor. The room didn't seem to belong to any one of the Lokheran Mages in particular; when he asked Keshaia, she confirmed his suspicions, explaining that the Circle-Mages took turns using it for personal business.[11]

"Deni also?"

"Oh, yes," she said. "He talked with his legalist and his financial adviser at least once a quarter."

Jerre had trouble picturing a Mage with a private financial adviser, and said so. Keshaia was an open and unsuspicious young woman— she really hadn't been a Mage for very long, he thought—and the artfully timed confidence worked as Jerre intended.

"Deni was a money whiz," she said. "He played with it, like some people do puzzles or—or build little models out of kits. For a game."

"Was he good at it?" Refayal Tavaet was claiming that the Lokheran Circle had killed Deni for his private money; maybe Refayal had a point, after all. Younger siblings who'd left the family altars didn't usually carry a great deal away with them, but a small competence could grow into a sizable fortune if properly tended. Jerre scrawled a question

11. Domestic and financial arrangements among the Mage-Circles have always been subject to considerable variation. Even in Circles tied to a particular area or institution, it was and is not uncommon for individual Mages to have occupations and business interests of their own, separate from the affairs of the Circle proper. Some Circles, of which the fictional Lokheran Circle was apparently one, live communally; others have only a meeting place in common and—in this latter day—may never have seen one another unmasked.

on his travel pad and sent the message off to Center Street with a flick of his stylus, then went back to taking notes.

Keshaia shrugged. "I suppose. He kept on doing it, and he seemed to be having fun."

"It takes all kinds," Jerre said. "I need some background here. How much can you tell me about the working?"

"The one where Deni . . . ? Not much. I was there, but I wasn't a part of it."

"How did that happen?" Jerre arranged his features into an expression of nonthreatening curiosity and waited. Given an expectant silence, people were more likely to fill it than not, and Keshaia proved no exception.

"The really big workings—nobody knows how long one's going to last once it starts. So you'll usually have a watchkeeper—somebody who stays out and keeps an eye on things."[12]

"What kind of things?"

"Trouble from outside. Somebody inside the working getting sick or hurt. Stuff like that."

"I see." Jerre checked his travel pad under the guise of making a note. Center Street had picked up his message; good. "So you—the Circle, that is—knew in advance that this was going to be a major working."

"Sort of. Grei *etaze* warned me it could go on for quite a while, but that was because things might get complicated. It was supposed to be a luck-of-the-town intention, and there's a lot of threads in one of those, he said."[13]

---

12. Much of what is known of Circle practice in the pre-Transitional period comes from passing references made by outsiders. Then as now, working Mages preferred to pass on their teachings through personal instruction, and entrusted very little to the written word or to any other archival medium. (As inconvenient as their reluctance may be for interested scholars, it should come as no surprise to anyone on this side of the interstellar gap; the Adepts' Guild has always been similarly unforthcoming about its own history.) The reliability of popular fiction as a source of information on the subject remains a matter for considerable debate.

13. On Eraasi and elsewhere, Mage-Circles interact with the universe through the manipulation of a complex of quantities and characteristics for which "luck" is the simplest and most usual (though perhaps not the most entirely accurate) translation. The luck is most commonly described, by those Mages willing to speak of it to outsiders, as complex patterns of silver, gray, or iridescent thread, which they call *eiran;* Eraasian philologists trace the word's origins to an unattested pre-Archaic root *ei* or *ai*, meaning, roughly, "to live."

"But no one expected it to grow into a great working?"

Keshaia shook her head. "It just happened."

Center Street was being efficient today, which was good. Jerre had the reply to his message before the afternoon was out. New information in hand, he went back to talk again with Grei Vareas in the latter's office.

"Lord syn-Casleyn." If the First of the Lokheran Circle was annoyed at having to speak with a man from the Watch twice in one day, he was hiding it well. "Is there anything further we can help you with?"

"Just a couple of things that I need to clear up."

"Of course."

Jerre made a show of consulting his travel pad. "First, Keshaia says that nobody expected the—what did she call it?—the luck-of-the-town intention to become a great working. Is that correct?"

"Yes. The Circle does such workings regularly, as part of our relationship with the town. We anticipated that this one might prove arduous, but nothing more than that."

"Does it happen often that a routine working turns out to demand a death?"

Vareas frowned. "Not a death," he said. "It isn't a death that the great working demands from us. It's a life."

"A life, then." From the Watch's point of view, Jerre reflected, it came to the same thing in the end—a man who'd been alive when the working started wasn't alive any longer—but he was willing to grant Vareas the distinction. "Do things like that happen often?"

"No. But we know that they always can."

"Thank you," Jerre said gravely. "I have one more favor I'd like to ask, etaze. If it doesn't do too much violence to your Circle's customs, I'd like young Keshaia to show me the room where the working took place."

The Lokheran Circle, it developed, carried out its workings and intentions in a large, windowless room on the building's second floor. The chamber had clearly been converted to its present use from some other purpose. The three tall windows along its rear wall had been bricked over and then, like the walls themselves, painted solid black. The hardwood floor was also painted black, with a white circle several yards across in the center of it.[14] The floorboards looked like they had recently been scrubbed clean, but Jerre knew that a good forensic team would find traces of blood on them just the same—Deni Tavaet's blood, shed in the working, and the blood of whichever member of the Circle had matched him.

Which would mean nothing at all, he reminded himself. Nobody was trying to hide the fact that Deni had died in the working, and the blood alone wouldn't be proof even of that.

He turned to Keshaia. "You were present in this room during the working, is that right?"

"Yes."

"Looking at it, but not seeing it from the inside?"

Rasha *etaze* had told him once that what she saw during a working was something other than the physical world—other, but not unreal. He was willing to take her word that there was a distinction; in the present case, it meant that none of Lokheran's Mages except for the youngest and most inexperienced counted as a reliable witness for his particular purposes.

"Yes," Keshaia said. "I had to stay out, to keep watch."

"Good. I want you to tell me exactly what you saw. Start with who was in what place when the working began, and go on from there."

"All right." Keshaia walked to a place on the perimeter of the painted circle. "The First was here." She crossed to the other side of the circle. "Chiwe *etaze*"—Jerre consulted his notes; Chiwe Raiath was Lokheran's Second—"was over here."

"What about Deni?"

She moved a few steps to the left along the edge of the painted circle. "He was here. Kneeling and meditating on the intention, like everybody else."

---

14. The typical meditation chamber, as described here by Teliau, has changed little over the intervening centuries. Similar circles were in use aboard Eraasian trade and exploration vessels, and in the hidden bases that made possible both the First Magewar and the Second. They are not, however, indispensable. During periods of conflict and repression—such as the Occupation following the end of the First Magewar, or the long struggle in the immediate pre-Classical period between the so-called Old Tradition and the rising power of the New Circles—Mages have often done their work without the use of these obvious and betraying diagrams.

"And that went on for how long?"

"I didn't have a timepiece; I'm not sure. A long time."

"Then what happened?"

"The *eiran* started pulling tight," she said. "I wasn't even inside, and I could see them. I wasn't worried yet, not really; the First had warned me it could be a hard working. I was expecting that he and Chiwe would raise the power, like I'd seen them do before, and that the worst that would come of it was that we'd have to patch one or the other or both of them up in the infirmary afterward."

"But it didn't happen that way," Jerre said. "Something went wrong."

"No, no—not wrong. Workings go the way the universe wants them to go; 'wrong' isn't part of it." Keshaia paused, then said, "But this one did go—not how we'd expected."

"In what way?"

"Well," she said, "first Grei *etaze* got up and said we needed more power, and who would match him. And Chiwe never got a chance to answer because Deni was already standing up and answering for him. And after that"—she swallowed—"after that, it was a staff-fight, like we do every day in practice, only this time for real, with the threads of the *eiran* going into it and weaving out again and the pattern drawing tighter and tighter until Chiwe got past Deni's guard and struck him dead. The pattern was done then, and that was the end of the working."

Two days later, Jerre syn-Casleyn paid a second social call on Refayal Tavaet sus-Arial. The two men spoke, as was courteous, of the weather and other trivial things until the red *uffa* was brewed and poured into the crystal glasses.

Then Jerre said, "I've made my final report to Center Street."

"And?"

"It was as the Circle told you. A death in the working."[15]

"That's all?" Refayal frowned. "I don't believe it, syn-Casleyn. I can tell when I'm not being told something, and you're not telling me something now."

---

15. Such deaths, according to statute law in most of the modern Eraasian Hegemony, still count as "by natural causes" provided the deceased is truly a Mage. Since the end of the second Mage-war, the precedent has also been applied elsewhere; see *Citizens of Gyffer v. Calentyk*, 1009 A.F.

"Very well," Jerre said. He set aside his glass of *uffa.* "You were intending to purchase Lokheran Premium Container and Packaging. The initial overtures are a matter of public record, and the Financial and Accounting Division at Center Street was able to find them for me with no difficulty. I'm told there was considerable worry in some quarters about whether you intended to break the company up and move its talents and assets elsewhere, or continue to operate it in its current location."

"I honestly hadn't decided yet," Refayal said. "It's all moot now, anyway. The Lokheran town council managed to top my offer—they scraped up enough money from somewhere at the last minute, apparently."

"Yes," said Jerre. Refayal Tavaet wasn't going to like what he heard next, but he'd asked for knowledge and it would come to him in the way that the universe willed—just as it must have come to Deni himself in the course of the working. Jerre wondered if Refayal would be as willing as his brother to accept that knowledge. Not Center Street's problem, thankfully; an Inquestor's work, as always, was merely to report the truth as he knew it and move on. "The money was a gift from the Lokheran Circle, for the health and welfare of the town of Lokheran."

# Cold Case

## Diane Duane

Diane Duane has written more than thirty novels, various comics and computer games, and fifty or sixty animated and live-action screenplays for characters as widely assorted as Batman, Jean-Luc Picard, Siegfried the Volsung, and Scooby-Doo. Together with her husband of fifteen years, Northern Ireland–born novelist and screenwriter Peter Morwood, she lives in a townland in the far west of county Wicklow in Ireland, in company with two cats and four seriously overworked computers—an odd but congenial environment for the leisurely pursuit of total galactic domination.

She gardens (weeding, mostly), collects recipes and cookbooks, manages the Owl Springs Partnership's Web site at *http://www.owl springs.com*, dabbles in astronomy, language studies, computer graphics, and fractals, and tries to find ways to make enough time to just lie around and watch anime.

fter Rob pulled up in front of the house on Redwood, he sat there in the front seat of the car for a few moments, drinking what remained of his coffee and looking the place over. It was the only single-family house left on this block, and one of very few remaining for some blocks around in this neighborhood—almost all of the rest of the buildings were apartment buildings now, or at the very least duplexes. As he swigged the second-to-last gulp of coffee, Rob tried to imagine what the neighborhood had been like when this house was built, fifty or even seventy years ago: wide lawns, wide new sidewalks, decorously spaced white stucco houses with red tile roofs, tidy front walks leading up to them, poinsettia and dwarf orange planted by the houses or on the lawns . . .

*Not anymore,* Rob thought. The frontages of the beige-painted terrace apartment buildings to either side of the house came up to within about two feet of the sidewalk, and the tiny strip of what could have been grass between them and the sidewalk was trampled to bare dirt. And the house that seemed to crouch between them had no lawn anymore, either—just a tangle of heat-blanched goatsfoot and crabgrass and a single incredibly stubborn patch of dusty, wilted pachysandra that had refused to die even though no one ever watered it now. The windows were all barred and curtained inside. The door had been barred, too, but the black iron screen-and-scrollwork gate hung sideways off its hinges, rammed through when the Drug Squad came in last week. Probably the neighbors had been glad to see the crack house go. *Most of them, anyway,* Rob thought. *The rest of them'll have found another source by now.*

He finished his coffee, crumpled up the paper cup, and chucked it into the garbage bag hanging off the cigarette lighter, then got out of the car and locked up. Rob made his way across to the front walk of the house, relieved at least that he wasn't going to have to go through the usual prolonged explanations to the present residents of the house. Just shy of the single step up to the cracked concrete of the front porch, Rob paused, gazing at the scarred paint on the door, the tiny window with the iron grille just visible inside, the newly split and splintered wood of the doorsills. *All right,* he said silently to the Lady with the Scales, *help me see what's going to get the job done here.*

The shift happened: the air got glassy clear, all the uncertainty and randomness of daily reality falling out of it in a breath's space to leave everything unnervingly fixed. That fixity had long since stopped bothering Rob, though: he worked in it every day. He stepped up onto the porch and tried the bell. It didn't work. Rob knocked on the door.

A pair of pale blue eyes, a little watery, looked out that little grilled window at him. "Yes?"

"Mrs. Eldridge?" Rob said. "Mrs. Tamara Eldridge?"

"Yes?" said the soft, uncertain voice.

Rob held up his ID. "I'm Detective Sergeant DiFalco from the LAPD, ma'am. Homicide. Could I speak to you for a moment?"

"Oh! Oh, of course, just a minute—"

There followed the sound of locks and chains being undone from the inside of the door, though one last chain remained in place. The lady standing on the far side of the door peered around it carefully, looking Rob up and down. "Here, ma'am," Rob said, and handed her his ID, being careful before he let it go to make sure that she could touch it.

She could. She held it in one hand, shaking a little, and looked down at it, while Rob looked her over and readily recognized her as the woman from the picture in the case file. Those watery blue eyes looked up at him again, and the crinkled face, framed by curly silver-white hair, smiled at him. "That's a terrible picture of you," she said. "It makes you look like a cartoon burglar."

Rob had to smile, for this was an accusation he heard often enough from his buddies back at Division. They claimed Rob could display five o'clock shadow five minutes after shaving; and he did have the kind of dark, craggy, brawny look that suggested he should be climbing out of windows in a striped shirt with a big sack labeled LOOT. "May I come in, ma'am?"

"Certainly, just a moment—"

She closed the door to take the chain off, then opened it again. "Please come in, Sergeant," she said, gesturing him past her into a small, tidy living room on the right-hand side.

The room was like her: neat, compact, a little worn but well kept— overstuffed chairs; a sofa with some brassware, half polished, laid out on it on newspaper; antimacassars over the sofa and chair backs; a worn but clean Persian rug in a reddish pattern; and curtains and wallpaper in an ivory shade. The lady herself, as she sat down across from Rob, struck him suddenly as so very frail as to almost certainly make this a wasted trip. *She'll never buy it,* Rob thought. *She'll throw a seizure or something, and I'll have to come back next week. And probably about twenty times after that.*

But he'd been down this road before, and patience had always won out. It would win out now. "Please sit down," Mrs. Eldridge said. She sat there perched on the edge of a big chair done in worn red brocade, looking very proper in a rather old-fashioned pastel tweed jacket and skirt, the effect of faded elegance somewhat thrown off by the tattered "comfy" scuffs she was wearing. "I'm sorry the place is a little messy at the moment: I was cleaning. What can I do to help you?"

"We're investigating a murder in the neighborhood, ma'am," Rob said.

She shook her head. "I don't know if I'll be able to help you much with that, Sergeant. I don't get out a lot: I don't really know any of the people living around here these days. And I don't know much about the neighbors, except that mostly they play their stereos too loud. Especially the people upstairs over at Fifteen Seven-twenty. I call and call their landlord, but he never does anything . . ." She shook her head in mild annoyance. "When did this murder happen? I didn't see anything in the papers."

"It's not recent, ma'am," Rob said. "There was very little physical forensic evidence to help us, so we're having to do neighborhood interviews and psychosweeps to see what else we can find."

Mrs. Eldridge looked at Rob with great surprise. "Why, you're a lanthanomancer!"

It was the usual mistake. "No, ma'am," Rob said, "that takes a few more years of training, and some paralegal. A lanthanometer, yes." He would have taken on a night job years ago if he'd thought he had any real chance of getting through the LMT course and making 'mancer. But his regular work left him tired enough, and Rob was also none too sure he could make it through the entry exams. He'd made it through the lanthanometry course only because of natural aptitude scores high enough to favorably average out the rather low score on his written tests. *I like what I do well enough,* Rob thought. *So why screw with what works?*

"So you can sense dead people," she said. "That must be very interesting work!"

There was a lot more that could be said about the job, but this wasn't the time to get into the technicalities. "Uh, it is, ma'am," he said. "Which brings me to the reason I came. Have you noticed anything different about the neighborhood lately?"

"Well, besides the noise from next door . . ." She laughed a little, shook her head. "The whole place has gotten so remote. I can remember when all the doors on this street would have been open: no one ever locked anything. If you did that now, you'd be dead in minutes."

Rob thought of saying something, restrained himself. "And if something happens to you," Mrs. Eldridge said, "well, you're probably just going to have to handle it yourself, aren't you? I remember when I fell down, right there, coming in the front door with the groceries. Nobody came to help. I had to drag myself in. It was awful."

"Can you tell me a little more about that, ma'am?" Rob said.

"What's to tell? I tripped, I fell down." Mrs. Eldridge gave him a wry look. "It's such a joke, isn't it? 'I've fallen and I can't get up,'" she said, in too accurate an imitation of the old commercial. "But that's all it was, dear, a fall. I got up."

"No, ma'am," Rob said. "You didn't."

She looked at him strangely. Now it would come: the part that always bothered Rob the most, but couldn't be rushed. Without her acceptance, his work could go no further—and Rob's memory was mercifully dulled as to how many of his cases had gotten stuck for weeks or months right here, at the point where truth met denial.

"What on earth are you talking about?" Mrs. Eldridge said. Her eyes suddenly went wide. "Whose murder are you investigating, Sergeant?"

"I think you know, ma'am."

She stared at him.

Rob waited. A change of expression, a twitch, at this point could blow everything out of the water.

"It's mine, isn't it?" she whispered.

Rob nodded, and waited.

Mrs. Eldridge simply sat there for some moments, looking down at her tightly interlaced fingers. They worked a little, and the knuckles were white.

"I don't understand," she said. "Who would want to murder me?"

"We were hoping you might be able to shed a little light on that, ma'am," Rob said.

Now, though, the shock was beginning to set in. "But I fell down," she said. "That was all it was."

"Ma'am," Rob said as gently as he could—for if at any point gentleness was needed, this was it—"as far as we can tell, you were coming into the house when someone came up behind you and struck you in the head. You did fall down. But not because you tripped." He stopped there, not yet being finished with his own disgust at the crime scene pictures, the tidy rug with its pattern blotted out across nearly half its width. It still astonished him sometimes how much blood even a small human body contains.

Her face was surprisingly still: the face of a woman who's just received one more piece of bad news in a life that has had its fair share of it. She looked up at Rob then and said, very composed, "Who killed me?"

"We don't know, ma'am. That's why I'm here: to see what you know about it. Unfortunately, the department is very backed up, and there were no witnesses in the neighborhood, so it's taken a while to get around to you. I was only brought on about two months ago to handle the backed-up cold cases—"

She blinked. "Cold cases?"

"Cases where we ran out of leads, ma'am, and didn't have the manpower right away to follow through. Your case was put 'on ice' until someone could be spared to look into it again."

The look in her eyes gave Rob a whole new definition of "cold" to work with. "Which has been how long, exactly?"

"You've been dead for about three years."

Her eyes widened. "And you're only turning up here *now*?"

"Budget, ma'am," Rob said, truly ashamed. "We're a very small department yet. The other kinds of forensics have been established longer, and they get most of the funds. I'm sorry for any inconvenience."

She looked at him more with disbelief than horror, which was a relief. "Bullshit!" she said.

Rob's mouth dropped open.

"The only reason my murder hasn't been solved sooner is that I don't have any sons or daughters making it hot for somebody on the city council!" Mrs. Eldridge said; and though she was annoyed, it wasn't at him. "Or somebody else down at Parker Center. When you say 'budget,' you mean there's one kind of law for the poor—excuse me, the low-income—and one for the noisy rich. Isn't that it? There's no big rush looking into the murder of an elderly widow with no living relatives, living on SSI. And I've been here being dead for three years when I could have been—"

She had to stop for a moment. "What *could* I have been?" Mrs. Eldridge said. "I mean, I've always been a churchgoing woman. I thought that—"

"We're not allowed to get into that, ma'am."

"Well, why in God's name *not*?"

This was not the usual dry resignation Rob was used to from the vast majority of his murder cases. "Lack of personal experience?" Rob said, maybe a little more roughly than he'd intended.

She let out a breath. "Sorry. This does make you uncomfortable, doesn't it? I'm sorry I snapped at you."

Rob also wasn't used to his victims being quite this perceptive—or so perceptive of others' reactions, anyway. Mostly, they immediately got totally absorbed in the personal implications of being dead. "Ma'am, there are various things that can keep someone from moving on to their final destination. Trauma. Confusion—"

She gave him a look that suggested she was not confused. "My final destination? Next you're going to tell me to fold up my tray table and put my seat in the upright position. Young man, I'm not so sure how final my destination is, even if I am churchgoing. You're saying I'm dead, but I haven't moved on. Fine. So what do I need to do so that I *can* move on? Since there are probably some people wondering where I am. I'm not the kind to be late."

And then she stopped and gave him a wry look. "That was a pun," she said. "Isn't there humor after death? You're not laughing."

Rob took a long breath: this interview was getting out of hand. "Ma'am," he said, "sometimes, in my line of work, it's smarter to wait awhile and make sure you're *supposed* to laugh." He did have to smile then. She was going to be an easier job than he had originally feared.

She looked around her, bemused. "And what about my house?" Mrs. Eldridge said. "If I've been dead for three years—"

"Ma'am, this is your *image* of your house," Rob said. "After your murder, your real house was put up for auction to pay off funeral expenses and death duties. It was bought by some people who sold it to a consortium of cocaine dealers. Until last week this was a crack house."

Now it was Mrs. Eldridge's turn to open her mouth and close it in shock.

"Let me see," she said.

She stood up.

"Ma'am," Rob said, "there's one thing we have to do first."

He fumbled about his left wrist, feeling for the slight sizzle of power that meant contact with his heartline. He didn't get the sizzle, possibly because he was so thrown off balance by the way this whole interview had gone; but the heartline he found, and drew it out—a thin silver thread, glowing even in the warm afternoon light of Mrs. Eldridge's living room.

"While this is connecting us, you can walk in the land of the living," he said, holding it out between his wrist and the fingers of his other hand. "And I can walk where you take me. Ideally, that would be back to the hours just before you died. You may not have been able to see who murdered you, but I will."

She looked at the line of silver light. "'Or ever the silver cord be loosed,'" she said, "'or the golden bowl be broken . . . .'"

Rob nodded.

Mrs. Eldridge held out her wrist. Rob draped the free end of the heartline over it. This time he got the shock, stronger than he expected; but that was in line with the kind of psychic energy bound up in someone who was so newly in touch with her status as a murder victim, and so thoroughly annoyed.

Mrs. Eldridge looked out the window at her tidy, close-mowed lawn, went to the door with Rob very much in tow, opened the door, and went out onto the porch.

There she stood for some moments, staring out at what her front yard had become. From somewhere next door, to the left, came the sound of loud heavy-metal music.

Mrs. Eldridge shook her head.

"Well, since you've taken this long getting into my case," she said, "we'd better get going, because I'm certainly not staying in *this* dump a moment longer than I have to."

And she looked at him.

"Ma'am?" Rob said.

"I'm waiting for you to offer me your arm," she said.

Rob did, helping her down the step. "There's this to be said for being dead," Mrs. Eldridge said, looking with distaste at the "lawn": "I don't feel my rheumatism so much. What do we do now?"

"We retrace your steps," Rob said. "Where were you coming from, that last day, when you had the groceries?"

"I'd been around the corner, at the Ralph's," Mrs. Eldridge said. "I couldn't get the delivery people to come up here anymore: my orders weren't big enough. I had to walk." She sighed. "And it wasn't a pleasant walk, as it was when I first had the house. The neighborhood's just not what it was . . ."

Rob nodded and mmm-hmmed and let her talk. This was just what he would have had to encourage her to do, anyway—immerse herself in her memories of her last day. While in circuit with a lanthanometer, her experience would briefly reshape Rob's perception of the world. *This is going pretty well. At last we should get some kind of result in this case,* Rob thought. It was a relief to him, for the case seemed to have been going on for so long now. They all did, though—all the cold cases with which he was routinely saddled. Not that it mattered, really, so long as they got solved: so long as Justice in Her majesty was eventually served. *It just seems to take so long sometimes. And this one more than most.*

"I don't see what the point is in talking to you when you're off in a world of your own," Mrs. Eldridge said, squeezing his arm.

"Uh, sorry, ma'am," Rob said. They were halfway along the long block, making their way past more lanai apartment buildings, up toward Sherman Way. Slowly, slowly, the landscape around them was beginning to shimmer and change—uncertainty descending over things in a silvery fog as, on a local basis, anyway, the past shouldered the present aside. Cars shifted position without warning, the sky started to get patchy about its weather, cloudy in one spot, clear and sunny in another.

"I said, Sergeant, do you have family?"

"Uh, no." That sounded a little bald: the change around them was taking quite nicely, and Rob didn't have to concentrate quite that hard on it. "It didn't seem fair," he said after a moment. "What I do can be dangerous."

"Other men have families . . ."

Rob nodded. "It wasn't right for me, though," he said. "Maybe later, when I have some more seniority. Is this the way you came, ma'am? Through this parking lot?"

"That's right."

"All right," Rob said. He stopped at the edge of the parking lot at the end of the block, and paused there, waiting for the change to settle fully, for the present to lie down under the weight of the past. That glassy clarity set in again all around the two of them. "Is this the time of day it was?" Rob said.

Mrs. Eldridge looked around in calm wonder at the way broad, blazing afternoon had reshaped itself into late afternoon, shading into dusk. "That's right," she said. "It was just before six. I realized I didn't have anything left in the fridge for dinner. I can't keep a lot of stuff in there anymore. It's on its last legs, poor thing. It has trouble keeping more than a quart of milk cold."

She laughed then as they started across the parking lot together. "I guess I don't have to worry about my fridge anymore," she said. "So now what do we do? I just show you what I did?"

"That's right, ma'am. As far as possible, you ignore me and just do whatever you did that evening. I'll take care of the rest."

She nodded and headed for the doors of the supermarket. The doors slid aside for them, and as Mrs. Eldridge picked up a hand-basket, Rob looked over his shoulder at the parking lot. People there were loading groceries, driving in, driving out; none of them showed any sign of having noticed the small, thin woman walking in.

Rob let the heartline stretch between them, looking around at the supermarket staff, the other people wheeling carts up and down the aisles. "You go ahead, ma'am," he said. "The people here can see you, just as they saw you that day. It's all happening again; just let the flow of it carry you along. No one can see me. I'm just your invisible friend."

"Well, I would talk to myself half the time when I was shopping," she said, wandering down the bakery aisle, "so no one's going to think twice if I do it now. Did I get bread? Yes, I think so. That sunflower rye . . ."

Rob dropped back as he would have on any surveillance involving the living, watching to see who noticed Mrs. Eldridge, how the people she interacted with behaved. She picked up the loaf of rye bread she wanted, chatted briefly with the young paper-hatted girl behind the bakery counter, and then headed back toward the dairy case. "I can never decide what kind of milk to get," she said softly. "All the different kinds they have now, it just gets confusing. What kind do you get?"

"I'm not much of a milk drinker, ma'am," he said. "Mineral water mostly, or beer."

"But what do you take in your coffee?"

"I drink it black."

Mrs. Eldridge rolled her eyes at him as she picked up a quart of skim. "Not sure you're human," she said with a mischievous look. "But maybe a dead lady shouldn't be casting aspersions."

Rob had to smile at that as she made her way into the next aisle. For a while he followed her up and down, while Mrs. Eldridge chose a head of lettuce here, a couple of potatoes there, hesitated for some minutes over the comparative virtues of two different brands of beans. "These are cheaper," she said, "but the others taste better." She sighed and put the cheaper can back. "If I'm going to be murdered before I get in the door with these," she said, "I'll at least be found with the better-tasting brand. And you'll see the murder, you think?"

"The murderer, too, I'd expect."

"That must be hard for you," Mrs. Eldridge said, heading into the paper products aisle. "Never able to stop a crime. Always having to watch it happen, and not be able to prevent it."

"It has to be done. But just finding out what happens," Rob said, looking around as Mrs. Eldridge turned into another aisle, "makes a big difference."

"And not just to you, I take it." She went through her basket, saw that everything she needed was there, and headed for the express checkout.

"Routinely, ma'am," Rob said, "when the murderer's found and brought to Justice, the soul of the murdered is released from whatever trauma it may have suffered, and it then goes . . ." He trailed off.

"Still can't get into detail about that, Sergeant?" Mrs. Eldridge said under her breath while waiting her turn. She smiled: she was teasing him now.

"The destinations would appear to vary, ma'am," Rob said, "and any answer I gave you could prejudice the course of action you take. Once Justice has taken Her course, you'll be free to go . . . wherever."

She got to the checkout, paid for her groceries, and picked up the bag. "It's just a shame I can't make you carry these for me," Mrs. Eldridge said. "This was always the bad part. But I guess I should think of it as the last time."

They went out through the sliding doors, Mrs. Eldridge first, Rob a short distance behind. And as they walked out into the parking lot,

Rob saw someone standing out by a car, watching the door, and something sang down Rob's nerves—recognition, certainty. The guy was in the sloppy baggy pants a lot of kids were favoring at the moment, a huge T-shirt, the inevitable baseball cap on backward: a tall kid, maybe seventeen, eighteen years old, hatchet-faced, with a thin little excuse for a mustache just growing, his hair blond, longish, shoved back under the hat. He watched Mrs. Eldridge the way a cat watches a mouse: the way a murderer watches a prospective victim.

"You shouldn't turn, ma'am," Rob said as they walked toward the edge of the parking lot, where it met the sidewalk of Mrs. Eldridge's street. "Not obviously, anyway; it'll disturb the flow. Seen this guy before? A tall kid, blond hair, rap rags, kind of a hooked nose?"

Deliberately, Mrs. Eldridge stopped and put down the plastic bag, as if the handle was cutting into her hand; then picked it up once more and started walking. "He lives in the apartment house to the right of me," Mrs. Eldridge said, having turned her head just enough to catch a glimpse of the casual shape following her. "He has a motorbike. Always revving it up and down the alley in the back; the noise of it would deafen you. Another one with the late parties and the loud music."

"You ever complain about him?"

She shrugged. "Lots of times, but not recently . . . Not that that would matter, I guess. But is that what we're coming to, Sergeant? That someone complains about noise, and you kill them?"

"Not what we're coming to," Rob said softly. "Where we've been for a long time now. People . . ." He shook his head.

They walked quietly down the street, in the gathering dusk, under the palm trees. Rob walked backward behind Mrs. Eldridge, watching the tall skinny shape following them, all casual innocence. Rob saw that one side of the baggy pants was hanging unnaturally low, and the kid had his hand in that pocket and was watching Mrs. Eldridge with care.

She merely kept walking.

"Do I have to go through it again?" she said then.

For any other similar case Rob had worked with lately, that would have been the first question. For this woman, it was the last. Rob wished he had had a chance to know her. "Of course not," he said.

Mrs. Eldridge turned into her front walk, went up onto the porch, put the shopping bag down, and fumbled in her little purse for her keys. She got them out, started going through the keys for the right one in the darkness of the porch, under the light fixture with the dead bulb. After a moment she found the key, opened the door—

Rob stepped in the door behind her and snapped the heartline between them. The air went glassy again. Somewhere out in the land of probability, a few feet away but nonetheless nearly invisible to Rob and Mrs. Eldridge, a teenager drugged half out of his mind and desperate for money for more came up behind the nasty old lady who could afford to live in a whole house by herself, smashed her skull in from behind with a lug wrench, kicked her the rest of the way in through the door, closed it, and set about ransacking the house.

The gossamer form of the murderer headed for the back bedroom; a form even dimmer and harder to see lay on the hall rug, twitched a couple of times, and went still. "So that was it," Mrs. Eldridge said softly.

"That was it," Rob said.

"And now what?" Mrs. Eldridge said.

"Now . . ."

Rob stopped himself. He knew better than to try to give the woman directions: souls knew their own way. All the same, he was suddenly going to be sorry to see her go. He couldn't get rid of the sense that there was something incomplete about this interview, though everything had gone as well as could have been expected.

"Now one of us goes on," Rob said.

Mrs. Eldridge looked at him kindly, almost with pity. "Not just one," she said.

Rob stared at her.

"But this is always the bad part, isn't it?" Mrs. Eldridge said. "Where truth meets denial . . ."

Her voice didn't sound the way it had before—and suddenly, she didn't look much like a little old lady, either.

"You were always the brave one," said the tall and radiant figure standing there. "Always charging in. Always sure you were in the right. Well, you charged in one time too many, six months ago. It wasn't that I knew for sure it was going to happen, but I'd had my suspicions for a long time. Why do you think I've been waiting here for you all this while?"

She waved around her, at the house with the seedy lawn and the down-at-heel guttering and the peeling stucco. "You had solving her murder on your mind that whole time. You came up that walk so sure you knew where all the guns were. But you never saw the one across the street, the one that surprised everybody. The paramedics were on another call: they got here exactly three minutes too late. But you were so intent on doing your job, and keeping the guys behind you from getting hurt, that you barely noticed your own Murder One. You've been coming up this walk for a long time, again and again and again; remaking your image of the day, though for a long time your soul was too shattered by the trauma to be able to finish the walk. This is the first time you made it to the door." She smiled. "But I knew you'd manage it eventually. Giving up was never your style."

He stared at Her, and the world whirled.

"You're a good cop," She said. "You always did your job, no matter how unfair it seemed, no matter how you seemed to get passed over when the promotions came around. None of that matters anymore. There are other places that can use you now."

"You're my guardian angel," he said. The words came out hoarsely: there was something about the look of Her, standing there, that made him want to cry—and not because he was sad.

"Not just yours," She said.

"Where is she?" Rob said, because it was all he could think of to say.

"She's gone now, a long time," the woman said. "Your boss was furious: he put Mike Gonzalez on the case right after they buried you. Not that any power on earth could have stopped Mike from taking the case, anyhow. He duplicated the results you produced just now. Mrs. Eldridge identified her killer, and a month or so later they caught up with him in New Mexico."

Rob let out a long breath of satisfaction, though without question it was bittersweet. "Where is he now?" Rob said.

She gave him a grim look. "Potter's field in Albuquerque," She said. "He tried to shoot one of the arresting officers. He missed." She let out a breath. "And after that, you know how it goes. The operations of Justice have a way of reverberating through things. Mrs. Eldridge, her murder solved, took herself off somewhere else—and the only one who had to be brought home, secondary to that case, was you."

"You waited for me," he said softly, awed.

"I wait for everyone," She said. "Come on, Rob. I can always use a steady worker at my end of things, and we've got a lot of work to do yet . . ."

From the sofa, She picked up the newly polished brassware, which Rob was now wryly amused not to have recognized immediately as a set of scales. From under the newspapers that had been protecting the sofa from the brass polish, She slipped out a sword, two-edged and bright. Then, together, She and Rob DiFalco went off into the day, into the realms of uncertainty again, where Justice and those who serve Her are needed the most.

# Snake in the Grass

## Susan R. Matthews

Susan R. Matthews's fiction is informed by her military background
and her professional experience as an officer, a janitor, an auditor,
and an accountant. Her favorite recreational reading is history and
adventure literature, both of which she mines shamelessly for plot
mechanics; she has published six science fiction novels (the seventh
is on its way, in October) and has very recently taken the anthology
route into the short-story market.

She and her partner, Maggie, have been keeping house for
nearly twenty-five years. They have two Pomeranian companion
animals and live in Seattle.

itting cross-legged on the bare earth of the ritual space out
in the backyard underneath the willow tree, Galen sorted
through the abandoned altar-set slowly, wondering. The
brazier, the embroidered cloth for the altar, the ritual dishes were as
beautiful as any she had ever seen—but they were all wrong.

Austin had never used the Taber rite in all of the years that Galen
had known her. Taber rite was powerful but dangerous; and Austin had
never been one to respond to the allure of the forbidden powers. Yet it
had been a Taber rite that killed her, Galen's friend Austin.

The startling details of Austin's death had yet to sink in past the
shock of the phone call, the sight of Austin's body in the morgue, her
face contorted with agony and her extremities turning black.

The story looked simple enough on the surface: the Taber rite required a Kinsey snake, and Kinsey snakes were poisonous and notori-

ously willing to share their venom. That was one of the reasons that Kinseys couldn't be legally imported: they were too dangerous to be kept outside of strictly controlled environments like zoos and research programs. The other reason was that they were endangered in the equatorial zone to which they were native and had never been successfully persuaded to reproduce in captivity.

It was true that Kinsey snakes and Folliet snakes looked alike. It took an expert to distinguish them. And a Kinsey snake was not beneath attending the Merris rite, though the Folliet snake had no such compunction. Austin had had a Folliet snake for years, an old wise patient soul whose bite was no more noxious than that of a horsefly. Austin was a priestess of the King-snake. Her pet was an important part of her ritual relationship with the god; but Austin had never stepped across the line from service into sorcery.

Until the night before last, when the Kinsey snake killed her.

Galen heard the subtle hissing of scales coming across the short brown grass that separated the ritual space from the house behind her, and stiffened. She knew that sound. She hadn't heard it for years; she and the King-snake had fallen out decades ago, when she was still a very young priestess, and the god had let her go. He had touched her once, though. She knew that it was him.

*You slander her memory,* the King-snake said, the words reproving and patient in her mind. *You should have more respect, after everything that she has done for you.*

Galen had to pause in her cataloging, closing her eyes in frustration. This was just the kind of nonsense that she and the King-snake had fallen out over, years ago. *I didn't ask for this,* she thought; but she knew better than to think it very hard. Instead, she focused her mind on her friend Austin and the debt she owed Austin for kindness and friendship. Austin hadn't meant to saddle her with this kind of confusion when she'd made Galen her executrix and heir.

"What am I to think, then?" Galen said aloud to the quiet of Austin's half-wild back acre, so that the King-snake would know that she meant for him to answer her. "Found dead of the bite of a Kinsey snake, surrounded by Taber furniture. I'd have sworn that she wouldn't even have let Taber into her house. What had she done to you?"

She braced herself for an angry hiss; but none came, just the sound of shifting coils on the ground. *Don't put that away*, the King-snake said. *You'll be wanting it soon.*

He wasn't answering her. He never had. Galen shook her head and turned back to her task; the doorbell rang. Austin had a bell on the back of the house just so she would know when someone came to the door, even if she was out in the field with her workings. The King-snake had gone.

Rising to her feet, Galen dusted her hands off on her denim skirt and went through the house to the front door. There were policemen there and a reporter. Three policemen; one of them very tall, very slender, with long-fingered hands and the hint of a hissing of scales in his wake as he came up the walk from the patrol cars and joined the others on the front porch.

"Miss Galen?" the oldest of the policemen said. "Sorry to trouble you. We'd like to discuss a neighborhood concern."

Galen let them in because they were police and she had always tried to respect authority. The police in Seelie had never harassed pagan people for being pagan. So long as the applicable ordinances were observed and the peace not disturbed, the police left them alone.

"What's the problem, Officer?" she asked once the door was closed behind them. She had an unhappy feeling in her stomach that she knew; that people were not going to tolerate a priestess in their midst any longer. But if the King-snake thought she was going to levy sanctions on decent if misguided people for the crime of being stupid, he had another think coming, Galen told herself firmly, glaring at that very tall policeman. The King-snake came in many forms to many people. To her he had come as a tall white man, French she'd decided for no particular reason, with a preference for plum-colored fabric and a cynical cant that she'd found very attractive. At one time.

"It's the snake, Miss Galen," the senior policeman said. "We never had complaints about Miss Austin, but people trusted her. Now Miss Austin's dead and the snake has gone missing. Nobody knew it was poisonous in all that time. And it could be anywhere."

Austin's backyard was a full acre of savanna scrub, with a pond she'd put in fifteen years ago and a watercourse to nourish the willow tree. There was a thick hedge there for privacy, but the neighborhood had gotten built up. People had children. Galen could see what the officer was getting at.

"The snake always kept to his own set of places before." She'd known that snake. He'd been perfectly equable, very mild-spirited, personable to the extent that that could be said of a snake. She hadn't seen him since she'd got the call to identify the body. By tradition he would have returned to the underworld to mourn the loss of his friend, but he should have shed his skin if that was what had happened, and she'd found no shed skins. She'd looked.

She still could hardly believe that he'd been a Kinsey snake all along. Cherig at the pet shop had been trying for years to get people to believe that her brightly colored, supple little Folliet was actually a Kinsey snake; and she'd gained a certain degree of influence among the more gullible members of the local snake-loving community through the deception.

Now with Austin's sudden horrible death, Galen was willing to wonder: too late to do Cherig any good. Customs had audited Cherig's shop not five days ago. The Folliet snake was a Folliet snake, no more, no less. It was bound to be a terrible blow to Cherig's prestige, but Cherig was putting a good face on things, from what little Galen had bothered to notice.

"What do you want me to do, Officer?" He'd know that she'd searched. The police wanted the snake to validate their theory about Austin's death by misadventure, with contributory negligence. There were insurance issues, as well as public relations to consider.

."We don't want to come with a mongoose, Miss Galen. But we've got to quarantine the snake. Now, I don't mean to insult you, I'm a Presbyterian myself. But I understand that part of your religious observance is to feed the snake. And that it's accustomed to coming when it hears drums."

Not her observance. No, she and the King-snake had parted company. Austin had taught her other things; but Galen had indeed helped Austin with her setup, out of affection and courtesy. She was Austin's heir, at least as far as the material estate was concerned. It was up to her, she supposed. Cherig would probably do it if she asked, but Austin had never liked Cherig; which made it all the more difficult to understand why Cherig would have been the one who discovered the body.

"I don't know anything about Taber rite, though, Officer." Nor did she wish to. She'd never wanted to engage with that kind of energy; it was so easy to become beguiled by it. Seduced. The King-snake in his dark aspect was beautiful, perfumed with blood and iron. There was too much power there. People lost their way and became venomous.

"I'm sure the snake doesn't know the difference, miss," the tallest policeman said. Galen knew that she was the only one who could hear the hiss in his language. "We can have a licensed herpetologist standing by. It's either bring the snake in or flush it out, Miss Galen. Your neighbors don't want to take it against you."

If he weren't a policeman and she hadn't been trying to avoid confrontation, she'd have a thing or two to say to him about that. *The snake doesn't know the difference.* He could hardly have been more insulting; but he was the one with the snake in him. King-snake was being provoking. He had a vicious streak, but there had been a time she hadn't minded.

"I'm not touching that stuff," Galen said firmly. "Not without backup. You can come to the work, Officer." She addressed herself to the oldest of the policemen. She had nothing to say to any snake-policeman. "Bring your herpetologist. I'll have company. They'll stand back." There were rules to be obeyed, etiquette to be observed. Old gods were very precise about manners.

Whether or not the snake had killed Austin, someone had to call him in—in front of Austin's extended family of friends and coreligionists—and announce the death of the priestess to him. Maybe he hadn't shed his skin and gone to ground because the announcement hadn't been made yet. "You can capture him then. Safely."

Why had the snake killed Austin? Had she been safe with him so long as she didn't succumb to the temptation to tap into darker energies than she had ever negotiated with before? Austin had been strictly Merris rite. Galen still couldn't understand it. But she knew better than to ask the snake. The snake had no particular investment in telling her the truth.

"When will that be, Miss Galen? Because we do need to resolve your neighbors' concerns as quickly as possible."

*He'd told her, too, hadn't he?* Galen reminded herself with disgust.

He'd just said that she was going to want the Taber furniture. He was so superior.

"I'm very sorry, Officer, but I can't tell exactly. I don't know much about the ceremony. I'll have to write to Austin's mother-in-rites for instructions." Who would probably be as shocked by the very idea as Galen was. She wasn't looking forward to it, either. Writing to Austin's spiritual mentor for such information would have constituted an act of slander had it not been for the evidence of Austin's death. Galen knew she had a difficult enough task in front of her as it was.

"One of the locals is an authority, though, Miss Galen. As I've heard, anyway," the tallest policeman said blandly. She could have spat at him. Cherig was an authority, all right, mostly on how powerful and important she was. "Hasn't she lectured on the same ritual? Maybe she could help."

Now the reporter looked interested, for the first time all visit. "Pet store priestess, that one?" the reporter asked. "I'm sure she'd help. I covered her press conference day before yesterday. Strong stuff, too, federal imposition on small businesses, harassment. Her hands were clean, after all. The audit proved it. Very impressive."

Someone had called that audit in on Cherig, Galen was sure of it. Her sly claims to custody of a Kinsey snake would be evidence of illegal trafficking in endangered species, after all . . . if that were true. Cherig had always annoyed Galen with her superior attitude and her self-satisfied air of importance. The last thing Galen wanted was to have to ask Cherig for any favors; it had been hard enough to be civil to her when she'd met Cherig at Austin's house on occasion.

If she was forced to ask for Cherig's help, Galen swore to herself, it would be the last occasion. And Cherig could have Austin's Taber furniture along with whatever else she'd been storing in Austin's back room, and be damned. Galen didn't want it in the house.

"Excellent suggestion," Galen said, hating it. "I'll give her a call and see what I can get scheduled, directly. And I'll let you know. I'll make it as soon as I can, Officer."

It would bring closure of a sort. Maybe. Cherig could walk her through the steps; Cherig had done something of the sort before, for summer programs in comparative religion. Born performer, not to say raging egoist. Cherig would be looking forward to watching Galen make a mistake, too, because Austin's community would be there; and with Austin gone, Cherig confidently anticipated taking Austin's place and her position of influence within the community.

It didn't matter, Galen told herself firmly. The neighborhood was worried about a poisonous snake out loose somewhere in Austin's back lot. Austin wouldn't want her neighbors to have to worry.

"Thank you, Miss Galen," the oldest of the policemen said. "We'll be waiting to hear from you."

Galen let the policemen and the reporter out the front door. The tallest of the policemen nodded to her very politely on his way past. His smile was mild and inscrutable, and she might have imagined the flash of nictitating membrane blinking down over his coffee-black eyes.

Austin's backyard was as crowded as Galen had ever seen it: Cherig had seen to that. There had to be thirty people here, Galen thought nervously, not counting the policemen with the herpetologist. That one policeman was here, but he was keeping back. After all, he hardly needed to watch to know what was going to happen.

She wanted more time to practice. Cherig insisted, though: it had only been three days, but the snake planets were in transit to the waterfall constellation, and it had to be done now. So far as Galen knew, Cherig was just making it all up, but maybe that was unfair to Cherig. Galen didn't like the woman, but at least she seemed sincere about her religion.

*If you could call Taber religion,* Galen thought bitterly; and heard the annoyed shifting of coils across the grass, behind her, to her left, where the policemen were waiting for the service to begin.

It was cool twilight in the back of Austin's house, and the coarse grass of the lawn was prickly beneath Galen's bare feet. Austin had had feet like leather, but the snake had bitten her on the hand, in the webbing between her thumb and her forefinger. Austin's entire arm had been swollen to grotesque proportions, but she had apparently been dead for at least twelve hours by the time Cherig found her, coming to pick up some gear she'd dropped off for temporary storage.

Cherig struck the wood blocks together sharply. The people gathered on the lawn quieted down and settled themselves to watch. There was no time like the present to be started. She wanted to get this over with; the Taber ritual furniture in array in the worship space made her nervous. Galen clapped her hands three times and then three times twice more, and then Galen stepped into the ritual space. The cool earth felt soft against her bare feet after the painfully coarse grass, dry and stubbly in the late summer heat.

The half-harp was waiting on its stand on the bare earth. Galen drew her hand across the strings, letting the sound soothe her. Austin had been her friend, even though they had never agreed about the King-snake. Austin had died horribly. The snake that had done it was not at fault, but had to be removed, for everybody's safety and peace of mind.

The silence behind her deepened as she stroked the half-harp, starting the call. Three notes, very simple; the snake wouldn't hear at all, not as a human would understand it, but vibration was vibration whether transmitted through the air or through the ground. The snake would come to see what had been brought for his supper. He had had no milk for days now. He might be hungry.

"Up-tempo," Cherig admonished Galen from behind. Galen had offered Cherig the chance to conduct the rite herself—to display her talents in a positive environment. Cherig had declined. No, Cherig was looking forward to a spectacular public failure on Galen's part, to strengthen her own position; as if Galen had any ambitions in that direction.

She kept her tempo the way she liked it. Snakes liked periodicity. She could hear Cherig's exasperated sigh at her left shoulder; she didn't care. She heard the slithering sound of the King-snake's approach, behind her, behind Cherig, and listened to see whether Cherig would say anything. Didn't Cherig hear?

*Come on, you bastard,* Galen thought, but with a touch of genuine desperation. *You always said you wanted me back. Here I am. Take me. Make it work, for Austin's sake.* She touched the strings of the half-harp, and the sound vibrated in her ears like an itch that was almost scratched but needed just a little—just a little—just a little bit more. She started to hum with it, drumming with her feet on the cool damp earth to call the snake.

"Sigils, *please,*" Cherig said from behind her.

Galen stooped over the low altar in front of her and took up the little leather bags of corn flour and wheat flour, rye flour and ground malted barley, making the sign around the altar with lines of ground grain. She was beginning to feel good, even with Cherig here. The snake had started to crawl up her spine. She'd sworn she would never deal with him again, but for old times' sake, maybe this once. It had been so good. Once.

*Don't you think it's time you called?* Galen heard the words and danced herself down onto her knees to bow down low to the ground and whisper to the bosom of the earth. *Let the snake come, Mother. Please. Open up the gate, and let me pass through to him, so that we may consort together, and I may gain in wisdom to serve your children better.* She had the eggs ready; she had decorated them herself with paprika and ink, determined not to succumb to the temptation that the Taber rite represented. She would do it clean.

Galen sang and Galen chanted, but nothing was happening, and she could sense the confusion of the spectators even as she fought to concentrate. It wasn't working. She couldn't do Taber. Taber couldn't be cleanly done. She offered whiskey and gunpowder and cayenne and nothing happened except that the sky grew darker as twilight deepened, and Cherig sounding bored and contemptuous behind her paced her ritual with clear disgust, fatalistic resignation. *Of course you can't do it, Galen. You don't have what it takes to dance Taber.*

But Austin hadn't, either. It took hatred and resentment and frustration to call out the Kinsey snake, and Galen had never wanted that energy in her life. She didn't want that energy in her life now, but the snake had her. He rose halfway up her spine, and she began to see the red mist in front of her eyes and took the dish up in her hands with savage abandon.

She'd never dealt in blood in her whole life, though when she'd been much younger, she had flirted with it—blood, and the King-snake, beautiful and savage and destructive, the joy there was in being absolute mistress of her own environment even at the expense of those around her. Austin had known the call; she'd wisely turned her back to it. How could Austin have lost her moral compass—

*It wasn't the snake's fault,* the King-snake whispered to her. *Cherig left him half-wild.* Galen couldn't quite grasp his meaning, but she didn't care; she had more important things on her mind. She had to be careful. There was so much power here, it could go wrong so easily; but she was drunk on him.

She spilled his drink out across the picture she had made, the crude geometric lines appropriate to the sigil of the King-snake in the Taber rite. She heard him, but in front of her now, and she could hardly believe it—she hadn't thought she had it in her to dance Taber, especially with so little preparation. The snake was coming. Galen knelt down and sang to him, passionately longing for his forked-tongued kiss, and saw him coming through the underbrush to taste his dish. The snake.

He looked just like Austin's cheerful self-contained Folliet, just like him. But a Folliet snake would never come to a Taber working. So he wasn't a Folliet snake, after all; he was a Kinsey snake, he had killed Austin.

"Shit," Galen heard Cherig say behind her. "I don't believe it—" Of course Cherig didn't believe it. Cherig would never have expected Galen to have what it takes to call the snake out in a Taber rite.

Or was there another meaning behind Cherig's curse? Galen wondered; but she didn't have much time to think about it, because as the snake came out of the underbrush to coil itself around its dish and taste the offering to bless it, the herpetologist reached over Galen's shoulder with his viper hook and snagged it around the body just behind its head.

Nobody had taken the herpetologist by the hand to lead him in; Cherig hadn't warned her. The sudden break in the ritual space shattered the chords of the sacred dance. The collapsing energies struck Galen like a blow to the stomach; the snake was gone. It wasn't supposed to happen this way. There were things to say, charges to deliver, energy to direct—an incomplete ritual was the worst hangover she had ever had. What had happened to Cherig?

The tall policeman raised her gently by her elbows, helping her up off the ground, walking her through to the house with his arm around her to support her and to shelter her, settling her down in her favorite of Austin's chairs in the front room. She didn't see Cherig anywhere, but it wasn't Cherig's fault, not really. She should have planned for this, Galen realized, half-addled. She should have realized that the ritual would not run its course. And now she owed the King-snake for having spoiled his ritual; she, who wanted nothing to do with him.

She hadn't believed it could have been a Kinsey snake, not even with the evidence she had seen, Austin's agonized form and the coroner's report. She hadn't believed that Austin had really done it. And she hadn't believed that she could, either. Nor had Cherig, Galen was sure of that. Where was Cherig?

Now Austin was lost to her so much more completely than the mere fact of her death in the body. An Austin who could have been seduced into the Taber rite wasn't Austin at all.

Galen wept with the sorrow of her bereavement. The women of Austin's circle gathered around her and wove the safety net, catching the rogue energy that she had to purge from her body in sticky-threaded chant, seeing that it harmed no one.

*Now she's not sure,* the King-snake said very quietly, for her ears alone. *She knows she traded snakes safely when she found Austin's body. But now she has to go and check again. And it is her fault that my priestess is dead.* King-snake was always talking in riddles. Galen didn't have the energy to wonder what he was on about. She curled up in the chair and went to sleep, with women chanting soothingly around her.

The police came back early in the next afternoon, with the snake and the herpetologist in tow. "There'll be a report in the evening papers," the senior policeman said. "We've removed the Kinsey snake from the pet shop. This one's Miss Austin's Folliet, after all."

Yes, the snake looked like Austin's Folliet; he was smiling sleepily at her, wanting to go back into his backyard. But to have a dish of milk first. "I don't understand," Galen said. Her body ached from head to foot; as she had feared, this was the worst hangover she had ever had. This if nothing else would have convinced her that the Taber rite was not for her. "If Folliet isn't a Kinsey snake, what killed Austin?"

The policeman exchanged a glance with the herpetologist, who shrugged. "Your associate was keeping a Kinsey snake at the pet store, it seems," the herpetologist said. "One of the part-time employees found it on her body in the back room when she opened the shop this morning. This snake—" The herpetologist lifted Folliet out of his travel cage and handed him to Galen. "This one I took last night, this snake is legal. All I can think is that she thought she could just switch the snakes to pass the audit. It didn't work very well in the long run."

And he didn't want to talk about it. So much was obvious. There were things unspoken that Galen didn't understand; the policeman excused himself and left her alone with Folliet, who nosed around her face looking for milk. Austin used to hold milk in her mouth for Folliet. Galen wasn't about ready to go that far; but if this was truly Folliet, if Folliet was an honest snake, why had he come to a Taber rite?

She carried Folliet out to the back, stopping in the kitchen as she went through for some milk. Pouring him a dish, a plain dish, an honest kitchen dish, Galen set him down beside the willow for him to find his favorite place.

The sound of the scales hissing in her ears from behind her did not surprise her. "What happened?" Galen asked the still air. "I don't understand."

*You did your part,* the King-snake said. *Cherig was willing to put my priestess at risk to hide the snake. Now the balance is restored.*

Reality blinked away from Galen's eyes like the membrane across the eye of the snake, and she saw it all. Cherig's snake. Austin dead when Cherig came to smuggle Folliet home and take her Kinsey back, after the auditors had gone. The Taber furniture, so that was what Cherig had been storing here; a cover-up. It was hard to tell the difference between Kinsey snakes and Folliet snakes, especially in a hurry.

When Folliet had come to Galen last night, Cherig had run to check, to be sure, to confirm for her peace of mind that she'd retrieved the Kinsey snake: and it had killed her. "Austin never touched the Taber rite," Galen said, more glad than she could explain. "It was a frame."

She heard his scales whispering across the ground. There was a shadow on the far side of the willow tree: a tall white man, with long hands. *My priestess is avenged, Galen. And Folliet has always liked you. Who will sing to him now?*

Folliet had finished his milk and crept away to nap. Galen looked out over Austin's back lot, remembering how it had been when she was much younger. It hadn't been the King-snake's fault. He could still move her when he took her. He'd proved it. "Well," Galen said, "I suppose I could give it a chance."

A breeze lifted the skirts of the willow tree. The King-snake passed, leaving her with a contented floating feeling in her body and the only very mildly mocking sound of his words in her ear. *I knew you'd come around. We'll do very well together, I can promise you that, priestess.*

He'd used her, yes, but he did have a right to protect his own. *Priestess.* She was Austin's heir in fact, perhaps Austin had always wanted her to reconcile with the King-snake.

Galen picked Folliet's dish of milk up off the ground and went into the house.

# Double Jeopardy

## M. J. Hamilton

M. J. Hamilton began crafting fantasy at an early age. While other little girls dreamed of becoming nurses or mommies, M. J. wanted to grow up to be Tinker Bell. When wings failed to sprout from her back, she turned her creative mind to writing.

*And she taught her all her mysteries*
*and gave her the necklace, which is the circle of rebirth.*

ou must pass the amulets to your successors within twenty-four hours to prevent any permanent damage to the balance of good and evil. Full responsibility is yours until your duty is fulfilled."

I really didn't want to assume full responsibility. I didn't have a choice. I adjusted the receiver on my ear and met my grandmother's steady gaze. "I'll honor my vows."

"Flight reservations have been made for you," Vesta continued as if I hadn't spoken. "I will meet you at the gate and take you to the farm. Everything will be ready when you arrive. After your private ritual, we'll celebrate success and your induction into the Council."

I jotted down flight numbers and time schedules as they were recited to me, then let my mind linger for a moment on the upcoming transfer of power. On a hill in the remote English countryside, I would perform a ritual to pass the talismans to the next set of identical twins fated to serve the gods. And assume my role on the Council.

I knew what that meant. When I passed the amulets on, my grandmother would die. I would take her place on the board of remaining twins.

"You *must* succeed," my grandmother said when I lowered the receiver to the cradle. Tears coursing through the wrinkles in her pale cheeks, she lifted a gnarled hand, palm out.

"I will." I pressed my hand to hers to seal the pledge, then hugged her frail body and gave her one last kiss. Grief and anger battled with duty and responsibility as I left the room and hurried from the elite nursing home.

Light rain fell from the murky sky. Malice and greed slithered through the mist. The chill of danger snaked down my spine.

Turning up the collar of my denim jacket, I jogged to my car, sinking one Reebok in a puddle in my haste. As I slipped the key into the lock, the side door on the van parked beside me slid open.

The face of my murdered twin flashed before me, and her voice called out a warning.

I whirled around, reaching for the gun in the holster at the small of my back. A fist slammed into my temple. The blow would have knocked me to my knees, but a huge muscular arm closed around my waist and yanked me into the van. A needle stabbed through my jeans and into my thigh, followed by the sting of fluid flowing into my leg.

A man who looked remarkably like Popeye's nemesis, Bluto, quickly bound my wrists and ankles with duct tape, slapped a strip across my mouth, then climbed into the driver's seat.

I teetered on the edge of consciousness during a long and bumpy ride, the ethereal voice of my twin giving me strength for my coming ordeal. The amulet between my breasts emitted a pulsating warmth that healed my wounds. But it couldn't melt the ice from my soul.

The van eased to a stop and Bluto honked the horn. Moments later the sound of a large metal door rolling on tracks drowned out the noise of the idling engine. Bluto pulled the van forward, then turned off the ignition. The door rolled again and the light dimmed. The goon got out, opened the side door, and leered down at me.

A short fat man stepped up beside him, his bald head gleaming under the overhead lights. "Put her over there in the corner," he said with a wave of his hand. "And no rough stuff."

"Sure, Arty." With a smack of his lips, the thug leaned down, threw me over his shoulder like a sack of potatoes, and carried me to a back corner. He moved his big hairy hands over my body as he lowered me to the floor, then stood at my feet, his mouth pulled into a feral grin. "Now, ain't you something? Worth a million bucks and I get a quarter of it."

I held my wrath in check, biding my time. He was a lesser villain in this play for power. Not worth the expenditure of energy this early in the game.

"Tony! In the office!" Arty yelled, his voice echoing off the walls.

Tony? "Bluto" better suited him.

I closed my eyes, felt him hesitate, then sighed with relief when he turned and walked away. The fact that I was still alive reinforced my convictions. This wasn't a simple case of rape, murder, and theft. It was much bigger than any mortal crime.

After several minutes, I opened my eyes and brought my surroundings into focus. Not an easy task when tripping on a drug powerful enough to put most people under. Wooden barrels reeking of dill and brine tainted every breath I took. No hope of rescue, even less for escape if I were an ordinary individual.

Ordinary I'm not. And I took personal offense at the manhandling used to subdue and dump me in the pickle warehouse. I'm a good P.I. Natural talent aided by the supernatural makes a dynamic combo. But sometimes it's best to assume a Columbo personality. I would have been a willing abductee if he'd given me a chance to cooperate. Oh well—I now didn't have to waste precious hours finding the site and possibly missing the transfer.

All part of plan A.

The injection had come as a total surprise.

Plan B drifted in and out of my mind, concrete one moment and elusive the next.

I sat quietly, listening to the voice of my sister gently coaxing me to stay calm and gather momentum, waiting for the drug to wear off. Not much else I could do under the circumstances. Although I have special talents, I am human. But I wasn't as comatose as I pretended.

I heard heavy footsteps approaching. Tony coming to check on me. The thought of his oily black hair and bad teeth made my stomach lurch. The moron sauntered through the maze to ogle my body again. I knew he didn't expect me to make a run for freedom, not bound with duct tape.

I wouldn't. Not this time.

He stopped at my feet, his thick black eyebrows drawn together and his nostrils flared in anticipation. "Ooh, she's got her eyes open. Feeling a little feisty? Maybe I'll get me a piece of you right now while I've got the chance. Arty don't care. I doubt his client will, either, since I'm supposed to kill you and stuff you in a barrel with enough concrete to sink you to the bottom of the bay." He straddled my legs and rubbed his crotch. "I bet you're even better than your sister was."

I gazed up at him, blinking as if I couldn't quite bring him into focus. Not far from wrong. Rage distorted my vision.

Hoping for a little more time to gather my strength, I closed my eyes and let my head loll to one side, praying he wouldn't force the issue. Willing him to leave me alone and let me do my job. I had to face the enemy and restore the balance. I had a lot to lose if I failed. Had lost too much already.

Mankind stood to lose even more.

"Tony!"

Arty was obviously the boss of this operation. Which meant he had the amulet. A small teardrop made from strands of intricately woven silver. Worn by Isadora, my twin, on a long silver chain. Identical to the one I wore, with one exception: the stones inside the teardrop. We received the ancient talismans at age twenty after our Great-Aunt Mauve died in a car accident.

Isadora had died only hours ago, and already I sensed a change in the atmosphere. Storms brewing within every nuance of nature. Natural disasters building to shake the earth. Unnatural changes in store for the flora and fauna of the future.

An impending doom that had nothing to do with the pervert standing over me. But I would not be raped. I peered at Tony through my lashes, waiting.

Tony unbuckled his belt, staring down at me, salivating. He unzipped his fly.

I would kill him if necessary to achieve my goal, and accept the consequences. If I had to pay threefold for taking his life, so be it. Nothing the Council could say about Fate would erase the fact that he murdered my sister. My grandmother would be taken from me at midnight. With the amulets in the wrong hands, freedom would become an archaic word in Webster's dictionary.

Fortunately, my captors knew nothing about the power of the amulet. They knew it was important enough to steal. Important enough for Arty to hire Tony to commit murder. The promised proceeds were great enough to feather their retirement nests against the worst scenarios.

I doubted they knew or cared what would happen to our everyday world if Arty turned the amulet over to the woman who orchestrated the plot. The Witch who sought to rule the world.

I hated both men. The Council demanded I spare them my wrath. If it hadn't been Arty and Tony, someone else would have taken the job. I had to play it their way if possible, use my inborn abilities aided by the amulet I wore, and bring my nemesis to justice.

Or die. Those were my choices.

Anger, hatred, grief, and a wary fear fueled my psychic energy, escalating its potency.

Whatever it took, I had to recover the amulet and eliminate the threat. Simple in thought. Much harder when it came to killing a member of the family. Morgan, a cousin who resented the fact that her twin died at birth, keeping her from possibly inheriting the position of power she coveted. Something I learned after breaking the news of Isadora's murder to my grandmother.

I had one chance to make this simple. My reason for sitting on the cold concrete floor for the last hour. I had to come face-to-face with her after she donned Isadora's necklace, but before she took mine. I suspected I knew, but had to verify how she learned of our positions on earth.

No one had attended the ritual when Isadora and I took our oaths before the remaining twin, our grandmother, who presided over the initiation. Only the three of us had been there that awesome winter night when Beth became Isadora, who aided the gods in keeping harmony between nature and mankind, and I became Lilith, entrusted with the task of keeping lust and magic in balance.

On the hilltop in the center of a circle of ancient stones, we pledged our lives and talent to keeping harmony in the universe. As we shared a chalice of warm mulled wine to seal our fate, the first snowflakes of the season swirled in the moonlight. A beautiful night filled with love and devotion.

Other than members of the Council, no one was supposed to know of our existence as liaisons to the gods. Until now, no one knew of the lineage of Witches who produced the twins destined for service. Someone let the ancient secret slip. Chaos loomed in the near future.

I blinked my eyes again and gazed up at Tony, planting the seed of thought that he should save me for later.

He pulled his thick lips into a disgusting smile and winked. "I'll be back."

I breathed a sigh of relief when he hurried off to answer the summons, then tried to find a more comfortable position. I needed to stay bound until I knew Tony wouldn't be back. He was a scumbag, but I really didn't need his death on my record.

"What the hell you think you're doing?" Arty bellowed. "She's due any minute. Now, get your ass in place. I'll up your share to half if we get the money *and* keep the necklace."

The verbal warning came at the same time I felt her presence and the unmistakable hostility surrounding her.

After a few moments of silence, a door opened and closed several rows of barrels away. Leather-soled high-heeled shoes snapped against the concrete.

Morgan had arrived.

My heart doing double time, I used the adrenaline to warm the tape around my wrists, stretching it until it snapped. Silently cursing, I peeled away all the tape, rolled it into a sticky ball, and eased from the corner. In a matter of seconds, I crouched low behind a pickle barrel near the office.

"Mr. Blum?" Her resonant alto voice held a note of amusement.

"Yeah. What can I do for you?" Arty asked, cautious but excited.

"I'm Mrs. Johnson. I believe you have something for me?"

"The necklace is locked in the safe and the woman is secured. Show me the money and we'll deal."

"Show me the merchandise or you'll die," Morgan demanded. Her Scottish burr did nothing to soften the malice in her tone.

Arty gasped and yelled, "Tony!"

I eased my head around the barrel and peered at my cousin Morgan.

She stood with her back to me, tall and erect, her red hair piled on top of her head adding several inches to her height of five feet nine inches. A formidable woman dressed in a black pantsuit and high-heeled shoes, a briefcase in one gloved hand and a gun in the other.

Tony stepped from an aisle between the rows of barrels a few feet from me, a gun in his hand. My gun, I realized after a moment. I ducked back and listened, debating whether to let them shoot it out, or intervene. I preferred the first choice, knew I had to do it the hard way. It was time for Morgan to recycle her soul, but Fate had other plans for Arty Blum and his sidekick.

"Put the gun on the floor nice and easy," Tony snarled.

"I don't think so," Morgan crooned, her voice heavily laced with disdain. "But I will make a wee concession since you boys don't really know with whom you're dealing. Keep the gun, Tony. And I'll keep mine. When I'm satisfied the necklace is genuine, we'll put down our weapons and you'll be rich." She aimed the gun between his eyes. "Cross me and you'll die."

I said a silent thank-you to the Goddess for the small reprieve. Again I eased around the barrel, my gaze riveted on the scene.

Arty's oversize face glowed an unhealthy shade of red. Sweat poured from his meaty forehead and dripped off heavy jowls onto the collar of his dingy western shirt. He nodded to Tony, then turned on the worn heels of his cowboy boots and strode into the office. The plate-glass window in the wall allowed me to watch him as he moved to the corner of the office. He dropped from view—I assumed to retrieve the amulet.

Morgan motioned her gun toward the interior of the office. Her voice dripping with sweetness, she smiled at Tony. "After you."

Since Arty seemed ready to do business on her terms, Tony didn't have much choice. He scowled at her, but entered the office, my .38 Special aimed at her head.

If I couldn't stop her, neither man would emerge from the pickle warehouse alive. Morgan wouldn't leave witnesses behind.

Dumb as dirt! Too caught up in their image of themselves to realize they'd been had. I doubted they'd even get the chance to learn that the briefcase she set on the floor beside the desk was empty.

When Arty reappeared behind the glass, I slipped around the barrels and approached the office. Back pressed to the wall beside the door, I waited and listened.

I could feel Morgan's purr of satisfaction and knew she looked upon the amulet.

A gut-wrenching spasm of grief passed over me.

Morgan touched the teardrop.

It was show time.

I stepped into the doorway.

She held the silver chain in one hand, a nine-millimeter Glock in the other.

"Don't do it, Morgan," I warned.

She gasped and spun around, her gun aimed at me. "You're an imbecile, Arty Blum," she snarled through clenched teeth.

"Tony, you stupid shit! Why the hell did you let her loose!" Arty exploded.

Face pale and eyes wide with shock, Tony shook his head. "I didn't, boss. I swear I didn't."

"Surprise." I tossed the ball of tape on Arty's desk and smiled, enjoying their panic.

Morgan recovered first, her red lips curling into a sneer. "I don't suppose it matters how you got loose. You're still here and we have the guns."

I returned her sneer with gloating pleasure. Surely a mark against me with the Council. I hurt too much to care.

"It does matter, Morgan. You made a fatal mistake when you had Isadora murdered."

With a disgusted shake of her head, Morgan looked down at me. "You can't lie your way out of this one, darling. I *know* you're Isadora. I also know you don't have the power to stop me."

I glanced at Arty, then pinned Tony with a heated glare and sent a current of energy zinging to his privates. When Tony dropped the gun and clutched his crotch in agony, I smiled at Arty. The moans of anguish coming from his trusted goon turned his face as ashen as my victim's.

Morgan looked at me, her features twisted with hatred, and tightened her finger around the trigger.

Revenge is so sweet when approved by the gods.

I shrugged. "Murdering either of us was bad enough, but you had to go and murder the wrong twin. Don't put on the necklace, Morgan. Our duplicity isn't the only thing you didn't learn in your hasty research."

"Bitch," she screamed at me, and pulled the trigger.

Nothing happened.

Morgan looked from the gun back at me. Her mouth opened and closed. I could see the rage building behind her eyes.

I shrugged again, taunting her. "I told you. You see, Beth took on the role of Isadora. Not me. *I'm* Lilith. You had Isadora murdered while she slept. Your time is up, Morgan. Give me the amulet." I held out my hand. "Don't make me take it."

She wavered in indecision for only a moment. "I don't believe you," she rasped, quickly slipping the chain over her head.

The earth shifted slightly on its axis, causing a ripple of energy to spark the air. The faint scent of ozone burned my nose. My heart pounded in jubilation. Reverse psychology had worked. Morgan was completely at my mercy.

Arty and Tony were unaware of the tilt toward mayhem. They watched us with a mixture of fear and curiosity.

But Morgan's eyes widened with anticipation when she sensed the change. Taking it as a good sign, she aimed the gun between my eyes and pulled the trigger again.

Another useless click in the quiet room.

The desire to kill her then almost overruled my better judgment. Evil pulsed around her, adding to the stench in the small office. But before I could rid the earth of her corruption, I needed answers.

"No!" Morgan tossed the gun to Arty and closed one hand around the amulet.

Although caught off guard, Arty managed to catch the gun before it hit the desktop, and fumbled it toward me. The Fates rarely explained the destiny of their subjects, leaving me to wonder what they had in store for the short, squat, bald man.

I met Morgan's steel-gray eyes. Time for show-and-tell. What she didn't tell me, she'd show me in mental images. A minor talent of mine.

Confident that his boss had it under control, Tony retrieved my gun, crabbed his way behind the desk, and eased into Arty's chair.

I let him.

Arty stood stock-still, watching us, the Glock trembling in his hands. That was good, too. Neither gun would work until somebody removed the jammed cartridges. I didn't need distractions.

Morgan stroked the teardrop as if waiting for a burst of power.

I almost felt sorry for her.

*Almost.*

My twin's life had been sacrificed for this woman's greed. I would be thousands of miles away when my grandmother took her last breath. There was no time to deal with my grief until true balance was resumed. Not one person deciding the destiny of the world, but a balance of two. Two different views working for the continuance of the future.

Morgan could rule the world alone, as I was prepared to do until I could pass the responsibility to the waiting twins. But her misdeeds would eventually cause her demise.

In other words, what goes around comes around.

"I've notified the Council and told them what I've learned. You signed the guest register at Summerland when Grandmother was sick last month, but not since. She doesn't remember your visit or anything else that transpired during those days. A couple of the nurses told me you visited often during her illness, that Grandmother hallucinated frequently during the worst hours of pain. She relived that monumental night several times, according to what I've been told. You were there for at least one of the retellings."

Hatred blazed in Morgan's eyes. "She was quite explicit with the details, so don't try to bluff me. Beth possessed the power to defeat me. You don't."

"There's much you didn't learn from her ramblings. Beth and I exchanged roles at our initiation. Beth was better suited as Isadora, and I have the heart of Lilith. Since we were identical except for the birthmarks covered by our robes, Grandmother never knew. The Council learned of our duplicity today. Under the circumstances, they needed to know the truth."

The long silver chain felt hot to my touch as I drew it from beneath my blouse. "I'm sorry you let greed destroy your heart, sorry you've forced me into this position. The Council has ordered your execution. I have no qualms about obeying their order." I grasped the teardrop and took a deep breath. "Good-bye, Morgan."

Morgan's eyes widened, then rolled back in her head as she crumpled to a heap on the concrete floor.

The balance made another slight shift. The hardest part of my task was almost over.

Tony raised my gun and pulled the trigger. Nothing happened. With a low growl, he hurled the piece at me. It hovered in front of me for a split second, then clattered on the floor at my feet.

I picked up the gun, pointed it at the ceiling, and squeezed off a round. The noise echoed through the warehouse.

Tony looked from me to Arty. "The fall must have fixed it."

"Yeah, sure." Arty looked at the gun in his trembling hand, then at me. He didn't quite understand that he'd witnessed a death executed on a psychic level, but he had enough sense to be scared out of his wits. He dropped the Glock onto the desktop, clasped his hands behind his head, and waited for me to call the shots.

I would. When I got my bearings. I needed a moment to revel in relief. I had a few hours before my scheduled departure for Heathrow. Until then, I would play the part of a key witness in the death of Alicia Harding—"Morgan," to the pagan world.

Tony had enough sense to lace his fingers behind his neck.

"I'd rather not kill either of you, so just stay put while I call the police."

Neither moved a muscle as I shoved the Glock into the holster at the small of my back. Dumb as dirt but not stupid. The .38 trained in their direction, I laid the receiver on the desk, activated the speaker, dialed 911, then plucked one of Blum's business cards from a plastic holder on the desktop.

After making my report, I called a familiar number, lowered the .38

to Tony's crotch when he took a side step, and pulled my mouth into a half-smile. "Don't even think about it, scumbag, or you'll be the only eunuch on death row. If you don't have a heart attack before your trial."

The homicide detective investigating my sister's murder answered his cell phone on the second ring. "Yeah, who is this?"

"Geez, you're rude. What happened to 'hello'?"

There was a pause on the other end of the line. When he answered, genuine concern replaced his belligerent tone. "Where the hell are you? I've been trying to track you down for the last two hours."

"Sorry, I've been tied up. I've got the two men responsible for my sister's murder in custody." Again I read off the address of the pickle warehouse. "And send an ambulance. We've got a possible heart attack victim."

"How the hell . . . ? Never mind. I'm on my way. Just don't pull any Houdini escapes until I get there."

"Sorry, you already missed it, but I will hang around. Just hurry up. I wouldn't put it past either of them to try something stupid. I'd hate to have to shoot them." I crossed mental fingers, hoping this case would intrigue him less than the last one.

Detective Heath would love to know my secrets. Or at least he thought he would. I had my doubts about his ability to understand.

"Did you call 911?" he asked.

"Of course. As a matter of fact, I hear a siren. Get your ass in gear, Heath. I'm on a tight schedule." I hung up and pointed the .38 at Arty. "I want the necklace . . . now."

Arty glanced at Morgan's inert body, his mouth working in silent protest, then back at the .38. "Yeah, sure. Sure. No problem." He sidled over to Morgan. "Tony, hold her up so's I can get it over her head."

"Just slide the chain around until you find the clasp, Arty. Unfasten it, take it off, refasten it, lay it on the corner of the desk, and step back." I aimed the .38 at his head. "Now."

The siren sounded like it was right outside. Which meant I needed to wrap up loose ends.

As soon as Arty stepped away from the desk, I snatched the amulet, slipped the chain over my head, and tucked both talismans under my blouse.

The essence of every previous Isadora warmed my soul. The earth righted itself on its axis, balance restored.

The twin amulets secure between my breasts, I began crafting a watered-down version of what had transpired and planting the story in the minds of the two men staring at me. By the time uniformed officers crossed the warehouse to the office, Arty and Tony no longer remembered the necklaces or my confrontation with Morgan. A necessary revision of the facts.

Otherwise, Isadora's amulet would spend months in a plastic bag as evidence required for trial, and Morgan's parents would be devastated by her evil plot. Not to mention the strain that having to single-handedly preserve cosmic harmony would cause on my nerves.

Morgan's body would be flown to Scotland for burial after an autopsy confirmed she died of cardiac arrest while helping me capture Beth's killers.

Only the Council and the gods would know the truth.

*I have heard, at still midnight,*
*    upon the hilltop remote and forlorn,*
*The note that echoed through the dark,*
*    the haunting sound of the heathen horn.*

# Witch Sight

## Roberta Gellis

Roberta Gellis has been a very successful writer of fiction for several decades, having published about thirty-five novels since 1964. Gellis has been the recipient of many awards, including the Golden Porgy from *West Coast Review of Books*, the Golden Pen from *Affaire de Coeur*, the Romantic Times Lifetime Achievement Award for Historical Fantasy, the Romantic Times Reviewers Choice Award for Best Novel in the Medieval Period (several times), and the RWA's Lifetime Achievement Award. Currently, Gellis is writing historical mystery—*Bone of Contention,* the third book in the Magdalene la Batarde series, will be published by Forge Books in September 2002—and coauthoring with Mercedes Lackey a series of fantasies set in Elizabethan England. Her home on the Web is *http://www. robertagellis.com.*

ell, of course, Brenda is a witch."

Brenda winced and her eyes flicked once to Dame Hillyard. The plump woman looked less at ease than usual, seated in one of the straight chairs in a study room rather than behind her imposing desk. Her voice was flat and without expression, but the turned-down lips of her small, pursed mouth betrayed her distaste for the words she had uttered.

The tall man seated beside Dame Hillyard looked with interest at Brenda, also noting the civil guard who had brought her into the room. She knew she was not a very prepossessing sight. Her eyes and nose must be red with crying, and her dress was limp and creased—not surprising because she had slept in it for three days. She clutched the beautiful knitted shawl Amy had given her tighter around her shoulders as she realized this man must be the person who was going to investigate Amy's death.

She glanced up at him quickly and down again. Yes, this must be the person. The murder of which she was accused had been reported by telex, because they had no telepath in the village, and it had taken him two days by train and carriage to get to Smallbourne.

"There's nothing wrong with being a witch," the tall man remarked, his brow creasing in a frown.

Brenda's heart leaped with hope, but she suppressed that hope at once. What he had said was a required response. Brenda knew there were laws prohibiting discrimination against witches, no matter how repulsive they looked.

"Oh, well." Dame Hillyard's voice drew her attention, and she looked up to see the woman shrug. "I suppose there isn't. I've been told that they're very useful in predicting the weather and in things like cursing locusts so they don't ruin the crops." She snorted lightly. "But I notice they don't ever kill *all* the locusts." A slight shrug and a snicker. "That would put them out of a job, wouldn't it?"

"It might also unbalance the ecology," the man said.

Dame Hillyard snorted again. "Well, it wouldn't matter in this case, since Brenda Willcoming can't curse away a flea, much less kill a locust. She's a witch according to the testing procedures, but she can't do a thing"—she sniffed—"except see things no one else can see."

"Can she?" the man asked, sounding interested.

"Yes, I can," Brenda put in. Her voice was a little hoarse but firm.

Now the man looked directly at her; his eyes were a bright brown, lively and curious. "I am Detective Inspector Maxime Farber," he said, but was then interrupted.

"So you say, Brenda," Dame Hillyard snapped, "but no one else ever saw . . ." Suddenly, her eyes widened. "Maybe you *can* see what no one else can. Maybe you saw where Amy Lightfeather hid her money. *That's* why you killed her! For her money."

"I *didn't* kill her," Brenda cried. "I didn't. I wouldn't hurt Amy. She was my friend." She had sworn to herself that she would be calm and simply insist on being sent to Centertown where she could be truth-spelled, but she couldn't help sniffling, and tears ran down her face. "I wouldn't hurt anyone," she sobbed.

"You knew that she had money hidden?" Farber asked.

"Everyone knew." Brenda swallowed another sob. "She was careful. She didn't dress in fancy clothes or put on expensive jewelry, but she did get things that no one else had. When the elf traders came through the village last year, she got one of their gossamer scarves. No one saw her buy it. I was with her at the fair and I saw her admire the scarf, but she didn't buy it. She didn't even ask the price. But a week after the traders left, she had the scarf. And then there was the amulet . . ."

Brenda couldn't help it. She burst into sobs anew and wavered on her feet. Farber gestured to the civil guard and told him to bring Mistress Willcoming a chair.

"Very well, Dame Hillyard," Farber said, taking a pad and writing tool out of the large purse hanging at his hip. "I've already examined Amy Lightfeather's body. Now I would like you to tell me what you did and saw—what you saw yourself, not what you were told by others. We'll get around to the others soon enough."

Brenda could feel her eyes widen in surprise. She had thought that he had already heard Dame Hillyard's tale and accusation and that he had accepted her guilt. When he sent for her, she had been overjoyed, hoping to appeal to him to be tested in the city. If she were left to local justice . . . She drew the shawl closer about her.

"It was Tiw's day," Dame Hillyard began, "just at noon meal, and Amy wasn't in her place. Brenda had been killing time setting the tables for more than half an hour, so I sent Brenda to fetch Amy. I knew Amy couldn't have gone far because I'd seen her when I told Brenda to set the tables just before the first lunch bell. Amy was in the garden, staring at flowers through that stupid amulet."

"Why send Brenda, if she was busy setting the tables?"

"She was the most likely to know where Amy would be. Amy was becoming impossible. She *wanted* to be a witch, and ever since she got that amulet, she would wander into the woods with it. Maybe the amulet was only an excuse. Maybe she had her money hidden there. Anyway, Brenda was most likely to know, so I sent her after Amy."

But Brenda hadn't been the first to look for Amy. She shifted slightly in her chair, wondering if she should mention that Amy's uncle had come to the school looking for her. Brenda had seen him through the window talking to Abel in the garden. Her head lifted; her lips parted; but then she decided not to speak.

"Then Brenda *was* Amy's friend?" Farber asked.

"Friend!" Dame Hillyard sniffed. "No one wanted to be Brenda's *friend*. Amy wanted to be a witch. Maybe Amy hoped if she spent time with Brenda, the witchcraft would rub off."

"So the girls were together a good deal? Would you say that Brenda knew Amy well?"

"I suppose so."

"Yes. Then go ahead. Brenda went out to look for Amy and . . . ?"

"And about five minutes later Abel Springwater—he isn't a student; he's one of the gardeners—came running in and said someone was screaming. Then, of course, we all rushed out. We found Brenda kneeling over Amy with the amulet in her hand. She killed Amy and was about to steal the amulet!"

"No!"

It was a strained whisper, but both Dame Hillyard and Detective Inspector Farber looked at Brenda. She shook her head and swallowed. She wouldn't speak again until asked.

"Do you know how Amy died?" the inspector asked.

"By magic, of course," Dame Hillyard said before Brenda could answer. "There wasn't a mark on the girl."

"Do you mean to say that Brenda killed Amy in five minutes by magic?" Farber raised his brows in patent disbelief. "If so, she must be an incredibly powerful witch . . . and an incredibly stupid one, too, since she would be the most likely suspect. And didn't you just tell me that Brenda couldn't even drive away a flea, much less kill a locust?"

Dame Hillyard's lips thinned. "It must have been her." She flashed a look of intense dislike tinged with fear at Brenda, who was staring at the detective inspector with her mouth open. Shrilly, Dame Hillyard continued, "She was the only one there. She had her hand on Amy's neck and was about to steal the amulet. I wouldn't be surprised if she's been hiding her power all along for just such a purpose."

"Are you a witch, Dame Hillyard?"

"No! Of course not!"

Farber nodded. His face showed nothing as he turned toward Brenda. "Now I would like to hear from you just what happened, Mistress Willcoming. Dame Hillyard asked you to find Amy and bring her back to the school to have lunch. Did you know where Amy would go?"

"Not for sure, sir. If she was looking through the amulet, she would have followed the spirits of the air wherever they went. But they did like the stream in the woods, which is why I went that way." She shuddered suddenly, and her eyes filled with tears again. "She was there, just where the wall around the school turns." Her throat closed, and for a moment she thought she wouldn't be able to continue. She swallowed hard. "There's a little shelter—I think it was once a guardhouse—at the corner. I looked in—"

"Why?"

For a moment Brenda considered not answering, but she had to if she was going to request examination under truth spell. Maybe the inspector was using a truth spell now—although he didn't look like a witch. She could feel color coming into her face, and she looked down at her soiled gown.

"Because she used to meet Abel there sometimes," she whispered at last. "You can't be seen from the school in the little house, and there are bushes. You can slip behind them before anyone coming along the path could see you."

"Liar!" Dame Hillyard exclaimed. "It was against the rules to fraternize with the help."

"No, I'm not lying." The tears that had filled Brenda's eyes dried up in the heat of her anger. "I'm not lying, and I'm not saying anything bad, either. I never saw them doing anything they shouldn't, only talking."

"I thought Abel was in the garden," Farber said. "Dame Hillyard said he ran in when he heard you scream. It was you that screamed, wasn't it?"

"Yes, sir." Tears filled her eyes and overflowed again. Brenda wiped her face with the heel of her hand.

Detective Inspector Farber took a kerchief from his sleeve and handed it to her. She wiped her face and blew her nose, letting her hands drop to her lap, holding the kerchief tight, as if it were a lifeline.

"Did you scream as soon as you saw Amy?" he asked.

She blinked. "No, I didn't. I didn't know she was dead. I thought she had tripped and fallen, and I knelt down and took hold of her shoulder. She didn't respond, and I was afraid she had hit her head when she fell, so I tugged her over onto her back. It wasn't until I touched her face that I realized she was dead." Brenda shuddered again and bit her lip. "It was then that I screamed."

"How did you know she was dead?" the inspector asked.

Brenda stared at him. "I . . . I don't know," she answered uncertainly.

"Did you See that there was no life force?"

"I don't know what life force is," she whispered.

Farber looked displeased. "Your tutor doesn't seem to have taught you anything," he said.

"Tutor?" Brenda repeated, looking puzzled. "I do as well as all the other students. I'm good at reading and writing and ciphering. I can spin and weave and sew. I don't need a special tutor in anything."

"I see," Farber said.

But Brenda's mind had gone back to the original question, and she said, "It was . . . her skin was different, cool and . . . and not rough the way skin gets when you're chilled. It was smooth, maybe a little clammy."

Farber looked interested again, but all he said was, "So then you screamed. Had you already picked up the amulet?"

"No. I did that right after. I only cried out once, but then I thought if I looked through the amulet, I would be able to hear the spirits of the air and I could ask them what happened to Amy."

"Hmmm." Farber did not look convinced. "Did you plan to steal the amulet?"

"No!" Brenda exploded, but then she looked down again, and her cheeks felt hot. "I did want it, but I knew taking it would be silly. I wouldn't be allowed to keep it. It must have been very costly, and Master Lightfeather would want to sell it."

"She says that now." Dame Hillyard's voice was flat. "But we caught her with it in her hand, just before she tucked it away into her clothing. It would have been easy to say Amy wasn't wearing it when she arrived."

Farber nodded, but Brenda protested, "No one would have believed that. Amy always wore it, even to bed. I *didn't* kill her. Why should I? I can already see the spirits of the air and the pixies and sometimes even a unicorn . . ." Her voice faded, and for a moment she was again looking through the trees at that magical beauty.

Brenda sighed and continued, "Why should I kill her? All I needed to do was to borrow the amulet for an hour or two. I'm sure I could have learned to understand them, and then I wouldn't have needed the amulet at all. Why should I kill my friend for it?"

"Maybe because she wouldn't lend it to you." Dame Hillyard sighed and looked at Farber. "I don't see the purpose of this. Brenda is the only witch in the village, and Amy died from no known cause. You looked at her body, Inspector. Did you see a crushed skull? Any knife wounds? She wasn't strangled; her face wasn't purple, and her tongue was in her mouth. Our apothecary swore she wasn't poisoned."

"No," Farber said. "She wasn't poisoned, but if you have no other witch in the village, I don't see where Mistress Willcoming could have learned the spell she would need to kill Amy with magic."

"Amy had a grimoire," Dame Hillyard said, grim and angry.

"But there was no spell in it for killing people," Brenda protested tremulously.

"Did you use the grimoire?" the inspector asked Brenda.

"I tried," Brenda admitted. "Nothing worked."

"Do you know where Amy got the grimoire?"

Brenda shook her head. "She just had it one day, like the gossamer shawl and the amulet."

"Do you know where the grimoire is, Mistress Willcoming?" Farber asked next.

"Yes, sir," Brenda whispered. "It's in my room, just on the bookshelf with the other books."

"Did you take the grimoire first and kill Amy to prevent her from complaining of the theft?" Dame Hillyard cried. "And then decided to steal the amulet, too?"

"No! Amy couldn't use the grimoire, so she left it with me for safe-keeping. She . . . she didn't trust her uncle William or her cousin Marcus."

"Brenda, that is an outrageous thing to say!" Dame Hillyard exclaimed. "Master Lightfeather took her in when her parents died, and raised her with the same care he gave his own son. You are only trying to make others seem guilty of the crime you committed."

"But Mistress Willcoming denies that she committed any crime, and I haven't seen any evidence yet that she *did* commit one," Farber said. "In fact, it seems unlikely, since Amy must have died as much as half an hour before Brenda found her and she, according to what you told me, Dame Hillyard, was in the dining room setting the table for about half an hour before she found the body."

Dame Hillyard's mouth opened, then closed, then opened again to gasp in outrage while her face got quite red. "Well!" she exclaimed indignantly. "I am shocked and disappointed in the Peacekeepers. I have always believed that they were astute enough to rely on the knowledge of those who knew best. Constable Willis agreed with me completely when I said the girl must be kept under restraint until the procurator of justice could send a warrant for her removal."

"Begging pardon, ma'am," the civil guard said softly. "I did agree that Mistress Brenda be kept under restraint, but that weren't because I thought she killed Mistress Lightfeather . . . at least 'er no more'n anyone else. It were because Master Lightfeather were talkin' quite wild about hangin' 'er."

"This would be Marcus Lightfeather, the victim's cousin?" Farber asked.

"Yes, sir. And 'is father were worse. He wanted to put 'er to the torture to make 'er confess and *then* hang 'er."

"Torture?" The horror in Inspector Farber's voice was enough to make Constable Willis shrug apologetically.

"We got no witch to do a truth spell, and it costs a pretty penny to bring one from Northbourne. And I been constable for . . . ah . . . goin' on twenty year and I never 'ad a crime that called for more'n pointin' my finger."

"How fortunate," Farber breathed. "And what were you going to do about this crime?"

"Nothin', sir. I know when I'm in too deep. I sent the telex. I figured Justice Procurator'd send someone."

"You sent a telex!" Dame Hillyard hissed.

"And it's just as well he did," Farber snapped. "If a removal had been done without an authenticated report from a truth-spell-trained witch or a justice-recognized investigator, those involved would have found themselves in serious trouble."

"Constable Willis is fully empowered—"

"No, ma'am, I ain't. I'm a civil guard, appointed by the village council, that's all. I can't do removals."

Brenda, who had been frozen stiff with horror when she heard what Dame Hillyard and the two Lightfeathers had planned for her, gasped when a sharp rap on the door immediately preceded the entry of both William and Marcus Lightfeather.

"You the inspector?" William asked sharply.

"Yes," Farber said.

"You've seen my niece's body, the constable's man said. Now I want the key to that room where Willis's been keeping her. Time and over time for her to be buried."

There was a silence in the room while the investigator looked carefully at William Lightfeather. Then he said slowly, "Why are you so eager to have your niece buried? Is there something about her body that you do not wish to be revealed?"

"There's nothing to reveal," Marcus yelled, voice shaking. "Amy was good as gold. The witch killed her with magic. You've got the witch. Burn her like she should be, and let us put poor Amy to rest."

"But Mistress Willcoming doesn't seem to have been anywhere near Mistress Lightfeather when she died."

"Who knows when she set the spell?" William snarled. "We know Centertown keeps witchs' evil secret so they have use of it. I want my niece's body now!"

"You cannot have it, sir," Farber said quietly. "It must wait until my Reader arrives. She will be here tomorrow, I believe, and tell me all sorts of things from an examination of the body. Now, perhaps, you can explain to me—"

However, the inspector did not bother to finish his sentence because William rushed out; Marcus fled on his heels, slamming the door behind him. The civil guard half rose to his feet, looking very worried, but Farber shook his head. Brenda swallowed, frightened again. If the inspector wasn't willing to act on such suspicious behavior, had his comments about her innocence only been some kind of trap?

"What if they flee?" Constable Willis asked.

"Where would they go?" the inspector replied. "Into the forest? They would not last a week. To the next town? They would be swiftly apprehended." He smiled. "Now, if it were Mistress Willcoming who tried to flee, I would be on her heels at once. Since she can see the spirits of the forest and the air, she might do well in the forest."

"I am not going to flee," Brenda said. "I demand to be taken to Centertown and questioned under truth spell."

Farber smiled more broadly. "So you say. However, I am not going to take any chances. I will keep you under observation . . . but not in the constable's gaol. You may return to your own room, and I will set a guard on it."

Dame Hillyard, who had been slumping sullenly in her chair, sat up looking brighter, but Farber disappointed her again. He took Brenda to the eating room and requested a meal for them both, and to Dame Hillyard's clear disapproval sat with Brenda asking her what the spirits of the air and the pixies and other forest dwellers looked like. Eventually, he requested that one of the teachers watch Brenda while she had a bath, and then he saw her to her room and locked her in.

She was not to have a peaceful night, however. Sometime well after dark the night erupted into a clangor of bells and shouts and the pounding of running feet. Brenda leaped from her bed, but the door was still locked. She ran to the window to scream for release and saw the red glare of fire—but it was no threat to the school. The school was quiet except for the students who were old enough running out to fight the blaze.

Still, Brenda was too anxious to go back to bed. She drew on a robe and sat watching out of the window as the red glare died. Eventually, the students began to troop back into the school, but before Brenda gave up her post to try to sleep again, there was a knock on her door and the key turned in the lock.

"Get dressed," Inspector Farber called through the door, "and come down to the study room. I have more questions."

He did not wait for her, however; Brenda was allowed to make her way alone. She found the room a good deal more crowded this time, and everyone but she was filthy with ashes and stained with smoke. As soon as she entered, Farber gestured to her to come closer and told Constable Willis to close the door.

"William and Marcus Lightfeather," he said, "you have been apprehended in the act of trying to burn down the place reserved for the keeping of the victims of unnatural death."

Those in the room shifted this way and that and made a low, unhappy noise, but they mostly looked at Brenda.

"Why do you say that?" Dame Hillyard cried. "*She*"—she gestured venomously at Brenda—"the witch could have set the fire from a distance. She certainly didn't try to fight it."

"Could you set a fire?" Farber asked Brenda.

"I can light a candle if I'm close," she said, somehow much less frightened of Farber now, "but not streets away."

He nodded. "Anyhow, Dame Hillyard, the whole back of the gaol stank of lamp oil, and so did the Lightfeathers, who had empty buckets nearby and torches in hand." He looked back at William and Marcus. "Did you kill Amy Lightfeather?"

"No!" Marcus cried. "Sometimes Amy made me crazy, the way she flirted with Abel, but I'd never hurt her."

William shook his head. "I had no reason to harm her."

Farber's lips tightened, and he turned to Brenda. "You were Amy Lightfeather's friend. I suspect you know why the Lightfeathers wanted to destroy her body."

Brenda swallowed hard, and color rose in her face. "I suppose it was because Amy was not . . . was no longer a maiden. She told me she had known men, but I never understood how she would find a time and place. She hardly left the school except to visit—" Her glance flew to William; her eyes widened. Then she covered her face with her hands. "Oh God, that was how she got all those things. Master Lightfeather got them for her to keep her quiet."

"Witch! Bitch!" William screamed, and leaped toward Brenda, but he was intercepted by his own son, who fell upon him and began to strangle him, weeping hysterically, moaning that he knew someone had meddled with Amy.

The inspector now drew two silvery ribbons from his purse and stepped toward the battling men. He separated them with surprising ease and thrust Marcus at Constable Willis, who grappled with him while Farber rolled one of the ribbons around William's wrists. A moment later he had Marcus similarly secured.

"We are all dirty and tired," Farber said, glancing around at the now shocked and silent people, "but it happens that all the town notables are gathered together, and I would like to settle this matter now so that I can leave with my prisoners tomorrow morning. Abel Springwater, come forward."

"Wait," Constable Willis said. "Don't you need the Reader's evidence? You said she would be here tomorrow."

"No Reader is coming," Farber said. "That was a test, which the Lightfeathers failed."

The civil guard's mouth opened, but before he could speak, Abel Springwater had made his way to the center of the room. The gardener was a handsome man, big-boned like Willis, but fair-haired and blue-eyed. He nodded easily to the inspector, still rubbing his ash-stained hands along the sides of his leather trews, and said, "Don't know nothing but what I said afore. Heard her"—he cocked his head at Brenda—"screaming and told Dame Hillyard."

Farber asked, "How long did the screaming continue?"

Abel's easy stance stiffened. He glanced at Dame Hillyard and then swiftly at Brenda. He cleared his throat. "Don't know," he said. "Shocked me, it did, that yelling."

"But Brenda says she only screamed once."

Sullenness replaced Abel's earlier expression of easy attention. "Could be. Said it shocked me. Went to tell Dame Hillyard 'thout waiting to see how long it would go on."

"You mean you have never heard a student in this school cry out for stubbing a toe or dropping a book or merely in play, that you rush to tell Dame Hillyard at every shout you hear? If this is your pattern—"

"No. 'Tain't the way I do usual. I—I don't know why I ran in to Dame Hillyard. Somethin' in the voice . . . Yeah. Somethin' in the voice scared me."

"Perhaps," Farber said, eyes and voice cold. "But I think you had been in the little guardhouse and seen Mistress Lightfeather's body already."

"No," Abel cried, his voice rising in panic. "No, I never went in. I only saw from the doorway . . ."

His voice trembled and faded as he realized that he had admitted Amy was dead before Brenda had seen her. He glanced at Dame Hillyard and then, quickly, at the closed door behind him. Constable Willis stirred as if to move to block the doorway, but he did not.

"Abel Springwater," Farber began.

"No!" Constable Willis and Dame Hillyard cried out together.

"The witch did it!" Dame Hillyard continued alone. "She did! I saw her! I'll give evidence. She—"

Her voice came to a gasping stop as Constable Willis drew his sword and backed toward the door. "No. Brenda didn't do nothin'," he said as he opened the door with one hand behind him. Farber didn't speak or move. "Nor did Abel, poor fool. I killed Amy Lightfeather."

"Why?" Brenda cried, tears rising to her eyes.

Willis turned to her. "You innocent!" he said scornfully. "You cared for 'er, but if ever there were a black soul, it were 'ers. What 'er uncle did were wrong, but she tempted 'im into it, and she tortured 'er poor cousin . . . and my Abel. She tormented 'im, too."

"Killed her how?" Farber breathed, the words hardly audible.

"I knew she were waitin' fer someone in that place—didn' know it were Abel or I wouldn't of . . ." He shuddered. "I went to tell 'er to say no to Abel and leave 'im be. She laughed at me. Me, the civil guard. And she knitted to the end of a row and poked the needle at me to push me back, laughing, sayin' it were Abel's turn to bring 'er somethin' pretty. So I took that damn needle out of 'er hand and shoved it right up the back of 'er head, just like I dreamed of doin' every time I heard Abel sobbin' in 'is room. Didn' make a sound. Didn' shed hardly a drop of blood. All I had to do was pull the needle out, drop 'er, and walk away."

There were exclamations of horror from the listening and watching group, but no one moved to intercept Willis, who stood in the open doorway, sword in hand. Abel Springwater was staring openmouthed at Constable Willis, and Dame Hillyard cried out, "Fool!"

"Fool? Me?" Willis said, moving the sword in a tight, threatening circle. "You're the fool, tryin' to say it were Brenda! I been a law keeper all my life. I weren't havin' no murder put on an innocent in my village."

And while the words still hung in the air, he was out of the door, which he slammed shut behind him. Everyone was frozen with shock, except . . . Brenda looked up at Detective Inspector Farber's face and saw that he was smiling slightly and was not shocked at all.

A few moments later a hubbub broke out of shocked exclamations and plans for pursuit. Farber made no move to follow Willis and took no part in the discussion until the others had talked themselves out; then he said calmly that it did not matter, that he would arrange with Centertown to have the constable found.

The people muttered and mumbled, but no one dared contest the inspector's authority, and with uneasy glances at Farber the room began to clear. Ignoring the others, Farber directed Brenda to one of the chairs around the study table and Dame Hillyard to the other.

"You are now clear of any accusation against you, Mistress Will-coming," he said, "but this is a very backward place. Are you sure you wish to remain in this village?"

"Wish to remain?" Brenda echoed. "Do I have any choice?"

Farber explained that, being a witch, Brenda had always had the right to attend one of the schools for the Talented in Centertown. "The schooling is free," he said, "and you need not worry about a living allowance because Dame Hillyard will be paying that—exactly the amount that has been paid to her to hire a tutor in witchcraft for you. She will pay it every single month, until the full sum she stole is cleared."

"The money is gone. I cannot pay," Dame Hillyard cried.

Detective Inspector Farber showed his teeth in what was not a smile. "Well, then, I can arrange for you to be taken as a prisoner to Centertown. You will then work for the authorities, likely scrubbing toilets, and your stipend will be paid to Mistress Willcoming. You as well as Brenda have a choice." He turned to Brenda with an entirely different smile. "Go back to bed now, or, if you cannot sleep, pack for the journey tomorrow."

Brenda nodded but did not move. Instead, she said, "You're a witch yourself, aren't you, Inspector Farber? When you asked me about the spirits of the air and forest, you were only making sure I *could* see them."

"Yes," he said, still smiling.

"And you *can* hear and understand the spirits of the air and forest?"

He smiled more broadly. "Yes."

"You knew! You knew everything right from the beginning. Why did you let the Lightfeathers almost burn down a building? Why did you make Constable Willis confess?"

"Mistress Willcoming, if I had simply said that some invisible people had told me the long-trusted constable of the village had murdered Amy, would anyone have believed me? They would have been even more sure you were guilty and that witches were evil. And the Lightfeathers would have escaped punishment—one for debauching his niece, although I hardly know who was the more guilty in that. You *are* an innocent, Mistress Willcoming."

"No," Brenda said, pulling the beautiful shawl Amy had made for her tighter around her shoulders. "I was not innocent. I was desperate. I knew Amy could be vicious, but she was very kind to me . . . and I had no one else."

Inspector Farber gently steered Brenda toward the door. "Get some sleep," he urged. "You will have many friends soon," he assured her. "You are coming home, to your own people now."

# Overrush

## Laura Anne Gilman

Laura Anne Gilman was born in New Jersey, left briefly to go to college in the wilds of New York State, then returned to her old stomping grounds. Ignoring all advice from her family and friends, she began her writing career in 1997 with a sale to *Amazing Stories*. Since then, she has published more than a dozen short stories, three media tie-in novels (two *Buffy the Vampire Slayer*, one *Poltergeist: The Legacy*), been reprinted in high school and middle school textbooks, written two nonfiction books for teenagers, and edited two anthologies (*OtherWere* and *Treachery and Treason*). Her first original novel, *Staying Dead*, featuring Wren and Sergei, is in stores now. She is married (Peter), with one cat (Pandora).

ou didn't say anything about a body!"

Well, that got his attention, anyway, Wren thought, seeing the startled look in her partner's eyes.

"Excuse me?"

"Body. As in dead. I thought we agreed, no more dead people?" She collapsed bonelessly in the large leather sofa opposite Sergei's desk. But she couldn't meld with the butter-soft material the way she normally did. Not with that much adrenaline coursing through her system.

"Walk me through it."

That was the thing about Sergei. You could flap him for maybe, oh, ten seconds. Then he was back in the groove. Which was good. She needed grooveness right now.

"Body. Dead. Propped up in front of the painting like a rag doll, only ickier. Blood, pooled and dried." She could feel herself calming down as she recited, the act of talking it out giving her some distance. "Head wound, looked like. He was wearing slicks"—the outfit of choice for the well-kitted burglar—"but his hood was back, like he'd stopped; like he thought he was in the clear."

She had been cruising up until then. It was a flyby, an easy job. They'd been hired by an insurance company who suspected that their well-to-do client hadn't actually been relieved of certain heavily insured paintings in a recent robbery as he claimed. So they'd come to Sergei, who had a certain . . . reputation . . . of being able to retrieve missing objects, and offered him a hefty check to ascertain the truth of the matter. Quietly, of course. Bad business to look as though you doubted the word of a wealthy client.

So Sergei took their check, shook their hands, told them they'd have an answer by the next Monday. And then he'd called her. He was the money guy, the deal guy. The face people saw.

She did the dirty work. The physical stuff. Ego aside, when it came to Talent, there were maybe fifty Mages who could manipulate current the way she did, with the results she got. Skills, maybe another twenty thieves working today who could finesse the way she did. There were maybe ten other people in the world who combined the two. And only one of them was better than she was.

But she was the only one who kept it legal. Ish. And dead bodies had no place in a legal game.

Wren didn't believe in ghosts. Dead was dead was dead. But . . .

She exhaled once, slowly, letting all the remaining tension flow from her neck, through her shoulder muscles, down her arms and legs until she could practically feel it oozing out of her feet and fingers like toxic sludge. And with it, the buzz of unused current-magic still running in her system was drawn back into the greater pull of the earth below her.

When she opened her eyes again, the world seemed a little more drab somehow, her body heavier, less responsive. Current was worse than a drug; it was like being addicted to your own blood, impossible to avoid. All the myths and legends about magic, and that was the only thing they ever really got right: you paid the price with bits of yourself.

She reached almost instinctively, touching the small pool of current generated by her own body. It sparked at her touch, like a cat woken suddenly, then settled back down. But she felt better, until she looked up and saw Sergei staring at her, a question in his eyes. And the ghostly presence she had felt on seeing the stiff weighted on the back of her neck again.

*What?* she asked it silently. *What?*

Wren bit the inside of her lip. Scratched the side of her chin. Then she sighed.

It didn't matter if you believed in ghosts or not, if they believed in you.

They had stored the body in one of the rooms in the basement, where Sergei kept the materials needed to stage the gallery's ever-changing exhibits: pedestals, backdrops, folding chairs. Wren opened the door and turned on the light, half expecting the corpse to be sitting up and looking around.

But the body lay where they had left it, on its back, on the cold cement floor. "Hi," she said, still standing in the doorway. That sense of a presence was gone, as though in bringing it here she had managed to appease its ghost. But it seemed rude somehow, to poke and pry without at least some small talk beforehand . . .

"I don't suppose you can tell me what happened to you?" She closed the door behind her and locked it. Sergei's gallery assistants were gone for the night, but better overcautious than having to explain.

Wren swallowed, then put the book she was carrying down on the nearest clear surface. No point trying to recall anything from her high school biology courses—that, as her mentor used to say, was what we had books for. "Rigor mortis," she said, and flicked two of her fingers in its direction. The book opened, pages riffling until the section she needed lay open. Taking a small tape recorder out of her pocket, she pressed "record" and put it next to the book.

"The body is that of an older male, maybe a really rough fifties. He's wearing jeans, sneakers, and a long-sleeved button-down shirt. Homeless, probably—his skin looks like he hasn't washed in a while." She walked around the body, trying to look at it objectively. "Hair, graying brown. Long—seriously long. This guy hadn't been to the barber in a long time."

She stopped, stared at the corpse, trying to decide what it was that struck her as being *wrong*. "There are no signs of trauma. In fact, there's no sign of anything. Unless he died from an overdose of dirt." It might have been a heart attack or something internal, she reminded herself. The only way to tell would be to cut him open . . . "Ew," she said aloud. "Rigor mort. Tell me about it."

There was a faint hum, like that of a generator somewhere starting up, and a voice rose from the book: "The stiffening and then relaxing of muscles after death, as caused by the change in the body's chemical composition from alkaline to acid. Process typically begins in the face and spreads down the body, beginning approximately two hours after death and lasting twelve to forty-eight hours. A body in full rigor will break rather than relax its contraction."

Wren flicked her fingers again, and the voice stopped. "The body was stiff but not rigid when I picked it up," she said thoughtfully. "And it stretched out okay when we got it in here—nothing broke off or went *snap*." She grimaced, then bent down to touch the skin, at first gently, then jabbing harder. "The skin is plastic, not hard. So I guess it's safe to say rigor's pretty much wearing off. So he's been dead at least half a day, maybe more. Not too much more, though—he doesn't smell anywhere near that bad."

Sitting back on her heels, she looked at the book. "Next paragraph," she told it. The voice continued: "Also to be considered is liver mortis, or postmortem lividity. When a person dies, the red blood cells will settle at the lowest portion of the body. This can be identified by significant marking of the skin. Markings higher on the body would indicate the victim was moved after death."

Wren made a face, then she sighed, gave herself a quick, silent pep talk, and reached down to take off his shirt.

"There better not be anything disgusting hiding in there," she warned him. "Or I'm so going to throw up on you."

Her fingers touched the skin at the base of his neck, and the jolt that went through her knocked her backward on her rear and halfway across the room.

"The hell?"

"What am I looking for?"

Wren shook her head. "If I tell you, you—just touch him."

Sergei shot her a look, but knelt to do as she asked. He was still wearing a tie, but his shirtsleeves were rolled to his elbows. Long, manicured fingers touched the corpse's hair, then the side of his cold cheek, flinching slightly away from the feel of dead flesh. You never got used to it, he thought.

"Go on. His torso."

Sergei placed the palm of his hand flat over the corpse's chest, where Wren had left the shirt half-undone. He waited. Then frowned. "What the hell?"

"You feel it?"

Sergei nodded, astonished. He was reasonably sensitive to the natural flow of magic—magic was how they'd first met—but this was different somehow. "I feel . . . something. What is it?"

"Overrush."

Sergei pulled his hand away, wiping it on his slacks as though that would erase the taint of death. "Which is . . . ?"

"Current. Only, more than that. There's current residue in him that's impossibly high. This guy's—God, I don't know how to explain it. I don't even know what it is! But it feels right. That's what you're feeling. It's the only thing that could explain—"

"Genevieve!"

He hated shouting at her, but it seemed to do the trick; she pulled herself together. "Right. It looks like he got caught up in current, major mondo current, pulled it in—and got ungrounded. Which is impossible. I mean, any lonejacker worth their skin knows how to ground. You don't make it past puberty if you can't."

"So this fellow should have been able to ground and dispel any current he couldn't use."

"Unless," Wren said, even slower than before, "unless somehow, he was stopped . . ."

Sergei stared at the body. "How? By whom?"

Wren shrugged, hugging herself. "Damned if I know. I didn't think it was possible. Grounding's as much mental as physical—like breathing. Which he's not doing, either, anymore."

Sergei sat down heavily on a velvet-covered stool and rubbed the bridge of his nose. "You couldn't have just left him there?"

She didn't even bother glaring at him, looking at her watch instead.

"Almost seven," she told him. "You'd better get upstairs and meet our new client. I'll see about finding the old boy a more final resting place."

Sergei caught her by the arm. "Be careful," he told her. "I don't like this."

She put her hand over his. "That makes two of us, partner."

Sergei never asked what she'd done with the body. She never offered to tell him. He told her, instead, about the new client. "It's something a little different," he said. Different was good. Different required planning, plotting. That was what they did best, the different ones. The difficult ones. That was why they were the best Retrievers in the business, on either side of the law.

And different distracted her from the memory of a man torn apart from the inside by too much of the stuff she depended on to exist.

Talents were all current junkies. Didn't matter that you were Mage or lonejacker; it got in your blood, your bones, and if you could jack, you did. And if you jacked too much . . .

Her mentor had gone crazy from current. She had always thought that was the worst thing that could happen. Maybe it wasn't.

Sergei's hand touched her waist, his breath warm in her ear. "Stop thinking. We're on."

Wren nodded once. It wasn't the usual run for Sergei to be with her on a job, but you had to mix it up every now and again. If they start expecting one, give them two. If they expect two, don't hit them at all that night, that week, that place. And when they expect stealth, walk in the front door.

"Mr. Didier, a pleasure, a pleasure indeed . . ." Wren tuned out the host's nervous bubbling. If lonejackers were bad about hanging around each other, gallery owners were worse. At least a lonejacker would let you see the knife before it went into your back. She detached herself from Sergei's side and began to wander around the gallery. It was larger than Sergei's and more eclectic. There was a series of oddly twisted wire shapes that she thought she might like. Then she saw them from a different angle and shuddered. Maybe not. Snagging a glass of champagne from the tray of a passing waiter, she took a ladylike swig, licked her lips, and in a heartbeat effectively disappeared from the awareness of everyone else in the room. There wasn't any real magic to it—herd-mentality clothing, a perfectly ordinary body and face, and a strong desire not to be noticed, sewn together by the faintest of mental suggestions that wafted along the current that was humming in the lights strung along the room, illuminating the exhibits.

Walking slowly, she made a half-circuit of the main floor, then moved up the short, straight staircase against the back of the wall. Nobody saw her lift the velvet rope barricading the steps, nobody saw her move up into the private areas of the gallery.

She barely paused at the primary security system at the top of the stairs. Her no-see-me cantrip was passive, neither defensive nor aggressive, and she passed through the barrier of current without a hitch.

Wren cast one look back down the stairs, picking Sergei out of the crowd with ease. He was leaning in to hear what an older woman was saying, his shoulders relaxed, his right hand holding a glass, his left gesturing as he replied, making the woman laugh. If you didn't know what to look for, you'd never recognize the break in the line of his coat as a holster. The one time Wren had picked up the compact, heavy handgun, she'd spent the next hour dry-heaving over the toilet. Psychometry wasn't one of her stronger skills, but she could *feel* the lives that gun had taken.

But hating something didn't mean it wasn't a good idea to bring it along.

Moving down the hallway, Wren counted doorways silently, stopping when she came to the seventh. A touch of the doorknob confirmed that there were elementals locking it. Trying to use magic to force them out would bring smarter guards down to investigate, exactly what she didn't want.

Going back to the stairs, she leaned against the wall, just below the protective barrier, and took a deep breath. As she exhaled, slowly, she touched the current, sending a wave of disturbance racing down the stairs.

The twinkling lights in the gallery window went out with a satisfying *pop,* followed in quick succession by the lights over the exhibits. As the crowd milled about in confusion, Wren raced back down the hallway and slipped inside the seventh room, trusting the chaos downstairs would hide her own intrusion.

Inside, the room was dimly lit, three paintings stacked against the wall like so much trash. Sergei would have had conniptions if he'd seen them treated like that. But Wren wasn't interested in their artistic value. A razor let her slice the bottom painting out of its frame and remove the piece of carved bone pressed between two layers of canvas. The relic went into a small, rubber-lined case that fit in her pocket, and the painting was placed back into the frame. A finger run along the serrated edges and a tiny drawdown of power, and the two layers sealed themselves together again. Done, and prettily, too, if she did say so herself.

"Sssst!"

She managed not to freak by the skin of her teeth, turning to glare at Sergei standing behind her.

"They're frisking everyone downstairs," he told her, heading off any questions. "We need another exit."

"Right. This way."

"This way" ended up being a long hallway without a single door off it until they came to a T-intersection. Sergei looked decidedly unhappy, his gun now out and ready in his hand. Wren barely spared it a glance, too busy listening to the hum of current throughout the building. It was alert now, singing in activity. The building was locking down, tucking itself up tight. "No, down here," she said suddenly, grabbing his free hand and tugging him to the left, concentrating on the patterns. Down the hall, through a heavy fire door, a pause on the landing to determine up or down, then up to another fire door and into a hallway that was the exact replica of the one they'd left behind. They took a corner at a full-out run and stopped.

"Oh hell."

Wren stared at the blank wall. She could smell the sweat on her skin, Sergei's. She could feel the thrum of blood racing in her veins. Panic bubbled just below the surface. But Sergei's voice, next to her, was calm.

"Get us out of here."

She knew what he was asking.

*I can't!*

*We're dead either way. Or worse . . .*

She reached, grabbing every available strand of current, draining every power source in the building, siphoning off Sergei until he staggered. Filled and overflowing, practically sparking and glowing from within, she grabbed her partner in a bear hug and *threw*—

There was no transition. Her chin to the ground, palms abraded by macadam, vomit pouring from her mouth. Her body ached and quivered, and she was drenched in cold, sticky sweat.

When the torrent finally released her, she fell to her side, panic filling her brain.

"Serg?"

"Da."

Utter relief filled her at the sound of his voice, faint and worn-out, somewhere behind her. "I told you I was no good at this," she said, wiping her face with her filthy sleeve. There was a scrape of flesh against pavement, then a slow stream of curses in Russian.

"You 'kay?"

She managed to find the energy to roll over and watched as Sergei fussed with his cell phone. Throwing it down in disgust, he reached into his inside jacket pocket and pulled out his PDA. He glared at it, then her, then threw the equally useless device next to the cell phone.

"Oops?" she offered.

He closed his eyes, picked up the gun from where it had fallen when they translocated. It seemed to click and spin in all the right places, and some of the lines on his face eased as well. He replaced it in the holster, then leaned forward and took her hand, pulling her up with him as he stood.

They leaned against each other for a few moments, listening to the sound of their still-beating hearts. In the near distance, a car hit the brakes too hard, squealed away. Farther away, the hum of engines, horns, sirens wailing—all the normal sounds of the city at night.

"You got it?"

She nodded, touching her pocket. "Got it."

"Then let's get the hell home." He paused. "You have any idea where we are?"

Wren tried to laugh, couldn't find the energy. "Not a clue."

They came to the end of the alley and paused to get their bearings. "Wow. I managed to toss us farther than I thought."

"In the wrong direction."

"Bitch, bitch, bitch." She paused, her head coming up like a dog catching a scent. "Sergei?"

A strangled scream answered her, and they whirled: bodies, exhausted or not, tensing for a fight. A figure staggered toward them, its skin crackling with fire like St. Vitus' dance, blue and green sparks popping and dancing along his skin. He jittered like a marionette, jinking first to the left, then right, forward and back, moaning and tearing at himself all the while.

"Oh God . . ." Wren went to her knees, her already depleted body unable to withstand the barrage of current coming off the man in front of her. "Oh God, Sergei . . ."

The burning figure lurched forward again, and Sergei reacted instinctively. A sudden loud *crack* cut across the buzzing of the current in Wren's ears. The figure jerked backward, his eyes meeting Sergei's with an expression of relief, gratitude, in an instant before he pitched forward and fell to the ground.

The lights disappeared, and Wren heard a faint *whoosh,* as though all the current were suddenly sucked back inside his skin.

Sergei went to the body before she could warn him not to, flipping it onto its back. Long fingers tipped the man's head back, and then Sergei nodded once, grimly, and released him, getting back to his feet and putting the pistol away.

Wren looked at what her partner had been looking at: a pale blue tattoo under the dead man's chin. "A Mage."

"That the same thing that killed the other stiff?"

Wren touched the rapidly cooling skin just to make sure, but it was a meaningless gesture. "Yeah," she said with certainty.

"Right. We're out of here." He put one large palm between her shoulder blades and steered her toward the sounds of traffic and cabs. Neither of them looked back.

Wren was still nursing her first cup of coffee when Sergei arrived at their usual meeting place the next morning, sliding into the booth across the table from her. The waitress brought over a carafe of hot water, tea bags, and a mug without being asked, and Wren watched him as he went through the ritual of testing the water, then stirring in the right amount of milk. She couldn't stand the stuff herself, but she liked watching him make it.

Finally, he took a sip, then looked at her.

"His name was Raymond Pietro," she told him. "Twelve years with the Council. Specialized in research, which is their way of saying he was an interrogator. Truth-scrying, that sort of thing. Only the past tense isn't just because he's dead. Rumor has it he went over the edge last month."

"Over the edge" was a gentler way of saying he had wizzed. That the chaotic surges of current had warped his brain so much that he couldn't hold on to reality any longer. But that didn't explain his death. Wizzing made you crazy, dangerous, but your ability to handle current actually got better the more you gave yourself over to it. That was why wizzarts were dangerous. That, and the raving psycho loony part.

"They dumped him?" It might have seemed like a logical explanation to Sergei, but Wren shook her head.

"Council takes care of its own. They have a house; really well warded, totally low-tech, so he wouldn't be distracted by electricity. He disappeared from the house two days ago. Council was freaking—the guy I talked to actually thanked me for bringing news, even though it was bad.

"They also said Pietro wasn't the first of their wizzarts to go missing. They never found the others."

Her partner's face, not exactly readable at the best of times, shut down even more. She finished her coffee, putting the mug down firmly on the table in front of her. "One might have been an accident, or a particularly crude suicide, but not half a dozen. Someone's killing wizzarts, Serg. Pietro, our stiff, the others. Who knows how many others? Council thinks—and I think they're right—we've got somebody fine-tuning a weapon. Goes right through the nulls, but fries Talent."

"And they're testing it on the wizzed population?"

"Nothing else makes sense. Nobody cares about the ones who've wizzed. You can't, not really. They're as good as not there anymore. So they're easy victims."

She was rather proud of how steady her voice was until she made the mistake of meeting her partner's eyes. The quiet sympathy she saw there destroyed any idea she might have had of remaining calm.

*Oh, Neezer . . .*

John Ebenezer. Two short years her mentor. Five years now since he started to wiz. Since he walked out of her life rather than risk endangering her.

*Are you out there, Neezer? Are you still alive?*

"And if he—she, that—are?" His voice matched his face: stone. "From everything you've told me, what I've seen, wizzarts are wild cards, dangerous, to themselves and others. And quality of life isn't exactly an issue."

Wren bit back on her immediate reply. He wasn't trying to goad her; it was, to his mind, a valid question. And she had to give him the respect of an equally valid answer. "Because that could be me someday. Council might poke around, but they don't care about lonejackers. If they discover anything, they might not even do anything so long as they can cut a deal to protect their own." She hated asking him for anything, but they had to take this job. She would do it alone—but their partnership had been founded on the knowledge that their skills complemented each other; she didn't want to handicap herself by working solo if she didn't have to.

A long moment passed. Finally, Sergei sighed. "It's not as though the Council will ever admit they owe us anything, least of all payment," he groused, signaling to the waitress for a refill of Wren's coffee. "First things first—is there any way to keep track of wizzarts in the area?"

"Already ahead of you," she said, her hodgepodge memory turning up what they needed. "It's not pretty, but once I have them in sight, I can tag them; monitor their internal current pool. If anything—anyone—tries to mess with them, I'll know."

Sergei looked like he had a bad taste in his mouth. "How much risk is there to you in this?"

"Negligible," she said, lying through her teeth.

Sergei tapped a finger on the space bar, studying the screen in front of him, skimming the list of John Does brought into the local hospitals for unexplained expirations. Of the seven names, two had cause of death listed as lightning strikes. One more had internal damage consistent with lightning, but the cause of death was liver failure—apparently, he had been a long-term alcoholic.

None of the men matched the description of John Ebenezer. His lips thinned as he entered another search, widening the area to include Connecticut and New Jersey. Assuming Neezer stuck around. Sergei wouldn't put any of his money on that.

Behind him, Wren made a sound of disgust, changing the channel of the motel room's TV without using the remote. They had spent two days driving through the area, walking into homeless shelters and into run-down apartment buildings until she could See the wizzarts scattered there, siphoning the faintest trace off their auras until she could weave a leash from them to her. She had found seven, but had only managed to create three leashes before collapsing from exhaustion. Just the memory of her shaking, sweating body made him angry all over again.

"Drink more of the juice," he told her, not looking over his shoulder to make sure she obeyed him.

The screen displayed a refreshed list of names. Nothing.

"Serg?"

He was at her side before he consciously realized he'd heard her voice. The juice lay splattered on the carpet, the glass rolling off to one side, unbroken. He determined that there was no physical danger and cupped her face in his hands, all in the space of heartbeats.

"I'm here, lapushka," he told her. The pulse at her neck was thready, and her eyes were glazed, pain lines forming around them. He waited, cursing whatever idiotic impulse had ever led him to agree to this, as she struggled to maintain the connection.

"Got him!"

They had lost the first one that morning, the leash snapping before Wren could do more than be aware of the attack. She had cried then, silent tears that left her eyes red-rimmed and her nose runny. She had never been able to cry gracefully. His fingers tightened on her chin. "Easy, Wren. Hold him. Hold him . . ."

It was dangerous touching her. The overrush of current could easily jump to him, and he'd have no protection, no way to ground himself. But he wouldn't abandon her to do it alone.

Sweat was rising from her skin now, dampening her hair against her face and neck. But she felt cool, almost clammy, tiny flicks of electricity coursing off the dampness, sparking in the air.

"Ah—yes, that's it, come on, lean on me . . . lean on me, dammit!"

She was chanting instructions to the wizzart, trying to reach into his current-crazed mind. Trust wasn't high on a wizzart's list, though, especially for voices they heard inside their own heads.

A bolt rumbled through her, almost knocking them to the side. Sergei planted himself more firmly, his grip keeping her upright. She'd have bruises on her face when they were done. He'd have them, too, on the inside: lightning burns, internal scarring. Pain ached through his nerve endings. This was insane. For some literal burnouts they'd never have anything to do with . . .

For John Ebenezer, he reminded himself. For Genevieve.

The air got heavy, and he could almost smell the singeing of hair and flesh, of carpet fibers cracking underneath his knees, the fusing of the wiring in the walls, the phone, his computer. A lightbulb popped, but all he could focus on was her labored breathing, the voice crooning encouragement to someone miles away.

Her eyes, which had been squinted half-shut, opened wide, and she stared into his eyes endlessly. He felt as though he were falling, tumbling straight into an electric maw with nothing to stop his fall. He *was* her, was him, was the current flowing between them. He Saw through her eyes the wizzart let go, felt the current being pounded into him, flowing into her, and being grounded. He understood, finally, for that endless second the elegant simplicity of grounding, and reveled in the surge of power filling the matter of his existence.

The wizzart slumped, fell unconscious in a puddle of his own urine. *Get him,* Sergei urged into her open mind. *Find whoever did this.*

He felt her stretch back into the wizzart's self, backtracking the current that had been pumped into him, striking out like the lightning it rode in. A shudder of anger, hatred, disgust slamming into hard walls, confusion, and time stretched and snapped back, knocking him clear across the room and headfirst into the wall.

When he came to, the room was dark. He didn't bother to turn on the lights—they'd blown, each and every one of them. Crawling forward, he reached out, finding the top of Wren's head. She was curled into a ball, silently shaking.

"I screwed up," she said. "I couldn't get them. It was too far away. I couldn't reach the bastards . . ."

He sat there, in the dark, and rocked his partner back and forth while she cried.

"It was a good control group," Sergei said around a mouthful of toast. "Small enough population to monitor, and nobody to care if a few bodies went missing." He shook his head, less astonished at the ways of mankind than impressed at the planning it had taken. Planning and resources and a certain bloody-mindedness.

"You're a bastard, Sergei." He had dragged her out to have breakfast, but she wasn't eating. Scrambled eggs congealed on the plate in front of her. Sunglasses perched on the edge of her nose even though the diner itself was shaded and cool.

He put his fork down. "What do you want me to say? It's over, Wren. We got too close . . . we scared them, at least. That will make them pull back, be cautious."

"So they'll just move shop to another town? Sergei, I can't—" She stopped. "I couldn't do anything last night. I didn't have enough juice, wasn't good enough. We can't stop them. We don't even know who 'they' are."

He ran a hand through his hair, wincing a little as he touched the bandage on his forehead. "We know the how, what they're doing, the kind of people they're looking for. A few well-placed words and people will be looking and paying attention. They'll be able to protect each other."

"It's not enough." He could see the tears building again and watched her force them away.

"It's all we can do." He didn't have anything more to offer her. Sometimes all you could do was make sure your own neighborhood was clean. Sometimes that just had to be enough.

Wren didn't look convinced. But she picked up her fork, shoveled a mouthful, and chewed, swallowed.

For him, that was enough.

# PART III

# Murder Most Genteel

# Captured in Silver

## Teresa Edgerton

Teresa Edgerton is the author of nine novels and a handful of short stories. As her connection with the twentieth and twenty-first centuries—not to mention reality in general—is somewhat tenuous, she had no other choice but to become a writer of fantastic fiction. She loves books, gardens, and old, old houses.

Her most recent novel is *The Queen's Necklace,* a big, strange, fantasy swashbuckler that ranges across years and continents with reckless glee. This story is set in an obscure corner of that universe.

The lady stood with her hands clasped tightly before her: nails scoring the delicate flesh, knuckles as white as her muslin gown. Under a close bonnet with a silky ostrich feather, she looked ill, haggard. Though the face itself was beautiful, the bone structure flawless, there were purple shadows under her eyes, and her skin had the color and transparency of old wax. "There is a man who has wronged me and my family," she said. "I desire his death."

The old man looked up at her from under sparse white eyebrows. He wore his hair unfashionably long, powdered and clubbed behind, and there was a jagged scar on one lean cheek. According to the sign outside his shop, he was an apothecary; he had, however, a reckless, buccaneer air about him, quite out of keeping with that respectable profession.

So much the better, thought the lady. She had no use for an honest man. Growing impatient at his prolonged silence, she spoke again. "I desire nothing on this earth so much as his death."

"You have come to me for poison," said the apothecary, making himself busy with something behind the high counter.

"No, nothing so simple as that. He's been poisoned before. There are those who believe he's made a pact with dark, occult forces; there have been many attempts on his life, yet he goes on living.

"And do not," she added with a convulsive movement, "suggest that I seek out some bully swordsman, any ordinary assassin. Attempts have been made, I tell you. He has men to guard him now, and he trusts no one."

There was another long silence but for a log collapsing on the hearth with a snap and a crackling shower of sparks.

"You say he has wronged you," the old man answered at last. "Perhaps you have some recourse within the law? The courts—"

"The courts are a travesty, the judges senile and deranged. Surely you know that as well as I. There is no justice in Tourvallon—there has not been any these ten years."

"And so you turn to sorcery?" said the apothecary. His appearance was shabby—his nails dirty and ragged, the elbows of his coat inexpertly patched—yet a gold ring with an immense rough-cut indigo stone adorned one hand. He smelled of camphor and of ambergris, of dust and chemicals, mildew and tallow.

"Yes. Someone—someone gave me your name. They told me you could kill anyone—anywhere—anytime."

"That is not precisely true. Yet it is possible that I can be of assistance to you. The price, however, is very high. You understand that I don't speak of payment in banknotes or gold."

He made a broad gesture, indicating his small, dark, crowded shop. Some of the stoneware jars on the shelves were cracked; a once handsome tiled floor was scuffed and muddy; yet there was a glimmer of cobalt-blue glass in the shadows, and the fire burned with unnatural intensity. Like the man himself, the room was dingy, but somehow suggestive of wilder, grander things. "If it was material wealth I desired, I'd hardly spend my days in these surroundings."

"Name your price," she answered with a desperate abandon. "So that the man dies, I scarcely care what becomes of me afterwards."

*     *     *

By some engineering feat of the Goblins who built the city—long ages before the race of Men rose to knowledge and power—the river divided into two perfect channels just north of the town and encircled Tourvallon like a shining ribbon—a ribbon that sometimes drew as tight as a noose, when the bridges were raised and the Duke sent his mounted troops out into the streets to root out dissent. Yet dissent still flourished: lampoons and scurrilous ballads, printed on cheap yellow paper in smeary ink, appeared on crumbling brick walls and rusty iron lampposts; earnest young men, in attics and garrets, turned out a flood of revolutionary pamphlets.

"Give us justice," cried the people, "give us life"; but there was no justice, and life was reduced to a hopeless struggle. The Duke had surrounded himself with a corrupt government and a sinful, luxurious court. Even more than the surrounding countryside, the city suffered. Children might starve, gutters run foul, and disease reduce the population in the poorer parts of the town by almost half, but public monies continued to flow into private coffers.

Greediest of the greedy, most insatiable of the insatiable, was the First Minister, Prosper de Rouille. When word of his death ran through the city, there was widespread rejoicing. He had gained enemies even among the nobility, for he had robbed and oppressed the rich as readily as the poor.

In one house, however, the news was received with mixed feelings. Gabriel-Louis-Constant Jaucourt, the Lord High Constable, was entertaining his friend Simon Montjoye, with a late-night supper of oysters and crayfish, when his servant came in with a letter on a tray.

The letter was brief, but Jaucourt read it twice. "You were wondering, on Monday," he said to his guest, "why de Rouille was absent from the autumn fete? Out of favor, you asked me then, or out of the city? I couldn't answer you at the time, but I can now. He is out of this world entirely."

"Murdered at last?" asked Montjoye. He raised his goblet of opalescent glass and took a dainty sip of the lemon-scented wine. But under the Constable's steady regard, he felt suddenly ashamed of his jest. "I beg your pardon. That was in execrable taste." Montjoye fumbled with the jeweled eyeglass he wore on a chain around his neck. "If de Rouille *had* been assassinated, it would be up to you to do something about it."

"He has been assassinated," Jaucourt replied, "though what I can do remains to be seen. The circumstances, it seems, are extraordinary." Folding the letter in half, he rose from the table and stood with one strong, square hand on the curved back of his chair, looking down at his guest.

They made an odd pair, the tall, grave Constable and his little frivolous, dandified friend, but Montjoye was at least honest and Jaucourt valued him. "If you wish to know more, you're welcome to accompany me to Château Lezardž."

The gaudy third-floor bedchamber was stifling, with the rotten hothouse odor of decaying flesh. Feeling a little faint, Montjoye took out a perfumed handkerchief and held it to his nose, but the Constable and his deputy, Lieutenant Buffon, were men of a sterner fiber and did not even flinch.

The body was lying between sheets of honey-colored satin, on a bed with four silver posts. There was a long, deadly spike of polished dark ivory piercing his chest and a stain of dried blood on his silken nightshirt.

"Impaled by the horn of the unicorn!" said Montjoye in a slightly muffled voice. "Who would have imagined it?" He indicated, with one unsteady hand, the delicate spiral of the murder weapon.

"No, sir. By the carved horn of a black monoceros," answered the practical Buffon. "The victim, it seems, collected curiosities." There was an open cabinet made of rare woods at one end of the room, and a gleam of silver and crystal within. "The servants, at any rate, claim to recognize it."

"I am afraid that poor Montjoye is waxing poetic," Jaucourt explained. "Or do I mean ironic? No one believes in unicorns anymore— or in virgins, for that matter."

Glancing over the room with an expert eye, he became all business. "Your letter was somewhat obscure. Tell me everything you've learned."

Buffon nodded. Leading the others across the room, where the air was somewhat better, he began his account.

"According to the servants, the First Minister entered this room three nights ago, locking and bolting the door behind him. All this was according to his custom—de Rouille lived in perpetual fear of assassination and he never slept but in a sealed room. There were two hired mercenary guards outside in the corridor—he employed six men, who took their duty in shifts—but they were never permitted to enter the bedchamber. Likewise, though he occasionally entertained female visitors, he never allowed any of them to stay through the night—having a fear, it would seem, of being murdered in his bed."

"Not without reason, as it appears," said Jaucourt. "But do you tell me that no one was surprised when he failed to leave his room the following morning?"

"He had restless nights; to make up for that, he often slept late. The servants had standing orders not to disturb him; not one of them dared to disobey. By evening, of course, his household steward began to fret—but still he was reluctant to act. It was as much as his position was worth, he told me later. And worse: those who knew de Rouille's habits, the routines of his household, had a habit of disappearing or meeting with accidents after he dismissed them."

Jaucourt and Montjoye exchanged a disgusted glance. "Obsessive," said Jaucourt, "and more unsavory, even, than I suspected. Yet what did it gain him?"

"Because of all this," Buffon went on, "no one sent for me until early this evening, at which time de Rouille had been in his bedchamber for seventy-two hours. I determined it would be best to knock down the door. That done, we found the body just as you see it now. There were no signs of a struggle, no way that I could see for an intruder to enter the room except through the door, which was of sturdy oak and a formidable barrier. We had the devil of a time knocking it down."

Jaucourt began to pace. He was searching the room with more than his eyes, listening with more than his ears. A student of magic—whose time at the university had passed, if not with honors, at least with distinction—he also possessed some slight ability to receive impressions from inanimate objects.

But the bedchamber, the furniture, the dead man's possessions, they were all mute. Unnaturally mute, it seemed to Jaucourt.

Very well, then, the Constable concluded, Prosper de Rouille had been murdered in his sleep—which explained, at least, the lack of psychic dissonance caused by his passing. But how had the *assassin* managed to leave no impression?

There was no answer for that, so far as he knew, so Jaucourt turned once more to his ordinary senses and to more practical questions.

The only windows were small and narrow, set high in one wall. They were not made to open, and the pale amber glass remained intact. Even had it been otherwise, there was not much chance that the smallest assassin—a child or a Goblin—could squeeze through so tiny a space.

Jaucourt said as much to Buffon.

"As you say, sir," the Lieutenant agreed. "I don't much fancy the windows as a means of entrance or egress myself."

"And the walls are of solid stone—no wooden panels, no secret doors." Just to make certain, Jaucourt had some of the furniture shifted. The walls behind were blank, solid, impenetrable. When the body was removed, the bed pushed aside, and the expensive figured carpet rolled up, the floor proved equally innocent of trapdoors.

The Constable knelt down and carefully studied the polished wooden planks, as though he could scarcely believe their silent testimony. "A very pretty puzzle." He rose heavily to his feet, dusted off his knees, adjusted the modest lace ruffles at his wrists, then turned to Buffon. "*When* do you suppose the murder took place?"

"By the evidence of the lights: within hours of retiring." The deputy indicated a pair of ornate candelabra in heavy silver, on a stand by the bed. "He distrusted the dark and always burned candles throughout the night. As you may see, only one branch was lit and allowed to burn down. The candles were never replaced."

Once more, Jaucourt began to pace. "And the guards outside heard nothing—on that night or at any time after?"

Buffon shook his head.

"And though there were women who . . . visited . . . from time to time, there was no one admitted the night in question?"

"According to the guards, there was a lady four or five nights ago who stayed very late. I say a *lady*," Buffon was careful to explain, "because she came in and went out still heavily veiled."

At this, there was an explosion of laughter from Montjoye. "Much good that would have done her if de Rouille still lived! He liked to boast."

Jaucourt ignored him. "I suppose, Lieutenant, that we can trust the word of the mercenary guards? At least provisionally?"

"Their employer distrusted them—as a matter of policy—but I see no reason why we should also. Three of the six are former city guardsmen who served with honor under the late Duke.

"Besides," Buffon added with an expressive shrug, "if there *was* a visitor, male or female, how do we explain the locked and bolted door?"

"We don't," said Jaucourt with a grim smile. "But I hope we may do so eventually."

Ordering the door repaired and locked, he prepared to leave. "When you are finished, send me the key at my lodgings."

Outside, in the cool, clean air, Jaucourt and Montjoye hired a passing fiacre to take them home.

The hour was late—or early—and the streets were otherwise deserted; the lamps on every corner were growing dim.

"A hired assassin of no little resource." Montjoye spoke in the darkness of the carriage. "You'll have a pretty time assigning the blame. There's half the court had a grudge against de Rouille." There was a jolt and a bump as the wheels passed over a stretch of rough pavement. "He all but ruined poor Champavoine. Belrivage, Mont Azur, Moncriff—they all hated him. Laurent, Chamfort—have I forgotten anyone?"

"You are forgetting the ladies," said Jaucourt. "Madame de Ambreville—her father is dead, her brother an exile, thanks to de Rouille. Madame de Fontenay—there is some history there, though I don't know the details. Madame Deffant—he published her letters out of idle malice."

The carriage turned a sharp corner, and light from one of the lamps briefly illuminated the interior. "A woman scorned—or violated," said Montjoye. "I rather lean toward that notion myself, considering the circumstances."

"The horn of the black monoceros, *not* the unicorn," Jaucourt reminded him. He opened a window and a draft of damp air invaded the carriage; they were approaching the river. "But how was it accomplished? How did the assassin enter? How did he leave?"

Montjoye laughed. "But my dear Gabriel, surely that part is perfectly obvious. The assassin came into the room *before* de Rouille, wearing a cloak of invisibility. Such cloaks are rare these days, it's true—but still to be found, if you know where to ask, in the Goblin Quarter. Concealed in his cloak, the murderer waited, and struck when his victim fell asleep. After that, he had nothing to do but to wait for Buffon and his men to break down the door—and steal away in the confusion afterward."

Jaucourt, however, was unconvinced. "Your conclusion is logical enough. But it flies in the face of Human—or Goblin—nature. Do you really believe that the murderer would elect to remain in that room for seventy-two hours *with the body of his victim* when he could have left by the door that first night and successfully evaded the guards?"

"It was caution. He could not be *certain* of evading the guards, invisible or not."

There was a clatter of iron wheels on cobblestones as some swifter conveyance raced by.

"Inhuman caution," rejoined the Constable. "Inhuman determination—as the hours went on and the body began to decompose. Not to mention most uncommonly careless: to provide himself with the cloak but no weapon and rely instead on whatever came to hand. Improbable, Simon!"

Montjoye sniffed in the darkness, not best pleased at hearing his theory demolished. "But what other explanation can there possibly be?"

"I begin to believe," said Jaucourt, "that the assassin did not leave the room because he *could* not—in which case, he may be there still."

The little man protested with an incredulous laugh. "No, really. The way we were all swarming around that room, how could anyone remain undetected—no matter how invisible—without someone tripping over him sooner or later?"

"But let us suppose," said Jaucourt, "he were not invisible, merely, but incorporeal."

"I would never suppose anything of the sort," replied the irritated Montjoye. "You suggest the impossible."

"Perhaps." The carriage came to a halt, and the Constable obligingly opened the door. "But in examining such problems as this one, when you have eliminated the improbable, whatever remains, *no matter how impossible,* must be the truth. Any magician would tell you that."

Montjoye hesitated before stepping down. "And how do you propose to prove this incredible theory?"

Jaucourt looked out. A pale streak of light was growing on the eastern horizon. Somewhere across the river, a clock tower chimed the hour of four. "Tonight, at Château Lezardž. You are welcome to meet me there if you choose. Let us say—at a quarter past eleven."

Shortly after eleven, the two friends met in the dead man's bedchamber. While Montjoye watched, Jaucourt drew up two high-backed mahogany chairs to the hearth, where a small, hot fire was already burning.

"What is the meaning of this?"

"Only that we may have some little time to wait," said Jaucourt, throwing incense on the fire. Though the corpse had been removed so many hours earlier, there was still an unpleasant suggestion of *something* in the room.

Taking one of the seats, he gestured to his friend to do likewise. "You are here to help me observe what occurs, and I would ask you to be particularly alert around the hour of midnight."

The next three-quarters of an hour dragged by, as the two men made halfhearted attempts at conversation. As the time passed, Montjoye experienced an increasing sense of oppression; he wondered what had possessed him to accept Jaucourt's invitation. When a longcase clock in the corridor outside began to strike, both men fell silent.

As the last chime continued to reverberate, Jaucourt reached out to touch his friend on the sleeve. Across the room, over by the cabinet of curiosities, something intangible stirred in the air; then, slowly, slowly, a misty form began to take shape.

The form lengthened, broadened, became the semitransparent figure of a powerfully built man. He was clad in a filmy shadow of elaborate court dress: long-tailed coat, knee breeches, and silver buckles.

At Montjoye's exclamation of surprise and dismay, the head of the specter turned his way. For the length of a heartbeat the living and the dead gazed deep into each other's eyes. Then the translucent shape began to fray and dissolve into mist.

Jaucourt sprang to his feet, but the phantom went out like a blown candle before he could reach it.

Montjoye gave a shaky laugh. "Is that what you were expecting? But, my dear Gabriel, you can't arrest a ghost, you can't charge him with murder—he is quite beyond your ken."

"It is not *exactly* what I was expecting, no," said Jaucourt with a troubled glance. "I was expecting a ghost, certainly—but this particular ghost? How could I?"

At Montjoye's look of blank incomprehension, he went on. "You did not, perhaps, recognize our recent visitor. It was Damien Alincourt, the late Duke's chamberlain, who died five years ago."

The Constable resumed his seat by the fire. "I was expecting, you see, the restless spirit of someone who suffered a violent death in this very house, this very room. That would explain why he was bound to this particular spot and could not escape. But why a man who died in his own home—on the other side of the city, of natural causes—should be haunting this bedchamber, that I can't comprehend. Unless—" He furrowed his brow, sat several moments in concentrated thought.

Suddenly, Jaucourt jumped to his feet again. "Unless there is some devilry at work that I never suspected!" Crossing to the curio cabinet, he flung open the doors and began rummaging through the clutter of exotic and dubious objects on the shelves.

"A necklace of crystals—no! The knucklebone of a giant—hardly! A thunderstone, a miniature portrait, a tiny sandstone idol—no, no, no! Ah!" With an exclamation of surprise and disgust, he turned back toward Montjoye. "Tell me, Simon, what you think of this."

Approaching the cabinet with a doubtful step, Montjoye saw that his friend was holding out a slender silver object, a flask or a phial, sealed with a great knob of crimson wax and decorated with magical symbols: the figure of a sphinx, an eye wreathed in fire, a five-pointed star.

"I have no idea what to make of it, but by the expression on your face, I would imagine that you do."

There was a flame of fury in Jaucourt's eyes, which Montjoye had never seen there before, yet when he spoke, his voice was soft and controlled.

"It is, in common parlance, a soul trap—a device for capturing a spirit as it departs the body. Once the ghost is captured, it becomes totally enslaved to the magician's will. Whatever its master requires, the spirit must do, no matter how immoral, how degrading the task. You thought such things were only a myth? The magicians who trained me at the university thought otherwise, though it has always been assumed that the spell was lost."

"Yet now rediscovered," said Montjoye in an awed voice. "By de Rouille? Surely not. I have heard him accused of any number of vile things, but never of sorcery."

"Rediscovered by one of his countless enemies," said Jaucourt. "Or at least—at least the spell *somehow* fell into the hands of someone with a grudge, who did not scruple to use it."

Placing the phial back on the shelf, Jaucourt covered his face, pressing the heels of his hands to his eyes. "Do you know, until this moment, it seemed to me that it did not matter very much whether the guilty party was punished or not. Oh yes, as a matter of professional pride—or of personal honor, whatever that means in this day and age—I thought it necessary to make the effort, though it's difficult to feel any genuine outrage because de Rouille was murdered."

He dropped his hands. "But *this*. Whoever was capable of this monstrous thing—that even the dead should suffer, in Tourvallon, that even they should be violated and degraded! For once, I'm determined to see justice done."

"And how will you do that?" asked the increasingly bewildered Montjoye.

A shudder passed over Jaucourt's sturdy frame. "By the use of spells little better than those of the magician I seek to discover. By summoning and binding. May I be forgiven for what I do, in a just cause."

Pulling a fine linen handkerchief from his coat pocket, he took up the soul trap again. "But I've not the means for drawing the pentacle here. I must go home and assemble the necessary materials."

Moving swiftly toward the door, he paused on the threshold, glanced back at his friend. "No blame to you, Simon, if you'd rather not accompany me. Indeed, I would not ask it."

Montjoye drew a deep breath, seemed to gather resolution. "Yet I *will* go with you, if you don't mind. Having come this far, I believe I should like to see the thing through to the end."

Two days later, in her sumptuous mansion beside the river, the beautiful Albine de Ambreville was reclining on a sofa draped with leopard skins when a servant came in to announce visitors.

The Countess declined to rise when Jaucourt and his friend entered the room, though she did extend a pale, somewhat damp and trembling hand to the Lord Constable.

He sketched only the briefest of bows, and Montjoye hung back by the door, looking haggard, haunted, and sleep-deprived. They had spent the last forty-eight hours experimenting with unclean magics, and the taint was still on them.

"I take it," said Albine to the Constable, "this is not a social call?" The hand he had so pointedly ignored was withdrawn. It fell into her lap, where it lay like a broken piece of shell, against the sand-colored satin of her gown.

"Madame, it is not," Jaucourt answered sternly. "I have come to arrest you for the murder of Prosper de Rouille. Though there may be charges of fouler things as well, by and by."

She regarded him with heavy-lidded eyes. "But why, Jaucourt, should you suspect me? What brings you here?"

"Not what, but who: Damien Alincourt. I had some difficulty bending him to my will; the spell that was on him was amazingly powerful. Then, too, I began by asking the wrong questions. I wanted to know who it was that enslaved him, but that was a name he was unable to speak. When I finally thought to ask who carried the soul trap to Château Lezardž, he gave me your name readily enough."

"I see," said Albine with a lazy movement. "But why, after all, should I deny anything? I'm not ashamed of what I have done. That is," she admitted with a faint blush, "one need not apologize for crushing a snake like de Rouille, though the means I employed were far from clean. About that much I do feel some shame. But I had a father and a brother to revenge. And I mean to release Alincourt's spirit eventually—which is better than he could have expected from the man who sold him to me!"

She rose slowly to her feet, her hands extended before her, her almost impossibly slender wrists held together. "What, Lord Constable, no chains? No manacles? But this is a *most* genteel form of arrest!"

"Madame de Ambreville," said Jaucourt, "there will be chains and manacles enough, later on. In any case, I am not your gaoler. Out of respect for the Count, your husband, I thought we might accomplish this in a dignified fashion."

He felt, rather than saw or heard, Montjoye make an embarrassed movement by the door. "But before we go, perhaps you will answer one question for me: who *was* the black magician that sold you the soul trap?"

She tilted her head, regarding him obliquely. "If I give you his name, would it go easier with me later?"

Jaucourt shook his head in quick denial. "Unfortunately, I can make no such promise. Indeed, madame, I can promise you nothing."

The lady shrugged. "Nor would I have believed you, whatever you promised. Yet it appears I've wronged you: you are an honest man. Who would have supposed that any such—" She gasped and was unable to finish the sentence as a deadly weakness suddenly assailed her.

He caught her as she fell, and lowered her gently to the floor. Every vestige of color had drained from her face, and her breath came in short, ragged gasps.

Moving at last from the door, Montjoye hovered indecisively. Even to his inexperienced eye, it was plain that the Countess was in genuine distress.

"Madame de Ambreville," said Jaucourt with a terrible ferocity, "what have you done to yourself?"

Her lips moved silently, as though she would answer him but lacked the strength. She continued to struggle for several minutes. At last, she rallied a little and forced herself to speak. "Poison. When I heard—you were at—my door." She laughed weakly, and tears rolled down her cheeks. "Vanity, perhaps—to wish not to be exposed at a trial."

"You were about to tell me," said Jaucourt, "the name of the magician."

"Was I? Perhaps—I was." A spasm passed over her, and it seemed for a moment she had left it too late. Then, with a final effort, she gasped out the words: "The apothecary—Doctor Palestrina—at the sign of the phoenix."

Later that same afternoon, Jaucourt was in a carriage with Buffon and two muscular uniformed guardsmen, heading across the city. He had, with some difficulty, located the apothecary shop, on the fringes of the Goblin Quarter.

"We can only imagine," he said to Buffon, "the extent of his wickedness. A doctor—even a simple apothecary—is called in so often to ease the dying. And when he seems to be offering comfort—a word, a moment, a gesture—and the spell is wrought, he catches their souls and binds them to his will."

Buffon nodded without making any comment, and the carriage clattered on. Meanwhile, the Constable experienced a restless discomfort, a frustrated impatience; this trip across town was taking far too long.

When the carriage finally lurched to a stop, Jaucourt was out of the door on the instant, moving toward the modest little shop of brick and timber. "At the sign of the phoenix," he said under his breath. "Where the dead rise, not to new life, but to slavery and degradation."

A swift, comprehensive glance around him, and he knew that he had arrived too late. The windows were shuttered, but the door stood half-open and the interior was dark.

Pushing the door aside, Jaucourt moved past it, into the shadows. The hearth was cold; a lantern above the door unlit. On the high counter, a shattered oil lamp lay on its side amidst crystal shards of glass. The shelves had been cleared of bottles and jars—the shop was empty.

He stepped back into the street, grinding his teeth in sheer frustration. "There must have been someone watching outside of de Ambreville's house. Still, had we acted more quickly, we might have caught him."

Buffon shrugged. To him, the matter of the apothecary seemed of minor importance. A man firmly rooted in the mundane details of daily existence, his business was with the living, not with the dead. "But the lady has punished herself," he replied with stolid satisfaction. "We needn't do so. Moreover, we've been spared the uproar of a trial, the ugly excitement of an execution."

The wooden sign with its picture of the mythical bird creaked overhead; a vagrant breeze caused a stray bit of yellow paper to skitter past, over the paving stones.

"De Rouille is dead—and the beautiful Albine," Jaucourt said with a bitter laugh. "But a man more wicked than either of them has escaped."

He bent at the waist, scooped up the torn scrap of paper. The printed words were blurred by rain and sun, but he guessed that it was part of one of the revolutionists' pamphlets.

The Constable sighed and turned away from the shop. As usual, there would be no real justice in Tourvallon.

# A Night at the Opera

## Sharon Lee and Steve Miller

Sharon Lee and Steve Miller are best known for their Liaden Universe® novels and their several short stories featuring a bumbling wizard named Kinzel. Steve was the founding curator of the University of Maryland's Kuhn Library Science Fiction Research Collection; Sharon has been executive director of the Science Fiction and Fantasy Writers of America and has also served as president of that organization.

They live in Maine, with lots of books, almost as much music, more computer equipment than two people need, and four muses in the form of cats. As might be expected of full-time writers, Sharon and Steve spend way too much time playing on the Internet and have a Web site at *http://www.korval.com*.

he was old money. He was old magic.

Together, they were a force to be reckoned with on the social circuits of half a dozen capital cities. It was said that they might reverse a fashion, make a playwright, or declare an early end to a tedious season. They were patrons of the arts—scientific, magical, and creative—and stood on terms of intimacy with the scions of several royal houses.

Despite all that—or because of it—they were popular hosts: full of wit and fire, certain to have an opening-night box at the brilliant new play, after which they would preside over an animated table of friends in a little-known gem of an eatery. It was therefore not at all unusual, when the daring new opera *The Fall of Neab* opened at Chelsington Opera House, where her family had kept a box for several generations, that they should host a party.

Nicholas—Lord Charles to most; Nick or Nicky to some few inti-mates; and "Nicky dear" to one alone—had early discovered that the hidden tax on old money was the absolute necessity of sharing the more public extravagances with others—and as many of those others as possible. It mattered little that he found the tax neither convenient nor fair; if he and his lady wished to go on more or less as they pleased, then these small payments to society must be made.

Since he very much wished them to go on more or less as they pleased, the inconvenience of hosting a theater party now and then did very little, really, to blight his horizon.

He did grumble, of course—a gentleman did not like to disappoint his wife—on this occasion as he knotted his tie, glaring quite fearfully at his reflection, one eye on the wife under discussion, who was nicely *en déshabillé* and clearly visible in the glass.

"I don't see why we have to play host to the National Zoo at these affairs," he said, his long, clever fingers deftly manipulating the ivory silk. "It would be very enjoyable, I think, to once attend the opera tête-à-tête with my wife."

In the glass, Denora was sliding a confection of silver-shot mid-night blue up over her legs, her luscious thighs, her delicious belly . . .

"Now, Nicky, you know you like Carrington, and the last time we had Brian, I swear the two of you spent the whole evening in each other's pockets. I was very much the jealous wife that evening."

He concocted a fierce frown for the mirror. "And I suppose the at-tentions of Beyemuir to yourself are only what the husband of a beauty of the first water should resign himself to bear?"

She laughed, easing the cloth over the dizzying mounds of her breasts. "Certainly, it would be, were you the husband of a jewel. As it is, you must allow poor Beyemuir to demonstrate a gentleman's natural charity to a matron of limited charms." She wriggled one last time, em-phatically. The blue dress was a tight, clinging sheath from breast to hip, where it softened into a wide, inverted tulip shape, allowing Nora her length of stride while still displaying an alluring tendency to cling to her long limbs. In all, it was something of a marvel, this dress, and Nicky gave it full honors, gazing into the glass, his hands quiet amid the intricacies of his tie.

Nora turned her back to the mirror, showing the unsealed row of tiny silver buttons; and smiled at him over her shoulder. "Do me up, please, darling?"

"Certainly." He winked, the air heated briefly, and the silver buttons glittered, sealing from bottom to top. He was rewarded with another smile as she wriggled appreciatively and adjusted the fabric for maximum fashionable décolletage.

He turned away from the mirror and reached for his coat. She spun, the tulip petal skirt floating above her ankles, the silver threads flashing like meteors through a midnight sky.

"Do you like it?"

"I admire it without reservation," he told her. "As will every other gentleman in the house—and those not so gentlemanly, too."

She arched a sable eyebrow. "Oh, come now, Nicky! At the opera?"

"Rogues are found everywhere," he replied. "Recall where you found me."

"Too true! Who would have thought Balliol harbored such vice!"

He bowed and went to fetch their cloaks.

The party was complete, with the exception of one, which of course engaged Brian's attention.

"Our esteemed Dr. Hillier not here yet?" he asked, twinkling at Nicholas over the rim of his wineglass. "Home sulking, do you think?"

Nick raised an eyebrow. "Now, why sulking, I wonder?"

"Ah, you haven't seen the latest *Magician Internist*? Mine arrived today."

"I've let the subscription lapse," Nick said, flicking an imaginary fleck of dust from his sleeve. "All that learned discourse—too fatiguing, Brian! Not to mention all those rather graphic descriptions of disease and malformation." He shuddered, deliberately, and fortified himself with a sip of wine.

Brian laughed. "Trust me, you'll want to look this issue up and take a look at Wolheim's refutation of our dear Hillier's pet theory."

"Not the spellchucker again?"

"No, dear boy—you are out of touch! Hillier's got himself a new pet theory. Mind you, he hasn't given up on the spellchucker, but if you'll recall, that little bit of legerdemain required an organic host—and a very specific host at that. Now he's gone the next step and declared that it is possible to store—*store*—a spell! Rather like a battery, you see. Well, as you might expect, Wolheim was all over that. The usual thing: states that his own tests, following Hillier's method, did not produce the results described, prosed on about the philosophy of magic, the theory of conservation of energies—oh, and the obligatory insult. Rather a nasty one this time. Said he hoped Hillier is a better engineer than he is magic-worker, else the city is in for a rash of bridges falling down."

"Well, that was too bad of him," Nicky said. "But, really, Brian, there's no need to suppose Hillier to be sulking. He and Wolheim have been at each other's professional throat for years now. Nora swears that they each live for the opportunity to refute the other's newest favorite theory or method."

"Oh, it's worse than that!" Brian said earnestly. "Wolheim lost Hillier a perfectly good assistant a few years back. You and your lady were traveling at the time, I believe."

Nicky frowned. "You mean Sarah Ames? I remember hearing about that. A tragedy, of course. But I really don't see how Wolheim can be blamed for the lady's decision to end her own life."

"Wolheim had cost her a fellowship, as I heard it. Hillier was badly broken up for—well, here's the fellow now!" he cried, turning his head with a wide smile for the tardy guest. "Hillier, old thing! It's been an age."

"Or at least a week," the latecomer returned, removing his top hat. He nodded cordially at his host. "Nicholas."

"Benjamin. Denora was concerned."

"Then I'd best make my apologies at once," he said, and stepped energetically forward.

"Benjy!" Denora looked around Beyemuir's shoulder and held out her hands. "You are so terribly late! Look, the lights have gone down once already."

Hillier kissed both hands, with flair and a careful eye to a husband's pride, and stepped back, smiling. "My apologies, dear Lady Charles! That a mere inconvenience of traffic should cause you an instant's worry!"

"At least it was worry rewarded," Nora said, smiling brilliantly upon both Hillier and Beyemuir. "Elihu, do pour Benjy something while he tells me how his daughter goes on."

"Aletha goes on quite well," the doctor said promptly, with another smile for her sweet courtesy. "Her talent for the Arts Magical is growing. Her tutor is quite encouraged."

"I am gratified to hear it," Denora said warmly. "So she is responding well to the treatment?"

Hillier's face darkened as he glanced aside to take his glass from Beyemuir. "Thank you, Elihu." He sipped and looked back to Nora.

"The treatment is not panacea, and not even those who love her best believe that she will ever embrace a normal life. Indeed, her tutor speculates that her affliction adds potency to her talent. I find no corroboration in the literature, and one does not like to subject her to any further testing . . ."

"Certainly not!" Denora said warmly, and met her husband's eyes across the box. "Nicky dear, I think we should get everyone seated, don't you? I do believe the lights have gone down again . . ."

It was Nicholas and Denora's pleasant habit, on the mornings when they were both at home, to breakfast together in their private room, sharing buttered toast, coffee, and the *Times* between them.

Two days after the opera party, they sat cozily together in the window nook, she in her carmine silk robe, he in the kimono Lord Murasaki had given him for his assistance in repairing a certain irregularity in His Lordship's love life. The window was open in the nook, admitting an agreeable bustling from the street below. The late morning sun bathed the table and remains of breakfast in languorous yellow light.

Nora, her father's daughter to the fingertips, was immersed in the business section, one slim hand curled round her coffee cup. Nicky slouched in his chair, lazily perusing the world news. According to the *Times,* the world was going to pot—no surprises there.

He turned the page to city news, one hand groping toward the table in pursuit of his cup—and froze.

"I say," he began, and paused as he read it again.

"Nicky?" Nora's hand dropped lightly to his sleeve. "What is it?"

He lowered the paper to meet her deep brown eyes, and found his voice. "Wolheim's dead."

Her eyes widened. "Oh, no, darling! An accident, I suppose?"

Anyone who knew of the nature of Dr. Sir John Wolheim's experiments with the Force Magical would certainly suppose an accident. Nicholas glanced down at the paper. Yes, the damning phrase was there . . .

"Nicky?"

"Suspicious circumstances, it says here."

"Blast." Nora crumpled her paper onto her lap with a frown. "Dickon will be calling, won't he?"

Dickon—that would be Prince Richard—would most assuredly be calling, Nick thought sourly. The wonder was that he hadn't called already. He sighed, folded the paper, and dropped it on the table.

"I'd better dress," he said, pushing out of the chair. He smiled down into her eyes and playfully tapped a finger against her cheek. "Come, now, darling; it's not as if I'm being sent to Timbuktu."

"This time," she said darkly just as the phone rang.

It was midday when Nicholas arrived at the house of the late Dr. Sir John Wolheim. The police were there before him, of course, but Dickon's office had been kind enough to let them know to expect the prince's sorcerer.

Despite the news report, Nicky had more than half expected to confront the remains of a catastrophic release of magical energy. Wolheim's spells always carried a taint of brute force; a hint of rather too much power used. It was a flaw that would have earned him the most stringent censure of the dean at Balliol, Nick's alma mater. Wolheim had been an Oriel man, however, and after all these years remained primarily a student of the philosophy of magic, rather than a practitioner. Benjamin Hillier, who had as deft a touch with a spell as anyone of Nick's acquaintance, himself a graduate of Balliol, had read practical magic, with a second in engineering. So it was that Hillier kept a house in the city and was no more a danger to his neighbors than the heedless town traffic, while Wolheim held to a country estate, where his frequently explosive explorations endangered no one but himself and his peculiarly devoted house staff.

Nick was let into the house by one of Appleton's men and escorted to the laboratory at the back by another.

"Here you are, sir," his escort said as they reached a doorway filled by a stern and wide-shouldered policeman. The door leaned against the opposite wall.

"Had to take it off the hinges," the guard said. "Locked from the inside, it was. Housekeeper called us when he didn't answer the house phone." He stepped aside, giving Nick room to pass.

"Lieutenant!" he called into the room. "It's His Lordship."

Even here, in the belly of the beast, there was no overt damage. Nicky paused on the threshold to admire the neat ordinariness of the room. Tools were hung away; vessels lined up by kind and capacity; books shelved; poisons behind glass; the famous collection of windup toys tidily arranged on their special shelf, except for one—a chimp mounted on a tricycle—sitting quietly, its energy spent, in the center of the otherwise empty worktable.

From behind that spotless work surface arose the long and dour form of Inspector Appleton. "Your Lordship," he said. "Here it is, sir. We've left everything as it was found."

Nick did not number precognition among his talents, but there was something in Appleton's face that put him on his guard. Carefully, he walked forward, steeled for the worst.

It was well that he was, for the object lying on the floor bore no relationship to the dapper and impatient little man Nicky remembered meeting at various professional symposia across the years.

The corpus was hirsute and thick, where Wolheim had been bald and thin. Rags of what had once been a laboratory smock and corduroy trousers clung in ribbons to bestial arms and trunk. The head was misshapen, showing a curved growth of horn from the temple, sweeping back around an oddly elongated ear. The face . . . Nicky sank carefully down on his heels. The face was as hairy as the rest of the body, the features thickened into something apelike or worse.

Nicky looked up to Appleton. "You're certain this is Sir John?"

"Sergeant Beerman cast the True-See, sir. Housemaid identified the ghost."

Nicky nodded. Sylvia Beerman was a first-rate 'caster. Wasted in the police force, really. He rose and stood staring down at the thing on the floor.

"Beerman said you was to check her, sir. Said she didn't believe it herself."

"Well, then. We mustn't disappoint a lady, eh?" Sighing, Nicky slid his wand from its long pocket inside the lining of his jacket and held it poised, eyes half-closed, gathering energy. The tip of the wand glowed a ridiculous bright green, which had pained him in his youth when he first learned that the wand light's color reflected the magician's life force. He had been quite the aesthete in those days and would have given his soul for a wand-glow of icy blue or starry silver. Thank God Nora had come along and knocked that nonsense out of him.

He glanced at Appleton, who held the police department's camera obscura at the ready.

The glow from the wand tip was steady. Nick drew the pattern in bright green fire around the corpse, murmuring, "I will see with the eyes of truth."

The pattern flared, bathing the monstrous corpse in a brilliant wash of color. Superimposed on the bestial body, emblazoned in brilliant green, was the image of a thin and tidy little man in rumpled lab coat and at-home corduroys, his face hairless, his features contorted in agony.

"Got it!" Appleton said over the snap of the shutter closing. He fiddled with the camera a moment, then nodded and held up a glass slide. "Same as Beerman caught, sir. Hers was a little fainter. Shall I run this past the maid?"

"It can't hurt, I suppose. Please express my compliments to Sergeant Beerman. First-rate work, as always."

"Will do, sir."

The green image above the horrid body was fading. Nicky stood with the wand between his palms, watching the last of the spell dissolve. He glanced at Appleton.

"I'll need some room, Lieutenant."

"Of course, sir. I'll be right outside the door."

Nicky stood, his attention focused on the . . . thing . . . on the floor. His next order of business was to identify the magician responsible for the spell—or spells—that had beset Wolheim during his last hour of life. This was work of high order, less energy-intensive than the

True-Seeing, but more wearying for the magician. It was not Nicky's favorite spell, though it was certainly among the enchantments he worked most often.

It had become something of a challenge among mages of a certain level of skill (and mischief) to conceal—to attempt to conceal—one's magical signature. In some circles it was a parlor game. Among the criminal element it was far from a game, and there were those who were quite ingenious in their methods. But it all and always came down to cover-up, obfuscation, and misdirection. No one—no matter how skilled—could completely erase all trace of their own signature.

Sighing, Nicky had recourse once more to the wand, this time enclosing himself and the corpse within the same circle of glowing green fire. He spoke a Word and the flames leaped upward, meeting over his head, sealing out the world and any random magics still afloat in the late doctor's laboratory.

He closed his eyes, feeling the wand vibrating in his hand; the air, warmed by power, caressing his face. Invoking the trance was a matter of a measured breath, the deliberate forming of a Word in the blackness behind his eyelids.

As always, it was as if he passed through a door, leaving a shadowed room and stepping into full, glorious daylight. All about him, he perceived the cords of power, the lines of magic that knit the world of the spirit to that of the flesh. There was no deception in this place, nor was there mercy. Those who came seeking truth here had best be canny and skillful—and wise. If one could not be wise, caution might do.

Nicky, who had studied caution at the feet of a master, brought his attention to the sorry tangle of cord and discord before him. Even in the remoteness of the sorcerous viewpoint, he felt a thrill of astonishment as he counted the layers of spell wrapping that which had been John Wolheim. So numerous were they that the shine of each melded into the next, rendering the whole a blot of meaningless, shapeless power, obscene in this place of orderly peril.

So, then. The sorcerer girded his will, lifted his wand, and set about the tedious and dangerous task of separating the layers, one by one, subjecting each to the closest scrutiny before allowing it to evaporate back into the common reservoir of magic.

\*    \*    \*

Some hours later, baffled and sweat-soaked, his ears ringing with exhaustion, Nicky leaned against the worktable. He had scrutinized each of the eighty-five separate and distinct high-level attacks upon Wolheim's person, and yet discovered no smallest trace of the magician who had conceived and implemented those attacks. It was as if a textbook spell had suddenly become maliciously animate, repeating itself over and over. Or a machine . . .

He closed his eyes. Memory replayed Brian's voice, cheerful with gossip: "declared that it is possible to store—*store*—a spell!"

"Oh," Nicky murmured. "Blast."

He was known to Benjamin Hillier's butler, and so was shown to the upper parlor while that worthy went off to roust his master from his work. Restless and exhausted, Nicky stalked the bookshelves—novels, mostly, with Benjy's more interesting books reposing in the research library upstairs, next to the laboratory.

Sighing, he turned from the shelves—and caught himself up. Curled into the corner of a wide damask chair was a towheaded girl of about twelve years, her dress rucked up to expose thin knees. There was a book on her lap—the bestiary, he saw—but she was staring at him out of frowning blue eyes.

"Good afternoon, Aletha," Nicky said softly. "How are you today?"

The frown extended to her face, drawing the light brows together. "I'm reading," she stated. "Why are you here?"

"I'm here to see your father," he answered, and moved carefully to sit in the chair opposite hers. Quick motions frightened her, and loud voices. Music, she could not abide, nor birds, nor dogs. Despite this, she had a fascination with pictures and books on the subject of all kinds of animals, and would spend hours immersed in one page of her bestiary. Indeed, it was this characteristic of absorption in her own projects to the exclusion of any other stimulus that sat at the core of her affliction. Benjamin had the best and most learned doctors—psychological, magical, and spiritual—attend to her, and some progress was made in the direction of encouraging her to interact with other humans. It was rare to find her in so talkative and gracious a mood, however.

"Your father tells me that you are progressing in your magical studies," he said, choosing a topic of conversation that might be expected to engage her interest.

Aletha stared at him, blue eyes unblinking, then abruptly shut her book, slipped to her feet, and walked away. A moment later, he heard the door to the parlor slam.

"How very maladroit of me," Nicky murmured around a sigh. He allowed his head to fall back against the chair and closed his eyes, wishing that Benjy would come.

The chair was comfortable and he was very tired. And it really would *not* do to fall asleep before he had a chance to speak to Benjy. Grimly, he pried himself out of the chair and wandered back to the shelves.

He was browsing the novels when a gleam caught his eye, back among the dark books. Aletha liked to hide those things she had identified as precious, according to Benjy; and her taste appeared to run to the shiny.

At great peril to his sleeves, Nicky reached back and slid the object out, discovering nothing more precious than a silver cigarette case. He frowned down at it, noting Benjy's initials, and a slight shimmer across the surface, as if—

Behind him, the door opened. He turned, slipping the case into his pocket.

"Nicholas! A thousand apologies for keeping you cooling your heels!"

Nicky smiled. "It wasn't as long as that."

"Well, you're kind to say so," Benjy said, running a hand through his already disordered hair. "I suppose it's about Wolheim? The news report said the circumstances were suspicious, and I thought of you."

"Yes, it's precisely about Wolheim," Nicky said. "Listen, will you, and see what you make of this."

Quickly, he described the scene as he had found it: the grotesquely transformed body, the cocoon of spells, the lack of signature.

By the time the tale was told, Benjy was shaking his head. "I can't help you, I'm afraid. Wolheim didn't confide in me, if you're thinking that this is one of his own projects gone hideously wrong." He frowned. "Though I don't know how he might have achieved that effect. And there would have been a signature in that case—his own."

"Too true. I'm wondering, though, something along the lines of your stored spell system . . ."

Benjy blinked, then shook his head again. "No, old man, it's not like that. Even if Wolheim had managed to completely overload his vehicle, the spell would still have shown a signature—his." He moved his shoulders. "A stored spell is the same as any other—just held in abeyance for a bit. I'd show you just how it is, but my prototype's gone missing."

"I see." Nicky frowned, wishing he weren't so desperately weary. "Do you know of any enemies Wolheim may have had?"

"Besides myself, you mean? Only half of the practical magicians on the town—and half of the philosophers, too."

Despite his weariness, Nicky smiled. "Explosive on all fronts, the late doctor."

"That he was." Benjy shrugged. "Not very helpful, am I?"

"Not yet, but I expect you will be. I would appreciate a list of those people you know Wolheim had offended."

Benjy sighed. "Is tomorrow morning soon enough? You understand, it's a project which will consume some time."

"Thank you," Nicky said with a weary smile. "Tomorrow morning will be soon enough."

"Nicky?" Nora's voice wafted into his dressing room. "Whose cigarette case is this, darling?"

He shrugged into his jacket and walked out into the main room. Nora, adorably tousled in her carmine robe, was fiddling with the catch on the silver case.

"Oh, it's Benjy's," he said. "There was something odd about it and I wanted—"

Across the room, the case sprang open with a loud swell of music and an expanding yellow cloud of a thousand tiny butterflies.

Nora squeaked and dropped the case; Nicky leaped forward and caught it before it hit the rug. On a higher plane, the butterflies reached the sky-blue ceiling and melted into snowflakes, embracing the two of them in a brief indoor snowstorm. The snow dissipated, leaving behind a lingering sense of cinnamon—the magical signature of Benjamin Hillier.

"What in heaven's name!" Nora gasped, but Nicky was holding the silver case, his face perfectly blank. She sighed, rather unsteadily, and went over to the table to pour herself a cup of coffee. By the time she had added cream and brought the cup to her lips, Nicky had blinked back to everyday awareness.

"It works," he said in soft wonderment.

"What works, darling?"

"Benjy's spell-storing system," he said, staring down at the case as if he had never seen anything like it before in his life. "This will revolutionize the Arts Magical."

"Well, good," Nora said. "Benjy deserves some—"

A knock at the door of their suite interrupted her. Nicky slipped the expended cigarette case into his pocket as he crossed the room and opened the door, finding their butler bearing a tray with a single envelope on it.

"Special delivery, Your Lordship," he said.

"Thank you, Jensen," Nicky replied, and took the envelope, recognizing Benjamin Hillier's hand. *The list of possibles, then. Splendid.* "That will be all."

He closed the door, slipped his finger under the seal, and pulled out a single sheet of paper.

It was not a list, but a letter.

> *Dear Nicholas,*
>
> *By the time you receive this, matters will be in hand. I apologize for leading you a little dance yesterday afternoon. Yesterday afternoon, I had not fully understood the problem— or the solution.*
>
> *But, there, you wish to know who killed Wolheim.*
>
> *I performed that well-earned deed. I and my accomplice.*
>
> *Certainly, there was no one else who deserved to die as much as Wolheim—for Sarah alone he deserved a dozen excruciating deaths, and she was only one of many, though dear to me. Very dear to me.*
>
> *The reason you could find no signature is that there was none to find. The phenomenon we call a signature is nothing more or less than the spin given any particular spell by the*

*mind of the magician. Wolheim's concoctions, for instance, were notable for the stink of unexpended power. Your own efforts have a silken essence, marking them out as the constructs of an unusually subtle mind.*

*The spells that transformed and killed Wolheim bore no signature because there was no interaction between the magician and the spell.*

*Allow me to explain.*

*My accomplice, Aletha, is an exceptionally strong and talented magician, but she is intensely literal. She cannot alter what she is taught by as much as a breath. Therefore, I used the process that I have perfected to prepare a perfectly ridiculous mechanical monkey. I then placed Tanister's book on transformation magic, open to the page where the base spell is written, before Aletha. As she read those words, over and over and over, I guided her thought—aimed her, if you will, at the toy. Then I went to the opera, leaving her to it.*

*When I returned home, Aletha was asleep and the monkey was fairly shimmering with energy. I wrapped it up and put it with the other mail, which was in due time taken down to the post office.*

*I confess that I hadn't expected the matter to go forth so quickly. Wolheim must have wound the toy up the moment he received it. The spells would have been released when the mechanism was engaged. With what exceptional results we have seen. I had not expected it to work nearly so well as it did. Eighty-five transformations! I hope each was an agony.*

*So the thing was done. Wolheim was dead. The monkey, its energy expended, would scarcely invite the scrutiny of the prince's sorcerer. I thought that would be an end to it. Alas, I had reckoned without my accomplice.*

*Last night, after I saw you out, I went in search of her. It is our custom to dine together on those days when I'm not engaged, and to work through some of those exercises the doctors had prescribed. I found her in the kitchen, torturing one of the cats. She transformed the poor creature into a monstrosity as I watched—as she watched, smiling delightedly,*

*then laughing aloud when it gave up its life in a shriek of
anguish, horribly, horribly misshapen.*

*It was then that I realized what I had done—and what I
must do.*

*On another subject, before I bid you adieu, the seek spell I
employed to locate my prototype reveals that it has come to
you. Nothing could be more satisfactory. You will by now have
understood it—and what it will mean for our art. The papers
are on file with my solicitor. I would be honored if you would
take up the work and see it made available. The process is, if I
may be forgiven a certain amount of pride in the child of my
own intellect, revolutionary.*

*And now I do bid you adieu, old friend. Pray assure your
lady of my everlasting regard, and make her see, won't you,
that this was the only way.*

*When you hear the engines go out of Station 9, you will
know the thing is done.*

*With respect and affection, your humble servant,*

*Benjamin Hillier*

He let the letter fall from nerveless fingers, seeing it—seeing it all
too clearly.

"Nicky?" Nora touched his arm lightly. "You look as if you've seen
a ghost."

"Very nearly. I must—"

From the street below, a sudden shouting of sirens. Nicky jumped
to the window and threw it wide, staring down as Engine Company
No. 9's scarlet pump truck streaked away. He raised his eyes, staring
across the rooftops, to a plume of smoke, dark against the egg-blue sky,
and flames, licking up from the fire. He turned away from the window
and looked into Nora's dark brown eyes.

She held up the letter he had dropped and wordlessly opened her
arms.

# A Tremble in the Air

## James D. Macdonald

James D. Macdonald was born in White Plains, New York, in 1954, the son of a chemical engineer and an artist, and raised in nearby Bedford. His last significant formal education took place at Archbishop Stepinac High School in White Plains, though he passed through the University of Rochester, where he learned that a degree in medieval studies wouldn't fit him for anything. He went off to sea "to forget," though he's forgotten exactly what.

As Yog Sysop, Macdonald ran the Science Fiction and Fantasy RoundTable on GEnie for two years (1991–93) and now is managing sysop for SSF-Net, an Internet presence provider and discussion site for genre fiction. He is also an EMT-intermediate with the local ambulance squad. Macdonald and Debra Doyle now live—still with various children, cats, and computers—in a big nineteenth-century house in Colebrook, New Hampshire, where they write science fiction and fantasy for children, teenagers, and adults.

rs. Roger Collins stood in the visiting room of her home. "Mansion" would have been a better word. The sun shone in through a bay window flanked by French doors. Filmy drapes kept the sun from bleaching the delicate cloth on the circular table in the center of the room. Spiced air from the gardens gently wafted in.

Mrs. Collins was expecting her friend Mrs. Frederick Baxter. She had something she wanted to talk to Shirley about. Last night the strangest thing happened. Mary Collins had known for years that the house was haunted, because there was a window on the second floor that would not stay closed if it wasn't locked. But last night, in the misty dark of twilight, while entering the upstairs guest bedroom, she saw the translucent shape of a young lady, and the apparition looked at her and she felt—

"Mary, dear!"

It was Shirley, being shown in by Mr. Collins. Mr. Collins had retired at the end of the war, and he had been very helpful during his wife's recent illness.

Mary had the tea things ready, and the tea itself, a nice oolong with a great deal of milk and sugar, occupied their time along with the small talk of doings in the town. Mr. Collins removed himself to his study. He had always played the stock market, and played it well. The war had left him wealthy, still quite young, for munitions had been greatly in demand. The prosperity that the whole nation now experienced made his investments more valuable by the day, while the contacts that he had across the nation gave him insights that perhaps other men didn't have.

Now was the time for Mary to tell the story, for that delightful frisson, in the bright afternoon.

"I'm sure you'll think I'm being silly," Mary said, "but I felt such a feeling of sadness coming from that woman. It was like a palpable wave. I gasped and took a step backward. Then I switched on the light, and she was gone!"

"You're so brave," Shirley said. "I'm sure I would have screamed and run."

"I was too surprised," Mary said. "And it wasn't until the light was on that I realized it wasn't a real woman at all; she was gone. She would have had to come past me to leave the room, you know. I looked under the bed and in the closet, and in the bathroom, but she was gone completely. It was only then that I realized I'd been able to see through her."

"You could? What are you going to do now?"

Mary's eyes sparkled, and she sipped her tea. "I thought it would be such great fun to have a séance."

"Are you quite certain? I mean, if you felt this sadness . . . that can't be good."

"She wants help, the poor thing," Mary said. "This is an old house. And after all those years of opening the window, she's finally gotten to trust me enough to appear and ask for my help."

"What does Roger say about your plan?"

"Oh, I haven't told him. You know what a stick-in-the-mud he is."

\*       \*       \*

On a gray afternoon, while a desultory breeze ruffled the remaining leaves on the trees around his home, Orville Nesbit sat in the overstuffed chair in his library, holding the letter that the morning post had brought. Mr. Nesbit styled himself a psychic researcher. He was entitled to call himself a master of science, master of arts, and doctor of philosophy, though he seldom did. His degrees were quite legitimate, in psychology and related fields. He had never had to use them. Family money supported the house and the grounds it stood on. His personal needs were simple and his wants were few; but he was a gourmand and had a weakness for old books, and these habits required that he occasionally turn his hand to trade.

His library contained books that required a particular turn of mind to comprehend, as well as fluency in the archaic forms of several languages. Many were the sole surviving copies. Royal and ecclesiastical censors over the centuries had exhibited little tolerance about certain things, and such volumes were expensive.

The letter, on unlined white notepaper with a blue border—high rag content and a watermark—told of a Ouija board that had spelled out the letters M-U-R-D-E-R, and of a feeling of oppressive hatred experienced before the candles (burning low and blue) had mysteriously blown out. The letter ended with the familiar plea "Please come at once" and the heartening words "I will pay any fee."

The signature and the return address told Mr. Nesbit that the writer could, indeed, pay any fee. If he took the case, it would provide a welcome break from authenticating documents for the National Archives, in which dreary pursuit he had been engaged for the last several months.

Mr. Nesbit rose and exchanged his silk dressing gown for a tweed jacket and a chesterfield coat, and set off into town to make arrangements to travel to California for an unknown period. Leaving the raw autumn weather behind would be a plus.

The Collins car met Orville at the station and carried him some ways south, through the town and into rolling hills, where swooping drives led to estates well out of sight beyond gated walls. Nesbit had the top button of his shirt unbuttoned and his neck draped with a loose silk cravat. He hoped that it wasn't too informal. His three heavy leather suitcases contained mostly clothing, with just a smattering of specialized equipment. His most important equipment, a notebook and fountain pen, nestled in the inside pocket of his linen jacket. The suit would need cleaning promptly after the transcontinental railway journey.

His quarters, he found on arrival, were in the guesthouse beyond the swimming pool, with a spectacular view of the Pacific below the cliffs. The driver had helped him with his bags, then left him with the words "Dinner is at seven."

Orville walked through the guesthouse—bedroom, bathroom, parlor, kitchenette, and wraparound porch, single-storied under a Spanish tile roof. He hung up his clothing in the bedroom wardrobe, then sat at the table in the parlor, in a wide wicker chair. After spending a few minutes in restful silence, he pulled out his pocket watch, consulted it, then took out his journal and began to write. The gold-edged steel of his fountain pen glided over the unlined paper in a sharply slanted Italian hand.

> *Journal of Orville Nesbit—*
> *I see before me a house in what is called the California Gothic style. Portions are clearly from the nineteenth century, though there have been renovations and additions since. The site is a secluded one, and the residents have not yet made themselves known to me. I hope to meet them tonight at dinner. Tomorrow I intend to go into town, in order to research the house and its various occupants from the moment of its construction.*
> *There are three events to consider, based on what I know now. First, a window. Second, an apparition. Third, a spiritualistic message. The three merit their own approaches. A plumb bob and a spool of thread for the first, a historical review for the second, and an interview with the participants in the séance for the third. I am particularly interested in chatting with the other person who touched the planchette.*

A knock on the open door and a shadow caused Nesbit to look up. A gentleman stood before him, neatly attired. The man took off his hat as he entered. "You're younger than I expected," he said.

Nesbit stood, placing aside his journal and capping his pen, and extended his hand. "Orville Nesbit, at your service."

"Oh, sit down," the man said, pulling a chair around with his foot and sitting in it himself. "I'm Roger Collins. Before things go too far, we have to have a chat."

"Of course," Nesbit said, resuming his seat. "How may I be of service?"

"I had my people check you out," Collins said, "and they say you're clean—that you really do have the degrees you say you have and that there are no scandals attached to your name. But the first thing you should know is that whatever arrangement you've made with my wife, you're not going to be getting a penny more. I expect you to do whatever mumbo jumbo you do and then go back to where you came from, pronto."

"Then we are agreed," Nesbit said, lacing his fingers and leaning a bit forward. "I have other commitments. I hope to investigate the affair that brought me here expeditiously. I shall submit my report and depart. Your cooperation—"

"Second thing," Collins said. "My wife has been . . . ill. One of your degrees is in psychology. I don't need to explain more. That's why she's seeing ghosts. You'll treat her respectfully. No digging around in her mind. She's delicate. And my men tell me you're discreet." Collins leaned forward himself. "See that you stay that way."

"—would be most helpful in arranging a rapid and satisfactory conclusion to this affair," Nesbit continued mildly, as if no interruption had occurred. "May I presume on your patience to ask a few questions, Mr. Collins?"

"I'm not happy that you're here," Collins said.

"I'm sure you aren't," Nesbit said. "Did the events that caused your wife to write to me happen in the main house there?"

"What? Yes."

"Ah, thank you. I'll be brief. How long have you lived here?"

"Seven years."

"Who lived here before you?"

"The place was empty when I bought it. It belonged to an old lady, who had it in trust from her husband, who made his money in railroads. I suppose you won't believe me if you don't see the deeds."

"That may not be necessary," Nesbit said, sitting back and reaching for a notebook. "Do you have servants or hired help?"

"Three. George is the gardener and chauffeur. You've met him."

"Not formally," Nesbit said. "And the others?" He opened his notebook.

"Dolores cooks for us. Helen cleans three days a week."

"Do the servants live on the grounds?"

"Just George. The others live in town."

"May I interview them?"

"Don't ask them impertinent questions. And don't waste their time. I'm paying them to do their jobs."

"Is George married?"

"No."

"I see. You and Mrs. Collins. How long have you been married?"

Collins thought for a moment, as if counting to himself. "Ten years."

"Three years before you moved here?"

"Yes. How is that important?"

"Have you ever personally seen any unusual events in this house?"

"No, I have not. And I don't believe in spooks."

"Nor do I," Nesbit said with a thin smile. "Your wife's letter spoke of a window that opened by itself. Have you ever observed that window doing anything out of the ordinary, as windows go?"

"I'm sure that it's just been Helen, leaving it open and forgetting that she'd done so."

"If you will indulge me." Nesbit looked down at his notebook. "Is there a particular time of day or day of the week when the window is more likely to be found open?"

"Not so I've noticed. Now if you'll excuse me, I'm a busy man. Good day, Mr. Nesbit." Collins stood, turned, and walked out into the brilliant sunshine, putting on his hat as he crossed the threshold.

Nesbit continued to write for a few more minutes before closing his notebook with a snap. At the bottom of the page, near the margin, was the word "affair?" underlined twice.

*Journal of Orville Nesbit—*
*Visual apparitions are rare, but among them the majority*
*are of the living. The friend who lives in a distant city and so*

*on. What kind of apparition we are facing here, if indeed there is one, remains to be seen.*

The woman who answered the knock on the door was tall, raw-boned, and saturnine. She wore a black dress with a white apron, and a white cap on her head.

"Orville Nesbit," Nesbit said with a slight bow. "Is Mrs. Collins in? I believe she is expecting me."

"Come in, sir," the woman said, stepping back from the door. Nesbit entered, removing his hat as he did so and pulling off his gloves. He stepped through the door into a hallway. A small table stood to his right, an umbrella stand to his left. To his right, a door opened onto a parlor where a grand piano glistened in the setting sunlight.

The servant took his hat and gloves, vanished into the parlor, and returned a moment later empty-handed to say, "This way, sir." She led and he followed back through the house. Gold-framed paintings hung on the walls.

"Excuse me," Nesbit said, "are you Helen?"

"Dolores," the servant replied, without breaking stride. "Helen is off on Tuesdays."

"Ah. Have you been working here long, Dolores?"

"Since last August."

"Only two months?"

"No, the August before that." They reached the far tea room, where bay windows overlooked the garden. "Wait here, sir," she said, and departed without another word or a backward glance through the door to the right.

Nesbit walked forward, brushing his gaze over the tea table with its beige cloth, and the airy white chairs around it. He walked over to the French doors to the right of a bay window. One of the doors was partly open. He pushed it open all the way. A formal garden extended beyond, a bee humming over the flowers of red and yellow. Shears clicked off to his left, and he saw the man who had driven him in the touring car, now dressed in boots, denims, and a soil-stained green apron, at work trimming the verge along the brickwork of the foundation. George, that would be.

"Good afternoon," Nesbit said pleasantly. "If I may be so bold, when do you get off work?"

"Eight, unless I'm called for," George said, not looking up from his task.

"May I call on you then?" Nesbit asked.

"Is it okay with Mr. Collins?" George asked.

"He promised me full cooperation from everyone," Nesbit replied. "I shan't ask any embarrassing questions."

"All right," George said, moving farther down the wall, shears still busy.

Nesbit heard a footstep on the floor and saw a bit of motion out of the corner of his eye. He turned back to the tea room and saw another woman enter. She wore a green pastel suit, the skirt coming just below her knees. Her stockings were silk, and her gloves and her open sandals matched her eyes, a cold sea-foam blue.

"Mrs. Collins," Nesbit said, stepping toward her, raising his hand to take hers. She lifted her own hand, allowing him to take it and lift it to his lips. "Orville Nesbit, very pleased to meet you."

"Enchanted," Mrs. Collins said. "Please, call me Mary."

"Mary," Nesbit echoed. "Orville."

"Well, Orville," Mary said, walking to the tea table and sitting at it, gesturing him to the seat across from her. He slid back the chair and sat. "I'm so delighted you could come. I'm sure I was just being silly and there's nothing that could interest you here."

"Since I came all this way," Orville said as Dolores appeared and set a tea tray on the table between them, "perhaps you can tell me about your adventures." He eased a notebook from his inner pocket and uncapped his pen.

Mary waited until Dolores had poured the tea and departed before she spoke again.

"I feel like I'm being watched," she said.

"Ah. And when did this start?"

"After I saw the ghost."

"You're quite sure that's what it was?"

"Completely."

"Tell me about the house, Mary."

And for half an hour, while he sipped tea, Orville heard about the house, the grounds, and the town. At last he asked, "And where did the séance take place, Mary?"

"Right here," she said, one hand sweeping over the table.

"Could I trouble you to show me the window?"

"Of course! How silly of me." She stood and led the way to a staircase, wide, with a curved mahogany rail, and a Marrakech carpet held down with brass bars at the foot of each riser. "Do you know what I think?" Mary asked as she climbed the stairs. "Sometime, many years ago, there was a poor servant girl here who was thrown to her death from that window. And only now is she feeling strong enough to ask me for help."

"A plea for help can motivate ghosts," Orville commented—not adding that revenge or protecting a place was more common still, and commonest among ghosts were those who simply did not know they were dead and kept rehearsing significant events from their earthly lives.

They came to an upstairs hall, bedrooms opening off both sides. "There," Mary said, gesturing to the double-hung panes at the far end.

"And is there a particular time of day when it opens?" Orville asked. The window was closed right now.

Mary became silent. After a moment she said, "Not so I've noticed."

"Well, is there a time when it never opens?"

They approached the window. It was locked. Outside and directly beneath the window he could see the garden.

"Not so I've noticed," Mary said again. "Do you always ask so many questions?"

"Sometimes," Orville said. He took a tape measure from his right-hand coat pocket and measured the window, writing the dimensions in his notebook. He closed his eyes and laid the fingertips of his left hand gently on the glass. Then he opened his eyes and, still with his left hand, briskly reached out and snapped open the lock. He took a step back and consulted his pocket watch.

"I was told that dinner is at seven," he said. "It's nearly time."

And so they descended.

Mr. and Mrs. Baxter were guests that evening at dinner. The two men talked business and politics, and the two women talked flowers.

Orville sat mostly silent, observing as George and Dolores served them and answering politely when spoken to. After dinner the men retired to the smoking room, where a billiard table beckoned. Orville accompanied the ladies to the parlor as Mr. Baxter and Mr. Collins left the dining room. The last word Orville heard was a muttered "Fairy" from Mr. Baxter.

In the parlor, Orville turned to the two ladies. "I wonder if you would indulge me," he said, "by re-creating your recent séance."

"Are you sure that's a good idea?" Mrs. Baxter asked.

"I will be present," Orville said. "I think it is a . . . necessary . . . idea."

"I'll fetch the Ouija board," Mary said, leaving the room, while Shirley cleared a dried flower arrangement from the table and drew the curtains.

Shirley took a pair of candlesticks from the mantelpiece and placed them on the table. Orville pulled a box of matches out of his pocket and said, "Allow me." He lit the candles. As he did so, he asked, "What was the nature of Mrs. Collins's illness of"—he took a guess—"a year ago last August?"

"Oh, that," she said. "She was in an automobile accident. The silly thing, trying to drive. She crashed into the gatepost at the foot of the driveway. She was taken to the hospital, and for three days Roger didn't leave her side. Such a devoted man."

"And the effects of her accident?"

"She was in a coma those three days, poor dear."

"Thank you." The candles were burning now, the flames tall and straight. He backed away.

With tapping of heels, Mary reappeared, a pasteboard box held before her in her hands. She opened it and removed the board, made of varnished wood with painted letters and numbers—the words "Yes" and "No" on either side, "Ouija" in larger letters in the center.

The two women sat, one on either side of the table. Orville switched off the lights. In the twin candle flames their faces changed to the visages of haggard crones.

Orville took out his notebook and his pen as the two put fingertips on the celluloid planchette. Nothing happened for a long time. Orville could hear the snick of billiard balls from elsewhere in the house. Then

the triangle of plastic began to move, indicating letters. *N* . . . *E* . . .
*D* . . . The planchette trembled, and the candle flames, hitherto steady,
flickered and burned low. *R* . . . *A* . . . A gust of wind from the French
doors snatched at the flames; the right-hand one went out.

"I'm so cold," Mary said, snatching her fingers from the planchette
and hugging her arms around herself.

"Upstairs," Orville said. He flicked on the light, then led the way
along the path Mary had led him on earlier. In the hall, the window
stood open.

> *Journal of Orville Nesbit—*
> *The recording accelerometer that I left in the guesthouse*
> *shows a slight tremble at 9:22 this evening, the very moment*
> *when the draft blew through the house—made possible, I*
> *suspect, by the opening of the upstairs window. I have a*
> *hypothesis that I will test in the morning. Tomorrow also I must*
> *check the newspaper archives in town, to see if any murders or*
> *suicides are associated with what is now the Collins house.*
>
> *My interview with George, the chauffeur, proved interesting.*
> *None of the servants currently employed have been in the house*
> *longer than Dolores, and she dates her employment from after*
> *Mrs. Collins's accident. The previous chauffeur, he states, was*
> *sacked for leaving the automobile running in the circular*
> *driveway in front of the house the day of that accident, after*
> *driving her from an appointment of some kind in town.*
>
> *When I inquire after the house, I shall inquire after the*
> *previous staff as well. Perhaps they will have stories to tell.*

Morning. Breakfast was a quiet one, with Dolores serving silently,
and little conversation between Mr. and Mrs. Collins. Orville said even
less. He was wearing a morning coat, a bit formal, but giving him what
he felt was an aura of power.

"So many kinds of power," he had written in his notebook. "The
earth, the wind, the fire. All that was missing last night was the water."

He took a sip now from the water goblet by his right hand.

After the plates had been cleared away, Orville stood and spoke to
the Collinses. "If you will indulge me, I have an experiment to perform

upstairs. Either or both of you may witness it. And if I may be so bold as to ask George to accompany us and bring his toolbox?"

"If it hurries the day this farce ends," Mr. Collins said, and Mary said sharply, "Roger!" Mr. Collins nodded to Dolores and said, "Fetch George."

When the gardener arrived, wooden toolbox in hand, the group proceeded upstairs. They walked to the end of the hall, Orville in the lead.

The window was closed and locked.

"Yesterday afternoon," Orville began as he snapped the lock open, "when I first saw this window, I unlocked it. And as I went down the hall, before coming to the nearest door, I secretly stretched a single long blond hair across the hall at knee level. Last night, when the window opened, that hair was still in place. No human had been down this passageway or opened it. But," and he slapped his hand on the wall, "the window opened"—another slap—"nonetheless."

Another slap. The window was creeping open, seemingly by itself. A sliver of light shone between the sash and the sill. Another slap and the window stood open an inch.

"George, if you were to open the side jambs, I believe you would find that the sash weights are a fraction too heavy. An earthquake tremble too light to be felt would still be enough to open the window."

"You mean there isn't a ghost?" Mary asked.

"The chill you felt last night, the candle that blew out—the opening window created a draft," Orville said. "A day or two longer should finish my researches, and I will be able to tell you whether a ghost is here or not."

"But you just said there wasn't one," Roger said. "Listen, Nesbit, I'll double your fee if you just take the next train out. I'm tired of your rigmarole."

"I was hired by Mrs. Collins," Orville said mildly.

"I'm still curious," Mary said. "Please, Roger, for me."

"You'll be sorry," Mr. Collins said, and turned on his heel.

*Journal of Orville Nesbit*—
*My researches today were fruitless, or perhaps not, if a negative answer can be considered to rule out possibilities. No*

*murders, no suicides, no stillbirths in the house. The police
blotter is clean, save only the accident in which Mrs. Collins
was injured, and one other thing. No suspicion of foul play
revolved around the accident. The question of the servants may
be simply answered—a police report and an insurance claim
dating from the following week, for a missing-presumed-stolen
emerald and gold choker necklace. Perhaps during the time Mr.
Collins kept vigil by his wife's side one of the servants took the
opportunity to indulge in larceny, and, unable to determine
which one, Mr. Collins dismissed them all. They are scattered
now, though it seems they were all given excellent references.*

The only one of the servants whom Orville had not yet interviewed
was Helen, the cleaning woman. He found her in the pantry, capped
and aproned, feather duster in hand.

He began his interview by asking how long she had been in the
Collinses' employ, although he already knew the answer. With notebook at the ready he asked about the house, about feelings she may
have had, about anything odd she might have noticed. He walked with
her as she made her rounds. She talked, he listened.

Helen was a dull woman, perfectly suited to drudgery. She did not
guard her tongue. She had been the first of the new servants to be
hired, and she had known the last ones. She wasn't worried about her
job. She had never seen anything odd in the house, but "that window,
I never touched it, sir, not like Mr. Collins said."

Orville's pen scarcely touched his notebook.

"Does the name Ned mean anything to you?"

"No."

"Which room was it where Mrs. Collins had her fright?" he asked.

"The tea room," she said. "That's where she screamed."

"No, before that," Orville said. "Where she saw the ghost."

"She never did any such thing," Helen said. "I'd have heard."

Of that Orville had no doubt. Servants hear everything. No man is
a hero to his valet. He had been hoping that the person who cleaned a
room would have something to say about that room. A thorough cleaning differs very little from a thorough search.

"Ah," Orville said, "thank you," and left her straightening the anti-macassars in the drawing room.

Mrs. Collins herself was in the piano room. He had avoided questioning her about the apparition. Mr. Collins had been right about her delicacy, that was certain, nor had Orville any reason to upset her with questions that could lead to questioning her veracity.

"Excuse me, Mary," Orville began without preamble. "There exist two more questions which I need to research. Your answers will help my efforts to give you a report by this time tomorrow."

"What do you mean?"

"I would appreciate it if you could show me the room where you saw the ghost."

"Upstairs, the guest bedroom," she said.

"Show me."

"I'd prefer not to," Mary replied. "I haven't been back in that room since that afternoon."

"Afternoon?"

"Night."

"Where were you standing?"

"In the hall—what difference does it make?"

"I would appreciate knowing. My research . . ."

"I don't—very well." With that Mary walked silently past Orville, up the stairs, and to the door, the first one to the left of the window that George had now repaired. The smell of fresh paint where he had touched up the stops perfumed the air.

"Was this always the guest bedroom?" Orville asked. An attached bathroom shone with mirrors and polished tile. He could see through its door from the hall. "It seems larger than your room."

"Since my accident," Mary said, her hand rising to touch the side of her head and smooth back her hair, "Roger and I have had separate bedrooms. This used to be the master bedroom."

"For the first five years you lived here."

"Yes."

*Journal of Orville Nesbit—*
*Helen tells me that the maid she replaced was young,*
*much younger than any of the current staff.*

*Mary is strangely reluctant to help me now. I plan to leave tomorrow, regardless of the state of my researches. I have come to suspect that there was no haunting here; merely an overly loose window and the imaginations of an ill woman. Perhaps her husband has prevailed upon her.*

*Still, from the description of the movements of the apparition in her initial letter, I have reconstructed its motion.*

*And from its motion, I know that the furniture could not now be where it stands.*

*The account is false. The account is true. I need to study this. I am still concerned about the missing element of water.*

*The Ouija board concerns me as well. I dislike conundrums.*

Orville Nesbit packed his bags in the guesthouse. Mary Collins had dreamed the ghost. A lifelike dream, remembered as real upon awakening. Such things were not unknown.

"Logical entities should not be unnecessarily multiplied," Orville said, fixing the last strap on his largest case.

The accident had happened at 3:55 P.M. The angle of the sun, then, would have been much as it would be at three o'clock today. Orville stood on the porch of the guesthouse and watched as Mrs. Baxter arrived. He hurried across to intercept her before she could raise the knocker on the front door.

"Excuse me, Shirley," he said. "You can help me, I think."

"What is it, Mr. Nesbit?"

"The spirit that Mary saw. I would like you to re-create its motion. Could you do that?"

"I don't know . . ."

"Come inside."

He opened the door and motioned her in. Together they mounted the stairway and walked to the guest bedroom.

"Here," he said. "Starting in the bathroom, walk across the room, to this spot." He pointed.

"Do I walk around the bed?"

"Yes."

He watched from the door as she moved. His pocket watch said 2:50.

"Excellent," he said. "Now, please, humor me. Would you put this on?" He held up one of the long black dresses and white aprons that the maid Helen wore about her duties. He had borrowed it from the wardrobe in the basement.

"Whatever for?"

"You're far too brightly dressed to be a ghost," he said. "You can put it on over your clothing."

"If you insist." Shirley wore a puzzled frown.

"Humor me. This could be important," he said. "It will help Mary." Knowing that he lied as he spoke.

She vanished into the bathroom; cloth rustled. She emerged black and white. "I feel like a fool."

"Now," Orville said, "walk across the room."

She did so, smiling nervously. "Is this necessary?"

"I believe so."

She did as he said.

"Now, I assure you that I am completely serious when I ask you to lie on the bed and remain there."

He walked down the stairs, into the tea room, and out the French doors. A garden hose lay coiled to his right, attached to a spigot in the brick foundation. He turned it on, extending the hose into the flower bed, and let it flow. The water stained his linen trousers. Then he walked back into the house.

He found Mrs. Collins in the parlor, sitting in a chair reading a book. Three o'clock by his pocket watch.

"Mrs. Collins, if you would indulge me one last time," he said. "I'm about to go to the station. There is one matter which still puzzles me, and I hope that you can find it in your heart to ease my mind in this tiny detail."

"Of course, Orville," Mary said.

"The upstairs hall. If you could merely walk the length of it?" He looked at his watch again. "I would like to time you." He smiled. "It's a small detail."

"Oh, if it helps," she said, rising from her seat. "Since you're about to leave."

"Just that one thing."

She walked up the stairs. He followed. At the end of the corridor that ran toward the window he stopped, letting her continue.

She started down the hall. At the door to the guest room she stopped as if frozen. She spun toward the door, her face twisting into rage.

"You bitch!" she screamed. "You bastard! How could you? In my own bed!"

Mary dashed into the room where Shirley was trying to rise. In an instant Mary was on her, pummeling her with her fists. Orville was close behind.

"Mary!" he shouted. "Mary, stop it!"

She threw him off her back where he was trying to stop her flailing arms with a bear hug. Then she turned and dashed for the door.

Orville landed on his back where she had thrown him.

Her feet pounded down the stairs. The front door slammed.

From outside, male voices shouted, "Mary, what in the name of heaven!" and "Mrs. Collins, no!"

By the time Orville—accompanied by Shirley Baxter—had limped down the stairs, George and Roger were pulling Mary out of the driver's seat of the automobile in which they had just arrived. George had her in a full nelson, still saying, "Ma'am, ma'am, don't."

"You," Roger said, turning and pointing at Orville. "This is your fault. I warned you. I'll sue you. I'll ruin you. You fraud. You quack."

"Perhaps," Orville said, going past him and around the corner of the house. He went back to the garden shed and found a shovel. Then he walked, still limping, to the spot where the water from the hose had run to its lowest level and was soaking into the ground of the garden, amid the red and yellow flowers.

He pushed the blade into the soft mud and pulled up the sodden earth. It made a plopping sound. Again he shoved the blade into the hole, pushing it deeper with his foot. All at once a foul smell burst from the earth. He retched. As the other members of the household arrived—Helen, Dolores, Roger, Shirley—Orville held his breath, bent, and shoved his hand into the muddy water.

He reached deep—feeling for something in the muck—and pulled.

His hand came up with a bone, long and white, and still hung about with scraps of rotting flesh.

"I think I've found your ghost," he said.

Roger stepped back, his hand darting into his pocket and pulling out a small chrome-plated pistol. "All of you, stand over by that man," he said. "Don't try anything; I have a round for each of you."

The little group did as they were told.

"Now I'll make ghosts of the lot of you," Roger said, raising the weapon.

He never fired. Instead, a sharp metal point appeared through the front of his shirt, a red stain surrounding it. Roger fell, the pistol tumbling from his limp fingers. And there was George standing behind him, edging shears in hand.

"You killed her," he said to the fallen man. "You son of a bitch, you killed her and buried her in my garden."

Orville shook his head. "Not exactly. But it will do."

*Journal of Orville Nesbit—*

*The apparition and the first message that the Ouija board gave have perfectly rational explanations. They were the subconscious memories of a woman who had arrived home unexpectedly to find her husband in the arms of another woman. She snapped, she attacked, and she unintentionally killed her rival. The girl fell, perhaps striking her head. No one who is alive remembers. The police found bloodstains in the backing of the carpet.*

*Mary ran from the room, perhaps not fully comprehending what she had done. She may have intended to kill herself when she hit the gate, or perhaps not. I do not know and she cannot tell, because the concussion and the coma stole her memory of that day.*

*Roger dismissed the servants. He couldn't have hidden a bloody carpet and a grave in the flower bed with observers present. The missing necklace was a ruse; it was in the shallow grave with the girl. A convenient, believable excuse. He waited anxiously by Mary's bedside, to make sure she wouldn't accuse him when she awoke. Perhaps he would have strangled her* had she remembered. He won't tell us now, not without the aid of the Ouija board—which I am not inclined to try.

But Mary's subconscious could not forget. The memory returned as a lucid dream of seeing the girl in her bedroom, and the subconscious recollection drove the movement of the planchette to spell out "MURDER."

As to what force caused the Ouija board to begin to spell "GARDEN" (backwards, I admit), information neither Mary nor her friend had or could possibly have learned—that I am not prepared to say.

# Murder Entailed

## Susan Krinard

Trained as an artist with a B.F.A. in illustration, Susan Krinard became a writer when a friend read a short story she'd written and suggested she try writing a romance novel. *Prince of Wolves* was the result. Within a year Susan had sold the manuscript to Bantam as part of a three-book contract.

Susan now makes her home in the Land of Enchantment, New Mexico, with her husband, Serge, her dogs Brownie, Freya, and Nahla, and cats Murphy and Jefferson. In addition to writing, Susan's interests include classical and New Age music, old movies, nature, animals, baking, and collecting jewelry and clothing with leaf and wolf designs. Her recent novella "Kinsman" was the winner of the SF Romance Sapphire Award. She is currently working on her first fantasy novel.

I f anyone in Albion was likely to be murdered, it was surely not Lord Roderick Featherstonehaugh.

Everyone loved Fen, as his intimates called him. Women adored him. His peers fought for the privilege of inviting him to their country house shooting parties to bag the best grouse and pheasant. Even servants, from grooms to housekeepers, hastened to do his bidding with uncharacteristic alacrity.

*And yet here he lies,* Lady Olivia Dowling thought, gazing down at the body sprawled on the Axminster carpet in the guest chamber of Waveney Hall. Fen was still quite imposing in death, though his expression of terror somewhat mitigated the impact of his girth. *Why is it that I cannot feel the proper grief? And how can I solve this terrible mystery before the constable must be summoned?*

For it would not do to involve the authorities, not until she was quite certain that none of her guests were guilty of the crime—or that one of them definitely was.

What made the situation even more vexing was the fact that no one was quite sure what family Talent Fen had inherited from his father, the former Viscount Featherstonehaugh. Society had long made a game of guessing its nature, but Fen had never told.

A windblown splatter of rain struck the window. Olivia pushed a loose tendril of hair out of her face and wrinkled her nose at the unmistakable smell of wet canine.

Lightning flashed, the window sprang open, and Kit Meredith climbed in. Though the guest rooms were in the east wing on the first floor of the mansion, scaling the brick walls of the Hall was no problem for Kit. His black hair was plastered to his face, but his black wool suit was conveniently unaffected by the miserable day outside. How fortunate that he did not need to leave his clothes behind when he called upon his wild magic. A naked man appearing in her home at any time of day was most inconvenient. Almost as inconvenient as a murder.

Kit slipped on his smoke-lensed spectacles and straightened to his full, lanky height. "Well?" he began. "What is—?"

His gaze followed hers to the body. He gave a startled *woof* and sank down in the nearest chair.

"Featherstonehaugh," he said. "Dead. By magic."

"Ah, Kit," she said fondly. "You always come just when I need you most—even if you prefer that no one knows *how* you come. I am very much afraid that you and I have a murder to investigate."

Kit could be every bit as practical as she. He wasted no time with questions, but dropped into a crouch beside the body and sniffed up and down its length. Olivia had long since ceased to be amused at his antics. One did not laugh at Old Shuck, even if one was the Black Dog's closest friend.

"As pitiful as my Residual gift may be," she commented, "I can See that he was strangled."

"Strangled?"

Sir Kenneth Ingleby stepped into the room, his face drained of color. "Fen! Is he dead?"

Olivia hastened to close the door behind him. "I fear so, Sir Kenneth. Is the news already abroad?" She sighed. "I did ask Amis to be discreet—"

"Your butler didn't speak of it," Sir Kenneth said with a grim twist to his mouth. "My room is just across the hall, and I heard voices." He stared at the body. "Good riddance."

"You do not seem very surprised, Ingleby," Kit remarked.

Sir Kenneth gave him a frosty stare. "I am not. No man deserved it more."

"Kenneth!" Olivia said. "How can you—?"

"I believe I know," Kit said. "Livvy, you must have heard the tragic story of young Mr. B., who took his own life a few months ago." He glanced with sympathy at Sir Kenneth. "I am sorry to be blunt, but the rumors said that the young man had so-called unnatural proclivities, and—"

"And he was my lover," Sir Kenneth finished. "You are surprisingly well informed, Meredith, given your distaste for London society." He looked at Olivia. "Bertram was my lover, but he was expected to wed a young heiress who would save his family fortune, so we agreed to end it. Unfortunately, Featherstonehaugh discovered our liaison and threatened to tell Bertie's family if he did not pay a considerable sum. Bertie knew he could not see his family ruined. He chose the honorable way out." Sir Kenneth smiled bitterly. "He did not come to me, damn him. But now Fen has been paid in full."

Olivia sat down in the nearest chair. "But Fen—everyone liked him! He could not have committed such a heinous act."

"But he did. He fooled all of us—and one can only conjecture what else he may have done to earn this death." He shook his head. "No, I did not murder him, Lady Olivia. Motive I may have, but not the means. I am half his size."

"It is true," Kit said. "There are no marks upon the body save those made by Fen himself during his struggles—here, and here, where he clawed at his own throat and chest. The shirt is torn, but there is no outward sign of strangulation. The manner of his death might remain a mystery if you could not See inside him, Livvy." He knelt again and ran his fingers along the victim's neck. "Sir Kenneth is an Invisible. He could have come upon Fen unaware, but his hands or a garrote would have left marks or bruises. There are none. Fen's skin is completely clear."

"A pity," Sir Kenneth said. "I hope you do not find the murderer—if, indeed, you still wish to. Good night, Lady Olivia. Meredith."

"You will not leave the grounds?" Kit asked.

"I would not wish to display a guilty conscience, would I?" Sir Kenneth saluted Kit with a crooked smile and bowed to Olivia, closing the door quietly behind him.

"Well?" Kit said, rising. "Who could have done it, Livvy? If what Sir Kenneth says is true, and Fen was capable of blackmail, he might have had any number of enemies."

"But one of my guests—it doesn't bear thinking of."

"Who else? A housebreaker? No common thief would be likely to possess skill beyond the Residual, and Residual magic could not kill. This was the work of entailed magic."

Olivia frowned and perched her weight on the edge of the massive oak half-tester, an informality she would not have ventured in other company. "You do not detect any particular scent?"

"Of the murderer, no. There is a rank odor of cologne—Fen's—which effectively obscures any other smell." He wrinkled his nose. "That is not so strange as the fact that I cannot tell if the magic is male or female. When exactly did he die, Livvy?"

She concentrated, willing her body-sense to replace normal sight. The Residual gift was erratic at best. "This would be so much easier if my grandmother had bequeathed her Talent to me," she said. "It is not as if she has any other heirs, or uses it herself."

"She only wishes to protect you from the pain of others' suffering. She has become a recluse to avoid sensing illness and disease she cannot heal."

"I am not my grandmother," Olivia said with a sniff. She glared at the body. "I can sense the damage inside his throat and chest. Definitely a lack of oxygen. He has not been dead more than two hours."

"Then you must know which guests have a ready alibi. Who is here, Livvy?"

"You would know if you had come to the party yourself," she chided. "There is Sir Kenneth, and Lord Angus Ware. Both have rooms in this wing, as does Jonathan Highet, who is next door, I believe. Also

Miles Chatham, Lady Isolde Swansborough, and Fanny Thursfield. And their servants, of course."

"But servants, like our theoretical housebreaker, would not have the necessary Talent."

Olivia nodded. For the past thousand years in Albion, members of the peerage and gentry with ancient connections to the royal house had passed on their family magic, whatever form it might take, to their chosen heirs—one male and one female in each generation. A father might choose the firstborn heir of his lands, or a different son entirely. A mother could select any of her daughters upon whom to bestow her Talent.

In such a way entailed magic had spread across Albion, even touching commoners to some small degree in the form of Residual gifts that every son or daughter of a Bearer received at birth. Residual magic might make for amusing parlor tricks or convenient shortcuts, but it could not murder.

"I cannot account positively for the whereabouts of any of my guests at the time Fen was killed," she said. "Most were in their rooms dressing for dinner. You said that you could not tell if the magic is male or female."

"Quite. But I would hazard a guess that strangulation is a man's work."

"Even if it leaves no mark?" She tapped her chin. "But that would mean Highet, Miles, or Lord Ware. It cannot have been Highet—his Talent is fire. I see no sign of burning, do you?"

"None whatsoever. But if Highet is roomed next door, he may have heard something." Kit joined her on the bed, swinging his legs in the air the way he had done when they were children. "Miles Chatham . . ."

"That is impossible! He loathes his own magic. Ever since the war . . . he carries an intolerable burden of guilt. And he is a man of the church."

"But he is a Puppetmaster. He can control the movements of others. Might he not have simply paralyzed Fen's lungs?"

Olivia shuddered. "He has no motive! None of them have an obvious reason to kill Fen."

"Neither did Sir Kenneth," Kit said dryly. He stared intently at the body and jumped down from the bed.

"What is it?"

"Water." He crouched by Fen's head and lifted a fingertip glistening with liquid. "Coming from Fen's mouth. Yes, and now I smell it as well. What is Lord Ware's Talent?"

"Water-summoning." She sucked in a breath. "Do you think—can he have drowned Fen from inside?"

"Or Fen might simply have drunk a glass of water before he was killed. Still, Ware must be questioned. They all must, Livvy." He straightened. "It might be less awkward coming from me."

"No. They are my guests. My responsibility." She slid down and straightened her skirts. "And I know how much you hate crowds."

"Well, then. I will stay here to see that the body is not disturbed. Perhaps I will discover something else I've missed."

She clasped his hand. "Thank you, Kit."

Though she could not make out his eyes behind the smoked lenses, she knew that their usual scarlet blaze had dimmed to a soft glow. "Take care, Livvy."

She slipped out of the room, assumed a dignified mien, and went downstairs to the drawing room.

All the guests were gathered there, dressed for dinner and looking uneasy. Lord Ware, Jonathan Highet, and Miles were engaged in desultory conversation by the mantelpiece. She was surprised that Ware had not cajoled the others into one of his perpetual games of cards. Sir Kenneth had just finished a tumbler of whiskey from the decanter at the sideboard. Lady Isolde and Fanny Thursfield glanced up at Olivia with obvious relief.

Announcing the murder was out of the question. She must speak to each man individually, without raising suspicion.

"Ladies and gentlemen," she said, "I am sorry to have neglected you. There has been a small disturbance which I am attempting to correct." She smiled. "Lord Ware, if I might have a word?"

The middle-aged gentleman excused himself from the others and hastened to her side. Olivia saw at once that he moved like a man afflicted by some guilt or shame.

She drew him into the adjoining library and asked him to sit. He remained where he was, fidgeting from foot to foot.

"You have discovered it," he moaned. "I knew you would. I am so terribly sorry."

Olivia was grateful for the chair beneath her. "Lord Ware?"

"It is an odious habit, I know," he confessed miserably. "But Featherstonehaugh trounced me at écarté on Thursday last—won everything I own. Who will believe he cheated? I have been desperate to find the money to pay him. He will ruin me if I do not." He mopped at his brow with a stained handkerchief. "Just a small, friendly game in the servants' hall—I saw no harm in it. I daresay that any footman is more plump in the pocket than I. But it was unforgivable, I realize that now."

"You were gambling with the servants?"

"With your coachman," he said, shamefaced. "And he beat me, too. It is no more than I deserve." A small rain cloud formed over his balding head and began to weep on his shoulders. "Fen has been casting me evil looks ever since I arrived at the Hall. When he comes for the money, I do not know what I shall do."

"Then you do not know . . ." She got up and paced the length of the room. Either he was an accomplished actor, or he did not know that Fen was dead. His guilt was of a much more mundane variety.

"Can you forgive me, Lady Olivia?" he said.

"Of course." Motive Ware had, and means if the water proved a clue, but had he the stomach for it?

"Oh, thank you," Lord Ware said. The rain cloud vanished, leaving streaks on his coat and droplets on the carpet. "I am sorry to have brought my personal misfortunes to your door. I will leave immediately if you wish—"

"No. No, I would prefer if you stay and behave as if nothing has happened. I will not speak of this, I promise."

Ware bobbed and kowtowed his way out the door as if taking leave of the Queen herself. Olivia remained behind, dreading the next interrogation. She had known the Reverend Miles Chatham since childhood; he was one of the gentlest souls in Albion.

With a heavy heart she returned to the drawing room. At the door she caught a flash of movement down the hall and saw a man and woman locked in a hasty embrace—Mary, Lady Isolde's maid, and Lord Ware's valet.

"George," Mary whispered. "I—" She glimpsed Olivia and flushed, breaking free of her lover's hold. George took a step after her and looked back at Olivia. He hesitated, bowed his head, and hurried away.

Olivia preferred to be blind to the servants' liaisons, as she was to those of her guests. She shook her head and entered the drawing room, glad she was not responsible for disciplining them.

The guests were arranged much as before, except that Lord Ware was the one drinking. She walked to Miles's side and touched his arm.

"Vicar," she said formally, "I have need of your counsel."

He exchanged a final word with Highet and followed her from the room. This time she could not sit, and Miles searched her face with concern, his high brow creasing beneath graying sandy hair.

"What is it, Olivia?" he asked. "What troubles you?"

"Oh, dear," she said. "I cannot . . . It is most distressing . . . Lord Featherstonehaugh is dead."

"I beg your pardon?"

Swiftly, before she could change her mind, she told Miles what she and Kit had discovered. He became more and more grave as she spoke, until he looked as though the very weight of the world rested on his narrow shoulders.

"I am so sorry, my dear child," he said. "How terrible for you. I will not ask why you have called me here. You have decided to investigate the crime yourself before calling the authorities, and I am, naturally, one of the suspects."

His frankness was both an embarrassment and a relief. "It is merely a formality," she assured him. "You were my father's dear friend. I know what you experienced during the war, and that you would never, never use your powers—"

"As I did so recklessly then. Yet, as much as I despise them and my own weakness, those powers are not gone. They remain within me." His expression grew strange and distant. "I could use them to reach inside a man's body. I could force him to play Punch at my command, dance in St. James's Square, turn a knife against his own flesh."

*Or freeze a man's lungs in his chest.* "But you did not. Could not. You have no reason."

"But I did have motive, my dear." He met her eyes with his clear, tormented gaze. "Fen served in the war, for a very short time, before his elder brothers died and he inherited both title and Talent. I was with him when he committed an act of unforgivable cowardice that led directly to the deaths of four of his men. I stood by when he charmed the Board of Inquiry into believing his lies." He made a sick sound in his throat. "Guilt is the devil's mount, and it runs where it wills."

"But not to cold-blooded murder!"

He opened his mouth to reply but was forestalled when Kit walked into the room, not troubling to knock.

"I wish I could have come earlier, to spare you both this unpleasantness," he said. "But what I have to tell you will clear Mr. Chatham of any complicity.

"It was not a man who committed this murder, Olivia. It was a woman."

Olivia sank into her chair. "But I thought you said you could not determine the gender of the magic."

"Yes, and that troubled me. My nose is usually somewhat keener than that." He glanced at Miles without the usual wariness, for the vicar had known of his "gift" since his childhood. "But perhaps my shortcomings may be forgiven. You see, Fen must not have arranged to bestow his Talent upon an heir before his death. When I examined the body more thoroughly to see what I might have missed, his magic was in the process of dissipation—freeing itself into the ether. Because it did not pass to a chosen recipient of his line, I was able to detect all of its nuances as it dispersed—including the taint of his killer."

"A woman?" Olivia demanded. "Who?"

Kit sighed and scratched his chin. "The signature was so muddled that I defy even the Lord High Magician to decipher it. That it is female I am sure. Beyond that . . ."

Female. Olivia felt the beginnings of a headache. She now knew enough of Lord Featherstonehaugh's vices to suspect that even a woman might have some motive to kill him. But here, under her own roof? Timid Mrs. Thursfield, frightened of all men? Lady Isolde, witty and bright . . . and one of the few who had avoided Fen with obvious dislike?

"Miles," she said quietly, "would you be so kind as to ask Mrs. Thursfield to join me?"

"Of course. And if I may be of any comfort, you know I am near." He let himself out of the room, and Kit took up a position behind

Olivia's chair. His fingers settled on her temples, attacking with precision the very portions of her skull that ached so abominably.

"Mrs. Thursfield," Kit mused. "She hardly seems a murderess. Rather more like a partridge hen stuffed with giblets, and about as formidable."

"Men always make the mistake of discounting women in any activity of moment," Olivia said, too relaxed to raise her voice above a murmur. "But even I have been guilty of that."

"'Guilty' being the operative word," Kit remarked, and cocked his head toward the door. Mrs. Thursfield crept into the room with tiny steps, her head bobbing ever so slightly. Unlike Lord Ware, who had worn guilt on his sleeve, she hid it among her skirts like a clandestine affair.

"Mr. Chatham said that you wished to see me," she said in a low voice, making herself very small—no mean task when nature had so inclined her to abundance. "Have I . . . have I done something to displease you, Lady Olivia?"

Olivia had felt sorry for Mrs. Thursfield ever since she had observed the nasty way Mr. Thursfield treated his wife at the Duke of Devonshire's ball. She had resolved then and there to invite the young matron into her circle, but Fanny Thursfield had a remarkable gift for fading into the background and remaining unnoticed no matter how often she was lured into games or conversation.

Her great asset—besides the figure her husband evidently did not appreciate—was her Talent of Preservation. On her first visit to Waveney Hall, she had presented Olivia with a single, perfect red rose, still lifelike yet frozen in a single moment for all time. Olivia did not understand the mechanism, but Kit had once referred to it as a "field" of some sort, perfectly molded to the shape of the rose and sealing it from air and decay.

Just as a person of Mrs. Thursfield's abilities might seal a man from air and life without so much as touching him.

"Not at all," Olivia said. "You have been a perfect guest. It is just that I have a small question or two regarding Lord Featherstonehaugh, and you may be able to shed some light on—"

Mrs. Thursfield's rather pretty eyes widened, and her legs began to buckle. Kit rushed to catch her. He delicately sniffed the air over

Fanny's lolling head and cast Olivia an unreadable glance. "Jonathan Highet," he said with unusual brusqueness. "Have you been with him, Mrs. Thursfield?"

Fanny's cheeks suffused with violent color. She gazed from him to Olivia in terror. "Do not tell my husband," she whispered. "I beg of you."

She had taken a lover? It was far more daring on Fanny's part than Olivia would have believed possible. "I will say nothing, but you must tell me all you know. Why did you swoon when I mentioned Fen?"

Her skin went from red to white. "He was . . . he was my—" She burst into tears. "He said he loved me. He held me in his arms and whispered such promises, and then he . . . he cast me aside like . . . like—"

"There is no need to further examine her," a masculine voice said from the open doorway. Jonathan Highet strode into the room and claimed Fanny's trembling hand. "I have heard that Fen is dead. Fanny knows nothing of it. Yes, Fen took advantage of her loneliness. He seduced her and amused himself at her expense, and she has good reason to hate the bastard, but she was with me—last night, and today, until we came down for dinner."

Fanny lifted her head. "It is true, and I am not ashamed!"

She had certainly proven to be something of a surprise, and if such a mouse was capable of taking two lovers in defiance of her tyrannical husband, she might also be capable of murder. Highet's obvious love for Fanny and his anger on her behalf was a motive as well. But they provided alibis for each other—a sticky situation indeed, though Olivia was certain that Fanny's terror was of her husband and not the result of an accusation of murder.

"If you doubt my word," Highet said stiffly, "you may ask Lord Ware's manservant. When Mrs. Thursfield and I returned from the garden to my room because of the rain, we found him skulking about inside, tying his cravat. What the devil he was doing there I don't know, but I could find nothing missing or disturbed. He had no business in my chamber. Ware should discharge him."

Lord Ware's manservant, George, was the young valet she had seen in the hallway with Lady Isolde's maid. "I shall inquire immediately. Kit, will you send for Mrs. Thursfield's maid and ask Lord Ware to summon his valet?"

Kit did as she asked, and Mr. Highet assisted Fanny into the hall, murmuring endearments to soothe her tears. When Kit returned, Lady Isolde Swansborough accompanied him.

Lady Isolde floated into the room as if borne on a mist. No man could hope to ignore such a golden-haired goddess, and Kit practically fell over himself showing her to a chair. Olivia raised a brow at his foolishness and turned to Isolde, all amusement fled at the grim prospect before her.

It could not be Isolde. Not her dearest friend.

"Isolde," she began, "I hardly know how to explain . . ."

"I have heard," Isolde said in her mellifluous voice. "Fen is dead. We are all suspects in his murder." She glanced at Kit. "You wonder who had both means and motive. He was killed by some form of strangulation, but without the use of outwardly physical means. A Mentalist, such as myself, could induce a man to forget how to breathe."

"And you can see what's truly within a man's soul," Kit said.

"You are more right than you know." Isolde laughed. "Yes, I saw what was in Fen's soul. I have always known of his corruption, his hypocrisy, his dishonor—just as I knew his unique Talent was to present a glamour of perfection, warmth, and generosity that deceived all but a very few of those who met him. His true nature was quite the opposite, and I disliked him heartily." She met Olivia's gaze. "I have no alibi, Olivia. I was alone in the conservatory all afternoon. But I did not kill him."

Olivia desperately wanted to believe her. There was a shining nobility in Isolde, the very essence of noblesse oblige that compelled her to take up causes of those less fortunate. If she had known of Bertram's suicide or Fen's treatment of Fanny, might she not be moved—

No. Any alternative was preferable. Olivia glanced at Kit. "I believe Lady Isolde. If we have eliminated the guests, then the murderer can only be a housebreaker or one of the servants. We dismissed those possibilities too quickly before."

Kit must have heard the note of urgency in her voice. "Commoners might inherit Residual gifts from noble or landed relations, but no heir to family Talent would be a servant."

Indeed—and certainly not one of her own! Yet even the rules of magic could be broken. One heard tales of hidden heirs, forbidden ceremonies, even male Talent passing to female heirs and vice versa in spite of the vast and often fatal risks involved.

While Kit waited for Lord Ware's valet to appear—Olivia had more than one question for him—she commenced inquiries about the recent whereabouts of each of the servants, which consumed a good hour. None of them had any obvious motive for murder, since few had dealt directly with Fen. But her heart beat a little faster when she learned that two servants were not accounted for during the time of Fen's death: George and Mrs. Thursfield's maid, Mary.

They were the very two she had seen together in the hall. Quite possibly, they would provide each other's alibi, just as Fanny and Jonathan Highet had done. But why had George been in Highet's room, when Lord Ware's chamber was two doors down?

She asked Mrs. Thursfield to send Mary to the library as soon as the girl had completed her immediate tasks. Lord Ware's valet still had not appeared, and she was about to send for him again when Kit escorted George into the room—or more accurately herded him, much as a shepherd's dog drove an unwilling sheep.

George was a very personable young man and quickly disguised any reluctance he might feel about being called before her. She could have sworn she caught a smirk about his lips in spite of his outwardly deferential manner.

"Where were you three hours ago?" she asked without preamble.

His eyes laughed at her. "I was with Mary, my lady, before Lord Ware called me to attend him."

Naturally. "What did you know of Lord Featherstonehaugh?"

"Only that he won a great deal of money from Lord Ware."

"Why were you in Mr. Highet's chamber this afternoon?"

His confident air vanished. "I . . . my lady . . ." He squared his shoulders. "I meant to find something to steal, to help Lord Ware. Mr. Highet and Mrs. Thursfield came in while I was there."

The explanation was so improbable yet simple that Olivia was taken aback. She glanced at Kit, who frowned. Kit was usually very good at detecting outright lies, but he was clearly stumped.

"Are you admitting to a crime for which you will, at the very least, be discharged?" she demanded.

"Yes, my lady." He hung his head. "I am sorry."

"And you claim you were with Mary before that, and Lord Ware afterward?"

"Yes. Lord Ware will say so, my lady."

The door opened, and Mary stepped in. Her gaze flew with alarm from Olivia to Kit and to George.

"Don't be afraid, Mary," Olivia said. "I have only a few questions for you. Did you know Lord Featherstonehaugh?"

"No, milady," she whispered. "Only as a guest."

"Were you with George three hours ago?"

She stared at George with a kind of horrified fascination. "Yes, milady."

"You must answer honestly, Mary. You will not be punished for dalliance, but the consequences of lying are considerable."

Mary began to shake. "I . . . was . . . with George."

Kit's expression affirmed what Olivia knew: the maid was lying, and badly. "Has George threatened you if you did not lie for him, Mary?"

She appeared very close to a swoon. Olivia was just about to ask Kit to watch George while she spoke privately with Mary when the door opened yet again, and Jonathan Highet entered.

"Forgive me for disturbing you," he said, "but I forgot to mention that I found—" He stared at George. "You!"

George's face was a blank. Highet strode past him and held out his hand. Between his fingers was a gold signet ring etched with a family crest—a slender woman's band.

Olivia took it gingerly. Even she could feel the magic in it. "I know this crest. Does it not belong to the Essex Belchams?"

Kit joined her and nodded. "The family of Fen's wife, Jane."

"But she died last October! Did you see Fen wearing this ring?"

"No." He glanced at Highet. "Where did you find it?"

"On the floor beside the wall, where *he*"—he gestured at George—"was standing when I caught him."

Olivia held the ring out to George. "Did you steal this from Lord Featherstonehaugh?"

"Wait," Kit said, holding up a hand. "Which wall, Highet?"

"Which—?" Highet's face cleared. "Why, the wall between my room and Fen's."

"Livvy," Kit said, "wasn't Lady Featherstonehaugh a *passe-muraille*?"

*Passe-muraille*—a wall-walker. One who could literally pass through solid objects, including walls. "But Lady Featherstonehaugh is dead," she protested.

She and Kit stared at each other. George began to back toward the door, step by slow step. "Did you steal this ring?" Olivia asked the valet. "Or was it yours all along?"

George stopped. His gaze swept the room, and then he smiled coldly. "It was my mother's."

"And your mother," Kit said, "was Lady Featherstonehaugh. Was Fen your father as well?"

"Are you saying that *he* walked through the wall adjoining my room with Fen's?" Highet asked. "How is that possible?"

"As I understand it," Kit said, "a wall-walker cannot bring anything with him when he travels through a solid object. You said he was tying his cravat when you found him, Highet? If he had to enter and exit Fen's room discreetly—via your room, if he knew you were to be out—he would have to undress in your chamber and retrieve his clothing after the deed was done. The ring would not pass, either."

"You are saying George murdered Fen?" Suddenly, she saw it. "If George is Lady Featherstonehaugh's son—"

"Unacknowledged, or we would know of him."

"—he could not have inherited her Talent. She is female, he is male."

"Is it truly impossible, Livvy? Cross-gender transference has been done, though it is usually fatal for the donor."

"And Lady Featherstonehaugh died in October." She gasped. "She sacrificed her life . . . and passed her magic to her son."

Kit dodged toward the door to block George's path. He showed his teeth in a smile. "Her illegitimate son. A bastard."

"No!" George gazed at them all in open defiance. "My father was Lord Featherstonehaugh, and *he* was the bastard."

Silence fell like a shroud. "Lady Featherstonehaugh gave you the ring?" Kit asked.

"Just before she . . . before she died." George stared at the band on Olivia's palm. "My *father* beat and abused my mother from the day they were wed. She took comfort where she could. Featherstonehaugh believed I was the son of one of his grooms, and my mother could not prove otherwise. She sent me to live with a country family out of fear for my life, and hers. She convinced my father that I was dead. But she didn't tell me that she was my real mother until . . . until just before she passed her Talent, and the ring, to me."

Olivia closed her hand over the ring. "And you have kept this secret since she died—that you are of gentle birth and magical Talent? Why?"

"Because he wanted revenge," Kit said. "And he might have gotten away with murder."

"Yes," George said. "My adoptive family saw that I got an education with the money Lady Featherstonehaugh sent to them. They had me trained to be a servant, a gentleman's gentleman. When I learned the truth, I found work with a member of Featherstonehaugh's circle. I knew my time would come."

"And no one would suspect any danger in a mere servant," Kit added. "We did not. And neither did Fen." He looked at George. "You waited until the right moment—until you knew Fen was alone and Highet's room was vacant, so that you had a safe and private place to prepare—and killed your father. But how?"

George made a fist of his hand. "I materialized this inside of his chest, and squeezed his throat and lungs until he strangled."

"My God," Highet whispered. "No outward marks—"

"And the false lead of the water in Fen's mouth, and the female magic," Kit said. "For his magic *was* female. It was the mingling of that with the male wielder I could not sort out."

"And he got Mary to lie on his behalf, making sure he was seen with her afterward," Olivia added. "Who can blame her for being frightened of what George could do if she did not agree!"

"You all know what he was," George whispered. "He beat my mother and would have killed me. He lied and cheated and blackmailed. He deserved to die."

George lunged at Olivia, snatched the ring with his right hand, and dove toward the nearest wall. His left arm passed through the painting hung there, disappearing up to the elbow, and the sleeves of his coat and shirt tore away in shreds.

Kit woofed. There was a puff of smoke, and a huge, shaggy black dog stood in the place where a man had been. It fixed its demonic red eyes upon the vanishing valet and leaped.

Cloth ripped. Kit's jaws closed on George's ankle. It hardly slowed the valet, whose clothes were heaped on the floor at the foot of the wall. But something else stopped him as Kit could not.

The ring. George's right hand remained visible, clutching the memento that he could not take with him. He lingered, and delayed, until his hand began to shake with the effort of his magic.

He let the ring fall. His hand vanished, and at the same moment Kit charged out into the hall.

Olivia hastened after him, followed by Highet. She found the stunned assemblage of guests in the drawing room, all staring at the naked man halfway emerging from the wall and the huge black dog looking up at George's expression of pain and horror.

A heartbeat passed, and then Kit was a man again, breathing fast. "George is dead," he said heavily. "He spent too long in the wall, refusing to let go of the ring. I am sorry, Olivia."

She felt a little faint, but Kit was there to support her. Lord Ware covered his eyes. The others found nothing to say.

"Look," Kit said. "The magic is dispersing."

Olivia raised her head from his shoulder. It was only a faint glow, a mist, a sigh that wreathed the air about George's head for a few seconds, but even she could sense the sorrow of magic lost forever.

"He had no heir," Kit murmured. "No one else will use Lady Featherstonehaugh's Talent to kill."

"I think it will be some time before I use this room again," Olivia said, her voice unsteady.

"You must come stay with me," Kit said close to her ear. "If you bring Lady Isolde, it will all be most proper."

She met his gaze. "Everyone knows your secret now, Kit."

"One of my secrets," he said, "but not all."

And he smiled in a way that made the world right again.

PART IV

# Murder
# Fantastical

# Dropping Hints

## Lawrence Watt-Evans

Lawrence Watt-Evans began a career as a full-time writer in 1979. He is perhaps best known for his fantasy work, including the Ethshar series and the Obsidian Chronicles, but has also written horror and science fiction. He has written and sold over a hundred short stories, more than thirty novels, and hundreds of articles.

Watt-Evans has been reading and collecting comics since childhood and is part owner of a chain of comic-book shops. He served two years as president of the Horror Writers Association (1994–96). He married in 1977, has two children, and lives in the Maryland suburbs of Washington, D.C. His latest novel is *Dragon Venom*. The Misenchanted Page is at *http://www.watt-evans.com*.

he young duke glanced around uneasily as he waited for the wizard's door to open; he was uncomfortably aware of how very little he knew about magic in general, and the wizard Rasec in particular. Magicians were notoriously eccentric, and it was obvious from the bizarre and haphazard architecture of Rasec's home that he was no exception. Rasec had always been a cooperative neighbor and had never given previous dukes any real trouble—but Lord Croy was not any of the previous dukes. He was the last duke's third son, acceding to the title only because of the recent plague that had taken his father and both his older brothers, as well as a good part of the local population.

As the new duke, it behooved Croy to pay a courtesy call on the wizard. It would not do to antagonize his realm's only real magician—especially when that magician might be able to assist in preventing any further outbreaks of plague.

Croy hoped he had not erred in choosing the size of his escort; he did not want to threaten the wizard, but it would not do for the duke to travel alone. Back at the castle, a dozen had seemed about right, but here on the stony hilltop, at the door of the wizard's home, the twelve guardsmen seemed like an entire mob.

The latch rattled, and Croy looked directly forward, composing his features. The door opened, and there was the wizard's inhuman servant.

Croy suppressed a shudder. The creature standing in the doorway stood between four and five feet tall, with gleaming gray hairless skin, naked and sexless. Its face was narrow and triangular, its eyes golden, its ears large and pointed.

"Please come in, my lords," it said, stepping aside. "My master awaits you in his chamber of art."

"Thank you," Croy replied as he stepped across the threshold.

He hoped he had the protocols right; he had never been trained for any of this, had never accompanied his father here. His elder brothers had both been taught a duke's duties and privileges, but no one had seen any reason to include a *third* son, and now he was forced to improvise.

He led the way into the house, his soldiers marching behind him, two abreast.

The servant directed them down a broad corridor, and another, identical servant waited at the far end, its hand on the handle of a great oaken door. Croy, startled, glanced from one servant to the other, looking for some distinguishing marks, some way to tell them apart.

He could see no difference at all; the two were so alike that he wondered whether Rasec might have found a way to have his servant in two places at once.

But then the second servant opened the oaken door, and Croy was struck dumb by the wonders of the wizard's sanctum.

The circular chamber was vast but windowless, lit by a ring of crystal skylights; the bright midday sunlight gleamed and sparkled from a thousand strange devices arranged on shelves, mounted on iron rods, or suspended from the ceiling on wires. There were tangles of polished brass and gleaming ebony, layered constructions of silver and ivory, mummified beasts pierced by golden wires, and things that Croy could not even begin to identify.

And in the center of the room stood Rasec, dressed in flowing robes of red and yellow silk, holding a golden scepter. Behind him stood his servant.

A *third* servant, Croy realized, indistinguishable from the others.

Croy hesitated at the door for only a fraction of a second before striding into the great room. He walked directly toward the wizard, along a red carpet laid out for him, and stopped at a polite distance, perhaps seven feet away.

The wizard bowed deeply, and Croy felt an immense rush of relief; Rasec had acknowledged his authority.

"My lord Duke," the enchanter said. "Welcome to my home; you honor us with your presence."

Croy bowed in return, though only a small formal bob. "Thank you, Sir Wizard," he said.

"May I ask, Your Grace, to what do I owe this honor?"

"Of course," Croy replied. "I have come to assure us both of the continued good will between our houses, and to discuss certain matters with you."

"I have only the best of intentions toward you, Your Grace, as I did toward your late, lamented father. I extend my most heartfelt condolences on your recent losses."

"Thank you; I am reassured to hear this. As I'm sure you will understand, I have found myself thrust into a role for which I was not completely prepared; I was not entirely certain just what arrangements might exist between my father and yourself."

"The arrangements are simplicity itself, Your Grace—but forgive me, before we continue this, might I ask why you have brought these others with you?" He gestured over Croy's shoulder at the dozen guardsmen.

"Merely an honor guard, Sir Wizard. If they trouble you, perhaps you could find a place for them to wait?"

The wizard nodded, then beckoned. "You!" he called. "Is it Nampach? See these gentlemen to the rose garden."

One of the gray servant creatures responded from the doorway,

"Yes, sir." Then it turned to the soldiers. "If you would follow me, please?"

"My lord?" Tilza, the squad's captain, asked uncertainly.

"Go with it," Croy said. "Enjoy the flowers, find a bench and rest your feet. I'll send for you when I need you."

The captain saluted, wheeled on his heel, and barked an order.

As the party marched away, Croy said, "If you don't mind my asking, Sir Wizard, what *are* those gray creatures?"

"Homunculi," Rasec answered. "I made them some time ago; I find them more reliable than human servants. They eat little, never sleep, and require no clothing. I have five of them, and they attend my needs quite effectively."

"I confess, they appear so similar that I cannot tell one from another."

"Yes, I cast them all in the same mold; I can't tell them apart by appearance myself. I'm not sure *they* can distinguish one another. Their personalities vary, though. Nampach is the brightest of them; it will make sure your men are safe." He lowered the scepter he still held, and asked, "Shall we make ourselves comfortable?"

"That would be fine," Croy replied, glancing around for somewhere to sit.

As he turned his head, he heard the wizard say, "Here, take this," and from the corner of his eye he glimpsed the wizard handing the scepter to the servant behind him.

Then a loud metallic ringing startled him, and his head snapped back.

The servant had dropped the scepter, and it had bounced on the stone floor; as Croy watched, it rolled under a nearby cabinet.

"Idiot!" Rasec bellowed. "Clumsy fool!"

The servant dove toward the cabinet, and in an instant knelt before it, groping for the scepter.

"Leave it for now," the wizard snapped. "Fetch two chairs from my study and *then* get it out."

"Yes, sir," the servant muttered. It got to its feet, essayed an awkward bow, then tried to back out of the room, but bumped into a framework of wires and brass rods that jangled and wobbled.

"Watch where—oh, just get the chairs."

"Yes, master," the servant said, bowing quickly before turning to hurry out.

"As you can see," the wizard said, "they aren't perfect. Every so often one of them seems to lose its wits temporarily and begin bumping into things or dropping them. It's very aggravating; there must be a flaw in the design, but I have no idea where it lies."

The young duke nodded as he watched the homunculus vanish, then looked back at Rasec and found the wizard staring at him expectantly.

"Ah," Croy said, gathering his wits. "Yes. Regarding any arrangements you might have had with my late father, uh . . ." He could think of no graceful way to complete the question, and after a moment's hesitation asked simply, "Were there any?"

Rasec smiled. "Our arrangement was quite simple, as I believe I started to say once before. He left me alone, and I left him alone. In exchange for being permitted to remain here untroubled and untaxed, I agreed to provide magical services when necessary, with the very clear understanding that such necessities could not be frequent."

"I see," Croy said. "It sounds straightforward, and I hope we can continue in the same fashion."

"Of course, Your Grace."

A movement caught Croy's eye, and he glanced over the wizard's shoulder to see the servant returning, hauling two chairs, one under each arm.

Rasec noticed Croy's gaze and turned in time to see the servant drop one of the chairs. It clattered on the stone floor, and the servant looked up, stricken.

"Imbecile!" the wizard raged, raising a fist—a fist, Croy saw with astonishment, that was *glowing*.

The servant cringed, then quickly set the undropped chair upright, positioned for the wizard's use, and hurried to retrieve the other.

The glow faded from Rasec's upraised hand.

"My apologies, Your Grace," he said. "I don't know what's wrong with them tonight." He looked down at the chair, then sighed. "And the stupid thing has given me the wrong chair; this is by far the better of the two, and therefore yours." He pushed the chair across, and Croy accepted it.

"Thank you," he said as he seated himself.

Then the servant placed the other chair, and the wizard settled into it. He rubbed at one of the carved wooden arms.

"It's ruined the finish here, do you see?"

Croy nodded, and cast a look at the servant who had brought the chairs, who was once again on its knees, groping under the cabinet where the scepter had rolled.

"You have heard of the plague, Sir Wizard. Do you have any idea, then, what might have *caused* it?"

"Foul air, I would guess," Rasec said. He turned at the sound of the servant's approach.

The creature had finally managed to retrieve the scepter, somewhat the worse for wear; cobwebs had wrapped themselves around the shaft, and one of the ornamental protrusions on the head was visibly bent. The servant held it out for its master.

"I don't want it," Rasec snapped. "Put it somewhere!"

The creature blinked. "Where, master?"

"Somewhere even *you* can find it again!"

The servant looked down at the scepter, closing both hands on the heavy shaft; it looked at the wizard.

Then with horrifying suddenness it swung the scepter up in a swift arc and brought it slamming down on the wizard's head.

Croy jumped from his chair with a wordless shout and caught Rasec as he slumped sideways.

The servant flung the scepter aside and ran; Croy, holding the wizard's crumpled body, was unable to pursue. Instead, he shouted, "Stop! Help!"

The servant ignored him and vanished through the nearest doorway.

"Help!" Croy bellowed. "We need help here!" He looked around the room but saw only inanimate devices; then he looked down at Rasec.

What he saw did not look good; there was a visible dent in the old man's skull and blood seeping from a hole made by one of the points on the scepter.

"Sir Wizard," he said, "can you hear me?" He lifted the wizard's shoulders, and the head flopped backward limply. Croy could not hear any breath, nor did the wizard's chest show any sign of a beating heart.

Rasec did not respond to his question; even if the wizard still lived, he was obviously not conscious.

"Help!" Croy shouted again.

This time he received an answer. "What appears to be . . . ?" a voice began.

Croy turned to see the servant reentering the room through a different door—or so he thought at first, but then he realized that this was probably *not* the servant who had wielded the scepter, but one of the others.

The newcomer caught sight of the wizard and did not complete its question.

"Fetch my men," Croy barked. "Bring them at once. Nampach took them to the rose garden."

"At once, my lord. And I'll send someone to tend to my master."

"Bring my men first," Croy barked. "I'll do what I can for your master, but I fear it's too late."

"Yes, sir."

Then the servant was gone, and Croy was alone with the wizard.

He knelt and put an ear to the narrow chest, then felt a bony wrist; he could find neither heartbeat nor pulse, and the flesh already seemed to be cooling.

The wizard Rasec was dead.

An hour later Rasec had been laid out upon his bed, and Croy's men had the five servants under guard in a bare stone storeroom. That was where Croy confronted them.

The soldiers had found the five scattered about the house and had brought them here. All five had vehemently denied killing the wizard and had not admitted to any knowledge of which of their fellows might have committed this heinous act.

It was up to Croy to decide what to do with them all.

The simplest thing would be to have them all put to death, on the grounds of conspiracy to commit murder—and as duke he certainly had the authority to do so—but these five were probably the only beings alive who knew anything about Rasec's magic, who knew their way around the household, who knew whether Rasec had any family.

And more important, four of them might be innocent of wrongdoing, and while they were not human, still they surely deserved whatever justice he could arrange.

He could have freed them all, pardoned the killer, perhaps let it be known that the wizard had died of the plague, but that would leave a murderer alive and loose on his lands, and furthermore, Rasec deserved better. That meant that Croy needed to determine which of the five had killed their master.

Looking at the five of them seated on the storeroom floor, however, he could see no way at all to distinguish one from another.

"Fetch me ribbons, or strips of cloth," he ordered one of his soldiers. "Tear them from draperies if you must. I need at least five different colors."

The man saluted and hurried away, leaving Croy standing in the storeroom doorway, looking in at the homunculi. Their inhuman faces were hard to read, but none of them appeared any more agitated than the others.

"This is a serious matter," Croy said. "Your master has been killed, do you understand that? I must question you to determine who is responsible. Lying to me in such a circumstance is grounds for execution."

"We understand, my lord," said one of them. The others nodded agreement.

That said, Croy tried to think what to ask, but the words did not want to come. He was distracted by footsteps and turned to see the soldier returning.

"I found the kitchen rag pile, Your Grace," the man said, holding out several strips of cloth.

Croy selected five—red, white, green, blue, and brown—and tossed them to the homunculi. "Now," he said, "each of you will wear one of these tied around your right arm at all times so that we can tell you apart."

The servants sorted out the tags and secured them in place, as ordered, with varying degrees of reluctance.

"I wonder," Croy said, "that your master never saw fit to label you. Could he tell you apart by sight?"

"No," said the nearest, who now wore a green band around its arm.

"He knew our voices," said the creature wearing the white band.

"I don't think he *cared* which of us was which," said the brown-wearing servant.

"He called one of you by name," Croy said. "Nampach."

"He had heard me speak just a few moments before," said the one wearing white.

"You are Nampach?"

"Yes, Your Grace."

Croy looked at the green-banded servant and asked, "Can *you* tell your companions apart by their voices?"

"Usually, my lord."

"Close your eyes."

The one in green obeyed.

"Now, tell me each name as you hear each voice." Croy pointed to the brown-banded creature.

"What would you have me say, my lord?"

"That's either Suturb or Nahris," the green promptly announced.

"I'm Suturb."

Croy pointed to the white.

"I take it I should not say my own name." The voice was somehow a little richer than Suturb's.

"Nampach."

Croy nodded, and pointed again, choosing red this time.

"I'm Suturb," the indicated homunculus said.

"Is it Suturb again?" the green asked. "You sound more like Nahris."

"It's Nahris," Nampach said.

"It is," Nahris admitted. "I was just seeing if I could fool you."

That left one who had not spoken, wearing a blue band; Croy pointed.

The blue-banded creature did not respond immediately, but Nahris prodded it with a thumb, and it said, "I can't think of anything to say."

"Thoob," the green-wearer pronounced as it opened its eyes. "And my name is Yar, my lord."

It occurred to Croy that perhaps he should be able to recognize the murderer's voice himself; after all, he had heard the creature speak. Unfortunately, he could not be certain; while there were subtle differences, the voices were fairly similar, and he had not been listening carefully when the killer replied to the wizard's commands.

He was fairly sure that it hadn't been Nampach, since Nampach had been sent to escort his men to the rose garden.

"Which of you answered the door and admitted us?" he asked.

"I did, my lord," Yar replied.

None of the others spoke up, but Croy asked Nampach, "Is that right?"

"I believe so, Your Grace."

That left three. "And which of you was assisting your master in the great chamber?"

The homunculi glanced at one another, but none spoke.

"Your Grace, we may not be as clever as true men," Nampach said after a moment's awkward silence, "and I can scarcely comprehend the thinking of one who would strike our master, but I do not believe you will catch the killer *that* easily! We all know that the one who was serving in the great chamber is the murderer."

"And do any of you know which it was? Nampach?"

"Alas, I do not, Your Grace."

"Yar?"

"No, my lord."

"Thoob?"

The blue-marked creature shook its head.

"Suturb?"

"I know only that I was not there."

"Nahris?"

"I say what Suturb said, my lord."

"One of you is lying."

"One of us is," Nahris agreed, "but I assure you, it is not me."

Croy stared at the five of them for a moment, remembering puzzles he had heard as a boy about men who always lied but might, by clever questioning, be coerced into yielding useful information.

Unfortunately, these creatures were not so limited; they could speak lies or the truth as they pleased. And presumably, only one of them knew who was guilty, so the others had no information to yield.

He had narrowed it down to three, in any case. That was a start. He could not spot the killer by appearance, nor by voice; what did that leave?

Actions, of course—actions, so it was said, spoke louder than words. The killer had been clumsy, constantly dropping things—but Rasec had said that all of them had spells of clumsiness.

Was there some *pattern* to those spells, some way to determine which of them was afflicted today?

"Yar," he said, "come with me." He gestured to the soldiers. "You two, with us. The rest of you wait here."

Leaving the remaining servants under guard, he led Yar and his two chosen men down the corridor and into the scullery. There he posted the two soldiers at the door, then turned and looked at the servant's wary face.

"You need have no fear," Croy said. "You and Nampach are not suspected, and even if we find it necessary to hang all three of the others, you two will be free to go your own way. In fact, it may be that we will find a comfortable place for you."

"Thank you, my lord," Yar said, bowing—but its expression did not entirely relax.

"I sincerely hope that we will *not* find it necessary to hang two innocents, but the guilty party cannot be permitted to live; I hope you understand that."

"I believe I do, my lord."

"Good. Now, I noticed something about the killer's behavior. Your late master said that there was a flaw in your construction and that sometimes you have spells in which you lose your wits and become quite clumsy. Are you familiar with this?"

"Of course, my lord; I have seen my companions drop fragile objects or trip over their own feet, on occasion."

Croy nodded. "And when did *you* last experience such a spell?"

Yar hesitated. "My lord, I do not remember *ever* experiencing one."

Croy frowned. "Speak honestly, now, or it will go ill with you."

"My lord, I *am* speaking honestly! I do not say I have never experienced such a spell, merely that I do not *remember* one. I have seen them affect the others, and perhaps one result of the unhappy event is that one does not remember it."

"Very well. But you have seen all the others afflicted?"

Yar hesitated again, then said, "I do not know, my lord."

Croy sighed. "Explain yourself," he said.

"I have certainly seen *someone* be clumsy, at least half a dozen times," Yar said, "but I don't know which of my fellows was involved in each instance. The clumsy one did not generally speak, and without a voice I cannot tell them apart any more than you can."

"Have you ever seen more than one be clumsy at a time?"

Yar thought that over carefully, then said, "No, my lord."

"Might it be that only one of you is *ever* afflicted?"

"Our master said there was a flaw in our design, my lord, and we were all made to the same design."

"But of your own knowledge, you cannot say how many have actually been affected?"

"No, my lord, I cannot."

"Have you ever seen one of your fellows lose its temper? It seemed to me that the blow was struck in a fit of rage, without planning or forethought; I cannot otherwise account for how anyone could be so foolish as to slay your master today, when my men and I were here, rather than on some private occasion when no witnesses were present."

"Indeed, my lord, I cannot imagine how it could be otherwise."

"Have you ever seen one of them lose its temper?"

"Often, my lord. Nampach was furious at the mice in the pantry, and the other day Thoob went shouting across the yard about something. Someone threw a pot at me once, but I never determined who was responsible. I fear we are all as prone to anger as any human."

"Do you have any idea who slew your master?"

Yar looked down at the floor for a long moment before replying, "I have no knowledge of who did it, my lord. Sometimes I think it might have been Nahris, as part of a joke gone wrong, but I have no evidence to support that suspicion."

"It appeared to be a fit of temper, not a joke gone wrong."

"And all of us are capable of fits of temper."

"Indeed. Thank you, Yar. You are free to go."

Nampach was the next to be questioned. Its responses were much like Yar's, right down to acknowledging that fits of clumsiness were common, but denying any memory of ever having had one itself.

"Nor am I aware of any gaps in my memory, Your Grace," it said. "But I suppose I might have lost the memory of such gaps, as well."

Croy had definite suspicions about the clumsiness now. "Can you say for certain which of your fellows *have* had these spells? I realize you cannot say with certainty who has *not,* but can you confirm any who *have?*"

Nampach had to think about that, and finally answered simply, "No."

Each of the others, in turn, denied any memory of experiencing bouts of awkwardness.

"I don't think I've ever seen Nampach drop anything," Suturb volunteered. "Nahris is usually quite agile, but there have been incidents that might have been its doing."

Nahris shrugged when asked who had been clumsy. "I'm afraid I just haven't paid attention, my lord."

"They always blame me," Thoob said, "but I never drop anything! I think it's mostly Yar, my lord."

Whereas Yar and Nampach had been released, the three still under suspicion were escorted back to the storeroom after questioning.

"Perhaps we could use the wizard's magic to determine the guilty party, Your Grace," Captain Tilza suggested. "These creatures have been assisting him; surely, they must have learned some of the art! Ask the two you trust to work a spell that will compel the truth."

Croy shook his head. He did not like the idea of inviting the homunculi to practice the arcane arts; it seemed somehow unholy. And besides . . .

"I have a simpler idea," he said, picking three apples from a bin. "One I really should have thought of sooner."

Fruit in hand, he returned to the storeroom.

The three suspects were seated on the floor, simply waiting; they looked up at his arrival.

"Catch!" he said, tossing an apple.

The red-banded homunculus, Nahris, caught the apple easily and looked up questioningly.

Croy tossed another, and Suturb, banded with brown, snatched it from the air. The third was lobbed toward blue-marked Thoob.

It bounced from Thoob's fingers, ricocheted from Nahris's shoulder, and was neatly captured by Suturb just short of the floor. Suturb handed it to Thoob.

"Now, toss them back," Croy ordered.

Suturb tossed its apple in a gentle overhand; Nahris glanced at the others, then used a sidearm snap to send its fruit back to the duke's hand.

Thoob demanded, "Why? What's going on?"

"Suturb, Nahris," Croy said, "please move back, away from Thoob."

"Why?" Thoob asked angrily as the others obeyed.

"You dropped the scepter," Croy said. "You dropped a chair. You couldn't catch the apple."

"I didn't catch the apple, but I didn't drop any scepter! That was one of *them* having an attack, it wasn't me!"

"No one has any attacks, Thoob," Croy said. "You're just clumsy. There's no design flaw in anyone else; it's just *you*. You're *always* clumsy and awkward. But you've been blaming the others when you break things, saying it wasn't you, so everyone, even poor Rasec, believed you and thought that you *all* had moments of ineptitude."

"We all *do*!"

"I don't think so."

"The master *said* so!"

"Because you fooled him."

"I didn't fool him! He knew it was me all along!" Thoob leaned forward, hands on the floor, as it shouted. "He said it was the others so they wouldn't realize he was always yelling at *me*, never at anyone else. He made me clumsy on purpose so he'd have someone to take out his bad temper on, and I put up with it for years. I played along. I let him mock me and abuse me in front of the others, but when he shouted at me in front of *you*, the new duke—"

Thoob suddenly stopped, realizing what it had said. It looked around, at the shocked expressions on Nahris and Suturb, the determined ferocity of the soldiers guarding the door, and the sadness on Lord Croy's face, and licked its lips.

"Kill it," Croy said, stepping aside to make room for the guardsmen.

The soldiers drew their swords and stepped forward to obey their lord's command.

# Au Purr

## Esther Friesner

Nebula Award winner Esther Friesner is the author of twenty-nine novels and more than one hundred short stories, in addition to being the editor of six popular anthologies. Her articles on fiction writing have appeared in *Writer's Market* and *Writer's Digest* books. Besides winning two Nebula Awards in succession for Best Short Story (1995 and 1996, from the Science Fiction Writers of America), she was a Nebula finalist twice and a Hugo finalist once. She received the Skylark Award from NESFA and the award for Most Promising New Fantasy Writer of 1986 from *Romantic Times*.

She lives in Connecticut with her husband, two children, two rambunctious cats, and a fluctuating population of hamsters.

didn't mind that the job paid nothing, or the way I was getting roughed up on a daily basis by a plug-ugly who just didn't like my looks, or being so close to my niece and nephew without being able to let them know I was there. That stuff I could handle. What really frosted my cauldron was all those blasted *mice*.

"Look, Joram, look!" little Niko exclaimed, tugging at the cook's apron and pointing proudly in my direction. He was my biggest advocate in what had once been my sister Magda's house. "Snowball's caught another one! Isn't she a *good* kitty?"

I sat with my forepaws together, posed in the most fetching way I knew how, a dead mouse dangling from my mouth by its tail. (I truly hated the mousing part of my masquerade—never could stand the taste of rodents, large or small, even when they were just a minor flavoring agent in one of my brews—but mousing was what *real* cats did. I couldn't let a little thing like personal taste foul up an otherwise perfect infiltration.) I knew I was the living embodiment of cuteness, an entry in the *Pictorial Dictionary of Adorable Felines* just waiting to happen, but to make sure of it I tilted my head slightly to the side and managed to utter one small, hopeful "Mew?"

"Snowball," the cook muttered peevishly through lips thicker than blood sausages. "It'd be Meatball if I had it my way." That plug-ugly I mentioned earlier? Him: Joram the cook. He had a brick-thick body, a brain to match, and a bad habit of throwing heavy pots at me whenever I ventured into the kitchen unescorted. He even managed to kick me in the rump once or twice, before I got my guard up. A nasty piece of work inside and out, that one, and he'd made it clear from my first day on the job that he had no use for me or for cats in general.

The big lug didn't dare lay a hand on me while I was with Niko, though. He could only express his hostility with witty sallies. It was like watching a troll try to make spitballs out of spiderweb.

"Snowball's a good kitty," Niko said, answering his own rhetorical question. He knelt down, threw his arms around me, and gave me a fierce cuddling, dead mouse or no dead mouse. "Why won't you let her eat in the kitchen? She'd take real good care of things down here. Lady Ulla keeps complaining that you've got too many mice running around and—"

"Lady Ulla likes to complain," Joram replied. "She hasn't bothered to examine my kitchen; she just assumes that because there's mice in the rest of the house, it's the same down here. Which it ain't! That's 'cause I keep a kitchen that's clean enough to eat off, and I don't need no blasted cats to help me do it!"

"But—" Niko tried to argue.

Joram turned his back on him and plunged both hammy hands into the wad of bread dough in the kneading trough before him. Great clouds of flour rose up all around. "Look, boy, in case you ain't noticed, I don't like cats," he said. "You're the master's son: you can order me to keep that mongrel's food dish down here if you want, but I wouldn't advise it. Ever wonder how come I *don't* have mice in my kitchen?"

"I—I guess it's 'cause—," Niko began.

"Traps," the cook said, snapping off the word as sharply as if it were the spring-loaded, back-crushing crossbar of those very devices. "Traps and . . . other ways. And if you're fool enough to care what becomes of that worthless beast of yours, you'll keep it out of my kitchen before it sticks its nose where it don't belong and gets it bit off clean!"

The big oaf's angry words frightened Niko badly. He scooped me up in his arms and held me tight to his chest. Tears were brimming in his eyes. I made a vow to repay the cook with interest for upsetting my poor, orphaned nephew so deeply.

"You wouldn't *really* let anything happen to Snowball, would you, Joram?" the child asked, his voice shaking. "I'll keep her out of your kitchen the best I can, honest I will, but what if sometime when I'm having my lessons she comes down here by accident? You'd keep her away from the traps, wouldn't you?"

The cook said nothing, but the floury clouds thickened around him as he pounded the devil out of the bread dough.

"Joram, *please* say you won't let Snowball get hurt!" Niko begged. "Please! You know how much—" A small sob shook him. "How much Mama would have loved her."

Oh, clever Niko! And clever without actually meaning to be so, which is always the best way. I had been living in my late sister's household long enough to know that Magda had been well loved by all of her servants, even the loutish Joram. The white clouds around him subsided as he paused in his yeasty labors and turned back to face Niko.

"Your mama was a great lady," he said. "We won't see her like again, that's certain. Never was a more loving heart than hers, nor one more ready to do a good deed for a helpless living creature. She changed all I ever thought about witches and how they're supposed to be so cold and cruel."

"That's 'cause you never knew any *real* witches until Mama," Niko said. Poor baby, you could tell his heart was breaking over the memories of his mother, but he'd managed to salvage pride out of the pain. "None of the ones that were her friends were bad, either, but she always said that it was just the bad ones that people remembered. Please, Joram, promise you'll be nicer to Snowball. It's what Mama would've asked you to do."

The cook's mouth hardened. He was torn between his usual boorish nature and his abiding love for my late sister. At last he said, "All right. I won't let nothin' bad happen to it while it's anywhere I can see. But that's all."

"You can't just *say* that, Joram; you have to *promise*." My little nephew could be as hard to shake as a bulldog. "You have to *swear on your honor* you'll look out for her."

"Good, good, I swear, I swear it already!" The cook raised the first two fingers of his right hand, licked them, and stroked both sides of his mustache. It was an odd gesture, but I remembered when Magda first introduced me to her new cook and told me he was a veteran mariner, newly come to her off one of the great ships in Ferdralli harbor. *Sailor-folk have odd ways, Alisande,* she'd said. *But Joram's got a good heart and a talent for cookery that's just this side of sorcerous.*

A good heart . . . I'd yet to see any evidence of that, beyond his fanatical devotion to my sister's memory. I didn't understand how Magda could have any praise at all for a man who made no secret of his hatred for cats.

Then again, I also didn't understand how my beautiful baby sister could be dead.

The news had hit me like a thunderbolt, a shock that arrived on the doorstep of my town house in the city of Crowfield in the innocent guise of a letter from her husband, Kopp. The fact that he had written it with his own hand should have forewarned me that something was gravely wrong: Kopp never wrote to me. Kopp never wrote to *anyone*. He was one of Ferdralli's wealthiest merchants, a man who left the tedious business of correspondence to his hirelings. For this, however, he had taken up the pen himself, in fingers more accustomed to forming numbers in a ledger than words on a page. He never was one to waste words any more than coins. No fine figures of speech or empty phrases of consolation cushioned the brutality of what his letter had to say. It was like reading a laundry list:

1. Magda was dead. He had come home from the waterfront to find her body sprawled across the kitchen floor.
2. He had made all the final arrangements, including her burial, and was sorry that these could not wait for me to make the long trip from Crowfield to Ferdralli and attend my sister's funeral, but it was summer, and he thought that a woman of my

intelligence didn't need to have some things spelled out for her.

3. He was leaving Ferdralli at once on a trading voyage to Beska.
4. The children would stay home, in the expert care of their governess, Lady Ulla.
5. I was welcome to come and visit anytime I liked. He hoped I would not wait for his return to do so, since he didn't think I wanted to see him any more than he wanted to see me.

That letter was Kopp all over, blunt as a barrel stave, practical as a pair of waterproof boots. He didn't like me because he'd been raised to believe that all witches were evil creatures. It didn't matter that he'd married one; you could tell just by looking at the love in his eyes whenever he gazed at my sister that he'd enthroned her in his mind as the exception that proves the rule.

I let out a groan fit to rouse the dead when I read that letter, a groan loud enough to bring my loyal servant Scalini running to see what was wrong. Scalini did not run, as a rule; for preference, he slithered. Scalini also did not work unless strictly enjoined, nagged, and browbeaten. Before my spells had summoned him from Underrealm, he had been the eldest spawn of Rax, the demon lord in charge of intentionally negligent schoolchildren. Scalini had appeared before me in a burst of flame, attended by a pack of homework-devouring hounds, and I'd slapped the indenture bondspells on him before fully determining what he was.

That was a mistake. It takes talent to raise a demon, and plenty of power to control him the instant he sets foot in this world; it's not one of those spells you can whip out on a whim. I summoned Scalini years ago, when I was still working on a limited budget but needed some serious help around the house and in my craftwork. Demons don't just *know* magic, they *are* magic, plus they do windows if you lay the bondspells on them properly. I thought that by summoning a demon I'd found the best and cheapest way to solve my problems. I put all my eggs into one basket, as it were, only to wind up with those same eggs all over my face. Scalini was loyal, but otherwise useless. However, he was also sympathetic, for a demon. The news of my sister's death moved him to tears.

Tears and more.

"*He* did it!" Scalini thundered. "That grabpenny husband of hers did this to her. It's no natural death she died, you mark me, mistress. Why else would the lubberlout have her poor body shoved into the ground and get himself out of town so quick? So you can't come and make the corpse talk to tell you how she truly died!"

I tried to assuage Scalini by telling him that I had never really gotten the hang of necromancy. Any corpse I came across would keep its secrets.

He was not to be comforted.

"And who's this Lady Ulla when she's at home, eh? Probably the husband's by-the-way bed warmer."

"Lady Ulla is an impoverished noblewoman whose family fled the kingdom of Tyrshen in the days following the Unpleasantness," I explained. For the life of me I never did understand why folks insisted on referring to the Tyrshen bloodbath as *the Unpleasantness*. Due to an unfortunate combination of circumstances, the crops had failed, the dam had burst, the peasants had revolted, the Queen had died without legitimate issue, the witches had gone on strike, and the wizards had decided to throw demon armies at one another all at the same time. It was like referring to the Baby-Eating Black Dragon of Koolai as *the skink*.

"Tyrshen!" Scalini echoed sarcastically. "That nest of would-be wand-wielders? My folk know all about people from Tyrshen, especially the aristocrats. They're never satisfied to leave magic to the professionals, oh no! They have to force every last one of their talentless brats to try a hand at it. So the nobles' kids learn a spell or two, which they generally bollix up past all recognition *if* they're lucky, and forever after they're trotted out when company comes to call and told, 'Show Auntie Inez how you turn a goldfish into a goat, darling.' They could accomplish the same thing if they'd just give the tykes spinet lessons, and then they wouldn't have to worry about what to do with all those goats!"

"Scalini, Lady Ulla no longer has to worry about goats, goldfish, or spinet lessons. Her whole family was wiped out and her lands seized. She's only a governess now."

"A governess who was taught magic in her salad days." There was no diverting my demon. "A governess who saw that the road to success led through your brother-in-law's bed! Your sister likely caught them at their games, made threats, and had to be gotten out of the way."

I rolled my eyes wearily. The news of Magda's death had dealt me a blow that drained me of all desire to debate the details of it. I decided not to waste my breath pointing out that Lady Ulla was a sting-tongued woman with an education that left her smarter than most men and an abiding belief that marital relations were the gods' painful, humiliating way of punishing mortals. She was hardly the foundation on which to build an adulterous fantasy, but I knew better than to take the road of reason with Scalini. There was no arguing with demons at the best of times, especially not with one whose sire, if not the Father of All Lies, was certainly the Father of All Excuses.

Before I could instruct Scalini to let the subject drop, he announced, "Your sister was always highly thought of among my folk. She never overworked any demon she invoked"—here he gave me a meaningful look—"and her pronunciation of our names was flawless. That sort of thing means a lot to us. By all unholy, I hereby vow upon the left hoof of Vadryn the Venomous that I will take a horrible vengeance upon the one who encompassed her death! Yea, upon him and all that is his, I swear it!"

And with that, he vanished in a puff of bloody smoke that reeked of sewage and rotten apples.

I did the only thing that I could do, under the circumstances: I went over to my friend Pella's house and had a cup of tea.

"Murdered?" Pella echoed after I had recounted the whole affair. "Are you sure of that?"

"I am now," I replied. Pella was not a witch—though she was a bit of a sorceress when it came to baking tea cakes—so I often had to explain professional matters to her. "Vadryn the Venomous is the most puissant prince of the Underrealm. When a demon takes an oath on his left hoof, its validity is instantly reviewed by the demon lord himself. If Vadryn decides it's just silly, he tears the oath-maker limb from limb."

"My!" Pella was impressed. "Not too well known for his patience, is he?"

"Nor for his forbearance *nor* forgiveness, but they're not demonic virtues, are they? On the other hand, if he finds that the vow in question serves his idea of justice, he grants the oath-taker full immunity from all other obligations until the pledge is fulfilled. The fact that Scalini was able to vanish from my sight, despite the binding spells laid on him when I first summoned him to my service, means that Vadryn approved his oath of vengeance."

Pella laid one finger to her lower lip in thought. "Which in turn must mean that your sister *was* murdered. Oh, Alisande, I'm so sorry!"

"Not as sorry as I'll be if Scalini's not stopped. He thinks that Kopp killed her, which is bad enough, but his oath includes vengeance on Kopp and on *all that is his.*"

Pella's hands flew to her face. "The children!"

I nodded. "Scalini never thinks things through. He certainly didn't when he made that oath. Not that it matters now; he's bound to it."

"Um . . ." Pella toyed with her teacup, looking ill at ease. "Are you sure Kopp *didn't* kill Magda?"

"Oh, *please.* He adored her."

"But that letter he sent you, the one you showed me just now. It was so—so cold."

I shrugged. "What if we judged every soul by how well they poured their heart's blood out on parchment?"

"But he fled the country!"

"And his grief, I'll wager. I'm thankful for that. Scalini abhors salt water. It comes from all that slug blood on his mother's side of the family. He can't touch Kopp until he returns to Ferdralli."

"But the children! The children are still there. Won't he—?"

"He swore to destroy the murderer and all that's his. *In that order.* I've dealt with demons long enough to know that they set unnatural store by the letter of the law. Niko and Mira are safe enough while their father stays out of Scalini's reach."

"Yes, but when he does come home again . . ."

"Well, by that time let's hope the real murderer's identity has come to light." I smiled, but there was no joy behind it. "I'll be most grateful for a box of your tea cakes for the road, Pella, and a couple of loaves of your best bread. It's not a long journey to Ferdralli, but it's hungry going nonetheless."

I made my first visit to my late sister's house in my own guise, just to get the lay of the land. The children were overjoyed to see me, poor lambs. I found Lady Ulla to be less than welcoming, with a shiftiness in her eyes that made me suspicious. Perhaps Scalini's melodramatic ravings weren't so far off the mark, after all. The otherwise impoverished governess wore a gold locket around her neck. When I admired it aloud, she opened it readily and showed me the painted face of her great-niece, a lovely girl living in the same genteel poverty afflicting Lady Ulla and all highborn Tyrshenese refugees. Even if the governess herself had no designs on a newly single Kopp, could I swear she did not covet him and his wealth for her pretty kinswoman? The lady would bear watching, but I was not in a position to do it effectively if I remained under that roof as a human houseguest.

A cat, on the other hand . . .

As soon as I left Magda's house, I ducked down an alleyway, shucked my clothing, and assumed a cat's shape and seeming. I took care to dirty and draggle my white coat by rolling around in the muck of the alleyway before showing myself to anyone within, the better to elicit pity. I even called up a short cloudburst so that when I climbed the ivy vines outside and scraped my claws against the window of my niece Mira's room, she would have no choice but to take me in. It worked like a charm.

It was the last thing about the job that worked well at all.

I had been nosing around the house for the better part of five months, turning up nothing but Joram's hostility. A cat may prowl where she will, so I made it my purpose as often as possible to slip into Kopp's office, Magda's library, Lady Ulla's chamber, and any other room of the great house that might contain written records of a revealing nature. I could have saved my breath to cool my porridge. Kopp's records were all business, Magda's journals spoke only of domestic joys, and Lady Ulla had apparently devoted her free time to the writing of a wench-and-wizard romance. It wasn't good, but it wasn't proof of murder, either.

Time was running out. One morning, as I sat on the doorsill, I caught the scent of sewage and rotten apples tainting the briny tang of the Ferdralli harbor air. Scalini was lurking nearby. Demons have an uncanny way of knowing when their prey is nigh. Kopp's ship must have been due to dock any day, and once it did—

Once it did, Scalini would slay him and then turn his attention to Niko and Mira.

I had failed in my self-appointed task to discover the true identity of Magda's killer, but I refused to fail in protecting what was left of her family. That very night, with Scalini's reek still strong in my nostrils, I padded up the stairs to the children's room and leaped onto each of their beds in turn, purring loudly in their ears and kneading furiously at their sleeping bodies with claws fully extended. They awoke grumbling, but they woke.

"Snowball?" Mira sat up, rubbing her eyes. She was eight, just two years older than her brother, but already I could see that she'd favor Magda when she was full grown. "What is it, puss?"

I mewed insistently and raced to the door, then back to the foot of her bed, then to the door once more. Short of standing up on my hind legs and announcing, "*This* way and hurry!" I couldn't have done anything more to demonstrate what I needed them to do.

The children exchanged a puzzled look, but they followed me. I scampered down the steps, bringing them to the kitchen. At the far end of that capacious chamber stood the entrance to the wine cellar. It would provide me with the best possible place to use my arts to conceal the children or, if it came to that, to defend them. I planned to lay a shape-change spell on the pair of them down there. Better a live wine cask than a dead dog, or something like that.

Of course the wine cellar door was locked, so without thinking I used a minor spell to cause it to unlatch and swing back on its hinges. That was a mistake: the children were not expecting their beloved stray to work magic. Niko whimpered and clung to Mira, who gasped and goggled at me.

"Children, come with me," I said. "You must. Your lives depend on it." The pair of them continued to regard me in trepidation. A witch's children knew enough to fear the presence of unknown magic.

Mira was the first to recover herself. "Who are you?" she demanded. "*What* are you? Keep away from my little brother, I'm warning you!" She shook off Niko's grasp and thrust her hands out at me. I saw the first faint tinge of magic illuminating her fingertips. She was all bravery and bluff, Magda's girl: she didn't command enough magic to hold off a mouse, yet she stood ready to face demons.

"Mira, it's me, your Aunt Alisande," I said. I would have cast off my disguise, but that would leave me standing before her naked as an egg.

On hearing my name, Niko stopped crying. He squatted down and brought his nose up close to mine. "Prove it," he said.

"I'm *talking* to you," I replied. "I'm a cat and I'm talking to you. Isn't that proof enough?"

"Maybe." He sounded doubtful. "But all shape-shifters can talk, and Lady Ulla says there's lots of things out there that can shape-shift. She says some of them are all right, like witches, but some you better not trust, 'cause they're up to no good, like—like demons and were-wolves and some wizards when they get all—all—I forget. Mira, what did Lady Ulla say about some wizards?"

"They get power-mad," my little niece replied. Her hands dropped to her sides, the twinkle of magic at her fingertips went out. Something wasn't right; her boldness had vanished. Niko had gotten over his initial fear of me (even if he was insisting that I produce proof of my identity; he'd make a great law-speaker someday), but Mira was shaking, and I didn't much care for the glassy look of apprehension in her eyes.

"Mira?" I said gently, taking a step toward her. "Mira, love, what's the matter?"

"Power-mad," she repeated to the air. "They thought that because they knew how to do some tricks, there wasn't anything they *couldn't* do. Lady Ulla said that was bad. Worse than bad; that it was *evil* of them. That only terrible things could come of—of overreaching yourself, of trying to be more than who you were, of—of forgetting your proper place."

"Yes, I'm sure that someone like Lady Ulla *would* be rather insistent that people remember their proper places, as long as hers stayed on top of the heap," I said dryly. "She can't help saying stupid things like that, darling: she's an aristocrat."

"She said that people who tried to get—to get above themselves were proud and that pride is always punished." Mira was taking two steps away for every one I took toward her. It lasted until she backed herself into Joram's big worktable in the middle of the kitchen floor. "She said that pride—pride would out, that the guilty would suffer, soon or late, that they might think it was over and their secret was safe, the price was paid, but when they thought they'd bought safety—"

"*Hogtwaddle!*"

The kitchen resounded with the thunderous echo of steel striking wood. The three of us jumped halfway out of our skins. My eyes flashed sparks, and I spat out a kindling spell that caused all the oil lamps to flare into life.

There, by the butcher block in the corner, stood Joram. He'd struck the thick beechwood tabletop a mighty blow with a cleaver the size of an eagle's wing. "Hogtwaddle!" he roared again, striding forward. "Hogtwaddle and catpiss!" Before I could react, he scooped little Mira up in one arm and cradled her to his hairy chest like a babe.

"I thought we'd settled your mind on that, m'ladylove," he said to her. His voice crooned sweetness, and my niece buried her face against his shoulder, gulping back dry sobs. "There, there, my nestling, you mustn't hold fast to blame. She'd never have wanted that. It was an accident, was all."

"An . . . accident?" I echoed, leaping up onto the butcher block, the better to see my niece and her ferocious guardian. My guts felt cold. "What's all this talk of accidents and blame?"

"Aye, an accident!" Joram rounded on me, shaking the cleaver a finger's span from my whiskers. My gift of speech had not flummoxed him for an instant; he knew me for who I was, and I don't think he liked me any better than when he'd believed I was an ordinary cat. "Care to pretend *you* never had one? Or did you come to the witch's trade when you were already old and full of wisdom, eh?"

"If you're speaking of my *craft*," I said coolly, "then know that my sister and I were both nine when we were first tested and admitted to the study of—oh!" A terrible thought touched me.

We were *tested*. We were brought before the local Gather and examined closely to determine whether we had what was needful for the making of a good witch. We had the brains, but it took more than brains to become one of the Knowing Ones. It took courage and patience and empathy, and above all, it took self-awareness. You had to know yourself: how much ambition you really had; how far you were willing to drive yourself, and for what cause; how much or how little pain, despair, and outright terror you could swallow and suppress if holding it in check meant the difference between a spell that you could harness or a spell that escaped your control and—

"What was it?" I asked Joram. "What kind of spell?" I tried to meet Mira's eyes, but she kept her face hidden. I wanted to let her know that it was all right—or as all right as such a thing could ever be—that accidents did happen, even world-shattering ones.

Even accidents that kill someone you love.

"It wasn't her fault," Joram said, still my niece's staunch defender. "That Lady Ulla, she ought to have her tongue tore out for her, the kind of notions she put into this poor infant's head. All her fine, high tales of witch-queens, spell-castin' girls done up in armor usin' sword and staff to win kingdoms!" He sighed and gazed at Mira's sleek, dark head. "How was she to know the fool was just romancin'? Mira loves her. She believes in her. Between those mad tales and Lady Ulla's harpin' on all she lost when her kin was forced to flee Tyrshen, the child thought to make her a gift of something that might win her back the family holdings."

What was the one thing strong enough to win back a kingdom where wizards battled one another with demon armies?

Another demon. A demon so great, so powerful, so exalted in the hierarchy of the Underrealm that he could clear the battlefield of lesser fiends with one casual sweep of his hoof.

His left hoof.

I erupted from my disguise without a second thought, too blinded by red rage to care about my nakedness. "Ulla, you *idiot!*" I shrieked loud enough to wake the dead.

"Hush, you rude creature." Lady Ulla stood in the kitchen doorway, her scrawny frame wrapped in a thin cotton night-robe, her hair done up in curling rags. "I hear you. The entire neighborhood hears you. What is the meaning of this untoward uproar?"

I couldn't put my fury into words. Instead, I lunged for the old harpy, my fingers curved like cat's claws, ready to tear that sour face clean off the front of her head. And I would have done it, too, if Joram hadn't set Mira down and hooked his meaty arm across my waist, knocking the wind out of me as he reeled me in.

"There'll be none of that in my kitchen!" he instructed us.

"Bitch!" I shrilled at the governess. "Brainless bitch, what were you thinking of, filling my poor niece's head with nonsense?"

Lady Ulla sniffed disdainfully, very much upon her dignity. "Stories are not nonsense if you're dealing with sensible people," she informed

me. "I took great care to teach these precious children the difference between tales and truth."

"If that's so, then why did Mira decide to use magic to give you
back your ancestral lands?" I countered.

"What?" Lady Ulla laid one bony hand to her equally bony breast.
"I never heard the like!"

"Don't play games with me, Ulla. I know what happened: Mira
called up a demon to serve your selfish ends—the demon lord Vadryn
the Venomous, no less!—only she didn't have the knowledge, the
power, or the endurance to lay strong enough bondspells on him once
he appeared. She was helpless against him, trapped, sure to die at his
hands. The only question was how slowly he'd destroy her, how much
he'd enjoy doing it. Magda must have heard the noise he made, must
have come running down here to see what was wrong. She threw down
all her craft as a fire wall between her daughter and the demon lord,
shielding Mira and banishing Vadryn at the same time. Only there
wasn't enough shielding magic left to save herself. *That's* what happened, *that's* how Magda died, and it's all *your* fault!"

*Almost,* said a voice like a thousand chirring locusts. It seeped from
the walls and the floors and the ceiling; it oozed up out of the darkness
beyond the wine cellar door and echoed inside my head. Vadryn the
Venomous, grand demon lord of the Underrealm, stepped out of
shadow and smiled.

*Hail, Alisande,* he said, inclining his horned head toward me with
awful grace. *As great a fool as your sister. She perished for her foolishness
over that brat of hers. So shall you all.* His eyes, bright with blue flames,
surveyed the five of us, and his tongue, which was itself a serpent,
passed hissing over his upper lip.

*It is true that the child summoned me and then lacked the skill to mas-
ter me,* he went on. *But she did not do so at that hag's bidding.*

"Young man, that remark was uncalled-for," Lady Ulla said huffily.
"When you speak of me, I will thank you to keep a civil snake in your
head!"

"You don't mean she decided to do it on her own?" I couldn't believe that in a million years.

*Children are creatures that dwell even more outside of human law than
demons,* Vadryn said. *They are born to nose about, to explore, to experi-*

ment, to dabble. *Even when you tell them not to touch a harmful thing, half may heed you, half will ignore your words, and the other half will regard your ban as an open invitation to embrace what you've forbidden.*

"Lovely," Lady Ulla muttered. "There goes *this* week's mathematics lesson, shot to the Underrealm."

"Are you telling us that Mira raised you because she was . . . experimenting?" I asked.

The fiend-king nodded. *She watched her mother at her craft and wanted to be like her. A shame that the girl did not have the woman's talent for clear pronunciation. She'd heard her mother complaining of the summer heat and was trying to perform a spell to make snow fall out of season.*

I knew that spell. Like all the rest of our repertoire, it was uttered in the Olden Tongue. My skin shivered over my flesh: the spell was rife with words and phrases that came perilously close to the Invocation of a Demon Lord.

"It was a *mistake!*" I exclaimed. "A simple mistake in pronunciation, and you would have killed the child for it?"

Vadryn's empurpled brow creased with perplexity. *Of course. Why not? Tell me that you would not devour a basket of tea cakes if it was delivered to your door by mistake! And a child is much tastier than a tea cake if you get it young enough.* He gazed at Mira and licked his chops.

That was when Lady Ulla hit him with the frying pan.

"How *dare* you, sirrah!" she declaimed. "How dare you stand there before my charges and advocate the illicit appropriation of property that does not pertain to you!"

"Yeah! Or swipin' stuff!" Joram put in. "Even when I was m'self, I never took but what belonged to me. A fine example for the kids!"

*The . . . kids, as you call them, will soon have no further need of ethical examples, good or bad.* Vadryn rubbed the side of his head where Lady Ulla had scored a healthy whack. It hadn't done much damage beyond leaving the demon lord testy. *Food is beyond morality.*

"Oh, no, you're not laying a tooth on them!" I cried, placing myself between the children and the fiend. My skin crackled with the energy of a hundred banishing spells. Even as I stood ready to launch them against Vadryn, I knew that such a sudden expenditure of magic would likely leave me just as dead as it had my poor sister. That didn't matter: I had to protect her children.

*Fool!* Vadryn stamped his hoof. *Any spell of banishment you can lay on me is temporary at best. You, like your sister, lack the full amount of power needful to bar me forever from this place and this prey. You'll kill yourself for nothing, and I'll allow it because it amuses me. Then I'll simply wait out the term of your puny banishment spell once more before coming back and finishing my business here. You can die, or you can be wise, get out of the way, and let me devour what's mine by right.* He took another step closer to the children.

Lady Ulla hit him with the frying pan again at about the same time that Joram chopped at his woolly leg with the cleaver. The demon king jumped back, roaring with rage. I saw lightning gather in his paws and knew that he would slay them both where they stood for their insolence.

Then I saw the sparks gathering at Mira's fingertips. My niece was no longer helpless with remorse and fear. She was angry. The women of my family do some of their best work when they're angry.

I reached out and grabbed one of Mira's hands in mine. "Follow my lead," I whispered. She met my eyes and nodded, looking less like a little girl and more like a battle-ready warrior woman. I felt the untapped depths of the power within her tiny frame and drew on it, weaving those first tender strands of awakening magic into an unbreakable chain with my own. Just as Vadryn leaped for Lady Ulla, I shouted out the words of Ultimate Banishment in the Olden Tongue.

I was *very* careful with my pronunciation.

Just as I spoke the final syllable, I felt someone claim my other hand. My eyes met Scalini's.

"Well, I *did* vow to take a horrible vengeance on whoever encompassed your sister's death," he said just as the demon lord exploded.

It was quite spectacular. The addition of Scalini's power to Mira's and mine made Vadryn the Venomous burst into countless flakes and blobs of radiant ooze that splattered every available surface of Joram's kitchen.

"Great," he said, looking around at the horrid mess in disgust. "That's what I get for givin' help where it wasn't wanted."

"Joram, *you*—?" I began.

He nodded. "Soon as I sensed what you were about doing with the girl, I sent my own mite o' power to join yours. I guess Lady Ulla did the same."

"Just so," Lady Ulla said primly. She lifted her free hand to her lips and blew away the strands of smoke wafting from her fingertips. "I received some instruction in the magical arts when I was but a girl back in Tyrshen. No more than was appropriate to my station, of course. I was raised to be a lady, not a mountebank. I thought I had forgotten it all."

"It's like riding a horse," I explained. "You just need to get back in the saddle for all of it to come back to you. *You*, on the other hand—" I turned to Joram. "How would a simple cook come to command magic? Beyond the making of a decent meringue, that is."

Joram lowered his head and mumbled, "Not just a cook." He looked up and twitched his nose at me. His mustache had gone all bristly, and there was a keen sparkle in his reddened eyes. The side slit of his nightdress parted slightly, revealing a long, hairless tail, which he gathered up in his rosy paws and twiddled nervously. His ears assumed the shape of fish platters, and his skin put out the sleek, black pelt of a fine wharf rat.

The crown on his head was worth a king's ransom, provided that the king in question wasn't afraid of rodents.

"At least that explains your hostility to cats," I remarked.

"Your sister saved m'life," Joram said. "We rats have our enemies— even us royal ones who've got some small measure of magic at our command. It was during a time of troubles that I had to flee my kingdom. Magda gave me the refuge of a human shape, and a place to stay, and a job to do. We rats hate idleness, you know. I'm proud to have had a paw in the destruction of her killer."

I stepped forward and, despite any weak-stomached scruples I felt, clasped his paw. "I couldn't have done it without you," I said. I meant it.

The kitchen proved harder to tidy up than the loose ends left behind by Vadryn's explosive demise. His death immediately threw the Underrealm into a political tizzy. Demons being demons, the tizzy evolved into all-out war before the last bits of Vadryn's shattered body finished dripping down from the kitchen rafters. Trifling matters such as human-demon contracts were cast by the wayside.

"I'm sorry I can't help you with the cleanup here," Scalini said. He wasn't sorry at all, but it was nice of him to lie about it. "Everyone's being recalled."

"Everyone?" Lady Ulla echoed. The two of us, plus Joram and the children, were down on hands and knees scrubbing the fireplace flagstones clean of Vadryn's leftovers. "Even the demon armies in the Tyrshen wizards' service?"

Scalini nodded emphatically.

Lady Ulla got to her feet slowly, stretched out a kink in her back, and announced, "Children, when your father returns from Beska, please convey my regrets that I could not afford him the customary two weeks' notice, but I do believe I have pressing business at home." With that, she set the frying pan on the floor, stepped into it, and after a few initial wobbles flew it straight up the chimney. Niko applauded.

So that, as I told my friend Pella when she came to visit me in Ferdralli, was why I sold the town house in Crowfield.

"*Someone* had to stay and look after the children after Lady Ulla went back home to reclaim her estates," I said as we sat together in the parlor enjoying a fresh pot of tea. We'd already drained two in the course of my narrative. "She remembered more of her magical training than she ever imagined possible. She or anyone else. The demonless wizards never stood a chance against her. Of course Kopp approved the change in domestic personnel. A governess he can trust who wants nothing more than bed and board? He's overjoyed to have me!"

Joram brought us another plate of his special cakes and gave me a kiss on top of my head before whisking himself back into the kitchen. Pella eyed him askance.

"Is *that* the rat?" she whispered. "The one who's king of all the rest?"

"Yes, and he's *my* rat, so have a care how you speak of him." I gazed fondly after Joram. "He's quite the charmer once you get to know him. We're to be married next spring."

"You can't be serious! Marry a *rodent*?" Pella cried.

"Many women do. At least I know what I've agreed to from the start." I sipped my tea complacently.

"But how can you—? What are you—? *Why* would you or any woman in her right mind ever—?"

I leaned across the table and popped one of Joram's cakes into Pella's mouth.

"Ohhhh," she breathed as a dreamy look of pleasure spread across her face. "He can *cook*."

# Getting the Chair

## Keith R. A. DeCandido

Keith R. A. DeCandido swore once to only use his superhuman powers for good, which he promises to do as soon as he gets some. He has written many stories in many universes, mostly *Star Trek* and *Farscape*, with some *Buffy the Vampire Slayer, Gene Roddenberry's Andromeda, Spider-Man, The X-Men,* and others thrown in for good measure. He is working on *Dragon Precinct,* a novel featuring Torin ban Wyvald and Danthres Tresyllione's further adventures fighting crime in Cliff's End, which Pocket Books will publish in 2004. Find out too much about Keith at his official Web site at *http://www.DeCandido.net.*

hat've we— Lord and Lady, what *is* that smell?"

Lieutenant Danthres Tresyllione of the Cliff's End Castle Guard stopped short in the doorway of the cottage. Behind her, Lieutenant Torin ban Wyvald, her partner, had to do likewise to keep from being impaled on the standard-issue longsword scabbard that hung from her belt. He found himself staring at the brown cloak with the gryphon crest of Lord Albin and Lady Meerka that Danthres (and Torin, and all lieutenants in the guard) wore.

Torin was about to ask what she was on about when he, too, noticed the smell.

Danthres was half-elf, so her senses were more acute. Torin could only imagine how much worse the stench was for her—it was pretty wretched for him. He detected at least four different odors competing to make his nose wrinkle, and only one matched the expected stench of decaying flesh.

The guard who had summoned the two lieutenants was a young man named Garis. Like most of the guards assigned to Unicorn Precinct—which covered the more well-to-do regions of Cliff's End—Garis was eager to please and not very bright. "Uh, that's the body, ma'am."

"Guard, I've been around dead bodies most of my adult life. They don't usually smell like rotted cheese."

"Uh, no, ma'am," the guard said.

A brief silence ensued. Danthres sighed loudly. "So *what* is the smell?"

"Ah, probably the rotted cheese, ma'am. It's on the table. Or it could be other food items we've found."

"Who found the body?" she asked, still standing in the doorway blocking Torin. Since she was half a head taller than him, and had a wide mane of blond hair, he had no view of the interior. Under other circumstances, he might have complained. Instead, he was happy to enjoy the less unpleasant aroma of the street a while longer. At least this murder wasn't in Dragon Precinct or, worse, Goblin Precinct, where a rotting corpse constituted a step up in the local odors.

"Next-door neighbor, ma'am," Garis said. "The, ah, smell got to her—"

"No surprise there."

"—and, ah, when he didn't answer the door, she summoned the Castle Guard. I came, broke the door in, and found this body. He's the only one here, and there's only one bedroom upstairs, so he probably lived here alone."

"You didn't ask the neighbor that?"

"Uh, no, ma'am, I thought that you—"

"Would do all your work for you. Naturally. Did you at least have the wherewithal to summon the M.E.?"

"Yes, ma'am, the magical examiner sent a mage-bird saying he'd be here within half an hour—and that was about a quarter of an hour ago."

Danthres finally moved into the house, enabling Torin to do likewise. He surveyed the sitting room, which seemed to take up most of the ground floor. To his left, a staircase led, presumably, to the second level. To his right was a wall taken up almost entirely with shelves stuffed to bursting with scrolls, parchments, and other items, interrupted only by two windows. The wall opposite where he stood was the same, those shelves broken only by a doorway. Directly in front of Torin was a couch, festooned with parchments, dust, writing implements, and wax residue from candles. Perpendicular to it on either side were two easy chairs, one in a similar state of disarray as the couch, the other relatively clean. A table sat in front of the sofa, covered with a lantern, scrolls, candles, bowls, and foodstuffs—including the cheese responsible for keeping Torin's nostril hairs flaring.

Lying facedown on the floor was the body of an elderly man, already decomposing, which meant he'd been dead at least a day. The corpse wore a simple—but not cheap—linen shirt and trousers. Most important, the man's head was at the wrong angle relative to the rest of his body.

"The question now," Danthres said, "is whether he broke his neck or if someone broke it for him."

"I'd say the latter." Torin pointed at the body. "Look how neatly he's arranged—almost perfectly parallel to the couch, with his arms at his sides. He was set there by someone."

Danthres nodded in agreement, then looked around. "Probably too much to hope for that it was a robbery. Not that we'd be able to tell if something was missing in this disaster." She turned to look at Garis, folding her arms across the gryphon crest—a match for the one on her cloak—on the chest of her standard-issue black leather armor. "Why haven't you opened a window?"

Garis seemed to be trying to shrink into his own armor, which was a match for Danthres's and Torin's, save that he wore no cloak and the crest on his chest was that of a unicorn, denoting the precinct to which he was assigned. "Well, er, uh, I didn't want to disturb the scene. I remember that robbery in Old Town last winter and I tried to close a window, and—well, ma'am may not remember, but ma'am tried to cut my head off for interfering with possible evidence before she had a chance to, ah, to examine it."

Danthres snorted. "That's ridiculous. I never would have tried to cut your head off—there'd be an inquiry."

Torin grinned beneath his thick red beard. "I think it will be safe for you to open it, Guard."

"If you say so, sir."

Garis walked to the window and found that it wouldn't budge.

"Honestly, they have *got* to raise the standards during those recruitment drives," Danthres said scornfully. Her not-very-attractive face looked positively deathly when she was angry, and Garis tried to shrink even further inside his armor. Danthres's features were rather unfortunate combinations of her dual heritage. The point of her ears, the elegant high forehead, and the thin lips from her elven father were total mismatches with the wide nose, large brown eyes, and sallow cheekbones she'd inherited from her human mother.

"I'm sure," he said before Danthres truly lost her temper, "that it's just stuck." He walked over and saw that there was no locking mechanism. That, in itself, was odd. True, this *was* Unicorn Precinct—people didn't need to virtually seal themselves into their homes for safety around here—but an unlocked ground-floor window was still unusual. Especially if this old man did indeed live alone.

Torin braced himself against the window and heaved upward. It still wouldn't budge.

"It won't work, you know."

Whirling, Torin looked for the speaker, his right hand automatically moving to the hilt of his longsword. The only people in the room were Garis, Danthres, and himself. And the corpse, of course, though he was unlikely to speak.

"Who said that?" Danthres asked. Her left hand was also at her sword's hilt.

"I did."

Torin realized that the voice came from the area of the couch.

"Come out from behind there." Torin walked around to behind the sofa.

"Uh, sir, there's nobody there," Garis said. "I checked."

Torin saw that Garis was right.

"It's the couch," Danthres said. "The couch talks."

"Brava to the woman," the couch said.

"Hell and damnation," Torin said, "our corpse is a wizard."

"And bravo to the man," the couch added. "Yes, my dear departed owner was a mage. His specialty, as you might have already deduced, was animating furniture. He also hated the very concept of fresh air, so he magicked the windows shut."

Another voice said, "You'd think just once he'd take pity on us, but no." This, Torin realized, was the lantern.

Then the cleaner of the two chairs made a noise. "All you *ever* do is complain. Efrak gave you life, and now that he's dead, you spit on his grave."

Danthres turned to Garis. "I don't suppose the M.E.'s mage-bird is still here?"

"No, ma'am, it discorporated as soon as it gave the message."

Another noise from the chair. "It really is a shame about poor Efrak."

"It's not that much of a shame," the couch said. "I mean, really, what did he do for *us*?"

"Well, he *did* give us life," the lantern said.

"I don't think—"

"That's *enough!*" Danthres bellowed, interrupting the furniture.

Torin added, "I'm afraid we're going to have to question each of you individually."

"What's the point?" Danthres asked him. "He's a wizard. The Brotherhood will claim jurisdiction, perform their own investigation, and keep us completely out of it, like they always do whenever one of their own is involved. And honestly, they're welcome to it. I *hate* magic."

"Don't be so sure of that," said another voice, this time from the doorway. Torin recognized this one: Boneen, the magical examiner. The short, squat old man was on loan from the Brotherhood of Wizards to provide magical assistance to the law-enforcement efforts of the Cliff's End Castle Guard.

"Good afternoon, Boneen," Torin said with a grin.

"What's so damned good about it? I was having a perfectly fine nap when one of those blasted children woke me with another damned thing for you lot." Several young children—troublemakers, mostly orphans that had been arrested and pressed into service in lieu of incarceration in the workhouses—served as messengers and/or informants for the Castle Guard. Most of the guard called them the Youth Squad, except for Boneen, who usually had less flattering terms. Garis had no doubt sent one such to fetch Boneen. "And what in the name of Lord Albin is that horrendous smell?"

"A combination of various slovenly habits," Torin said.

"Not surprising," Boneen said as he entered. "Efrak makes the gutter rats in the Docklands look positively pristine by comparison."

"You know him?" Danthres asked.

Boneen nodded. "A tiresome little old man who dabbles in useless magic for the most part. He's not actually a member of the Brotherhood."

Torin blinked in surprise. "I didn't think that sort of thing was permitted."

"With new wizards, it isn't." Boneen reached into the bag he always carried over his shoulder. "But Efrak's a couple centuries old. He predates the Brotherhood, and they let him be as long as he registered with them and stayed out of mischief." He pulled the components for his spell out, chuckling bitterly. "That certainly won't be an issue anymore."

Torin led Garis toward the back doorway, which presumably led to the kitchen. "Come on, let's give him some room."

The primary duty of the magical examiner at a crime scene was to cast a "peel-back" spell. It read the psychic resonances on inanimate objects and showed him what happened in the recent past. This generally meant he was able to see what happened, how it happened, and, most important, who did it.

Danthres followed him into the kitchen, which smelled worse than the living room. The place was an even bigger mess, with several part-full mugs of various liquids (or congealed messes that were liquid once), plates of unfinished food, and still more papers and books freely distributed about the table, chairs, countertop, and cupboard. The cupboard itself was the source of the worst stench. Torin recognized the sigil on the cupboard door as that of a freezing spell, but he also knew that it had to be renewed every few days—something Efrak was no longer in a position to do.

"Why would anyone want to have animate furniture?" Danthres asked.

Torin shrugged. "It gave him someone to talk to? If he lived alone, shunned even by other wizards, he probably didn't have much by way of social interaction."

"We should talk to his neighbors, starting," she said with a look at Garis, "with the one who called you. Take us to her."

The peel-back generally took half an hour or so, which left the lieutenants with the task of questioning potential witnesses. That pool was fairly shallow. The neighbor who summoned the guard referred to Efrak as a "stupid old man who talks to himself." His other neighbor said that he had very few visitors, usually people seeking out potions or other small magicks that they didn't want the Brotherhood to know about. "Y'know how these young folk are—they think if they don't tell no one, no one'll find out," he said with a wink. That neighbor hadn't seen anyone go in recently, though.

The house was across the street from a park Lord Albin and Lady Meerka had had built a year before as a children's playground. No one there was particularly helpful: the parents were too busy watching their children, the children were too busy playing, and, since they'd only all been there a few hours at most, it was unlikely that they saw anything useful to the investigation of a day-old murder.

Garis, meanwhile, tracked down two of the Youth Squad and told them to fetch a cadre of guards, since in addition to removing the body, they'd need to take the furniture in for questioning.

Boneen came out of the house after a half hour, looking even more sour than usual. "Bad news, I'm afraid. The peel-back was inconclusive."

Danthres's eyes flared. An inconclusive peel-back was a rare thing indeed. "Why?" she asked sharply.

"That damned furniture, that's why!"

Torin closed his eyes and exhaled. "Let me guess. They don't count as inanimate objects?"

"No," Boneen said. The peel-back spell only worked on unliving items. The living interfered with the spell's ability to work—a term that didn't apply to Efrak's corpse, of course, nor would it to, say, a zombie or vampire, but apparently did to magically animated furniture.

"We have to remove the furniture, anyhow," Danthres said. "Maybe after that—"

Boneen shook his head. "Won't work. Something about the way that old ass performed the spell interferes with the peel-back. I can tell you two things, though. One is that it's just the lantern, the one chair, and the couch. All the other objects in that house are *properly* inanimate."

"And the other?" Torin asked.

"Efrak died about a day ago, and there was someone else in the house yesterday. But I can't tell you if it was before, during, or after the murder." Boneen smiled—a most unpleasant expression that didn't remotely suit him. "Actually, it's good news for you two, isn't it? It means you have an actual mystery on your hands."

"Wonderful," Danthres muttered.

"Oh, I thought you detective types loved a good mystery." Boneen was still smiling.

"Actually, we hate them," Torin said, "with great passion and vehemence. They're irritating, they involve a good deal of effort, and they tend to be exceedingly messy."

Danthres nodded in agreement. "I prefer my crimes simple and my criminals stupid and easily found."

Three guards, each wearing armor with the Unicorn Precinct crest, walked up to the house. One of them said, "Afternoon, Lieutenants. Hear tell we're, whaddayacall, movers now."

Nodding, Torin said, "Yes, we've got a body, two large pieces of furniture, and a lantern to bring to main headquarters. They're witnesses."

"The, whaddayacall, body's a witness?"

"No," Torin said with a grin, "just the other three."

"I'm telling you, I didn't see anything!"

Danthres growled. "How could you not have seen anything? You're a *lantern.*"

"I can only see things when I'm lit. Efrak was in one of his—his moods. He was only using candles."

Danthres sat at the table in one of the interrogation rooms of Castle Guard headquarters. The headquarters were housed in the east wing of Lord Albin and Lady Meerka's castle, which in turn was located right at the end point of the Forest of Nimvale, the architectural centerpiece of Cliff's End. Three of the wing's interior rooms were lit only by a sin-

gle lantern and used primarily for questioning people. Torin and Danthres had found that suspects and witnesses tended to get nervous—
and therefore chatty—in rooms that had little light and many shadows.

She had to admit, however, that having two such lanterns—the one
hanging from the wall and the one sitting on the room's only table—di-
luted the effect considerably.

"Moods?" Danthres prompted after the lantern remained silent for
several seconds.

"Oh, he'd just get into one of these things where he'd be experimenting with some magic thing or other. It was always just a phase—
he didn't have *any* discipline, really. He'd always start something, throw
himself completely into it for a while, then abandon it unfinished. But
every time he did, all of a sudden it was just candles, candles, candles.
I'd sit for *days* without being lit—weeks, even. It was just *awful*. I mean,
can you imagine having to sit blind all the time?"

Danthres didn't answer—her first rule of interrogation was that she
asked all the questions. "What happened the night he died?"

"I told you, I didn't—"

"See anything, yes. But I assume you can still hear when you're not
lit, right?"

"Well, strictly speaking, yes, but—"

"So what did you hear?"

A pause. "Well, you see, I wasn't really paying close attention."

"You were sulking because he was ignoring you," Danthres said.

"I don't sulk!"

She pressed on. "You didn't like the way he was treating you, so you
decided to ignore him. He was treating you like a child, so you were
going to act like one."

"I'd hardly go *that* far, but—well, it isn't fair. I mean, if he was going
to make·my sight dependent on being lit, the absolute *least* he could do
was light me regularly. But no, he couldn't be bothered. He just *had* to
study by candlelight. 'It keeps me pure,' he used to say. Honestly, such
pretentious garbage."

Danthres got up from her chair and paced around the table, her
brown cloak billowing a bit behind her as she did so. "So what happened the day he was killed? You must have heard *something*, you were
right there."

"Just another one of those idiots that always come in. Even if I had been lit, I probably would've ignored him. They just want to use Efrak, you know, try to get around the Brotherhood, like *that* ever works. Honestly, it's just so—"

"Did you recognize the voice?"

"Not really, but you people all sound alike to me."

"People—or humans?"

Another pause. "You're right, it wasn't a dwarf or an elf—and he spoke Common, so it wasn't a goblin or anything like that. Besides, I'd've been able to tell by the smell, even in *that* pigsty. No, definitely a human."

"I saw the whole thing, Officer."

Torin smiled as he entered the interrogation room. The guards had placed the couch up against the wall and removed the papers and books, though it was still thoroughly stained and dirt-encrusted. At least Torin assumed that whatever encrusted it was dirt. He decided not to inspect it too closely, instead turning the seat at the table toward the couch and addressing it.

"I'm a lieutenant, actually."

"Look, I saw everything, Sergeant. It was a human, male, young, black hair, blue eyes. Or maybe it was brown hair, but either way it was tied back in a ponytail, and it was definitely dark red hair. And greenish blue eyes. Anyhow, he came in and started bothering poor Efrak. He wanted a charm for this girl he was attracted to. Efrak said he wasn't licensed for that kind of thing, and the boy went insane. He punched Efrak right in the face, then broke his neck. He seemed a little surprised after that, actually. Got all angry and started yelling at Efrak. At least that's what it sounded like."

Torin frowned. "Sounded like?"

"Well, it was hard to get a good look. Efrak tended to leave stuff lying around, and it makes it hard to see exactly—"

"Good sir, if you could tell me what color my beard is, I'd be grateful."

"It's red, of course. But I can see fine now. It's just—Efrak had all that stuff all over me."

"You don't have any idea what the murderer's hair color is, do you? Or what length it is?"

"Well, not as such, no, but I did hear everything that happened. I can tell you this, too, Captain: he didn't leave right away. I don't think he took anything, just threw some papers around."

"Did you try to stop him?"

"No. I think the chair might have, though. I heard them talking, but I couldn't make anything out. My hearing isn't always great with all that stuff, either, to be honest, but I definitely heard that blond-haired boy break Efrak's neck. Probably."

"It was just an accident."

"Really?" Danthres said, gazing upon the chair with annoyance.

"Total accident. Efrak tripped right after that boy who wanted the love potion left. Poor kid, he just wanted to impress a girl, y'know? Why do boys do that, anyhow? Try to impress girls?"

"Describe the boy."

"He was average height, straight brown hair, blue eyes. No beard, but he was obviously trying to grow one."

"And what happened when he was there?"

"Not much. He came in, asked Efrak for a love potion. Efrak explained about how those things have to go through the Brotherhood and he wasn't licensed. The boy whined the way boys do, and then he left, talking about how unfair life is and how he'd never get the girl of his dreams. Kind of tragic, really. Poor boy."

After several seconds, Danthres prompted. "*Then* what?"

"Oh, Efrak just tripped on the table and broke his fool neck. At least I assume that's what broke. His head hit the table, and then he didn't get up. Silly old man, he was always tripping over things."

"I hate magic, I really, really hate magic."

Torin smiled at Danthres's words as he entered Captain Osric's office. His partner was already seated in one of the captain's guest chairs and had made that comment to the head of the Castle Guard.

Osric sat behind his desk, his perpetually half-shaven face in its permanent scowl, made all the more doleful by a silk patch over his left eye. He, too, had a cloak and leather armor, both emblazoned with a gryphon crest; however, his cloak was red, and presently hanging on a hook on the wall.

Danthres continued ranting as Torin took the other guest chair. "It's ridiculous. How am I supposed to interrogate someone who doesn't blink, doesn't shrug, doesn't slouch, doesn't smile, doesn't—?"

"I get the idea, Tresyllione," Osric said. He turned his right eye onto Torin. "What did Boneen say, ban Wyvald?"

"To stop bothering him when he's trying to have a nap." Torin grinned. "However, I got him to admit that there's no way to tell if Efrak died by accident. The neck break and the bruising on the side of Efrak's head are both consistent with Efrak falling into the table, but *how* he fell is impossible to say."

"From the sounds of it," Osric said, "the only reliable witness is the chair."

"It's the only one who saw everything," Danthres said, "but I'm sure it's lying."

Osric's right eye bored into Danthres. "Why would a chair lie?"

"I don't know, but it's lying. Efrak was murdered."

"I agree with Danthres."

Osric snorted. "As if that's going to convince me. You two always agree with each other when you're sitting in this office because you don't want me to think that you ever argue."

"That's absurd," Danthres said archly. "Torin and I never argue."

"Yes, we do, actually," Torin admitted.

"No, we don't."

"In any case, she's still right. Efrak was murdered. Bodies don't, as a rule, fall down with arms on the side perpendicular to the other furnishings. Someone set him down."

"Probably our lovesick boy. I want to put his description out to the guard."

"What description?" Torin asked. "The chair's the only one who described him."

"True," Danthres said, "but it's the only one of the three who got a good look."

Leaning back in his chair, Osric said, "This still doesn't answer the question of why a chair would lie. What's the motive?"

Danthres shrugged, causing her blond hair to bounce. "Either way, the chair's description is the only one we've got. It's what we have to start with."

"It could take days to find him."

Again Danthres shrugged. "So it takes days."

The captain pulled out his dagger, grabbed the battered sharpening stone on his desk, and started running the blade up and down it.

Torin scowled under his beard. Osric only started sharpening his dagger when he had bad news to impart.

"The Brotherhood's letting us handle this—assuming we handle it 'quickly and properly.' Translated into Common, that means that we need this case closed by sunup, or they'll step in."

"Fine by me," Danthres said. "Let them have it."

"No." Osric leaned forward again and pointed at Danthres with the tip of the dagger. "It's bad enough that they crawl all over our damn cases from the start when their registered mages are involved, but I'm damned if I'll let them step on us because we're not solving the case fast enough to suit 'em. I want this case closed by sunup, is that clear, Tresyllione?"

"Yes, sir."

"What about you, ban Wyvald?"

"Quite clear, sir," Torin said quickly.

"See if you can get a better description out of one of the other two, if you're so sure the chair's not being truthful."

Danthres shook her head. "They couldn't see anything. They were all covered in clutter. The chair's the only one who got any kind of good loo—"

"That's it!" Torin said.

"What's it?"

Grinning, Torin said, "The chair's motive for lying."

"Did you find that poor boy yet?"

"We're still looking," Torin said as he and Danthres reentered the interrogation room where the chair sat. "We were wondering if you could answer a few more questions."

"Of course. I'm happy to do whatever I can to aid you good people."

"That's very considerate," Danthres said.

"Indeed." Torin nodded. "You've been much more helpful than your compatriots, in fact."

"Well, that's hardly surprising," the chair said. "They're just a couple of tiresome, filthy little worms."

"I'm glad you said that," Danthres said. "That they're filthy, I mean. We noticed that you were less stained than the other furnishings."

"*Any* of them," Torin added, "ability to talk notwithstanding."

"Oh, well, that's hardly surprising," the chair said quickly. "After all, I was Efrak's favorite chair. He always treated me better than the others."

"Funny, the others never mentioned that."

"Well, they're jealous is all."

Danthres looked at Torin. "I can certainly understand that."

"Of course," Torin said with a nod. "After all, if I were a piece of furniture in that house, and some other piece of furniture was singled out for such treatment, I'd be jealous also. But if the chair *was* his favorite . . ."

"Yet the other two gave no indication of this exalted status. In fact, they were also surprised when we told them how clean you were." On those last two words, Danthres turned to the chair. "In fact, the couch opined that that was why your poor, lovesick boy stuck around after Efrak's death. And why you two were talking."

"That's—that's ridiculous," the chair stammered. "I would never lie like that."

"Unless you had good reason," Torin said.

"Or a shallow one," Danthres added. "Like a promise to clean you up in exchange for lying to us about how Efrak died."

"Shallow?" The chair now sounded indignant. "You think it's shallow to ask for once—just *once*—to be treated with respect? To actually scrape off the food that dates back to the reign of Chalmraik the Foul? To not leave eight pounds of scrolls on top of my cushions? To maybe *sit* on me every once in a while instead of treating me no different than the table? I'm a *chair*—my function is to be sat on, not used as a receptacle for some stupid old man's garbage."

"So the boy did kill him?" Torin asked.

"It was an accident, but yes. They got into a shoving match, and Efrak fell down and broke his fool neck. And you know what? I'm glad that old fool's dead! The man had no respect for us! *None!* And it wasn't just me, you know—but those other two were just so grateful to be animated they let him walk all over them. How he treated the poor lantern—a disgrace, an absolute disgrace, keeping a lantern in the dark like that."

"We're going to need a full description of the boy," Torin said after a moment. "Then I'm afraid we'll have to turn you over to the Brotherhood of Wizards."

At that, Danthres turned to Torin. "What for? Why not just put him in a cell here? He *did* cover up a crime."

"Yes," the chair said in a panic, "why not in a cell here? The Brotherhood'll probably deanimate me or something. I don't want to die!"

"Besides, the Brotherhood gave us jurisdiction," Danthres said. "So it's up to our magistrate, not them, to decide what to do with him."

"I'll be a model prisoner!" the chair put in. "In fact, it'll be heavenly—people will actually use me to sit on for once."

Torin shook his head and smiled. "Fine, we won't turn him over."

"Oh," the chair said, "and the boy's name is Brant. He lives a few blocks from Efrak's house. He came by a few times, actually, and always talked to me. Very nice boy—short blond hair in a ponytail, brown eyes, and a thick full beard."

Torin gazed at the chair, then turned to Danthres. "So much for our accurate description."

"I'll have Garis pick him up," Danthres said. Then she sighed deeply. "I really hate magic."

PART V

# Murder
# Most
# Historical

# The Necromancer's Apprentice

## Lillian Stewart Carl

Lillian Stewart Carl finds herself inventing her own genre, mystery/fantasy/romance with historical underpinnings. Her work often features paranormal themes. It always features plots based on history and archaeology. She enjoys exploring the way the past lingers on in the present, especially in the British Isles, where she's visited many times.

Lillian has lived for many years in North Texas, in a book-lined cloister cleverly disguised as a tract house. She is a member of SFWA, Sisters in Crime, Novelists Inc., and the Authors Guild. Her Web site is *http://www.lillianstewartcarl.com.*

obert Dudley, master of the Queen's horses, was a fine figure of a man, as long of limb and imperious of eye as one of his equine charges. And like one of his charges, his wrath was likely to leave an innocent passerby with a shattered skull.

Dudley reached the end of the gallery, turned, and stamped back again, the rich fabrics of his clothing rustling an accompaniment to the thump of his boots. Erasmus Pilbeam shrank into the window recess. But he was no longer an innocent passerby, not now that Lord Robert had summoned him.

"You beetle-headed varlet!" His Lordship exclaimed. "What do you mean he cannot be recalled?"

Soft answers turn away wrath, Pilbeam reminded himself. "Dr. Dee is perhaps in Louvain, perhaps in Prague, researching the wisdom of the ancients. The difficulty lies not only in discovering his whereabouts but also in convincing him to return to England."

"He is my old tutor. He would return at my request." Again Lord Robert marched away down the gallery, the floor creaking a protest at each step. "The greatness and suddenness of this misfortune so perplexes me that I shall take no rest until the truth is known."

"The inquest declared your lady wife's death an accident, my lord. At the exact hour she was found deceased in Oxfordshire, you were waiting upon the Queen at Windsor. You could have had no hand—"

"Fact has never deterred malicious gossip. Why, I have now been accused of bribing the jurors. God's teeth! I cannot let this evil slander rest upon my head. The Queen has sent me from the court on the strength of it!" Robert dashed his fist against the padded back of a chair, raising a small cloud of dust, tenuous as a ghost.

A young queen like Elizabeth could not be too careful what familiar demonstrations she made. And yet, this last year and a half, Lord Robert had come so much into her favor, it was said that Her Majesty visited him in his chamber day and night . . . No, Pilbeam assured himself, that rumor was noised about only by those who were in the employ of Spain. And he did not for one moment believe that the Queen herself had ordered the disposal of Amy Robsart, no matter how many wagging tongues said that she had done so. Still, Lord Robert could hardly be surprised that the malicious world now gossiped about Amy's death, when he had so neglected her life.

"I must find proof that my wife's death was either chance or evil design on the part of my enemies. The Queen's enemies."

Or, Pilbeam told himself, Amy's death might have been caused by someone who fancied himself the Queen's friend.

Lord Robert stalked back up the gallery and scrutinized Pilbeam's black robes and close-fitting cap. "You have studied with Dr. Dee. You are keeping his books safe whilst he pursues his researches in heretical lands."

"Yes, my lord."

"How well have you learned your lessons, I wonder?"

The look in Lord Robert's eye, compounded of shrewd calculation and ruthless pride, made Pilbeam's heart sink. "He has taught me how to heal illness. How to read the stars. The rudiments of the alchemical sciences."

"Did he also teach you how to call and converse with spirits?"

"He—ah—mentioned to me that such conversation is possible."

"Tell me more."

"Formerly, it was held that apparitions must be spirits from purgatory, but now that we know purgatory to be only papist myth, it must be that apparitions are demonic, angelic, or illusory. The devil may deceive man into thinking he sees ghosts or . . ." Pilbeam gulped. The bile in his throat tasted of the burning flesh of witches.

"An illusion or deception will not serve me at all. Be she demon or angel, it is Amy herself who is my best witness."

"My—my—my lord . . ."

Robert's voice softened, velvet covering his iron fist. "I shall place my special trust in you, Dr. Pilbeam. You will employ all the devices and means you can possibly use for learning the truth. Do you understand me?"

*Only too well.* Pilbeam groped for an out. "My lord, whilst the laws regarding the practice of magic are a bit uncertain just now, still Dr. Dee himself, as pious a cleric as he may be, has been suspected of fraternizing with evil spirits. My lord Robert, if you intend such a, er, perilous course of action as, well, necromancy . . . ah, may I recommend either Edward Cosyn or John Prestall, who are well known in the city of London."

"Ill-nurtured cozeners, the both of them! Their loyalty is suspect, their motives impure. No. If I cannot have Dr. Dee, I will have his apprentice."

For a moment Pilbeam considered a sudden change in profession. His beard was still brown, his step firm—he could apprentice himself to a cobbler or a baker and make an honest living without dabbling in the affairs of noblemen, who were more capricious than any spirit. He made one more attempt to save himself. "I am honored, my lord. But I doubt that it is within my powers to raise your . . . er, speak with your wife's shade."

"Then consult Dr. Dee's books, you malmsey-nosed knave, and follow your instructions."

"But, but . . . there is the possibility, my lord, that her death was neither chance nor villainy, but caused by disease."

"Nonsense. I was her husband. If she had been ill, I'd have known."

Not when you were not there to be informed, Pilbeam answered silently. Aloud he said, "Perhaps, then, she was ill in her senses, driven to, to . . ."

"To self-murder? Think, varlet! A fall down the stairs could no more be relied upon by a suicide than by a murderer. She was found at the foot of the staircase, her neck broken but her headdress still secure upon her head. That is hardly a scene of violence."

Pilbeam found it furtively comforting that Lord Robert wanted to protect his wife's reputation from hints of suicide . . . Well, her reputation was his as well. The sacrifice of a humble practitioner of the magical sciences—now, that would matter nothing to him. Pilbeam imagined His Lordship's face amongst those watching the mounting flames, a face contemptuous of his failure.

"Have no fear, Dr. Pilbeam, I shall reward you well for services rendered." Lord Robert spun about and walked away. "Amy was buried at St. Mary's, Oxford. Give her my respects."

Pilbeam opened his mouth, shut it, swallowed, and managed a weak "Yes, my lord," which bounced unheeded from Robert's departing back.

The spire of St. Mary's, Oxford, rose into the nighttime murk like an admonitory finger pointing to heaven. Pilbeam had no quarrel with that admonition. He hoped its author would find no quarrel with his present endeavor.

He withdrew into the dark, fetid alley and willed his stomach to stop grumbling. He'd followed Dr. Dee's instructions explicitly, preparing himself with abstinence, continence, and prayer made all the more fervid for the peril in which he found himself. And surely, the journey on the muddy November roads had sufficiently mortified his flesh. He was ready to summon spirits, be they demons or angels.

The black lump beside him was no demon. Martin Molesworth, his apprentice, held the lantern and the bag of implements. Pilbeam heard no stomach rumblings from the lad, but he could enforce Dr. Dee's directions only so far as his own admonitory fist could reach. "Come along," he whispered. "Step lively."

Man and boy scurried across the street and gained the porch of the church. The door squealed open and thudded shut behind them. "Light," ordered Pilbeam.

Martin slid aside the shutter concealing the candle and lifted the lantern. Its hot-metal tang dispelled the usual odors of a sanctified site—incense, mildew, and decaying mortality. Pilbeam pushed Martin toward the chancel. Their steps echoed, drawing uneasy shiftings and mutterings from amongst the roof beams. Bats or swallows, Pilbeam hoped.

Amy Robsart had been buried with such pomp, circumstance, and controversy that only a few well-placed questions had established her exact resting place. Now Pilbeam contemplated the flagstones laid close together behind the altar of the church, and extended his hand for his bag.

Martin was gazing upward, to where the columns met overhead in a thicket of stone tracery, his mouth hanging open. "You mewling knotty-pated scullion!" Pilbeam hissed, and snatched the bag from his limp hands. "Pay attention!"

"Yes, master." Martin held the lantern whilst Pilbeam arranged the charms, the herbs, and the candles he dare not light. With a bit of charcoal he drew a circle with four divisions and four crosses. Then, his tongue clamped securely between his teeth, he opened the book he'd dared bring from Dr. Dee's collection and began to sketch the incantatory words and signs.

If he interpreted Dee's writings correctly—the man set no examples in penmanship—Pilbeam did not need to raise Amy's physical remains. A full necromantic apparition was summoned for consultation about the future, whereas what he wished was to consult about the past. Surely, this would not be as difficult a task. "Laudetur Deus Trinus et unus," he muttered, "nunc et in sempiterna seculorum secula . . ."

Martin shifted, and a drop of hot wax fell onto Pilbeam's wrist. "Beslubbering gudgeon!"

"Sorry, master."

Squinting in the dim light, Pilbeam wiped away one of his drawings with the hem of his robe and tried again. There. For a moment he gazed appreciatively at his handiwork, then took a deep breath. His stomach gurgled.

Pilbeam dragged the lad into the center of the circle and jerked his arm upward so the lantern would illuminate the page of his book. He raised his magical rod and began to speak the words of the ritual. "I conjure thee by the authority of God Almighty, by the virtue of heaven and the stars, by the virtue of the angels, by that of the elements. Domine, Deus meus, in te speravi. Damahil, Pancia, Mitraton . . ."

He was surprised and gratified to see a sparkling mist begin to stream upward from between the flat stones just outside the circle. Encouraged, he spoke the words even faster.

". . . to receive such virtue herein that we may obtain by thee the perfect issue of all our desires, without evil, without deception, by God, the creator of the sun and the angels. Lamineck. Caldulech. Abracadabra."

The mist wavered. A woman's voice sighed, desolate.

"Amy Robsart, Lady Robert Dudley, I conjure thee."

Martin's eyes bulged and the lantern swung in his hand, making the shadows of column and choir stall surge sickeningly back and forth. "Master . . ."

"Shut your mouth, hedgepig!" Pilbeam ordered. "Amy Robsart, I conjure thee. I beseech thee for God his sake, et per viscera misericordiae Altissimi, that thou wouldst declare unto us misericordiae Dei sint super nos."

"Amen," said Martin helpfully. His voice leaped upward an octave.

The mist swirled and solidified into the figure of a woman. Even in the dim light of the lantern Pilbeam could see every detail of the revenant's dress, the puffed sleeves, the stiffened stomacher, the embroidered slippers. The angled wings of her headdress framed a thin, pale face, its dark eyes too big, its mouth too small, as though Amy Robsart had spent her short life observing many things but fearing to speak of them. A fragile voice issued from those ashen lips. "Ah, woe. Woe."

Pilbeam's heart was pounding. Every nerve strained toward the doors of the church and through the walls to the street outside. "Tell me what happened during your last hours on earth, Lady Robert."

"My last hours?" She dissolved and solidified again, wringing her frail hands. "I fell. I was walking down the stairs and I fell."

"Why did you fall, my lady?"

"I was weak. I must have stumbled."

"Did someone push you?" Martin asked, and received the end of Pilbeam's rod in his ribs.

Amy's voice wavered like a set of ill-tempered bagpipes. "I walked doubled over in pain. The stairs are narrow. I fell."

"Pain? You were ill?"

"A spear through my heart and my head so heavy I could barely hold it erect."

A light flashed in the window, accompanied by a clash of weaponry. The night watch. Had someone seen the glow from the solitary lantern? Perhaps the watchmen were simply making their rounds and contemplating the virtues of bread and ale. Perhaps they were searching for miscreants.

With one convulsive jerk of his scrawny limbs, Martin scooped the herbs, the charms, the candles, even the mite of charcoal, back into the bag. He seized the book and cast it after the other items. Pilbeam had never seen him move with such speed and economy of action. "Stop," he whispered urgently. "Give me the book. I have to . . ."

Martin was already wiping away the charcoaled marks. Pilbeam brought his rod down on the lad's arm, but it was too late. The circle was broken. A sickly-sweet breath of putrefaction made the candle gutter. The woman-shape, the ghost, the revenant, ripped itself into pennons of color and shadow. With an anguished moan those tatters of humanity streamed across the chancel and disappeared down the nave of the church.

Pulling on the convenient handle of Martin's ear, Pilbeam dragged the lad across the chancel. His hoarse whisper repeated a profane litany: "Earth-vexing dewberry, spongy rump-fed skainsmate, misbegotten tickle-brained whey-faced whoreson, you prevented me from laying the ghost back in its grave!"

"Sorry, master, ow, ow . . ."

The necromancer and his apprentice fled through the door of the sacristy and into the black alleys of Oxford.


Cumnor Place belonged not to Lord Robert Dudley, but to one of his cronies. If Pilbeam ever wished to render his own wife out of sight and therefore out of mind, an isolated country house such as Cumnor, with its air of respectable disintegration, would serve very well. Save that his own wife's wrath ran a close second to Lord Robert's.

What a shame that Amy Robsart's meek spirit had proved to be of only middling assistance to Lord Robert's—and therefore Pilbeam's—quest. No, no hired bravo had broken Amy's neck and arranged her body at the foot of the stairs. Nor had she hurled herself down those same stairs in a paroxysm of despair. Her death might indeed have been an accident.

But how could he prove such a subtle accident? And worse, how could he report such ambiguous findings to Lord Robert? Of only one thing was Pilbeam certain: he was not going to inform His Lordship that his wife's ghost had been freed from its corporeal wrappings and carelessly not put back again.

Shooting a malevolent glare at Martin, Pilbeam led the way into the courtyard of the house. Rain streaked the stones and timber of the facade. Windows turned a blind eye to the chill gray afternoon. The odors of smoke and offal hung in the air.

A door opened, revealing a plump, pigeonlike woman wearing the simple garb of a servant. She greeted the visitors with "What do you want?"

"Good afternoon, mistress. I am Dr. Erasmus Pilbeam, acting for Lord Robert Dudley." He offered her a bow that was polite but not deferential.

The woman's suspicion eased into resignation. "Then come through and warm yourselves by the fire. I am Mrs. Odingsells, the house-keeper."

"Thank you."

Within moments Pilbeam found himself seated in the kitchen, slurping hot cabbage soup and strong ale. Martin crouched in the rushes at his feet, gnawing on a crust of bread. On the opposite side of the fireplace a young woman mended a lady's shift, her narrow face shadowed by her cap.

Mrs. Odingsells answered Pilbeam's question. "Yes, Lady Robert was in perfect health, if pale and worn, up until several days before she died. Then she turned sickly and peevish. Why, even Lettice there, her maid, could do nothing for her. Or with her, come to that."

Pilbeam looked over at the young woman and met a glance sharp as the needle she wielded.

The housekeeper went on, "The day she died, Her Ladyship sent the servants away to Abingdon Fair. I refused to go. It was a Sunday, no day for a gentlewoman to be out and about, sunshine or no."

"She sent everyone away?" Pilbeam repeated. "If she were ill, surely she would have needed an attendant."

"Ill? Ill used, I should say . . ." Remembering discretion, Mrs. Odingsells contented herself with "If she sent the servants away, it was because she tired of their constantly offering food she would not eat and employments she had no wish to pursue. Why, I myself heard her praying to God to deliver her from desperation, not long before I heard her fall."

"She was desperate from illness? Or because her husband's . . . duties were elsewhere?"

"Desperate from her childlessness, perhaps, which would follow naturally upon Lord Robert's absence."

So then, Amy's spear through the heart was a symbolic one, the pain of a woman spurned. "Her Ladyship was of a strange mind the day she died, it seems. Do you think she died by chance? Or by villainy, her own or someone else's?"

Again Pilbeam caught the icy stab of Lettice's eyes.

"She was a virtuous God-fearing gentlewoman, and alone when she fell," Mrs. Odingsells returned indignantly, as though that were answer enough.

It was not enough, however. If not for the testimony of Amy herself, Pilbeam would be thinking once again of self-murder. But then, as His Lordship himself had said, a fall down the stairs could no more be relied upon by a suicide than by a murderer.

The housekeeper bent over the pot of fragrant soup. Pilbeam asked, "Could I see the exact staircase? Perhaps Lettice can show me, as your attention is upon your work."

"Lettice," Mrs. Odingsells said with a jerk of her head. "See to it."

Silently, the maid put down her mending and started toward the door. Pilbeam swallowed the last of his soup and followed her. He did not realize Martin was following him until he stopped beside the fatal staircase and the lad walked into his rump. Pilbeam brushed him aside. "She was found here?"

"Yes, master, so she was." Now Lettice's eyes were roaming up and down and sideways, avoiding his. "See how narrow the stair is, winding and worn at the turn. In the darkness—"

"Darkness? Did she not die on a fair September afternoon?"

"Yes, yes, but the house is in shadow. And Her Ladyship was of a strange mind that day, you said yourself, master."

Behind Pilbeam, Martin muttered beneath his breath, "The lady was possessed, if you ask me."

"No one is asking you, clotpole," Pilbeam told him.

Lettice spun around. "Possessed? Why would you say such a thing? How . . . What is that?"

"What?" Pilbeam followed the direction of her eyes. The direction of her entire body, which strained upward stiff as a hound at point.

The ghost of Amy Robsart descended the steps, skirts rustling, dark eyes downcast, doubled in pain. Her frail hands were clasped to her breast. Her voice said, "Ah, woe. Woe." And suddenly, she collapsed, sliding down the last two steps to lie crumpled on the floor at Pilbeam's feet, her headdress not at all disarranged.

With great presence of mind, Pilbeam reached right and left, seizing Martin's ear as he turned to flee and Lettice's arm as she swooned.

"Blimey," said Martin with feeling.

Lettice was trembling, her breath coming in gasps. "I did not know what they intended, as God is my witness, I did not know . . ."

The revenant dissolved and was gone. Pilbeam released Martin and turned his attention to Lettice. Her eyes were now dull as lead. "What have you done, girl?"

"They gave me two angels. Two gold coins."

"Who?"

"Two men. I do not know their names. They stopped me in the village, they gave me a parcel and bade me bring it here."

"A parcel for Her Ladyship?"

"Not for anyone. They told me to hide it in the house was all."

Pilbeam's heart started to sink. Then, as the full import of Lettice's words blossomed in his mind, it reversed course and bounded upward in a leap of relief. "Show me this parcel, you fool-born giglet. Make haste!"

Lettice walked, her steps heavy, several paces down the hallway. There she knelt and shoved at a bit of paneling so worm-gnawed it looked like lace. It opened like a cupboard door. From the dark hole behind it she withdrew a parcel wrapped in paper and tied with twine.

Pilbeam snatched it up and carried it to the nearest windowsill. "Watch her," he ordered Martin.

Martin said, "Do not move, you ruttish flax-wench."

Lettice remained on her knees, bowed beneath the magnitude of her defeat, and made no attempt to flee.

Pilbeam eased the twine from the parcel and unwrapped the paper. It was fine parchment overwritten with spells and signs. Beneath the paper a length of silk enshrouded something long and hard. Martin leaned so close that he almost got Pilbeam's elbow in his eye. Pilbeam shoved him aside.

Inside the silk lay a wax doll, dressed in a fine gown with puffed sleeves and starched stomacher, a small headdress upon its tiny head. But this was no child's toy. A long needle passed through its breast and exited from its back—Pilbeam's fingertips darted away from the sharp point. The doll's neck was encircled by a crimson thread, wound so tightly that it had almost cut off the head. A scrap of paper tucked into the doll's bodice read: *Amy.*

Pilbeam could hear the revenant's voice: *A spear through my heart and my head so heavy I could barely hold it erect.* So the spear thrust through her chest had been both literal and symbolic. And Amy's neck had been so weakened it needed only the slightest jolt to break it, such as a misstep on a staircase. A misstep easily made by the most healthy of persons, let alone a woman rendered infirm by forces both physical and emotional.

It was much too late to say the incantations that would negate the death spell. Swiftly, Pilbeam rewrapped the parcel. "Run to the kitchen and fetch Mrs. Odingsells," he ordered Martin, and Martin ran.

Lettice's bleak eyes spilled tears down her sunken cheeks. "How can I redeem myself?"

"By identifying the two men who gave you this cursed object."

"I do not know their names, master. I heard one call the other by the name of Ned is all."

"Ned? If these men have knowledge of the magical sciences, I should know . . ." She did not need to know his own occupation. "Describe them to me."

"One was tall and strong, his black hair and beard wild as a bear's. The other was small, with a nose like an ax blade. He was the one named Ned."

*Well, then!* Pilbeam did know them. They were not his colleagues, but his competitors, Edward Cosyn, called Ned, and John Prestall. As

Lord Robert had said, they were ill-nurtured cozeners, their loyalty suspect and their motives impure.

Perhaps His Lordship had himself bought the services of Prestall and Cosyn. If so, would he have admitted that he knew who they were? No. If he had brought about his wife's death, he would have hidden his motives behind sorrow and grief rather than openly revealing his self-interest and self-regard.

God be praised, thought Pilbeam, he had an answer for Lord Robert. He had found someone for His Lordship to blame.

At the sound of a footstep in the hall Pilbeam and Lettice looked around. But the step was not that of the apprentice or the housekeeper. Amy Robsart walked down the hallway, head drooping, shoulders bowed, wringing her hands.

Lettice squeaked in terror and shrank against Pilbeam's chest.

With a sigh of cold, dank air, the ghost passed through them and went on its way down the hallway, leaving behind the soft thump of footsteps and the fragile voice wailing, "Ah, woe. Woe."

Pilbeam adjusted his robes and his cap. Beside him Martin tugged at his collar. Pilbeam jabbed the lad with his elbow and hissed, "Stand up straight, you lumpish ratsbane."

"Quiet, you fly-bitten foot-licker," Lord Robert ordered.

Heralds threw open the doors. Her Majesty the Queen strode into the chamber, a vision in brocade, lace, and jewels. But her garments seemed like so many rags beside the glorious sunrise glow of her fair skin and her russet hair.

Lord Robert went gracefully down upon one knee, his upturned face filled with the adoration of a papist for a saint. Pilbeam dropped like a sack of grain, jerking Martin down as he went. The lad almost fumbled the pillow he carried, but his quick grab prevented the witching-doll from falling off the pillow and onto the floor.

The Queen's amber eyes crinkled at the corners, but her scarlet lips did not smile. "Robin, you roguish folly-fallen lewdster," she said to Lord Robert, her voice melodious but not lacking an edge. "Why have you pleaded to wait upon us this morning?"

"My agent, Dr. Pilbeam, who is apprenticed to your favorite, Dr. Dee, has discovered the truth behind my wife's unfortunate death."

Robert did not say "untimely death," Pilbeam noted. Then Her Majesty turned her eyes upon him, and his thoughts melted like a wax candle in their heat.

"Dr. Pilbeam," she said. "Explain."

He spoke to the broad planks of the floor, repeating the lines he had rehearsed before His Lordship: Cumnor Place, the maidservant overcome by her guilt, the death spell quickened by the doll, and behind it all the clumsy but devious hands of Prestall and Cosyn. No revenant figured in the tale, and certainly no magic circle in St. Mary's, Oxford.

On cue, Martin extended the pillow. Lord Robert offered it to the Queen. With a crook of her forefinger, she summoned a lady-in-waiting, who carried both pillow and doll away. "Burn it," Elizabeth directed. And to her other attendants, "Leave us." With a double thud the doors shut.

Her Majesty flicked her pomander, bathing the men and the boy with the odor of violets and roses, as though she were a bishop dispensing the holy water of absolution. "You may stand."

Lord Robert rose as elegantly as he had knelt. With an undignified stagger, Pilbeam followed. Martin lurched into his side and Pilbeam batted him away.

"Where are those evildoers now?" asked the Queen.

"The maidservant is in Oxford gaol, Your Majesty," Robert replied, "and the malicious cozeners in the Tower."

"And yet it seems as though this maid was merely foolish, not wicked, ill used by men who tempted her with gold. You must surely have asked yourself, Robin, who in turn tempted these men."

"Someone who wished to destroy your trust in me, Your Majesty. To drive me from your presence. My enemy, and yours as well."

"Do you think so? What do you think, Dr. Pilbeam?"

What he truly thought, Pilbeam dared not say. That perhaps Amy's death was caused by someone who intended to play the Queen's friend. Someone who wished Amy Robsart's death to deliver Lord Robert Dudley to Elizabeth's marriage bed, so that there she might engender heirs.

Whilst some found Robert's bloodline tainted, his father and grandfather both executed as traitors, still the Queen could do much worse in choosing her consort. One could say of Robert what was said of the Queen herself upon her accession: that he was of no mingled or Spanish blood but was born English here in England. Even if he was proud as a Spaniard . . .

Pilbeam looked into the Queen's eyes, jewels faceted with a canny intelligence. Spain, he thought. The deadly enemy of Elizabeth and Protestant England. The Spanish were infamous for their subtle plots.

"B-b-begging your pardon, Your Majesty," he stammered, "but I think His Lordship is correct in one regard. His wife was murdered by your enemies. But they did not intend to drive him from your presence, not at all."

Robert's glance at Pilbeam was not encouraging. Martin took a step back. But Pilbeam barely noticed, spellbound as he was by the Queen. "Ambassador Feria, who was lately recalled to Spain. Did he not frequently comment to his master, King Philip, on your, ah, attachment to Lord Robert?"

Elizabeth nodded, one corner of her mouth tightening. She did not insult Pilbeam by pretending there had been no gossip about her attachment, just as she would not pretend she had no spies in the ambassador's household. "He had the impudence to write six months ago that Lady Robert had a malady in one of her breasts and that I was only waiting for her to die to marry."

His Lordship winced but had the wisdom to keep his own counsel.

"Yes, Your Majesty," said Pilbeam. "But how did Feria not only know of Lady Robert's illness but of its exact nature, long before the disease began to manifest itself? Her own housekeeper says she began to suffer only a few days before she died. Did Feria himself set two cozeners known for their, er, mutable loyalties to inflict such a condition upon her?"

"Feria was recently withdrawn and replaced by Bishop de Quadra," murmured the Queen. "Perhaps he overstepped himself with his plot. Or perhaps he retired to Spain in triumph at its—no, not at its conclusion. For it has yet to be concluded."

Lord Robert could contain himself no longer. "But, Your Majesty, this hasty-witted pillock speaks nonsense. Why should Philip of Spain . . ."

"Wish for me to marry you? He intended no compliment to you, I am sure of that." Elizabeth smiled, a smile more fierce than humorous, and for just a moment Pilbeam was reminded of her father, King Henry.

Robert's handsome face lit with the answer to the puzzle. "If Your

Majesty marries an Englishman, she could not ally herself with a foreign power such as France against Spain."

True enough, thought Pilbeam. But more important, if Elizabeth married Robert, then she would give weight to the rumors of murder, and might even be considered his accomplice in that crime. She had reigned for only two years; her rule was far from secure. Marrying Lord Robert might give the discontented among her subjects more ammunition for their misbegotten cause and further Philip's plots.

Whilst Robert chose to ignore those facts, Pilbeam would wager everything he owned that Her Majesty did not. His Lordship's ambition might have outpaced his love for his wife. His love for Elizabeth had certainly done so. No, Robert Dudley had not killed his wife. Not intentionally.

The Queen stroked his cheek, the coronation ring upon her finger glinting against his beard. "The problem, sweet Robin, is that I am already married to a husband, namely, the Kingdom of England."

Robert had no choice but to acknowledge that. He bowed.

"Have the maidservant released," Elizabeth commanded. "Allow the cozeners to go free. Let the matter rest, and in time it will die for lack of nourishment. And then Philip and his toadies will not only be deprived of their conclusion, they will always wonder how much we knew of their plotting, and how we knew it."

"Yes, Your Majesty," said Lord Robert. "May I then return to court?"

"In the course of time." She dropped her hand from his cheek.

He would never have his conclusion, either, thought Pilbeam. Elizabeth would like everyone to be in love with her, but she would never be in love with anyone enough to marry him. For then she would have to bow her head to her husband's will, and that she would never do.

Pilbeam backed away. For once he did not collide with Martin, who, he saw with a glance from the corner of his eye, was several paces away and sidling crabwise toward the door.

Again the Queen turned the full force of her eyes upon Pilbeam, stopping him in his steps. "Dr. Pilbeam, we hear that the ghost of Lady Robert Dudley has been seen walking in Cumnor Place."

"Ah, ah . . ." Pilbeam felt rather than saw Martin's shudder of terror. But they would never have discovered the truth without the revenant. No, he would not condemn Martin, not when his carelessness had proved a blessing in disguise.

Lord Robert's gaze burned the side of his face, a warning that matters of necromancy were much better left hidden. "Her ghost?" he demanded. "Walking in Cumnor Place?"

Pilbeam said, "Er—ah—many tales tell of ghosts rising from their graves, Your Majesty, compelled by matters left unconcluded at death. Perhaps Lady Robert is seeking justice, perhaps bewailing her fate. In the course of time, some compassionate clergyman will see her at last to rest." Not I, he added firmly to himself.

Elizabeth's smile glinted with wry humor. "Is that how it is?"

She would not insult Pilbeam by pretending that she had no spies in Oxfordshire as well and that very little failed to reach her ears and eyes. And yet the matter of the revenant, too, she would let die for lack of nourishment. She was fair not only in appearance but also in her expectations. He made her a bow that was more of a genuflection.

She made an airy wave of her hand. "You may go now, all of you. And Dr. Pilbeam, Lord Robert will be giving you the purse that dangles at his belt, in repayment of his debt to you."

"Yes, Your Majesty." His Lordship backed reluctantly away.

What an interesting study in alchemy, thought Pilbeam, that with the Queen the base metal of His Lordship's manner was transmuted to gold. "Your Majesty. My lord." Pilbeam reversed himself across the floor and out the door, which Martin contrived to open behind his back. Lord Robert followed close upon their heels, his boots stepping as lightly and briskly as the hooves of a thoroughbred.

A few moments later Pilbeam stood in the street, an inspiringly heavy purse in his hand, allowing himself a sigh of relief—ah, the free air was sweet, all was well that ended well . . . Martin stepped into a puddle, splashing the rank brew of rainwater and sewage onto the hem of Pilbeam's robe.

Pilbeam availed himself yet again of Martin's convenient handle. "You rank pottle-deep measle! You rude-growing toad!" he exclaimed, and guided the lad down the street toward the warmth and peace of home.

# Grey Eminence

## Mercedes Lackey

Mercedes Lackey has been an international supermodel, a psychic detective, an espionage agent, a rocket scientist, and a globe-trotting jet-setter, hobnobbing with the likes of Madonna and Elton John. She is currently nominated for both the Pulitzer and Nobel Prizes in literature and is coordinating and financing the effort to create the real-life version of International Rescue. She is five feet nine, with flaming red hair to her waist, an IQ of 250, and a flawless figure and complexion, and she thinks that if you believe any of this, you really need to get out more.

an Killian sat on the foot of her best friend's bed, with her feet curled up under her flannel nightgown to keep them warm. Sarah Jane's pet parrot, Grey, lay flat on Sarah's chest, eyes closed, cuddling like a kitten. Warm light from an oil lamp mounted on the wall beside the bed poured over all of them. It wasn't a very big room, just large enough for Nan's bed and Sarah Jane's and a wardrobe and chests for their clothes and things, and a perch with food and water and toys for Grey. If the wallpaper was old and faded, and the rugs on the floor threadbare, it was still a thousand times better than any place that Nan had ever lived in—and as for Sarah, well, she was used to a mission and hospital in the middle of the jungle, and their little room was just as foreign to her as it was to Nan, though in entirely different ways.

Sarah and Grey were from somewhere in Africa; Nan was a bit

vague as to where, exactly—her grasp of geography outside of the boundary of London was fairly weak. Sarah's parents were missionary doctors there, and as many parents did during the reign of Victoria, had sent their child to England, where, it was assumed, there were fewer diseases, better food, and better physicians, and it was altogether less likely that their darling would sicken and die. There were hundreds, if not thousands, of children like Sarah, sent off to "schools" that cared only to warehouse them and starved their minds, bodies, and spirits; or to caretakers who were as indifferent to the needs of a child all alone as the schools were. Fortunately, there were also good caretakers and, like this, the Harton School for Boys and Girls, good schools. On the outside, this school might not look like a "good" school—it was an old mansion, now on the outskirts of a neighborhood long since declined into a slum. It had seen much, much better days, and the Hartons had acquired it for a pittance, which was fortunate, since a pittance was all they could afford. They had spent their money on repairs, decent (if much-used) solid furnishings, and common comfort, and had advertised, as so many other schools did, that they took children sent back to England by their parents living and working in the service of the empire abroad.

This school, however, was just a little different from most of the others, to say the least. While only little Sarah had a pet from "home," pets and other reminders of absent parents were encouraged here. Mrs. Harton—whom everyone called Memsah'b, from the servants up to and including her own husband—employed a staff of servants almost entirely Indian, including the cooks, so children ate the curries and rice and strongly vegetarian fare they were used to, and only gradually had to adapt to English dishes that would have been very heavy and difficult for their tropic-adapted appetites. Toddlers too young for schooling had two Indian ayahs to tend them—familiar lullabies, familiar sounds and scents, all designed to make the horrible separation from Mama less painful. No one was punished for chattering to the servants in Hindustani, and no one forbade the exuberances that were bound to break out in children raised by the indulgent native nurses. There was a great deal of laughter in the Harton School, and the lessons learned all the surer for it.

And that was the least of the eccentricities here, in a school where not all of the lessons were about what could be seen with the ordinary eye.

Now, Nan was London-born, London-bred—poor child of a gin-raddled, opium-addicted mother who had finally descended (last Nan had heard) to the lowest rung on the social ladder her type could reach, that of a street whore in Whitechapel. She roamed the streets now with everything she owned on her back, without even a garret or cellar room, or even an under-stairs cubbyhole to call her own, satisfying first her craving for drink, before looking for the extra penny for a bed or a meal. She would probably die soon, of bad gin, of cold and exposure, of disease, or as her chronically damaged body gave out. Nan had no time or pity for her. After all, it had been her gran that had mostly raised her, not her mam, who'd only been interested in the money Nan brought in by begging—and anyway, the last contact she'd had with the woman was when money and opium had run out, and to get more, she'd sold the last thing of value she had left—which was Nan herself.

It was through the unlikely friendship she had with little Sarah here, and the intercession of Memsah'b herself, that she ended up here and not elsewhere. Since then, she had shared academic classes with Sarah and paid for her keep by helping the ayahs with the children still in the nursery. And she had another sort of "class" that she shared with no one—a class taken at odd times with Memsah'b herself, in using something other than the usual five senses to learn things. Sarah had a class of her own with Memsah'b; Sarah had a very special sort of bond with Grey—who Sarah insisted was a great deal more than "just" a parrot. Nan was in wholehearted agreement with that estimation at this point—after all, it was no more difficult to believe in than to believe that wolves could adopt a Man-Cub, and Nan was convinced of the truth of Mr. Kipling's stories.

Sarah had other lessons as well, for she could, on occasion, talk with, and see, the dead. This could be a very dangerous ability, so Memsah'b had told Nan, who had appointed herself as Sarah's protector.

Well, if Nan and Grey had anything to say about the matter, danger would have to pass through them to reach Sarah.

"Nan tickle," Grey demanded in her funny little voice, eyes still closed; Sarah was using both hands to support the bird on her chest, which left no hands free to give Grey the scratch she wanted. Nan obliged by crawling up to the head of the bed, settling in beside her friend, and scratching the back of Grey's neck. It was a very gentle scratch—indeed, more like the "tickle" Grey had asked for than the kind of vigorous scratching one would give a dog or a tough London cat—for Nan had known instinctively from the moment that Grey permitted Nan to touch her that a bird's skin is a very delicate thing. Of all the people in the school, only Nan, Memsah'b, Sahib himself, and Gupta were permitted by Grey to do more than take her on a hand. Sarah, of course, could do anything she liked with the bird.

"Wisht Oi had a friend loike you, Grey," Nan told the bird wistfully, the remnants of her cockney accent still clinging to her speech despite hours and hours of lessons. The parrot opened one yellow eye and gave her a long and unreadable look.

"Kitty?" Grey said, but Nan shook her head.

"Not a moggy," she replied. "Mind, Oi loike moggies, but—Oi dunno, a moggy don't seem roight."

Sarah laughed. "Then you must not be a witch, after all," she teased. "A witch's familiar is always a cat or a toad—"

Nan made a face. "Don' want no toads!" she objected. "So Oi guess Oi ain't no witch, no matter what that Tommy Carpenter says!"

Tommy, a recent addition to the school, had somehow made up his mind that she, Sarah, and Memsah'b were all witches. He didn't mean it in a derogatory sense; he gave them all the utmost respect, in fact. It had something to do with things his own ayah back in India had taught him. Nan had to wonder, given whom he'd singled out for that particular accolade, if he wouldn't be getting private lessons of his own with Memsah'b before too long. There was something just a little too knowing about the way Tommy looked at some people.

"But Oi still wisht Oi 'ad—had—a bird-friend loike Grey." And she sighed again. Grey reached around with her beak and gently took one of Nan's fingers in it; Grey's equivalent, so Nan had learned, of a hug. "Well," she said when Grey had let go, "mebbe someday. Lots uv parrots come in with sailors."

"That's right!" Sarah said warmly, and let go of Grey just long enough to give Nan a hug of her own before changing the subject. "Nan, promise to tell me all about the Tower as soon as you get back tomorrow! I wish I could go—maybe as much as you wish you had a grey parrot of your own."

"Course Oi will!" Nan replied warmly. "Oi wisht you could go, too—but you know why Memsah'b said not." She shuddered, but it was the delicious shudder of a child about to be regaled with delightfully scary ghost stories, without a chance of turning around and discovering that the story had transmuted to reality.

For Sarah, however, the possibility was only too real that, even by daylight, that very thing would happen. It was one thing to provide the vehicle for a little child-ghost who had returned only to comfort his mother. It was something else entirely to contemplate Sarah coming face-to-face with one of the many unhappy, tragic, or angry spirits said to haunt the Tower of London. Memsah'b was not willing to chance such an encounter, not until Sarah was old enough to protect herself.

So the history class would be going to the Tower for a special tour with one of the Yeoman Warders without Sarah.

Sarah sighed again. "I know. And I know Memsah'b is right. But I still wish I could go, too."

Nan laughed. "Wut! An' you gettin' t' go t' Sahib's warehouse an' pick out whatever you want, on account of missin' the treat?"

"Yes, but—" She made a face. "Then I have to write an essay about it to earn it!"

"An' we're all writin' essays 'bout the Tower, so I reckon it's even all around, 'cept we don't get no keepsakes." Nan ended the discussion firmly.

"I know! I'll pick a whole chest of Turkish delight, then we can all have a treat, and I'll have the chest," Sarah said suddenly, brightening up in that way she had that made her solemn little face fill with light.

Grey laughed, just like a human. "Smart bird!" the parrot said, then shook herself gently, wordlessly telling Sarah to let go of him, made her ponderous way up Sarah's shoulder and pillow, and clambered up beak-over-claw to her usual nighttime perch on the top of the brass railing of the headboard of Sarah's bed—wrapped and padded for her benefit in yards and yards of tough hempen twine. She pulled one foot up under her chest feathers and turned her head around to bury her beak out of sight in the feathers of her back.

And since that was the signal it was time for them to sleep—a signal they always obeyed, since both of them half expected that Grey would tell on them if they didn't!—Nan slid down and climbed into her own bed, turning the key on the lantern beside her to extinguish the light.

It was a gloomy, cool autumn day that threatened rain, a day on which Nan definitely needed her mac, a garment that gave her immense satisfaction, for up until coming to the school she had relied on old newspapers or scraps of canvas to keep off the rain. Getting to the Tower was an adventure in and of itself, involving a great deal of walking and several omnibuses. When they arrived at the Tower, Nan could only stare; she'd been expecting a single building, not this fortress! Why, it was bigger than Buckingham Palace—or at least, as big!

Their guide was waiting for them under an archway that had not one, but two nasty-looking portcullises, and the tour began immediately, for this was no mere gate, but the Middle Tower. The yeoman warder who took the children under his capacious wing was an especial friend of Sahib, and as a consequence, he took them on a more painstaking tour of the Tower than the sort given to most schoolchildren. He did his best—which was a very good "best," because he was a natural storyteller—to make the figures of history come alive for his charges, and peppered his narrative with exactly the sort of ghoulish details that schoolchildren loved to hear. Creepy but not terrifying. Ghoulish but not ghastly.

Nan was very much affected by the story of poor little Jane Grey, the Nine Days' Queen, and of Queen Anne Boleyn, but she felt especially saddened by the story of the execution of Mary, Queen of Scots, not for that unhappy lady's sake, but for that of her little dog that was hiding under her skirts when she died.

They walked all over the Tower, up and down innumerable stairs, from the old mint buildings to the armory in the White Tower even to the Yeoman Warders' private quarters, where their guide's wife gave them all tea and cakes. Nan felt quite smug about that; no one else was getting tea and cakes! Most of the other visitors had to blunder about by themselves, accompanied with maps and guidebooks, or join a crowd of others being given the general tour by another of the Yeoman Warders, and dependent on their own resources for their refreshment.

She tasted the heady wine of privilege for the first time in her young life and decided that it was a fine thing.

But the one thing that she found the most fascinating about the Tower was the ravens.

Faintly intimidating, they flew about or stalked the lawns wherever they cared to; they had their very own yeoman warder to attend to them because of the story that if they were ever to leave the Tower, it would be the end of England. But Nan found them fascinating; and kept watching them even when she should, perhaps, have been paying attention to their guide.

Finally, Nan got a chance to watch them to her heart's content, as Memsah'b noted her fascination. "Would you like to stay here while the rest of us go view the crown jewels, Nan?" Memsah'b asked with a slight smile.

Nan nodded; going up another set of stairs along with a gaggle of other silly gawkers just to look at a lot of big sparklers that no one but the Queen would ever wear was just plain daft. She felt distinctly honored that Memsah'b trusted her to stay alone. The other pupils trailed off after their guide like a parade of kittens following their mother, while Nan remained behind in the quiet part of the green near the off-limits area where the ravens had their perches and nesting boxes, watching as the great black birds went about their lives, ignoring the sightseers as mere pointless interlopers.

It seemed to her that the ravens had a great deal in common with someone like her: tough, no nonsense about them, willing and able to defend themselves. She even tried, once or twice, to see if she could get a sense of what they were thinking, but their minds were very busy with raven business—status in the rookery being a very complicated affair—though the second time she tried, the minds of the two she was touching went very silent for a moment, and they turned to stare at her. She guessed that they didn't like it, and she stopped immediately; they went back to stalking across the lawn.

Then she felt eyes on her from behind and turned slowly.

There was a third raven behind her, staring at her.

"'Ullo," she told him.

*Quoark*, he said meditatively. She met his gaze with one equally unwavering, and it seemed to her that something passed between them.

"Don't touch him, girl." That was one of the Yeoman Warders, hurrying up to her. "They can be vicious brutes when they're so minded."

The "vicious brute" wasn't interested in the warder's estimation of him. *Quork,* he said, making up his mind—and pushed off with his strong black legs, making two flaps that brought him up and onto Nan's shoulder. *Awwrr,* he crooned, and as the yeoman warder froze, the bird took that formidable bill, as long as Nan's hand and knife-edged, and gently closed it around her ear. His tongue tickled it, and she giggled. The yeoman warder paled.

But Nan was engrossed in an entirely new sensation welling up inside her, and she guessed it was coming from the bird; it was a warmth of the heart, as if someone had just given her a welcoming hug.

Could this be her bird-friend, the one she'd wished for?

"Want tickle?" she suggested aloud, thinking very hard about how Grey's neck feathers felt under her fingers when she scratched the parrot.

*Orrrr,* the raven agreed, right in her ear. He released the ear and bent his head down alongside her cheek so she could reach the back of his neck. She reached up and began a satisfying scratch; she felt his beak growing warm with pleasure as he fluffed his neck feathers for her.

The yeoman warder was as white as snow, a startling contrast with his blue and scarlet uniform.

The ravenmaster (who was another yeoman warder) came running up, puffing hard and rather out of breath, and stopped beside his fellow officer. He took several deep breaths, staring at the two of them. The raven's eyes were closed with pure bliss as Nan's fingers worked around his beak and very, very gently rubbed the skin around his eyes.

"Blimey," he breathed, still staring at them. He walked, with extreme care, toward them and reached for the bird. "Here now, Neville old man, you oughter come along with me—"

Quick as a flash, the raven went from cuddling pet to angry tyrant, rousing all his feathers in anger and lashing at the outstretched hand with his beak. And it was a good thing that the outstretched hand was wearing a thick falconer's gauntlet, because otherwise the warder would have pulled it back bloody.

Then, as if to demonstrate that his wrath was only turned against those who would dare to separate him from Nan, the raven took that formidable beak and rubbed it against Nan's cheek, coming within a fraction of an inch of her eye. She in her turn fearlessly rubbed her cheek against his.

The warders both went very still and very white.

"Neville, I b'lieve you're horripilatin' these gennelmun," Nan said, thinking the same thing, very hard. "Wouldjer come down onta me arm?"

She held out her forearm parallel to her shoulder as the warders held their breath.

*Quock,* Neville said agreeably, and stepped onto her forearm. She brought him down level with her chest, and as he rested his head against her, she went back to scratching him in the places where she was now getting a sense that he wanted to be scratched. He was a great deal less delicate than Grey; in fact, he enjoyed just as vigorous a scratching as any alley cat.

"Miss," the ravenmaster said carefully, "I think you oughter put him down."

"I c'n do that," she said truthfully, "but if 'e don't want to leave me, 'e'll just be back on my shoulder in the next minute."

"Then—" He looked about helplessly. The other warder shrugged. "Miss, them ravens belongs t' Her Majesty, just like swans does."

She had to giggle at that—the idea that anyone, even the Queen, thought they could own a wild thing. "I doubt anybody's told them," she pointed out.

*Rrrk,* Neville agreed, his voice muffled by the fact that his beak was against her chest.

The ravenmaster was sweating now, little beads standing out on his forehead. He looked to his fellow officer for help; the man shrugged. "'Ollis, you was the one what told me that Neville's never been what you'd call a natural bird," the first warder said judiciously, and with the air of a man who has done his best, he slowly turned and walked off, leaving the ravenmaster to deal with the situation himself.

Or—perhaps—to deal with it without a witness, who might have to make a report. And what he didn't witness, he couldn't report . . .

Nan could certainly understand that, since she'd been in similar situations now and again.

Sweating freely now, the ravenmaster bent down, hands carefully in sight and down at his sides. "Now, Neville," he said quietly, addressing the raven, "I've always done right by you, 'aven't I?"

Neville opened one eye and gave him a dubious look. *Ork,* he agreed, but with the sense that his agreement was qualified by whatever the ravenmaster might do in the next few moments.

"Now, you lissen to me. If you was to try an' go with this girl, I'd have ta try an' catch you up. You'd be mad an' mebbe I'd get hurt, an' you'd be in a cage."

Nan stiffened, fearing that Neville would react poorly to this admission, but the bird only uttered a defiant grunt, as if to say, "You'll catch me up the day you grow wings, fool!" The feathers on his head and neck rose, and Nan sensed a sullen anger within him. And the fact that she was sensing things from him could only mean that as the warder had said, Neville was no "natural" bird.

In fact—he was like Grey. Nan felt excitement rise in her. The fact was, a tough bird like a raven suited her a great deal more than a parrot.

But the yeoman warder wasn't done. "Now, on t'other hand," he continued, "if the young lady was to toss you up in th' air when you'd got your scratch, and you was to wait over the gate till her an' her schoolmates comes out, an' then you was to follow her—well, I couldn't know you was missing till I counted birds on perches, could I? An' then I couldn't know where you'd gone, could I? An' this young lady wouldn't get in no trouble, would she?"

Slowly, the feathers Neville had roused, flattened. He looked the warder square in the eyes, as if measuring him for falsehood. And slowly, deliberately, he nodded.

*Quok,* he said.

"Right. Gennelmun's agreement," the warder said, heaving an enormous sigh and turning his attention at last to Nan. "Miss, I dunno what it is about you, but seems you an' Neville has summat between you. An' since Neville's sire has the same summat with the ravenmaster afore me an' went with 'im to Wight when 'e retired, I reckon it runs in the family, you might say. So."

Nan nodded, and looked at Neville, who jerked his beak upward in a motion that told her clearly what he wanted.

She thrust her arm up to help him as he took off, and with several powerful thrusts of his wings, he took off and rowed his way up to the top of the main gate, where he ruffed up all of his feathers and uttered a disdainful croak.

"Now, miss," the yeoman warder said, straightening up. "You just happen to 'ave a knack with birds, and I just give you a bit of a talkin'-to about how dangerous them ravens is. An' you never heard me talkin' to Neville. An' if a big black bird should turn up at your school—"

"Then I'll be 'avin' an uncommon big jackdaw as a pet," she said, staring right back at him, unblinking. "Which must've been summun's pet, on account uv 'e's so tame."

"That'd be it, miss," the warder said, and gathering his dignity about him, left her to wait for the rest of the class to come out.

Memsah'b, Nan was firmly convinced, knew everything. Her conviction was only strengthened by the penetrating look that her teacher gave her when she led the rest of the Harton School pupils out to collect her. Since the crown jewels were the last item on their program, it was time to go.

"How did you get on with the ravens, Nan?" Memsah'b asked with just that touch of irony in her voice that said far more than the words did. Could someone have come to tell her about Neville being on Nan's shoulder? Or was this yet another demonstration that Memsah'b knew things without anyone telling her?

Nan fought hard to keep her accent under control. "I'm thinkin' I got on well, Memsah'b," she said with a little smile.

Memsah'b raised an eyebrow. If there had been any doubt in Nan's mind that her teacher might not be aware that there was something toward, it vanished at that moment.

She raised another when, as they made their way down the broad walk away from the Tower, a black, winged shape lofted from the gate and followed them, taking perches on any convenient object. For her part, Nan felt all knotted up with tension, for she couldn't imagine how the great bird would be able to follow them through London traffic. It seemed that the ravenmaster hadn't yet got around to trimming Neville's wing feathers, for the bird had them all but two, so at least he wasn't going to be hampered by lack of wingspan. But still . . . how was he to get from here to the Harton School?

They boarded a horse-drawn omnibus, and since it wasn't raining yet, everyone ran up the little twisting staircase to the open seats on top. After all, what child cares to ride inside when he can ride outside? They were the only passengers up there, due to the chill and threatening weather, and Nan cast an anxious look back at the last place she'd seen Neville—

He wasn't there. Her heart fell.

And right down out of the sky, the huge bird landed with an audible thump in the aisle between the rows of seats, just as the bus started to move. He folded his wings and looked about as if he owned the place.

"Lummy!" said one of the boys. "That's a raven!" He started to get out of his seat.

"No, it isn't," Memsah'b said firmly. "And no one move except Nan."

When Memsah'b gave an order like that, no one would even think of moving, so as Neville walked ponderously toward her, Nan crouched down and offered her forearm to him. He hopped up on it, and she got back into her seat, turning to look expectantly at Memsah'b.

"This is not a raven," their teacher repeated, raking the entire school group with a stern glance. "This is an uncommonly large rook. Correct?"

"Yes, Memsah'b!" the rest of Nan's schoolmates chorused. Memsah'b eyed the enormous bird for a moment, her brown eyes thoughtful. Memsah'b was not a pretty woman—many people might, in fact, have characterized her as "plain," with quiet brown hair and eyes and a complexion more like honest brown pottery than porcelain. Her chin was too firm for beauty; her features too angular and strong. But it was Nan's fervent hope that one day she might grow up into something like those strong features, for to her mind, Memsah'b was a decidedly handsome woman. Right now she looked quite formidable, her eyes intent as she gazed at Neville, clearly thinking hard about something.

"Bird"—she addressed the raven directly—"we are going to have to go through a number of situations in which you will not be welcome before we get home. For instance, the inside seats on this very bus—since I think it is going to rain before we get to our stop. Now, what do you propose we do about you?"

Neville cocked his head to one side. *Ork?* he replied.

Now, none of the children found any of this at all peculiar or funny, perhaps because they were used to Memsah'b, Sarah, and Nan treating Grey just like a person. But none of them wanted to volunteer a solution, either, if it involved actually getting near that nasty-looking beak.

"Oi—I—can put 'im under me mac, Memsah'b," Nan offered.

Their teacher frowned. "That's only good until someone notices you're carrying something there, Nan," she replied. "Children, at the next stop, I would like you to divide up and search the bus for a discarded box, please. But be back in a seat when the bus moves again."

Just then the bus pulled up to a stop, and slightly fewer than twenty very active children swarmed over the vehicle while passengers were loading and unloading. The boys all piled downstairs; they were less encumbered with skirts and could go over or under seats quickly.

The boys hadn't returned by the time the bus moved, but at the next stop they all came swarming back up again, carrying in triumph the very thing that was needed, a dirtied and scuffed pasteboard hatbox!

As their teacher congratulated them, young Tommy proudly related his story of charming the box from a young shopgirl who had several she was taking home with her because they'd been spoiled. Meanwhile, Nan coaxed Neville into the prize, which was less than a perfect fit. He wasn't happy about it, but after thinking very hard at him with scenes of him trying to fly to keep up, of conductors chasing him out of the windows of buses, and of policemen finding him under Nan's mac and trying to take him away, he quorked and obediently hopped into the box, suffering Nan to close the lid down over him and tie it shut. Her nerves quieted down at that moment, and she heaved a sigh of very real relief. Only then did she pay attention to her classmates.

"I owes you, Tommy," she said earnestly. "Sarah, she said last night she was gonna get a chest uv Turkish delight from Sahib's warehouse for her treat and share it out. You c'n hev my share."

Tommy went pink with pleasure. "Oh, Nan, you don't have to—" He was clearly torn between greed and generosity of his own. "Half?" he suggested. "I don't want to leave you without a treat, too."

"I got a treat," she insisted, patting the box happily. "An' mine'll last longer nor Turkish delight. Naw, fair's fair; you get my share."

And she settled back into her seat with the pleasant, warm weight of the box and its contents on her lap, Memsah'b casting an amused eye on her from time to time. Neville shifted himself occasionally, and his nails would scrape on the cardboard. He didn't like being confined, but the darkness was making him sleepy, so he was dozing when the box was on her lap and not being carried.

There were no difficulties with the rest of the journey back to the school; no one saw anything out of the ordinary in a child with a shop-worn hatbox, and Neville was no heavier than a couple of schoolbooks.

They walked the last few blocks to the school; the neighbors were used to seeing the children come and go, and there were smiles and nods as the now thoroughly weary troupe trudged their way to the old gates, which were unlocked by Memsah'b to let them all back inside.

True to her word, Sarah had gotten the sweets, and when the others filed in through the front door, she was waiting in the entrance hall, with Grey on her shoulder as usual, to give out their shares as soon as they came in. Nan handed hers over to Tommy without a murmur or a second glance, although she was inordinately fond of sweets. Sarah looked startled, then speculative, as she spotted Nan's hatbox.

"Sarah, you just gotter see—," Nan began, when Memsah'b interrupted.

"I believe that we need to make a very careful introduction, Nan," she said, steering Nan deftly down the hall instead of up the stairs. "Sarah, would you and Grey come with us as well? I believe that Nan has found a friend very like Grey for herself, but we are going to have to make sure that they understand they must at least tolerate one another."

There was a room on the first floor used for roughhousing on bad days; it had probably been a ballroom when the mansion was in a better neighborhood. Now, other than some ingenious draperies made out of dust covers, it didn't have a great deal in it but chests holding battered toys and some chairs pushed up against the walls. For heat, there was an iron stove fitted into the fireplace, this being deemed safer than an open fire. This was where Memsah'b brought them, and sat Sarah and Grey down on the worn wooden floor, with Nan and her hatbox (which was beginning to move as a restless raven stirred inside it) across from her.

"All right, Nan, now you can let him out," Memsah'b decreed.

Nan had to laugh as Neville popped up like a jack-in-the-box when she took off the lid, his feathers very much disarranged from confinement in the box. He shook himself—then spotted Grey.

Grey was already doing a remarkable imitation of a pinecone and growling under her breath. Neville roused his own feathers angrily, then looked at Nan sharply.

"No," she said in answer to the unspoken question. "You ain't sharin' me. Grey is Sarah's. But you gotter get along, 'cause Sarah's the best friend I got, an' my friend's gotter be friends with her friends."

"You hear that?" Sarah added to Grey, catching the parrot's beak gently between thumb and forefinger and turning the parrot's head to face her. "This is Nan's special bird-friend. He's going to share our room. But he'll have his own food and toys and perches, so you aren't going to lose anything, you see? And you have to be friends, because Nan and I are."

Both birds thought this over, and it was Grey who graciously made the first move. "Want down," she said, smoothing her feathers down as Sarah took her off her shoulder and put her on the floor.

Neville sprang out of his hatbox and landed within a foot of Grey. And now it was his turn to make a gesture—which he did, with surprising graciousness.

*Ork,* he croaked, then bent his head and offered the nape of his neck to Grey.

Now, in Grey's case, that gesture could be a ruse, for Nan had known her to offer her neck—supposedly to be scratched—only to whip her head around and bite an offending finger hard. But Neville couldn't move his head that fast; his beak was far too ponderous. Furthermore, he was offering the very vulnerable back of his head to a stabbing beak, which was what another raven would have, not a biting beak. Would Grey realize what a grand gesture this was?

Evidently, she did. With great delicacy, she stretched out and preened three or four of Neville's feathers, as collective breaths were released in sighs of relief.

Truce had been declared.

Alliance soon followed the birds' truce. In fact, within a week, they were sharing perches (except at bedtime, when they perched on the headboard of their respective girls' beds). It probably helped that Grey was not in the least interested in Neville's raw meat, and Neville was openly dismissive of Grey's cooked rice and vegetables. When there is no competition for food and affection, alliance becomes a little easier.

Within a remarkably short time, the birds were friends—as unlikely a pair as the street brat and the missionary's child. Neville had learned that Grey's curved beak and powerful bite could open an amazing number of things he might want to investigate, and it was clear that no garden snail was going to be safe come the spring. Grey had discovered that a straight, pointed beak with all the hammerlike force of a raven's neck muscles behind it could break a hole into a flat surface where her beak couldn't get a purchase. Shortly afterward, there had ensued a long discussion between Memsah'b and the birds to which neither Nan nor an anxious Sarah was party, concerning a couple of parcels and the inadvisability of birds breaking into unguarded boxes or brightly wrapped presents . . .

After the incident with the faux medium and the spirit of the child of one of Memsah'b's school friends, rumors concerning the unusual abilities Sarah and Nan possessed began to make the rounds of the more esoteric circles of London. Most knew better than to approach Memsah'b about using her pupils in any way—those who did were generally escorted to the door by one of Sahib's two formidable guards, one a Gurkha, the other a Sikh. A few, a very few, of Sahib's or Memsah'b's trusted friends actually met the girls, and occasionally Nan or Sarah was asked to help in some occult difficulty. Nan was called on more often than Sarah, although had Memsah'b permitted it, Sarah would have been asked to exercise her talent as a genuine medium four times as often as Nan used her abilities.

One day in October, after Memsah'b had turned away one of her friends, a thin and enthusiastic spinster wearing a rather eccentric turban with a huge ostrich plume ornament on the front, and a great many different-colored shawls draped all over her in every possible fashion, Nan intercepted her mentor.

"Memsah'b, why is it you keep sendin' those ladies away?" she asked curiously. "There ain't—isn't—no harm in 'em—least, not that one, anyway. A bit silly," she added judiciously, "but no harm."

The wonderful thing about Memsah'b was that when you acted like a child, she treated you like a child, but when you were trying to act like an adult, she treated you as one. Memsah'b regarded her thoughtfully and answered with great deliberation. "I have some very strong ideas about what children like Sarah—or you—should and should not be asked to do. One of them is that you are not to be trotted out at regular intervals like a music-hall act and required to perform. Another is that until you two are old enough to decide just how public you wish to be, it is my duty to keep you as private as possible. And lastly—" Her mouth turned down as if she tasted something very sour. "Tell me something, Nan. Do you think that there are nothing but hundreds of ghosts out there, queuing up to every medium, simply burning to tell their relatives how lovely things are on the Other Side?"

Nan thought about that for a moment. "Well," she said, after giving the question full consideration, "no. If there was, I don't s'ppose Sarah'd hev a moment of peace. They'd be at her day an' night, leave alone them as is still alive."

Memsah'b laughed. "Exactly so. Given that, can you think of any reason why I should encourage Sarah to sit about in a room so thick with incense that it is bound to make her ill when nothing is going to come of it but a headache and hours lost that she could have been using to study, or just to enjoy herself?"

"An' a gaggle of silly old women fussing at 'er." Nan snorted. "I see, Memsah'b."

"And some of the things that you and Sarah are asked to do I believe are too dangerous," Memsah'b continued with just a trace of a frown. "And why, if grown men have failed at them, anyone should think I would risk a pair of children—" She shook herself and smiled ruefully down at Nan. "Adults can be very foolish—and very selfish."

Nan snorted again. As if she didn't know that! Hadn't her own mother sold her to a pair of brothel keepers? Neville, perched on her shoulder, made a similarly scornful noise.

"Has he managed any real words yet, Nan?" Memsah'b asked, her attention distracted. She crooked a finger in invitation, and Neville stretched out his head for a scratch.

"Not yet, mum—but I kind 'v get ideers about what he wants t' tell me." Nan knew that Memsah'b would know exactly what she was talking about, and she was not disappointed.

"They say that splitting a crow's or raven's tongue gives them clear speech, but I am against anything that would cause Neville pain for so foolish a reason," Memsah'b said. "And it is excellent exercise for you to understand what is in his mind without words."

*Quork,* said Neville, fairly radiating satisfaction.

Nan now put her full attention on the task of "understanding what was in Neville's mind without words." It proved to be a slippery eel to catch. Sometimes it all seemed as clear as the thoughts in her own mind, and sometimes he was as opaque to her as a brick.

"I dunno how you do it," she told Sarah one day, when both she and Neville were frustrated at her inability to understand what he wanted. He'd been reduced to flapping heavily across the room and actually pecking at the book he wanted her to read. She'd have gone to Memsah'b with her problem, but their mentor was out on errands of her own that day and was not expected back until very late.

Grey cocked her head to one side and made a little hissing sound that Nan had come to recognize as her "sigh." She regarded Nan first with one grey-yellow eye, then with the other. It was obvious that she was working up to saying something, and Nan waited, hoping it would be helpful.

"Ree—," Grey said at last. "Lax."

"She means that you're trying too hard, both of you," Sarah added thoughtfully. "That's why Grey and I always know what the other's thinking. We don't try, we don't even think about it really, we just do. And that's because we've been together for so long that it's like—like knowing where your own hand is, you see?"

Nan and Neville turned their heads to meet each other's eyes. Neville's eyes were like a pair of shiny jet beads, glittering and knowing. "It's . . . hard," Nan said slowly.

Sarah nodded; Grey's head bobbed. "I don't know, Nan. I guess it's just something you have to figure out for yourself."

Nan groaned, but she knew that Sarah was right. Neville sighed, sounding so exactly like an exasperated person that both of them laughed.

It wasn't as if they didn't have plenty of other things to occupy their time—lessons, for one thing. Nan had a great deal of catching up to do even to match Sarah. They bent their heads over their books, Nan with grim determination to master the sums that tormented her so. It wasn't the simple addition and subtraction problems that had her baffled, it was what Miss Bracey called logic problems, little stories in which trains moved toward each other, boys did incomprehensible transactions with each other involving trades of chestnuts and marbles and promised apple tarts, and girls stitched miles of apron hems. Her comprehension was often sidelined by the fact that all these activities seemed little more than daft. Sarah finished her own work, but bravely kept her company until teatime. By that point, Nan knew she was going to be later than that in finishing.

"Go get yer tea, lovey," she told the younger child. "I'll be along in a bit."

So Sarah left, and Nan soldiered on past teatime and finished her pages just when it was beginning to get dark.

She happened to be going downstairs to the kitchen, in search of that tea that she had missed, when she heard the knock at the front door.

At this hour, every single one of the servants was busy, so she answered it herself. It might be something important, or perhaps someone with a message or a parcel.

Somewhat to her surprise, it was a London cabbie, who touched his hat to her. "Scuze me, miss, but this's the Harton School?" he asked.

Nan nodded, getting over her surprise quickly. It must be a message, then, from either Memsah'b or Sahib Harton. They sometimes used cabbies as messengers, particularly when they wanted someone from the school brought to them. Usually, it was Sahib, wanting Gupta, Selim, or Karamjit. But sometimes it was Nan and Sarah who were wanted.

"Then Oi've got a message, an' Oi've come t' fetch a Miss Nan an' a Miss Sarah." He cleared his throat ostentatiously and carried on as if he was reciting something he had memorized. "Mrs. Harton sez to bring the gur-rels to 'er, for she's got need of 'em. That's me—I'm t' bring 'em up t' number ten, Berkeley Square."

Nan nodded, for this was not, by any means, the first time that Memsah'b had sent for them. Although she was loath to make use of their talents, there had been times when she felt the need to—for instance, when they exposed the woman who had been preying on one of Memsah'b's old school friends. London cabs were a safe way for the girls to join her; no one thought anything of putting a child in a cab alone, for a tough London cabbie was as safe a protector as a mastiff for such a journey.

Nan, however, had a routine on these cases that she never varied. "Come in," she said to the cabbie imperiously. "You sits there. Oi'll get the gels."

She did not—yet—reveal that she was one of the "gels."

The cabbie was not at all loath to take a seat in the relative warmth of the hall while Nan scampered off.

Without thinking about it, she suddenly knew exactly where Sarah and Grey and Neville were; she knew, because Neville was in the kitchen with the other two, and the moment she needed them, she'd felt the information, like a memory, but different.

Stunned, she stopped where she was for a moment. Without thinking about it—so that was what Grey had meant!

But if Memsah'b needed them, there was no time to stand about contemplating this epiphany; she needed to intercept Karamjit on his rounds.

He would be inspecting the cellar about now, making certain that no one had left things open that should have been shut. As long as the weather wasn't too cold, Memsah'b liked to keep the cellar aired out during the day. After all, it wasn't as if there were fine wine in the old wine cellar anymore that needed cool and damp. Karamjit, however, viewed this breach in the security of the walls with utmost suspicion and faithfully made certain that all possible access into the house was buttoned up by dark.

So down into the cellar Nan went, completely fearless about the possibility of encountering rats or spiders. After all, where she had lived, rats, spiders, and other vermin were a matter of course. And there she found Karamjit, lantern in hand, examining the coal door. Not an easy task, since there was a pile of sea coal between him and the door in the ceiling that allowed access to the cellar.

"Karamjit, Memsah'b's sent a cab t' fetch me 'n' Sarah," she said. "Number ten, Berkeley Square."

Berkeley Square was a perfectly respectable address, and Karamjit nodded his dark head in simple acknowledgment as he repeated it. "I shall tell Sahib when he returns from his warehouse," Karamjit told her, turning his attention back to the cellar door.

He would; Karamjit never forgot anything. Selim might, but Karamjit never. Satisfied, Nan ran back up the stairs to collect Sarah, Grey, and Neville—and just for good measure, inform the two cooks of their errand. In Nan's mind, it never hurt to make sure more than one person knew what was going on.

"Why do you always do that?" Sarah asked when they were both settled in the closed cab, with Grey tucked under Sarah's coat and Neville in his hatbox.

"Do what?" Nan asked in surprise.

"Tell everyone where we're going," Sarah replied with just a touch of exasperation. "It sounds like you're boasting that Memsah'b wants us, and we're getting to do things nobody else in the school gets to."

"It does?" Nan was even more surprised: that aspect simply hadn't occurred to her. "Well, that ain't what I mean, and I ain't goin' ter stop, 'cause summun oughter know where we're goin' 'sides us. What if Memsah'b got hurt or somethin' else happened to 'er? Wouldn' even hev t' be anything about spooks or whatnot—just summun decidin' t' cosh 'er on account uv she's alone an' they figger on robbin' 'er. What're we supposed ter do if that 'appens? Oo's gonna lissen t' couple uv little girls, eh? 'Ow long'ud it take us t' find a perleeceman? So long's summat else knows where we've gone, if there's trouble, Sahib'll come lookin' fer us. But 'e can't if 'e don't know where we are, see?"

"Oh." Sarah looked less annoyed. "I'm sorry, I thought you were just—showing off."

Nan shook her head. "Nah. I show off plenty as 'tis," she added cheerfully, "but—well, I figger around Memsah'b, there's plenty uv things t' go wrong."

"Clever bird," Grey said, voice muffled by Sarah's coat.

*Quorak,* Neville agreed from within his box.

Sarah laughed. "I think they agree with you!" she admitted, and changed the subject. "I wonder why Memsah'b sent for us?"

"Dunno. Cabbie didn't say," Nan admitted. "I don' think 'e knows. All I know's that Berkeley Square's a respect'ble neighborhood, so it might be one of 'er fancy friends again. Not," she added philosophically, "that ye cain't get coshed at a respect'ble place as easy as anywhere's else. Plenty uv light-fingered lads as works Ascot, fer instance."

"Do you always look on the bright side, Nan?" Sarah asked in a teasing tone of voice that told Nan she was being twitted for her pessimism.

Nan was just about to let her feelings be hurt—after all, just how was someone whose own mother tried to sell her to a brothel keeper supposed to think?—when her natural good humor got the better of her. "Nah," she said dismissively. "Sometimes I get pretty gloomy."

Sarah stared at her in surprise for a moment, then laughed.

It was fully dark when they arrived, and the cabbie dropped them off right at the front door. "The lady sed t' go on in, an' up t' the room up there as is lit," he told them, pointing to an upper room. Light streamed from that window; very much more welcoming than the rest of the darkened house. Before either girl could ask anything further, he snapped the reins over the horse's back and drove off, leaving them the choice of standing in the street or following his directions.

Nan frowned. "This don't seem right. There oughter be servants about."

Sarah, however, peered up at the window. "Memsah'b must be with someone who's hurt or ill," she said decisively. "Someone she doesn't dare leave alone." And before Nan could protest, she'd run up to the door and pushed it open, disappearing inside.

Bloody 'ell. Nan hurried after her, with Neville croaking his disapproval as his box swung beneath her hand. But she hadn't a choice: Sarah was already charging up the staircases ahead of her. Something was very wrong here. Where were the servants? There hadn't been any furniture or pictures in the front hall, either.

She raced up the stairs, her feet thudding on the dusty carpet covering the treads, aided only by the light from that single door at the top. She wasn't in time to prevent Sarah from dashing headlong into the lit room, so she, perforce, had to follow, right in through that door left half-ajar invitingly. "Memsah'b!" she heard Sarah call. "We're here, Mem—"

Only to stop dead in the middle of the room, as Sarah had, staring at the cluster of paraffin lamps on the floor near the window, lamps that had given the illusion that the otherwise empty room must be tenanted.

There was nothing in that room but those four lamps. Nothing. And more important—no one.

"It's a filthy trick!" Nan shouted indignantly, and turned to run out—

Only to have the door slammed in her face.

Before she could get over her shock, there was the rattle of a key in the lock and a further sound as of bolts being thrown home. Then footsteps rapidly retreating down the stairs.

The two girls looked at each other, aghast.

Nan was the first to move, because the first thought in her mind was that the men she'd been sold to had decided to collect their property, and another girl as well for their troubles. Anyone else might have run at the door, to kick and pound on it, screaming at the top of her lungs. She put the hatbox down and freed Neville. Even more than Grey, the raven, with his murderous claws and beak, was a formidable defender in case of trouble.

And Neville knew it; she felt his anger and read it in his ruffled feathers and the glint in his eye.

Grey burst from the front of Sarah's coat all by herself, growling in that high-pitched, grating voice that she used only when she was at her angriest. She stood on Sarah's shoulder, every feather erect with aggression and wings half-spread.

Nan growled under her breath herself and cast her eyes about, looking for something in the empty room that she could use as a weapon. There was what was left of a bed in one corner, and Nan went straight to it.

"Sarah, get that winder open, if you can," she said, wrenching loose a piece of wood that made a fairly satisfactory club. "Mebbe we can yell fer help."

She swung the bit of wood, feeling the heft of her improvised club. With that in her hand, she felt a little better—and when whoever had locked them in here came back—

"Nan—"

At the hollow tone in Sarah's voice, Nan whirled and saw that she was beside the window, as white as a sheet.

"Nan, I don't think a stick is going to be much use now . . ." She faltered, pointing a trembling finger at the lamps.

And as Nan watched, the flames of the lamps all turned from yellow to an eerie blue. All Nan could think of was the old saying Flames burn blue when spirits walk.

Nan felt every hair on her body standing erect, and her stomach went cold, and not because of some old saying. No, oh no. There was danger, very near. Sarah might have sensed it first, but Nan felt it surrounding both of them and fought the instinct to look for a place to hide.

Neville cawed an alarm, and she turned again to see him scuttle backward, keeping his eyes fixed on the closed door. The lamp flames behind her dimmed, throwing the room into a strange, blue gloom. Neville turned his back on the door for a moment, but only long enough to leap into the air, wings flapping frantically, to land on her shoulder. He made no more noise, but Grey was making enough for two. His eyes were nothing but pupil, and she felt him shivering.

"There's something outside that door," Sarah said in a small frightened voice.

"And whatever 'tis, locks and wood ain't goin' t' keep it out," Nan said grimly. She did not say aloud what she felt deep inside.

Whatever it was, it was no mere ghost, not as she and Sarah knew the things. It hated the living; it existed to feed on terror, but that was not all that it was or did. It was old, old—so old that it made her head ache to try and wrap her understanding around it, and of all that lived, it hated people the most. That thing out there would destroy her as casually as she would swat a fly—but it wanted Sarah.

Grey's growling rose to an ear-piercing screech; Sarah seemed frozen with fear, but Grey was not; Grey was ready to defend Sarah with her life. Grey was horribly afraid, but she was not going to let fear freeze her.

Neither was Neville.

And I ain't, neither! Nan told herself defiantly, and though the hand clutching her club shook, she took one step—two—three—

And planted herself squarely between whatever was behind the door and Sarah. It would have to go through her, Neville, and Grey to reach what it wanted.

I tol' Karamjit where we went—an' when Memsah'b comes 'ome wit'out us . . .

She knew that was the only real hope: that help from the adults would come before that . . . Presence . . . decided to come through the door after them. Or if she could stall it, could somehow delay things, keep it from actually attacking—

Suddenly, Grey stopped growling.

The light from behind her continued to dim; the shadows lengthened, collected in the corners, and stretched toward them. There was no more light in here now than that cast by a shadowed moon. Nan sucked in a breath—

Something dark was seeping in under the door, like an evil pool of black water.

The temperature within the room plummeted; a wave of cold lapped over her, and her fingers and toes felt like ice. That wave was followed by one of absolute terror that seized her and shook her like a terrier would shake a rat.

"Ree—," Grey barked into the icy silence. "Lax!"

The word spat so unexpectedly into her ear had precisely the effect Grey must have intended. It shocked Nan for a split second into a state of not-thinking, just being—

Suddenly, all in an instant she and Neville were one.

Knowledge poured into her; and fire blossomed inside her, a fire of anger that drove out the terror, a fierce fire of protectiveness and defiance that made her straighten, take a firmer grip on her club. She opened her mouth—

And words began pouring out of her—guttural words, angry words, words she didn't in the least understand, that passed somehow from Neville to her, going straight to her lips without touching her mind at all. But she knew, she knew, they were old words, and they were powerful . . .

The light from the lamps strengthened, and with each word, she felt a warmth increasing inside her, a fierce strength pouring into her. Was it from her feathered companion, just as the words were? Or was it the words that brought this new power?

No, it wasn't the light behind her that was increasing! It was the light around her!

Cor—

A golden halo of light surrounded her, increasing in brightness with every word that spilled from her lips. And now Grey joined in the chanting, for chanting it was. She caught the pattern now, a repetition of some forty-two syllables that sounded like no language fragments Nan had ever heard. She knew what Italian, Hebrew, and Chinese all sounded like, even if she couldn't speak or understand them, for folk of all those nationalities thronged the slums where she lived. She knew what Latin, Greek, and French sounded like, too, since those were taught at the school. This language definitely wasn't any of those. But when Grey took over the chant, Nan stopped; she didn't need to speak anymore. Now it was Grey who wove an armor of words about her—and a moment later, Sarah's voice, shaking, faltering, but each syllable clear, if faint.

Then she went all wobbly for a moment. As if something gave her a good cuff, she experienced a sort of internal lurch of vision and focus, a spirit earthquake. The room faded, thinned, became ghostly. The walls receded, or seemed to; everything became dim and grey, and a cold wind buffeted her, swirling around her.

On the other side of that door, now appallingly transparent, bulked an enormous shadow; that was what was oozing under the door, reaching for them, held at bay by the golden light around her. The shadow wasn't what filled her with horror and fear, however—it was what lay at the heart of it, something that could not be seen, even in this half-world, but that sent out waves of terror to strike devastating blows on the heart. And images of exactly what it intended to do to those who opposed it—and the one it wanted.

Now the shadow was on their side of the door, and there was no getting past it. The shadow billowed and sent out fat, writhing tentacles toward her.

But Nan was not going to break; not for this thing, whatever it was, not when her friend needed protecting from this horror that was going to devour her and take her body for its own!

She brandished her club, and as the shining blade in her hand ripped through the thick grey tendrils of oily fog the thing sent toward her out of the shadow, she saw with a shock that she no longer held a crude wooden club. Not anymore—

Now she held a shining sword, with a blade polished to a mirror finish, bronze-gold as the heart of the sun. And the arm that swung the blade was clad in bronze armor.

She was taller, older, stronger; wearing a tunic of bright red wool that came to her knees, a belt of heavy leather, her long hair in a thick plait that fell over one shoulder. And Neville! Neville was no heavier than he had been, but now he was huge, surely the size of an eagle, and his outspread wings overshadowed her, as his eyes glowed the same bronze-gold as her sword and the golden aura that surrounded them both.

But the form within the shadow was not impressed.

The shadow drank in her light, swallowing it up, absorbing it completely. Then it began to grow . . .

Even as it loomed over her, cresting above her like a wave frozen in time, she refused to let the fear it wanted her to feel overwhelm her, though she felt the weight of it threatening to close in on her spirit and crush it. Defiantly, she brandished her sword at it. "No!" she shouted at it. "You don't get by!"

It swelled again, and she thought she saw hints of something inside it . . . something with a smoldering eye, a suggestion of wings at the shoulders, and more limbs than any self-respecting creature ought to have.

She knew then that this was nothing one single opponent, however brave, however strong, could ever defeat. And behind her, she heard Sarah sob once, a sound full of fear and hopelessness.

Grey and Neville screamed—

And the ghost door burst open behind the horror.

In this strange half-world, what Nan saw was a trio of supernatural warriors. The first was a knight straight out of one of her beloved fairy books, broadsword in hand, clad head to toe in literally shining armor, visor closed—though a pair of fierce blue eyes burned in the darkness behind it. The second bore a scimitar and was wearing flowing, colorful silken garments and a turban centered with a diamond that burned like a fire, and could have stepped out of the pages of the *Arabian Nights,* an avenging jinn.

And the third carried not a sword, but a spear, and was attired like nothing Nan had ever seen—in the merest scrap of a chemise, a bit of draped fabric that scandalized even Nan, for inside that little wisp of cloth was—

Memsah'b?

The shadow collapsed in on itself—not completely, but enough for the knight to slam it aside with one armored shoulder, enough for the jinn and Memsah'b to rush past it, and past Nan, to snatch up Sarah and make a dash with her for the now open door, with Grey flapping over their heads in their wake.

Nan saw the shadow gather itself and knew it was going to strike them down.

"Bloody hell!" she screamed—or at least, that was what the words that came out of her mouth meant, for she certainly didn't recognize the shape of the syllables. And, desperate to keep it from striking, she charged at the thing, Neville dove at it, and the knight slashed upward frantically.

Again it shrank back—not in defeat, oh no, but startled that they had dared to move against it.

And that was enough—just enough—for Memsah'b and the jinn to rush past bearing Sarah, for Nan and Neville and Grey to follow in their wake, and for the knight to slam the door shut and follow them down the stairs—

Stairs that, with every footstep, became more and more solid, more and more real, until all of them tumbled out the front door of number 10, Berkeley Square, into the lamplit darkness, the perfectly ordinary shadows and smoke and night sounds of a London street.

Sahib slammed the front door shut behind them and leaned against it, holding his side and panting. Gone were his armor, his sword—he was only ordinary Sahib again. Selim—and not the jinn—put Sarah down on the pavement, and Grey fluttered down to land on her shoulder. Neville looked up at Nan and quorked plaintively, while Memsah'b, clad in a proper suit, but with her skirt hiked up to scandalous shortness, did something that dropped her skirt from above her knees to street length again.

"Are you two all right?" she asked anxiously, taking Sarah by the shoulders and peering into her face, then doing the same with Nan.

"Yes'm," Nan said, and Sarah nodded.

"Faugh," Sahib coughed as he straightened. "Let's not do that again anytime soon, shall we? I'm getting too old for last-minute rescues."

Last-minute rescues—'cause we went off alone! "Oh, Sahib, Memsah'b—" Nan felt her eyes fill with tears as it suddenly came home to her that her protectors and benefactors had just put themselves into deadly danger to save her. "Oh, I'm sorry, I didn' mean—"

"Nan, Nan, you aren't to blame!" Sahib said immediately, putting one strong arm around her shoulders. "You did nothing that you shouldn't have done, and if you hadn't been so careful, we wouldn't have known where you were until it was too late! No, it was our fault."

"It certainly was," Memsah'b said grimly. "But it was someone else's as well . . . and there is going to be a reckoning. But let's get away from here first. I don't altogether want to find out if the bindings keeping that thing confined to this house will hold under provocation."

Sahib took Sarah's arm, giving her Grey to tuck inside her coat, and Selim lifted Neville onto Sarah's shoulder. As they walked quickly away from the house, Memsah'b continued. "Someone came to me a few days ago with a story about this place, how some haunt was making it impossible to rent out and he was in dire difficulty because of it. He wanted Sarah or me, or both of us together, to lay the spirit, but I have heard all of the stories about this address, and I knew better than to try. Something came to dwell there, over a hundred years ago, and it is not a thing to be trifled with. Men have died here, and more than one, and many people have gone mad with fear. Whatever that thing was—"

"Is old," Nan put in with a shudder. "Real, real old. I dunno how it got 'ere, but it ain't no spook."

"Well, evidently this person decided to force our hand," Sahib said thoughtfully, and as Nan looked up when they passed under a streetlamp, she saw that both his face and Selim's were grim. "I believe that I will have a private word with him."

"As will I—although I am sorely tempted to tell him that his devil has been laid, and suggest he spend a night there himself," Memsah'b said with deep anger in her voice. "And from now on, we will contrive a better way of bringing you girls if I should need you."

"Please," Sarah said in a small voice. "What happened to Nan and Neville? And you and Sahib and Selim?"

Sahib cleared his throat awkwardly; Selim just laughed, deep in his throat. "You saw us as we seem to be—"

"Are," Sahib corrected dryly.

"Are, then—when we are warriors for the Light," Selim concluded.

"Though how Nan happened to slip over into a persona and power she should not have until she is older—much older—I cannot imagine," Memsah'b added with a note in her voice that suggested that she and Nan would be having a long, a very long, talk at some point in the near future.

But for now, Nan was beginning to feel the effect of being frightened nearly to death, fighting for the life of herself and her friends, and somehow being rescued in the nick of time. She stumbled and nearly fell, and Sahib sent Selim in search of a cab. In a good neighborhood like this one, they were not too difficult to find; shortly, both the girls were lifted in to nestle on either side of Memsah'b, birds tucked under their coats with the heads sticking out, for Nan had left Neville's hatbox and was not at all inclined to go back after it. And in the shelter of the cab, Neville providing a solid oblong of warmth, and the drone of the adult voices above her head, safe at last, she found herself dropping off to sleep.

But not before she heard Memsah'b saying, "I would still like to know how it was that the child came into her Aspect without any training—and where she found the Words of Power for the Holy Light."

And heard Grey answer.

"Smart Neville," she said in her sweetest voice. "Very smart Nan."

# Afterword

ow that you've taken your trip into the shadows, I suppose you have a few questions. Why these murders? Why murders at all, for that matter? Why mix murder and magic?

It's a long story.

In one sense, every story is a mystery, even if it isn't intended to be a mystery for the reader. How do you get the characters from here to there, and the story from "Chapter One" to "The End"? So I suppose an interest in unraveling that sort of puzzle leads naturally to an interest in mysteries, but in point of cold hard fact, I was a mystery reader long before I began the daunting process of becoming a writer. Writers like puzzles and mysteries because they spend so much of their professional life solving them.

As for why *occult* mysteries, well . . . there's a basic rule of fiction that I've always followed.

If you want to keep a reader's attention, keep raising the stakes.

It's like this.

Murder is the most unnatural act, a crime that often requires the keenest and most insightful investigator, whether official or amateur, to solve it. The investigations, and the theories, are bounded by the laws of possibility, if not probability, and so the murderer is eventually identified and brought to justice.

But what if, once you eliminated the impossible, what you had left were still impossible? What if a killer could be in two places at once, kill from a distance, or enter a locked room without a trace? What if, in a world where magic was a fact of everyday life, a killer were to commit a crime by purely mechanical means?

I'm not the first person to have thought of this, of course. Crime and the supernatural have long been a popular mix. Nearly every detective worth the name has at least dabbled in a case touching on the occult at some point in his career—even Lord Peter Wimsey, in "The Incredible Elopement of Lord Peter Wimsey," undertook to solve a case of supposed witchcraft and demonic possession.

To do even the sketchiest history of the occult detectives would require a full book, not just a few pages. I'll try to hit one or two of the high points here, but in order to even begin to winnow things out, I need to stick to series where most of the detective's adventures focus on the occult, and to leave out single-title works entirely. So *Dracula* isn't here, or *The Exorcist*, although you could make a strong case for both Doctor Abraham Van Helsing and Father Lancaster Merrin being occult detectives.

Nor do I have the space to get into movies, comics, or television, though that means I have to leave out *Ghostbusters; The Exorcist* (the movie); *Doctor Strange, Master of the Mystic Arts; The Sixth Sense; Kolchak: The Night Stalker; The X-Files; Buffy the Vampire Slayer; Charmed;* and many more that would certainly otherwise be worth mentioning for their influence on the field.

The Occult Detective—often called a ghosthunter or Ghost Breaker—found his (almost always "his" in those early days) first true flowering in the world of the pulps and the proto-pulps, in an era when there were hundreds of magazines on the newsstands every month and thousands of stories published every year. And now, a few pages from our "angels gallery" . . .

Doctor John Silence was the creation of Algernon Blackwood, perhaps best remembered today as a horror writer. Silence first appears in 1908, with a final adventure dated 1914, though the early adventures may only have appeared in book form. Silence is an archetypal O.D.: like many of his successors, he is independently wealthy, a member of the professions, and possesses psychic powers himself, gained through rigorous years of study.

Jules de Grandin was the brainchild of pulp master Seabury Quinn, and appeared almost exclusively in the original incarnation of the magazine *Weird Tales*. Unlike Silence, de Grandin is all flamboyance and quirks, rather like a ramped-up Poirot. He's referred to as "the Sherlock Holmes of the Supernatural," and he makes his way with great verve and an immoderate body count through a host of zombies, vampires, and other ghoulies in the ninety-three adventures that appeared from 1925 through 1951. De Grandin is notable for having both connections to French Intelligence and a military background, both of which he exploits in his fight for good.

Carnacki the Ghost-Finder is the O.D. of William Hope Hodgson, who is best remembered today for his classic dark fantasy *The House on the Borderland*. Carnacki's first adventure appeared in 1912, and he flourished in various British and American magazines through 1947, his career overlapping those of both Doctor Silence and de Grandin. Like Doctor Silence, Carnacki is a psychic investigator, called in to investigate occult disturbances, but unlike other occult detectives, he always attempts to eliminate any mundane cause through the scientific method before turning to the "Black Arts" to solve the crime.

Doctor Taverner, who appears in twelve stories originally published in *Royal Magazine* at unknown dates, and first collected in 1926 in *The Secrets of Dr. Taverner*, is the creation of Violet Mary Firth, who wrote under the pen name Dion Fortune, a pen name taken from her family motto, *Dio et Fortuna*. Possibly unique among the ranks of the creators of the O.D.'s, Fortune was herself a practicing occultist, a member of the Golden Dawn. She claimed to have based Taverner on her mentor, Doctor William Moriarty, and said that her Taverner stories were "studies in little-known aspects of psychology put in the form of fiction because, if published as a serious contribution to science, they would have no chance of a hearing."

Beginning in the 1930s, Manly Wade Wellman gave us three classic O.D.'s: Judge Keith Hilary Pursuivant (1938–82), a retired judge who has devoted himself to a study of the occult; John Thunstone (1943–85), a renowned scholar of independent means whose passion is the occult (and who, oddly enough, possesses a blessed silver-bladed sword cane identical to Judge Pursuivant's); and Silver John (1946–87), sometimes known as John the Balladeer. Of the three, Silver John, a soft-spoken countryman who plays a silver-strung guitar and whose adventures are drawn from the folklore and mysticism of the American South, is perhaps best known. All three characters shared the same universe and met each other at various times.

Marion Zimmer Bradley was best known for her fantasy and science fiction novels, but she also wrote quite a large body of occult and gothic novels and stories. Colin MacLaren is her occult detective, who appears with his psychic partner, Claire Moffat, in four books: *Witch Hill, Dark Satanic, The Inheritor,* and the collaboration *Heartlight,* which was written with yours truly.

With the diminishing of the pulp market and the rise of the paperback novel at the end of World War II, the classic O.D. became less prevalent. But you certainly can't keep a good man (or woman) down, and the O.D. quickly found a new home in the SF and Fantasy field, shedding much of his pulp-horror background in the process.

A distinct subgenre of the O.D. is the tale set in an alternate universe where the ground rules are decidedly different, but the problems of detection and justice remain the same. Three examples:

Lord Darcy, whose original adventures appeared from 1964 to 1980, is the creation of SF master Randall Garrett. Darcy is an investigator for Richard, Duke of Normandy, in an alternate universe where magic works and the Plantagenet dynasty rules to this day over a low-tech Anglo-Norman Empire. Garrett gave us classic puzzle-based mysteries, sticking firmly to the rules of his "scientific" magic and filled with allusions to the classics of the mystery field.

Glen Cook provides an archetypal hard-luck hard-boiled gumshoe, also (coincidentally) named Garrett. Garrett has appeared in ten novels since 1987 and doesn't seem to have a first name as of this writing. The difference between Garrett and the classic mean-streets private eye is that Garrett hangs his hat in another world: the city of TunFaire, a decaying outpost of the Karentine Empire, a corrupt (in all senses of the word) city populated by elves, giants, centaurs, pixies, wizards, and just about anything else that ever escaped from a fairy tale. In a tip of the hat to Rex Stout, Garrett shares his lodgings with The Dead Man, a massive creature who isn't a man but is certainly dead. And quite grumpy about it. Philip Marlowe would certainly recognize Garrett's problems, if not their packages.

Anita Blake, vampire executioner, is the creation of Laurel K. Hamilton, and has appeared in nine novels since 1993. Anita lives in a world where vampires and other supernatural creatures have come "out of the closet" and into the mundane world, much in the tradition of Dean R. Koontz's 1973 classic, *The Haunted Earth*. Anita, who has the innate ability to animate the dead, executes rogue vampires for the state of Missouri. And to her surprise, she finds that the supernatural community has begun coming to her to investigate crimes.

And that brings us to the modern day, and the wonderful assortment of choices, both traditional and nontraditional, awaiting the connoisseur of the O.D., many types of which you find represented in these pages.

But all of this really doesn't quite explain how the anthology *Murder by Magic* came to exist. For that I owe a personal debt of gratitude to Debra Doyle, because without her, you would not be holding this anthology in your hands at all. A few years back, she and I were both guests at a DarkoverCon together, discussing, as writers will, the Great Unwritten Stories we wanted to write and never would, simply because there just didn't seem to be a home for stories that blurred the lines between fantasy and mystery. She mentioned a story she'd always wanted to write, about a "country-house" murder set in the Mageworlds universe, where magic was a fact of life. A mystery that—literally—could not have occurred—or been solved—anywhere else.

"But who would publish an occult mystery set in an SF universe?" she said, shrugging.

"You write it," I said. "I'll edit the anthology."

And so *Murder by Magic* was born. Thanks, Debra. I owe it all to you, and to the other fine writers who came along to play.

—Rosemary Edghill
Chez Edghill, January 2003

# About the Editor

Rosemary Edghill's first professional sales were to the black & white comics of the late 1970s, so she can truthfully state on her résumé that she once killed vampires for a living. She is also the author of over thirty novels and several dozen short stories in genres ranging from Regency Romance to Space Opera, making all local stops in between. She has collaborated with authors such as the late Marion Zimmer Bradley and SF Grand Master Andre Norton, worked as an SF editor for a major New York publisher, as a freelance book designer, and as a professional book reviewer. Her Web site can be found at *http://www.sff.net/people/eluki*.